A Third Life

A Novel

G. Owen McGinnis
MD, FACS

FIRESIDE FICTION
2007

FIRESIDE FICTION
AN IMPRINT OF HERITAGE BOOKS, INC.

Books, CDs, and more—Worldwide

For our listing of thousands of titles see our website
at
www.HeritageBooks.com

Published 2007 by
HERITAGE BOOKS, INC.
Publishing Division
65 East Main Street
Westminster, Maryland 21157-5026

International Standard Book Number: 978-0-7884-4125-6

Dedication

This book is dedicated to those men and women who have gone before and suffered untold hardships, struggled in a primitive land and died -- seeing little reward on this earth. We who live with comforts of this day are descended from these hard working people. The book is further dedicated to those who follow. May they cherish the struggles and pain of their forbears. May they hear and profit from voices of the past.

Contents

Author's Note

When I was about to go to the first grade, my mother asked me if I would like to be to be called by my middle name. I had been called by both, since I had my father's first name. I thought I wanted the same name as my father because he was a big person. I continued to be called by both given names by family and first name by friends -- and my wife – through college, medical school, residency, two years of army, and forty-four years of surgical practice in Anniston, Alabama – and still going.

I was just a dumb kid. I didn't know that Mother was proud of her family name and that I was the only grandchild. When I began to write this book nine years ago at the little farm where we live in Choccolocco, I vowed that if it were ever published, it would be under the name Mother wanted me to use. She gave me the love for words and gently goaded me to be the first college graduate in our family.

She *will* know.

Gaston   **Owen McGinnis**

Preface

Go back to a time when water was brought from a spring -- candles and torches lit the night. Go back to a time when mules and horses pulled the wagon and plow. Go back to at time when wood fires cooked the bread -- bears, wolves or mountain lions might cross the yard during supper. Go back to a time when the land was defeated, devastated and straining to recover. And if you do, you live in the pages of this book and see people who exist through their own labor. Like most of the South, they had no slaves and were not plantation society. You see a man suffer a lost cause, lost arm, and lost friend far from home. You see struggles of a war forced on a farm wife. You see the worst decision imaginable forced on parents. You also see how they survived.

But be warned that in this land, tragedy, struggle, painful decision, love of family, love of home, and love of neighbors is more intense than you have ever known.

I learned the ways and speech of this time by listening on long summer evenings on the porch and nights around the fire in winter. My grandparents grew up in homes of confederate veterans. They spoke the words of their parents. My mother wrote stories in longhand of a determined one-armed veteran of The Big War and of Billy at the spring. She gave me love letters from the nineteenth century. In the last week of his life, my father told me the story given to him long ago of the bite of the Devil Dog, the terrible results and painful decision.

This is my account of events handed down and of life long ago. It is a story of things that were and those that might have been.

About How they Talked

People in this land speak the dialect of North and Central Alabama and surrounding lands, not to be confused with the soft fluid speech of the Blackbelt and coastal areas--the speech which some take to extreme to make a caricature of our ways. Friends to the south eliminate the letter 'r' from their speech as in cout house (court house) or pronounce 'r' as -ah, as in rivah (river). In some circumstances i-r is pronounced as u-i, as in fuist (first). If the word begins with 'r', the letter is reluctantly pronounced.

Those in North Alabama speak the language of Upland South. We love our 'rs', and pronounce them with an emphasis of the letter. Our speech is flat in inflection. We leave out harsh syllables in the center of words and knock off sharp corners by dropping consonants at the end or the first letter of awkward utterances.

Our use of the letter 'i' is different. We don't often use the two-part sound, but say many words with a short and flat 'i'. This is not so severe as imitators would have it.

On occasions an 'a' is added to a word, which lost its 'g' at the end to indicate some ongoing activity as agoin' or astandin'. Words ending in -day and -ow are too harsh for gentle ears. Sunday and window are rarely heard. An -er is sometimes used for -ow endings. But substituting vowels as in Sundee and winda is soothing to the ear and is more common. Small expressions as you, your, and for are thought trivial and are smoothed over in the form of *ya* and *fa* unless emphasis is needed. Even when vital to a sentence, for frequently comes out as the easier to say: *far*.

Our speech is not uniform, but layered by socioeconomic status and education. Rules of grammar are strictly enforced only by the more educated.

People in this land wish to emphasize their negativity or their uncertainty, so there is common usage of double negatives and double conditionals--as in "might could" and "can't hardly." Double positives such as "raise the winda up" or "he left out" are less common.

To those who live here, Upland dialect is relaxed, honest, and kind to the ear. Speech flows with rhythm and smoothness and is filled with colorful expressions. Words are sometimes blended in this unhurried flow of speech. Those in the upland south use archaic word forms, fitting and descriptive, preserved hundreds of years, but long forgotten in other regions.

Words and patterns of speech learned at home or from the schoolteacher born nearby were passed generation-to-generation -- largely unchanged. With instant global communication, this speech will soon fade into memory, as have these people and their way of life.

Acknowledgement

The words of this book could not have been written without the love, patience, and understanding of my wife Betty and encouragement of Opal Lovett, who taught a small writing group for many years. They both took my writing seriously long before I did.

Although I tried to be historically accurate, a friend assured me that I have not offended people of color. I consulted Civil War experts, veterinarians, a Methodist minister and a white water boating expert.

I am grateful for the technical help and advice from my sister, Dr. Carol McGinnis Kay.

Chapter One -- Devil Dog

In mists beyond the tree, a body lies by a spring. One hand pulls feebly at a weed. Evening light fades to dusk and deer appear, halting, cautious, testing the air. The shape on the ground does not stir, and the animals move on, gliding soft as shadows touching grass. Fingers of clouds shroud the moon. An owl calls from the tree.
A whisper of wings floats through darkness, fades and dies away leaving stillness but for voices of the night.

****

"Come up ... one last time." The boy pulled upward and backward on the plow handles and the mule strained forward. The worn point jumped out of the furrow, skidded and bumped along the ground into the barn lot, past a shoulder high pile of rocks hauled from the pasture and fields over the years.

The setting dun was low beyond the weathered barn, but the air hot and still, even in shadows. Light glowed through the hall and sheds leaving the barn itself a wall of darkness. In a cloud of weariness, the boy did not see a strange shape rise from hiding beyond the rocks. The long creature crept from darkness, pressed low to the ground, gliding without sound. It stopped, nose quivering, every muscle tense, moved a few feet, hesitated, now showing teeth -- then began slinking toward the boy, with eyes fixed on its quarry.

Nate felt a strange presence and looked up an instant before he heard scratching claws and gasping breaths behind him. He jerked his head around to see a monstrous red dog with teeth bared springing toward him. The beast lunged through the air the last few feet, its low growl rising to a horrific snarl, scattering squawking chickens and ducks in every direction. Nate dropped the lines and threw up his right arm. Huge paws struck him full in the chest and both fell to the ground. The creature sank his teeth deep into the upheld arm.

The dog rose, towering over the boy, and crushing his flesh in an iron grip. Growling, head thrashing side-to-side, it slung and tore Nate's arm as if it were a helpless rabbit. Frantically, Nate threw up his left arm to protect his throat and tried to pull away, but the pain of teeth tearing flesh held him. He expected the next moment to be his last, but the dog growled once more as it shook the arm, then dropped its grip, snapped at Nate's face, and as suddenly as it came, disappeared in the dusk.

The attack took seconds, but to the boy gasping and shaking on the ground it seemed hours. Nate lay on his back, arms lifeless and trembling, as the mule bolted across the barn lot dragging the plow. The trailing point scooped and scattered clumps of dirt and rocks until it caught on a stump and brought the frightened mule to an abrupt stop, throwing her on her side. She lay there chest heaving, fanning the air with two legs and stirring dust with the others.

Nate brushed trash and grit from his eyes, sat up and stared at the shadows of the barn and beyond the rocks. Through settling dust he saw nothing but the cow and sheep staring at him from a distance. He struggled to his feet and crossed the lot unsteadily to the mule. A stream of blood coiled around his wrist and dripped off his fingers. Avoiding a kick from the flailing legs, he grabbed the reins on the second try and gained control of the mule's head. He spoke gently to her as he finished removing the harness and tried to calm the mule and himself. After several attempts and with continuous urging, she struggled to stand and limped a few steps. Nate ran his hand down the right foreleg. It seemed straight and solid, but she pulled away when he touched a spot near the hoof and she favored the leg when she walked. He left the plow and harness where they lay and led the limping mule to the barn.

The boy was covered with sweat and dust from his day in the sun-baked fields. At fifteen, Nathan was the baby of the family, but he gave promise of being six feet in a year or so like his father and older brother. The wide brim hat shaded careless red hair and sunburned face with freckles sprinkled across his nose. Fuzz on his chin had begun to grow -- the kind that laughing brothers said the cat could lick off. His was the face of a child, struggling to become a man.

While his mule drank water, the boy noticed that his arm and hand were wet and sticky and looked for the first time. The bite had ripped the sleeve and torn through skin deep into his forearm. Nate watched sinews and muscles tighten and slide as he moved his hand and trembling fingers. When he made a fist, blood poured from the depths, ran down his wrist, and dripped into a small pool at his feet. All of the tearing pain from the beast returned. Nate clinched his teeth and felt his stomach tighten.

As he guided the mule to the hall of the barn, he took the cloth from around his neck, and wrapped his arm. Holding his right arm against his side, he fumbled with his left to pour feed in the trough of a stall. He led in the mouse-colored mule with the drooping head.

"Maude, ya might could do with a soak in the branch, but I can't do it just now. Stay put and rest. It'll be cool in a little while."

Nate latched the east gate where he had finished the last row of the day and moved around the barn. He picked up a stick, then slowly took a few steps closer

and looked beyond the pile of rocks. He jumped when
a rabbit fled from the shadow. Nate moved toward the
north gate and the path beyond, pressing both hands
against his right side to stop the trembling. He could
not stop the gnawing fear in his stomach.

Nate knew about a strange dog that neighbors
had seen prowling the woods. He wondered if his arm
had been damaged permanently, if he might be like the
man who sat at the end of the supper table each night.
His steps were unsteady and came slower. He stopped
at the gate. Trees and barn spun about him. He rubbed
at his eyes and blinked. *It hurts, but I can't cry. Men just
don't. Pa wouldn't. Don't think I can make it. I've got to
rest. I don't know what's wrong.*

The boy leaned against a fence-post with eyes
closed. In his mind he saw again the red dog's open
mouth. Nate heard a faint running scratching sound
that grew louder. He forced his eyes open and in the
blur of shadows saw a dog bounding toward him. Nate
gave a small cry and struggled to open the gate with
his left hand.

The animal slowed, stopped at his feet, looked
up and wagged his tail. Bear was one of the family
dogs. With a sigh, Nate closed the gate and followed
the path toward the shed behind the house. He walked
deliberately, concentrating on each step, watching his
feet, and holding his cloth-wrapped arm stiffly against
his side.

His brothers had quit minutes earlier and were
in the shed washing away the dust of the day. Their
bath came from cedar buckets and tubs of water hauled
from the spring and warmed by the sun. Four changes
of clothing hung from pegs on the shed wall. They
were splashing and talking as they washed.

Jacob was twenty-two, but looked older. He had
been a good-looking man before the red scar that ran
from his left eye to his chin. On occasion, a twitch

pulled at his lower lid to remind him that the mark of the past was there. Benjamin, the middle brother, had plain, undistinguished features that often showed confusion and sometimes a smile. He worked hard and was pleasant. At nineteen he was a little shorter and a little slower than his brothers. Benjamin and Jacob had brown hair and several days' growth of beard. All three were thin.

Nate was almost to the shed, stumbling along the path. The cloth had slipped down his arm and blood dripped from his fingers onto his trousers. Every few steps, the attentive dog at his side looked up at him. As Ben glanced up from his towel, he saw the two and shouted, "Look -- look yonder! What's wrong with Nate?" He kicked over a tub as he ran the few steps to his brother.

"Lord God Nate!" Jacob yelled as he ran, "Ye've been near tore up!" They grabbed Nate's arms as his steps faltered and called, "Ma -- Ma!"

Martha McGinnis poked her head out the kitchen door, then ran down the dogtrot and across the yard. She touched Nate's shoulder as his brothers eased him down on a stump in the shed.

"Oh my poor baby! What happened? What hurt ya arm? Bear wouldn't do this." Martha was in her early forties. Her face was kind, but with a sadness which showed the years. Dark blond hair, streaked with gray, was twisted and tied in a bun at the back of her head. She wore a plain dress with a white apron over it. The shapes of yellow and brown were hardly evident as flowers on the faded print.

"Nate, just sit on there and put yer arm over that bucket. Let's clean it up a mite so we can see how bad it is. Ben, run get Pa. He'll be in the garden 'till good light is gone. Nate, we can let ya lie down if ya feel weak."

Nate glanced up at his mother. "No, Ma. I'm fine here. It was a dog, but it wasn't Bear. He was way bigger than Bear."

When Martha looked at her family, her hazel eyes hinted at the love and patience she felt for them. Now wrinkles of concern crossed her forehead and lids were pinched around her eyes. After wiping the blood from around the injury, Martha poured water directly into the wound. Nate flinched and she flinched with him.

"It must have been the dog folks was talkin' about at church the last two weeks," Jacob said. "People said they seen him afar off. Nobody had any i-dee where he come from. He wasn't a big wolf like some thought. Ears were wrong for that. Ever body said he was a great big 'ol red hound and they couldn't say what kind. They said he was uncommonly thick and strong lookin'. Some said they lost chickens and calves and some right good-sized dogs."

Between dousings with the water Nate caught his breath and said, "J. D. Butler said his pa shot that dog -- hit him too -- but he was back runnin' cows the next day. Said that dog chased their wagon and made the mules run away till the wagon turned over and near tore up. The Butlers are callin' him Devil Dog. They thank he's not a regular dog -- but maybe from Satan himself."

John McGinnis arrived a few steps behind Ben, breathing hard and frowning. He was tall and gaunt with a harsh expression fixed beneath long, mostly gray hair. His face was partially hidden by a long scraggly beard. A smooth white scar extended down his cheek and into his beard. He was in his early forties, but could pass for fifty. The palm of his left hand was thickly callused. He had no right hand.

As John stumbled into the shed, he pulled his galluses over his right shoulder to hitch up his trousers.

He wiped the sweat from his forehead and drew his hand across his faded cotton shirt.

He tilted his hat back, kneeled by the stump, and peered at the wound.

"And that wild dog done this? The one they call Devil Dog -- the one that might be a mad-dog?" He pointed at the wound, "Ya know we'll have to heat an iron and burn that place. Ya'all never noticed that deep bite on the side of his face. That oughta be burned, too." He looked up at Nate's twisted face, "Did he bite Maude?"

"No, but she ran and fell down. She's got a place on her front leg that's right touchous. She's lame, but she walked to the stall. Look at her, if you're a mind to." He glanced at his father's right arm and then turned away. " I don't want my arm burned, Pa..."

Martha stared at her husband. "Ya can't mean that, John! Look -- see them leaders when he moves his hand. It would mess up his arm forever. They's got to be some other way." She wrapped her arms around Nate. He looked down at the familiar hands that carried marks of biscuit dough, brush-brooms, and lye-soap.

John frowned and jerked his head in the general direction of a neighbor's house. "Robert Cooper saw that dog ... said he had slobber 'round his mouth. Folks killed several 'coons this spring they thought was mad. Robert Butler's best dog went mad last week. He had to shoot him -- and that no more'an a mile off."

Ben blurted out, "Ever 'body is talkin' about that dog. After church last week even the preacher said somthin' about him. He said, 'First the Yankees and now that Devil Dog. What've we done?'"

John ignored Ben and glared at Martha and Nate. "Burnin' that bite is better'n some ways. In the war, if somethin' was bad wrong with a fella's arm or leg, he lost it. If that was a mad dog that bit him, he'd be better off if Doc come and cut it off."

Nate spoke from within his mother's arms, "I don't want to be here without my right arm. Look at you, Pa! Ya can't plow...can't work iron... have trouble harnessin' a team. I couldn't be that way."

John stood and glared at his youngest son. "Don't get smart with me, Nathan! Long as yer under my roof, ya'll do what I say, ...*even* if I say cut it off." He pulled his hat down farther. His brows were pinched in the shadow under the brim. "I haul water; I milk the cow. I hoe crops; I plant and work the garden and tell all of ya what to do. I do as much work as the three of ya put together. Ya couldn't raise gourds if I didn't show ya how. I work slower, but I work longer."

Martha watched John's face as he spoke. Nate shuddered and she held him tighter. "John, ya still have some of that corn liquor. Couldn't we just pour it in that bite? Wouldn't that work as good as that -- that hot poker? We could wash it out with lye soap first."

John stared at his wounded son and the distressed mother. Both watched him, waiting for an answer. He looked into their eyes for a few moments, and then turned away.

"If he don't think any more of what his Pa says than that, and he wants to chance dyin' from a mad-dog bite, then do it. But I'm havin' nothin' to do with none of this."

Ben ran around his father to the house for the liquor and clean rags. The two brothers and anguished mother scrubbed and cleaned the gaping wound. Nate clinched his teeth and managed to give no more than low grunts as they cleaned the injury with soap and water. But he screamed when alcohol flooded the raw space and shouted, "Owee, that damn mess hurts like Hell!"

Martha jerked back and her mouth opened, but she said nothing and kept on washing the wound. The brothers watched as the liquor drained off the arm. Then red streamed into the water again.

"Ma, that place is still ableedin'. Ya want me to get some spider webs and sut?"

"No, Ben, wash out that liquor and get me two fresh eggs and more rags."

Martha cracked the eggs and separated the whites, poured them on the open wound, covered it with clean rags and tied them in place. "Somebody recite Ezekiel 16:6; or run and get the book and read it, if ya don't remember." Ben and Jacob mumbled and stammered the words. "Try to keep that arm still for a while. After the scripture, I'm sure the bleedin' will stop." She scrubbed the deep puncture wounds on Nate's cheek, coated them with more egg white and left them open. As the older boys headed toward the house, Nate held his injured arm across his chest and pushed up with his left. Martha grabbed his shoulder and pushed him back down. She looked at Nate with a serious, almost angry face.

"Now, before we go in and while it's fresh on my mind, I mean to talk to ya." Her voice increased in pitch as the boy squirmed. "Nathan Leander McGinnis keep sittin' on that stump! I don't want to have to stand on a milkin' stool to look ya in the face. Now turn this away and look me in the eyes when I talk. I want ya to hear this good. The very i-dee of usin' language like *that*, and in front of yer Ma, too. Ya may as well have called on the devil hisself as to use words like that! Ya didn't hear it from yer brothers or yer teacher or yer pa".

"But, Pa sometimes...."

"I know where ya learned such. Them Butler boys have been acomin' over here on Sundee when we're gone. Now let me tell you somethin' right now, young man! And you listen good. You'll hear cussin' and all kinds o' bad words long after I'm gone. When some folks can't thank of the right words to say, they cuss! They cuss 'cause they're not smart enough to say a word that means somethin'. I know you're smarter than that. So when ya hear somebody cuss, just thank to yaself, bad words -- empty head -- dumb as a froe. Don't *never* let me hear ya cuss again, or even use ugly words. Do it and I'll be on ya like a duck on a junebug. Yer not too old to have yer mouth washed out with lye soap." She took a jerking deep breath and sighed. "Bathe off some and come on in the house. Prop that arm on the table and try to eat some supper."

"Yes, ma'am. I'm sorry. I didn't go to say that." He sat on the stump looking at the ground, not offering to move until his mother walked up the back steps. Martha brushed past a young woman in the dogtrot holding back a small child.

In the early darkness, Nate glanced up to see both women go into the kitchen. He followed up the wooden steps, and through the dogtrot separating the rooms. He took slow deliberate steps down the passageway, steadying himself with his good hand. As his fingers passed over the surface, Nate marveled again at the walls of the double pen cabin. His father and his grandfather had built the entire house with their hands and tools in the shed. He thought of the strength and determination of these men. As much as he was in awe of his father, he admired him and he often wondered if he could ever be as strong as the men who had come before him. *Now I've got a hurt arm -- a bad hurt arm. I can't work with just one arm.* As he came to the kitchen door, Nate's weakness returned and he leaned against the entranceway and took quick shallow breaths.

After he rested, he raised his head. The kitchen-eating room was the same size as the big bedroom across the dogtrot. What he could not see by candlelight, he saw in his mind. Nate knew every log in the walls and everything in it. Hand hewn beams supported a rough lumber ceiling. The boards were mottled gray from a thousand candles on the table and a thousand fires in the stove. Walls were logs smoothed with a broadaxe. The split hardwood log floorboards were hand-planed to nearly flat and seemed to ripple in the flickering light.

A cook-stove, bought used for ten dollars, years earlier, was connected by a pipe to the stone chimney. It was old and patched, but Martha and her daughter-in-law managed to cook simple meals for the family. A window behind and slightly above the stove was open at times to clear the kitchen of fumes and heat. When the sun was up, the wavy glass let in light and a twisted view of the world. A worn candle mold and a box with the leavings of a tallow cake were almost hidden in shadows toward a north corner.

On the hearth near the stove, a broom leaned against the stones of the fireplace. Three feet long and tied with cords near the top, this bundle of broom sage was left loose at the bottom to form a cylindrical brush for the hearth. As Nate propped on the doorway his left hand brushed against the handle of the floor broom of dried broomcorn, hanging from a peg next to the shuck mop.

A small table for preparing food in the winter stood near the stove, and another for the summer sat in the north corner of the room, beyond the heat of the chimney. A larger table for eating extended along the wall to the west and was surrounded by simple straight chairs. The door on the west wall opened onto the dogtrot. Small windows on the north and east sides of the kitchen were now dark. Dried peas, flour, meal, baking soda, salt and other staples were stored in rough cabinets near one of the food tables. Dried fruit hung in cloth bags outside the shelves for the better ventilation. A bucket of water was kept filled on the cooler north table.

Nate took a deep breath. There was a comforting smell in the kitchen of smoke and dried peaches, of wood, corn meal, candles, and vapors of meals past. This was Nate's home -- the only one he had ever known. He knew every part of it and loved it. His arm hurt, but he felt safe and secure. Nothing could hurt him now. He was home.

Nate's father sat at the large kitchen table, his face barely visible in the flickering candlelight. He looked up as Martha put plates on the table. "Ya musta poured the liquor in. Heard him holler. Real man wouldn't carry on like that." Martha glanced at Nate, opened her mouth to speak, but then pursed her lips. John continued in a barely audible voice," I never made a sound when they cut off my arm. White hot iron woulda been better, but maybe liquor'll work."

John did not look at his youngest son propped against the doorway and pale in the candlelight. Instead, he stared at the dancing lights and shadows on the uneven logs of the blank wall, then looked down at the table, and in a low halting voice said:

"And if thine right hand offend thee,
cut it off and cast it from thee: for it is
profitable for thee that one of thy members
should perish and not thy whole body
should be cast into hell."

"I think on them words ever' mornin' when I wake up and see this here stump." He ran his fingers over the scar where his right hand should be. "But it hadta be, fa me to live." For the first time the older man seemed to see his son at the door. With little change in expression, he added quietly "Yes sir, Nate, wooda been better to cut it off or burn the evil out of that arm. But maybe yer ma's treatment will work."

For a time, no one spoke. There were no sounds but the sputtering of the candles.

Nate regained his balance and took cautious steps toward the table, avoiding the high spots in the floor. He knew the stove he passed had been cold since noon, yet he suddenly felt heat in his face.   His weakness came back and he almost fell in his chair.

Martha removed the cloth covering pitchers of sweet milk and buttermilk, a plate of cornbread, and one with a few pieces of cold ham. As the family gathered around the table, light from two tallow candles barely showed these remains of the noon meal. Jacob's wife, Bertha Mae, set out plates and glasses. The twenty-year-old mother was blond, but not a towhead like their son. She was not a beauty, but was pleasant and had good looks of youth and health. She showed signs of a child to come. In her soft voice she asked Nate about his injury and sat down at the end of the table to encourage her own son to eat. John B. was rubbing his eyes and pushing away his food. "No -- don' want it. It's not good!"

Bertha Mae held his hands while the others scraped their chairs across the uneven floor. When they were seated, adult heads bowed and John B.'s pushed over, John began, "Lord, we thank ya for our farm and home and our family. Save us from Satan and uh…his messengers. Thank ya for this food. Amen."

"John B., get your hand out of that glass!" Bertha Mae grabbed his hand and wiped it on her apron. The adults at the table looked at their food with little enthusiasm. In spite of his mother's pleadings, Nate drank milk, but ate nothing. John B. whined and complained about the food and about being held, then rubbed his eyes again.

John B. became quiet, his eyes nearly closed, As they sat in the stillness, light flashed through the windows. Almost immediately, a rumbling rattled dishes on the shelf. John B. opened his eyes, threw his hands up and gave a shrill cry. John sat up with a start, then leaned back and mumbled, "For a bit there, I thought it was....Weell, it's just thunder."

The wind began to moan about the old house, and they heard a far away howling, like the cry of an anguished soul. Nate sat straight up in his chair and jerked his head toward the sound. They heard Bear bark once and there were several bumps under the kitchen floor.

John moved his chair around and went to the front porch. He came back and looked in the doorway. "I'm gonna put them dogs in a stall at the barn. If that Devil Dog comes agin and if he's anywhere near as big as you say he is, he might kill 'em. It's comin' up a bad cloud to the north and commencin' to rain. Better go before it gets any worse and while I can still see."

On warm nights, the family sat on the porch in the moonlight, looked at the stars, listened to the sounds of the night, and talked, but not with a storm threatening. John and Ben left for the barn. Jacob cleaned the food from his hair and took crying John B. to his bed. The women cleared the table and washed the dishes.

Martha put a hand on Nate's shoulder, "Can I help ya get to the room?"

"No ma'am. I'm fine."

Nate lit a short candle, and carried it down the dogtrot. He leaned against the wall and shielded the flame with his hand against the breeze in the passageway. Two shed-roofed clapboard rooms had been added on the south side of the log cabin as the family grew. One to the west was for the two unmarried boys; the one to the east was for Jacob and his wife and child.

Nate sat at the small table near the window in his room where he wrote and studied when school was in session. Books and papers were scattered about the worn table that had been his father's when he was young and had a hand to hold the pen. His father never admitted it now, but Nate knew there was a better time when he wrote letters and read books. John now often said to his sons, "Won't make ya grow any more corn or cotton if ya read a hundred books. Just makes ya think ya're better'n the rest of us." The others read slowly and painfully -- usually the Bible.

Nate owned few books, but borrowed one from friends when he could. He had read and reread a thumb-worn *Ivanhoe*, while he dreamed of a time when men wore fine clothes, rode great horses, did noble deeds and did not plow and plant and gather crops all the time. Nate looked at things on the table and picked up a book, tilted it toward the candle, propped it on an inkwell and read a few lines, but the print was small and hard to read by flickering light. He wished for brighter light, but the lard oil lamp was gone.

With a start, he saw that he was rubbing his throbbing arm in the same way his father touched the scars of his stump. He gave up his efforts to read and stared through the window at the yard. Light from the moon came and went, sometimes bright enough to read by. The martin pole and stacks of firewood glowed, then faded into shadows as clouds gathered and rain began to fall.

Ben stomped in after helping his father and settled in for the night. Nate blew out the candle and went to bed. The heavy rain on the roof slowed to a gentle splatter. The door to their parents' room by Ben's bed was closed, but faint light outlined the crack at the edges. Sounds traveled from room to room in the stillness of night. Nate heard the scraping of a chair and an object being set aside. From a thousand nights before, he knew his father had just put down his Bible.

As the light around the door blinked out, Nate heard his mother say, "John, I do wish ya wouldn't be so harsh with our youngest. He's just a boy. He'll thank ya don't love him, and I know ya do. Ya just can't bring yaself to show it."

The bed creaked as the couple settled in. The deeper voice answered, "Big as he is, it's time he learned that life is hard. He has to grow up fast or it'll beat him down." The voices in the next room trailed off and the house was still.

He drifted off to sleep in the blackness of a cloudy night, listening to distant call of cows to their calves, a far-off dog howling at the moon, owls hooting, frogs celebrating rain. The wind moaned around the old farmhouse, creaking as it settled in the night air. In some far corner of his mind Nate heard these sounds of the night, heartbeats of the land, and even in sleep knew that all was well. After the happenings of the day and with his arm throbbing, Nate slept, though fitfully.

Chapter Two -- Night Visitor

Nate woke with a start. Had he really heard a faint scratching or did it come in a dream. Skies had cleared and moonlight flooded through his small window. The wind was still and there were no sounds – not even crickets. He drifted back toward sleep. His eyes had almost closed when a shadow crossed the window and he heard a dull thump. He jerked his right arm across his chest, pushed up on his elbows, forced his eyes fully open to see a huge head silhouetted in the window. Nate screamed. Martha rushed through the doorway as Ben, sleeping in the same room, struggled to sit up.

"Ma, it was that dog -- that Devil Dog! He was lookin' in the winda. His mouth was open and all white and slobbery. And his eyes ... his eyes were like fire. I could hear him pantin'. Why is he after me?"

While Martha was trying to console Nate, John stumbled in. "The very   i-dee! That winda is four foot off the ground," he snorted. "Ya didn't see no dog! Musta had a nightmare. Yer old enough to do better'n that! Real man wouldn't holler out over a dream." Martha's frown was evident even in the moonlight. Nate could feel her callused fingers squeeze his shoulders as his father ranted on, "Now let us get a little sleep. Ya got ever'body up. I can hear Jacob out in the dogtrot and John B is asquallin'."

But sleep did not come the rest of that night. Nate lay awake thinking about the strange dog coming a second time. *I wonder if I should have let Pa use that hot iron. I've had bites before and nothin' happened. But somehow that dog seems different from a regular dog. It's the worst bite I've ever had. Worst I've ever seen. Still -- whatever happens, I know I can't work on a farm without my right arm.* The thoughts were troubling, and he found no clear answers. Even when he reassured himself, it was not lasting.

* * *

At first light, John McGinnis dressed and left the quiet house. He moved down the dogtrot and stepped into the cool morning of drifting mists and heavy dew. He shivered in the damp air as he passed a small pile of fireplace logs, next to stacks and ricks of stovewood. Most was split pine, wrist to arm sized pieces, small enough to fit into the firebox of the cook-stove. John looked to the west at an eighteen-foot pole supporting two smaller cross members. Longneck gourds with a hole cut in one side hung in rows. A collection of purple martins shared this farm with the family in the spring and summer. They swirled in frenzied circles in the heat of the day, gathering mosquitoes and other insects to feed their babies.

In the bend of the path beyond the smokehouse, John stopped at the spring. He stood for a while watching the mist slowly swirl and rise. He drank a dipper of water, and filled a bucket to wash his hands and the cow's bag at the barn. Farther down the slope, he made a stop at the privy, almost hidden by muscadine vines with bright new leaves. As he opened the gate to the barn lot, he looked toward a tree-covered ridge in the distance to the south and across the flatter, plowed fields to his right and left. Mists covered the top of the ridge and flowed down into the valley. The farm was peaceful and still in the thin early light.

Inside the gate of the barn lot, John almost stumbled over a still form on the ground. He stooped for a better look. Frowning, he stood, muttered to himself and shook his head as he walked toward the barn. At the entrance to the hall of the barn he stopped again, kneeling to inspect something on the ground.

When he finished at the barn, John carried the bucket of milk to the springhouse in the crook of his right arm. He tipped it over with his stump as he held the bail with his left hand and strained the warm milk through white cloth into a jug then lowered it into the spring. Before going in the kitchen, he walked the yard around the cabin, carefully searching the ground.

John sat at the table with the rest of the family. Other than a mumbled greeting, he said nothing, nor did the others speak. Even John B. was quiet. Little was said until they finished their meal of eggs, side-meat, biscuits, and boiled coffee with eggshells to settle the grounds. Martha picked up the pot and said, "John that's the last of the coffee. I don't reckon we'll see any more till the crops come in?" John nodded.

After eating, John pushed back from the table and stared glumly at the blank wall, "That big brindle cat's dead, and one sheep, too. They're clean tore up. They's tracks all 'round the house -- prints big as that yella lion left at Ambrose's place last year."

Everyone gasped. Martha and her three sons dropped forks and knocked over chairs as they ran into the yard, leaving John B. and his mother at the table. Bertha Mae ran to the window for a look toward the yard. "Wanta see! Wanta see!" John B. yelled, as he climbed down from his chair.

John slowly walked out of the kitchen, down the dogtrot into the yard and watched the others circle the house pointing at tracks in the damp earth and muddy smudges covering the windowsill. They gathered around a set of pad prints facing Nate's window. The tracks were nearly twice the size of those of Bear, who sniffed the trail cautiously.

Nate looked at his father, "I told ya I saw a dog's head."

"Still shouldn't have hollered and woke everbody up. We mighta got a shot at him if ya hadn't scared him off." Martha gave Nate a quick smile and walked back to her kitchen. Nate turned away and tried not to let his father seee his face. John pointed, "Judgin' from them tracks, he's a right smart size. I saw one big as that...once. He was red, too. That was way back yonder and a long ways off."

As the rest of the family followed Martha back down the dogtrot, John said, "Nate, after yer Ma takes care of ya arm and if ya're able, feed the stock. Ya shouldn't have no trouble. If ya can't do it right off, ya'll have to learn. I do it with one hand all the time. After the rain, it's a mite too wet to plow. The other boys can split shingles. We need to fix the roof on the north side of our room. I was in the loft last week and daylight is showin' several places. Leaked some last night, too."

After the others left, Martha removed yesterday's dressing and wrapped Nate's arm with clean white rags. She stood in the dogtrot watching as he left. "Now, you be careful. Don't hurt that arm."

* * *

At the barn, Nate fed the two sound mules and then turned Maude out. Her limp was worse. She could bear no weight on the right front leg. It was badly swollen above the hoof, which angled slightly to one side. Nate held his bandaged arm across his chest and ran to the house to bring his father.

John examined the leg carefully. Any motion caused severe pain to the patient mule. "Nate, it's broke. You know, well as I do, what has to be done. I may as well do it."

"But yesterday it wasn't this bad. I looked at it."

"Don't make no difference. Today it's broke. Maybe ya didn't check good enough or it coulda been partly broke and she finished it off in the night. I'll go get the gun. We'll have to hitch up the other mules and drag her out to the woods so she don't stink so bad."

"No, don't do it! If it has to be, I'll do it. I plowed her more than anybody. We won't have to drag her. I'll take her to the woods. She'll walk three legged for me." Seeing his father opening his mouth to speak, Nate raised his voice as much as he dared, "I can do it. I don't want nobody else to do it."

To Nate, the distance from the barn to the house seemed longer than the day before. He followed his father into the big bedroom and watched as he took down the double-barreled muzzleloader from the pegs on the wall, loaded it, and put the cap in place. John did not speak or touch his son as he handed him the gun. Nate took the weapon with his left hand. It almost sank to the floor. "Don't miss." John said. "I just loaded one barrel. We're not gonna be able to buy powder and shot 'till the crop comes in this fall. And don't rurn that bridle. Take her up on the ridge. But don't put her downside toward the spring. Nobody uses it for water now, but we might some day. When we get time, we need to build Jacob a house of his own. He might want to live there."

Nate took a deep breath and made a small sound as he grabbed the stock with his right hand and raised the gun. He turned, took a few steps and stopped at the doorway. He shifted his grip on the gun and watched out of the corner of his eye as his father walked up behind him. John reached out his hand toward Nate, but before he touched his son's shoulder he drew it back again and held the stump of his right forearm, as if that were his intent from the first. "Go ahead and do the job. A man has to do what he has to do."

Nate mumbled, "Yessir." He stood staring at the gun for a moment, but said nothing, then stepped through the doorway and down the dogtrot.

Ben caught up with Nate at the barn. "Ya want me to go with ya? I'll hold the mule and you do the gun or t'other way round."

"No, I'd rather do it by myself. She'll stand still for me." Ben watched Nate lead the staggering mule from the barn. The boy and Maude plodded through the lot, across the pasture, over the wet weather branch and into the woods. They climbed the slope on an old road that was little more than a footpath, angling first to the right and then to the left toward the top of the ridge.

He tried carrying the gun with his right hand and leading Maude with his left. Pain in his arm caused him to shift the gun to the left and hold the bridle with the right hand. Sometimes Maude wobbled, stumbled, bobbed her head, and jerked Nates's wounded arm. He stopped several times for Maude to rest and to shift the gun from one side to the other. The way was steep for the limping mule, but patches of shade were dark and cool. Each time they stopped, Maude looked at him and Nate thought of the dog's attack. He could still see the beast rushing with teeth bared. He closed his eyes and heard the snarls and felt the pain in his arm and tightness in his chest. *My arm hurts, but Maude is gonna die. But if Maude had arms, we'd both have hurts in the same place. What could happen to me? What could be worse than death?*

The pair reached a level clearing where the trail turned left and climbed steeply. A lone outcrop of rock rose abruptly from the slope and held back the forest floor above. In a flat semicircle at the base of the rock, a few bushes and weeds sprouted from stony soil. Through stunted trees at the edge, Nate could look down and see the pastures, fields, and buildings of the farm. Spring greens of hardwoods shined against darker pines. Cows and sheep grazed with their little ones. The valley was alive and growing. Even rows of fresh plowed fields had dots of green. New life was everywhere.

The mule was willing, but her hops were labored and rests longer. She only covered inches with each step. Maude could go no farther. Nate led her into the clearing and took off the halter. Maude did not move. He lifted the muzzleloader to his shoulder and rested his thumb on the right hammer. His eyes passed over the mule from switching tail to drooping head. He hesitated, lowered the gun, took a few steps, and placed his hand on her head. "Maude, I thank ya for what ya've done; ya've worked real hard. I'm right sorry it's come to this. I don't know what else to do... or say... I reckon it's for the best."

He backed away and raised the gun to his right shoulder again. He had heard it said that mules were dumb and had no feelings, but when Maude lifted her head and looked at him, he could not have been convinced of that. He supported the gun with his left hand, cocked the hammer, and struggled to slide his trembling fingers toward the trigger. The long barrel wavered, but Maude did not budge. *Oh, if she just wouldn't look at me like that!* His right index finger closed on the trigger, but it wouldn't move, as if it were no longer part of his body. He closed his eyes. The blast of the gun jarred his wounds. The worst pain was not in his right arm.

*   *   *

From the garden, John straightened up and looked toward the ridge as the echo rolled across the farm. Fifteen minutes later, Nate plodded through the pasture to the barn to put up the halter. He found his father working in the garden. Nate carried the gun in his left hand, occasionally pushing up the barrel with his right. "I did it, Pa, and with one shot. I shot a friend. I'm gonna put up the gun."

John stood, glanced at the fresh bloodstains on Nate's rag dressing and looked down as he dusted his pants. He stared at the potato vines as he spoke. "I heard. Bertha Mae just got through pickin' a mess of greens. It'll be time to eat pretty quick. We'll knock off a spell." The path to the house seemed longer than ever to Nate. Martha was standing in the dogtrot, watching as they arrived in the yard. Nate's face was dry, but his cheeks had streaks of pollen and dust.

"Ya all right, Nate?"

"Tolerable, Ma. Just tolerable."

"Wash up and come in and set a spell. We'll eat d'rectly."

Nate stepped into the shed to wash his hands and throw water on his streaked face. He dried with a clean rag and moved into the workshop where his brothers were working. Jacob and Ben looked up as he entered.

"Right glad your job is over, Nate. We're might near through here." Piles of shingles were scattered about the shed floor, and behind Ben were stacks of cedar blocks. Ben picked up one of the blocks and placed it on the worn stump. Jacob held the wooden handle and rested the sharp side of the froe near the edge of the block. The topside of the wedge-shaped blade was thick and scarred. Jacob nodded. Ben struck the top with a maul. The shingle knife went halfway.

"Ben, ya gotta hit that thang just so. Hit it like you mean it and cut the shingle with one swing." Jacob took the hammer-like tool made from an oak sapling with a natural knot. He placed the shingle knife against the end grain of the wood and struck the froe sharply. A shingle of perfect size and thickness fell with a single blow. He handed the tools back to Ben. "Try again till ya get the feel of it. Just remember, don't never hit that froe with a regular hammer. Always use this here maul. It's been dried by fire an' feels hard to us, but wood is kinder to metal than a hammer--won't run the edges over so bad. It's been a long time since we've cut shingles. Ya've just forgot."

Bertha Mae and Martha were setting the table when the men arrived. They placed bowls of turnip greens, dried beans, and cornbread, and pitchers of milk on the large table. The rest of the family ate but Nate only picked at the meal. Martha touched his shoulder so that he looked up from his plate. "Nate, me and Bertha Mae worked hard to fix this dinner. Ya need to eat to get well."

Ben leaned over to look at the stained rag. "How's ya arm?"

"I'm not as bad off as Maude. Not yet, anyways."

Martha dropped her fork, "Don't say thangs like that!"

After the plates were cleared, John said, "Jacob and Ben got more shingles to split. Nate, just help me finish the garden. We got an arm apiece. Maybe we can get the job done."

"Pa, I can do a day's work. I got two arms. One's just hurt a little. I can plow."

"Too wet to work the fields anyways. Go to the garden with me." After the noon meal, John and his sons sat on the porch while the women cleared the table. Today the rest was silent.

Without a word, John got up from his chair and left for the garden. Nate followed. The two weeded and cultivated. Bertha Mae worked with them while John B. took a nap. Nate was kneeling down to pull weeds between the potato vines in the mid-afternoon heat when he stood up to straighten his back and glanced toward the south ridge. Huge birds were soaring on motionless wings in sweeping circles over the ridge. John followed Nate's gaze and then watched the pained expression on his son's face. "Nate, a man has to do what a man has to do. Them are buzzards. And buzzards have to do what buzzards do. That's all they're doin'. Buzzards and skippers; they're all part of God's plan."

"They don't waste no time doin' it."

"No, they don't. And men can't waste time neither. We best get back to it, if we aim to finish by dark."

In the late afternoon as they made their way home, Nate turned toward the ridge yet again. The sky was empty, the buzzards gone. Nate shuddered.

Chapter Three – WHY?

> *"We are a band of brothers*
> *And native to the soil*
> *Fighting for the property*
> *We gained by honest toil;*
> *And when our rights were threatened,*
> *The cry rose near and far –*
> *Hurrah for the Bonnie Blue Flag*
> *That bears the single star!"*
> *The Bonnie Blue Flag*

At the end of the day, John and his sons washed and changed for supper. After the blessing, the family picked at their food in silence. John B. 's eyes almost closed and his head fell to one side. In the deeper stillness that followed, the adults looked blankly at scraps on their plate or at the wall. Benjamin stared intently at his father's face in the flickering light, fidgeted in his chair then began hesitantly, "Uh -- uh -- Pa, could I ask ya somethin'?" John nodded, without looking up. "Way back yonder, we useta play and sing and go on with foolishness, sometimes. It didn't hurt nothin'. When ya came back home at the first of the war, you played and we sang *Bonnie Blue Flag* or *Turkey in the Straw,* and the like -- mor'n just hymns like we do in church. We useta go to doin's at school or folks' houses. 'Bout all we do now i s work and go to church. Is that all we're ever gonna do? Don't nobody ever laugh any more?"

His brothers looked at their plates or toward the wall, away from their father at the end of the table. John B. frowned and began to squirm. Bertha Mae tried to keep him still and quiet. Martha glanced at Ben, watching his father, waiting for an answer. She opened her mouth.

Before she could utter a sound, John looked up, scowled at his son and said, "Be thankful. Ya got a roof over yer head and food on the table. Lots of folks don't have that. Some are walkin' the roads. Some are starvin'. Some went west after the war. A heap are dead– shot, or dead to sickness, or starved. In the war, we lost more to camp sickness than to Minié balls. They died out from smallpox or slow fever or even measles. It's a wonder any of us made it home."

John's pulled at his trembling beard. He frowned as he pushed his left shoulder forward and moved his hand to cover the scars of his stump. Martha smiled at Ben and leaned into the light to see John's face. "Ben didn't question the food on the table, clothes on his back or how ya grow cotton. I thank he asked a fair question. Ya could give him more of a real answer."

As John glanced toward Martha, she pled with her eyes, "He asked why there's not much happiness any more. I'd like to hear the answer."

John studied the faces around the table in the dim light. Martha and Ben fixed questioning eyes on him. The others turned away -- silent and almost holding their breath. There were no sounds but the sigh of the wind and the sputter of the tiny candle flames in the breeze from the dogtrot door. John said nothing and stared at the wall, as if watching the past unfold in dancing lights and shadows. He rubbed the scars of his stump. After several minutes, he began slowly. "Ya'all just don't understand. Jacob saw enough of the war to get a scar on his face, but not much as me. I saw the whole thang. We lost -- still pains me to say it, and it always will. Most of the young men and lots of old men died out and the country was tore up and burned. Most folks' stock was stole and anythang worth somethin' hauled off. Now we got all them Yankees ever' where tellin' us when to jump and how high! Life now is not what life was and won't never be."

John's stared at the wall and his voice trailed away. Jacob spoke hesitantly, "Ben, ya don't see it on the farm, but we got them carpetbaggers and scalawags all over. I don't thank we'll ever get shed of 'em. Such bothers Pa...and...and me too."

John frowned, "The roads and the towns are full of 'em. Them folks is waitin' with a sackful of the money they made in the war. They're just awaitin' to grab up somebody's land if he has a bad crop and can't pay his taxes or note to the bank. Folks that fought for the South get put out of their house and on the road. And some Union man, who made a satchel full of money in the war, sits in that house and laughs. Scalawags're worse. They're from the South, but they were trash and they're still trash. They sided with the Union and ended up with money when the rest of us are pore. Both are circlin' like buzzards. Ever' time we get some news from somebody in town or church, we hear about more of our friends bein' put out of their house and on the road.

Yankees stole four years of my life. They took my right hand. Now they want my farm. They'd have it and put us out too, if they could. While there's life in me, I'll not let that happen. Family without land is nothin'. I'm not the man I was. You're not like you were when I left. By now you ought to be ready to farm on your own ... 'stead of askin' fool questions." John took several short breaths and looked toward the wall again. "I don't reckon I do laugh much any more. That much might could be true, but there's not much call for a one-armed banjo player.

The Yankees whupped us. Now they're grindin' us in the dirt. I don't see no end in sight. This farm is our land. Our sweat has gone in it, and my Pa's before me. And a right smart of our blood, too. I'm just tryin' to keep this place for you boys. If ya wasn't in war, ya wouldn't understand all that."

Ben glanced at his mother. She smiled, but said nothing.

"If it was so bad, Pa, why did we have the war? What did we fight about? Was it all about turnin' the darkies aloose, like some say?"

Nate and Jacob traded embarrassed glances. John never turned his head, but answered in a voice hardly loud enough to be heard, "Some says it was. But we never had no darkies and three out of four white folks in the south didn't have slaves or even work any."

"Does that mean that we're pore?"

John appeared startled and moved his eyes back and forth as if searching for an answer on the wall. Martha said, "Now, just one minute! This family is not low-down pore white trash! We don't have what rich folks have in them fine houses, but we have ever'thang we need. We own land and work hard; we just don't have other folks work far us. We're not rich, we're just plain folks."

John said, "In Ebenezer Springs and lots of other places not one in ten had slaves ... if that many. Slavin' hurt us 'stead of helpin' us and hurt most of our friends. Ol' Man Ham could grow more cotton and corn and take less for it than we could 'cause he had all them colored hands. I'd just as soon there wern't no slaves. Some might have fought to keep slaves, but not many. Fact is, fella with a passel of 'em got to stay home from the war. Slaves was part of the trouble between North and South, but that wasn't the biggest cause of the war. Man won't risk life and limb fightin' just so folks down the road can have slaves."

"Is havin' slaves wrong, Pa?"

"Ya know I don't hold with slavin'. The book says, 'In the sweat of thy face shall thou eat bread.' It don't say nothin' 'bout the sweat of another fella's face. My pa and uncle Ambrose was fathered by a man who come from the old country as a in-dentured servant before the first revolution ... which is about same as a slave four years, sometimes six. Them folks sold the only thang they had to get here -- they sold themselves. It was the only way pore folks could get across. Course some got sent when they didn't say "Yessir" just right to one of the king's men. Now all those slaves been turned loose and don't quite know which way to turn. Bein' free don't put food on the table without work. With time, they'll learn to look out for theirselves."

John B. stopped smearing food on the table and began rubbing his eyes and whining. Bertha Mae leaned over and whispered in Jacob's ear. He stood up and said, "Ben, you were big enough to remember the war and what went on. There's no call for all this. We're just plowin' the same ground over agin. We need to leave it be."

"Now, Jacob, be patient with Ben, Martha said. You know his hurt addled his thinkin' and rememberin' some."

"I know more about the war than I want to, now. Me and the wife and boy are goin' to bed." The scar tugged at his lid at rapid intervals.

The rest of the family mumbled "G'night," as they left.

John said nothing as he stared at the wall of changing shapes. Nate shifted his chair away from the table, but Martha motioned to him to be still. These words were the most the family had heard about the war since John came home, a broken man. He began again, "Most says that we was tryin' to get our independence like folks did from England, way back when. Some says the fight was about state's rights. The North was takin' our taxes and givin' us nothin'. We wanted to be aloose from them folks and go our own way. We're different from Yankees and didn't thank the other states should keep us in the Union aginst our will. Some said they were jealous of what we had. We wanted our own country. And we didn't want it like the North. It wasn't no overnight thang. We were fussin' and pullin' apart a good thirty year before the war."

"What's the difference? Ain't they just like us?"

"Folks in the north are interested in machines and factories and makin' money. They don't care who they step on to do it, neither. What's important to us is God and blood and land. Most fought 'cause the Yankees was here, and shouldn't be. The Yankees were on our land, and we were willin' to spill our blood on that land to run 'em out. Once the war got started, some just got carried away with speeches and bands and flag wavin'. Sounded like a man under fifty wouldn't be able to hold up his head in the county, if he didn't go."

"Why did *you* fight, Pa?"

"Wasn't much choice. When the first revolution commenced, my grandpa fought for a land he hadn't known long. I was born here. I *had* to go help get our freedom from the north. All I know is, once I got in, they was a line o' men to the north and one to the south. Ever'body had guns and swords and knives. I was atryin' to kill some Yankee mother's son 'fore he kilt me or my friends. I saw some fall when I shot. I have asked God to forgive me for killin' all them Yankees... O'course...I haveta ad-mit that I asked Him to let me aim straight when I was shootin'. Most times He did." John stopped to stare at the wall again.

Ben said, "Sam Simpkins says that God was on the Yankee side. That's why they won."

"Sam Sinpkins is a no 'count scalawag. When the war come, he deserted his kin and went north. Some of his family won't even call his name. Most likely they never will. If God was on the North's side, then He always picks the side with the most soldiers and the most guns. The Lord was with good men on both sides. Lots died when they had a limb cut off. Some lived. With all the killin' and terrible thangs on both sides, how could God pick a side? He's not gonna choose one side of Hell over the other. I b'lieve God turned his head and shed bitter tears while the war was on."

"We didn't have scalawags in our family, did we?"

John looked down at the table and moved his left hand over the scar on the stump of his right arm. He winced as if the wound were new. "It pains me to say it, but we had a scalawag...just one. Uncle Absalom joined the Confederate army when the war commenced. Then one day they couldn't find him. He just plain disappeared. We all thought somethin' had happened to him. Ya might say it had. He lost his right mind and went over to the Yankee army. We didn't hear nothin' about him 'til that steamer *Sultana* blew up on the Mississippi River with two thousand Yankees let out of prison camps. Ol' Ab was among 'em. He met his maker with a big D branded on his arm. It's right sad when folks die, but not many grieved over Absalom. Most of the family just go on like he never was born."

"Well, Pa, why did we lose? Seems like I remember folks makin' speeches in town sayin' that any man from the South could take on four or five Yankees.

John winced. He looked at the wall, then turned to Ben, "First off, we didn't have a lot of factories to make guns and thangs. I still don't think we wooda lost if we just fought the Yankees, but after we done good at the first of the war, they went off to Europe and brought in all sorts of fureigners for their army. They recruited and stol' slaves from the south and put them with northern Nigras and give 'em guns and put 'em in the army. Told 'em if they didn't win they'd go back to bein' a slave agin. At the end, they was more Nigras an' fureigners fightin' for the Yankees than all the men in the whole Confederate army. It's a wonder we lasted long as we did. The sufferin' of the home folks hurt us, too. It was 'specially hard for folks that didn't work darkies. Fields was grown up in weeds and people was starvin'."

Martha tried to interrupt, but John continued, "The gov'ment was havin' to give out food. Womenfolks wrote husbands and begged 'em to come home. In '65, some deserted and did go home. I don't reckon I blame 'em much, but I knew you kids and yer Ma would take care of our place. I stayed 'til the end, and got the scars to show far it."

John shoved his plate away with his stump. "Yankees had more votes'n we did in '60. They was gonna make us dance when they played the tune. Ol' Abe never even come south when he run for election. It was his meanin' to put us down. He wanted ever'thang run by that big fed'ral gov'ment from the north, just like now!" Martha quickly cleared the table and sat back down.

"We fought for our own country. And we had it four years. We built a gov'ment, army and navy startin' from nothin'. We lost the war. I still b'leve we was right to want our own land. And it was just as legal for us to leave the north as it was for the colonies to leave England. We thought God would defend us."

Ben nodded, but still looked confused, "After the war, didn't we go back to just the way we was?"

"Ben, you were old enough to remember that! The fightin' stopped, but the war's not over till yet. Yankee soldiers are in ever' town rulin' us like they was a bunch o' Philistines. The law is what they say it is. The Free'man Bu-ro come in and started feedin' the Nigras that run off from the farms and come to town. For white folks, it's root-hog or die. They let ever' darkie that could breathe have the vote, even if he couldn't sign his name. But right after the war, I couldn't vote, and lots of our friends couldn't 'cause we'd volunteered for the Confederacy. And I wouldn't swear an oath and say we were wrong. There never was a war like the Big War. Brother fought brother.

After the fightin' stopped, there wasn't any peace treaty 'cause the Yankees said we never were a country. So they put our president in chains and run our country like it's theirs. I don't hardly thank that we wooda put ol' Abe in shackles if we hada won. Now that we're down, the buzzards have come to pick us clean -- like they are after that mule on the ridge." As he stared at Ben, his voice became harsher and the words slower. "I don't see no call to laugh much these days. Ya never seen the war, boy. Ya can't really understand." He looked around the table. " None of ya do."

Martha studied the faces about the table. John's beard hid his face, but she saw despair in his eyes and heard it in his voice. Nate looked away. Ben continued to watch his father with open mouth and wide eyes. Nate pushed his chair back and stood.

Martha said, "If ya arm will let ya, Nate, sit back down. I want ya to hear this." She began gently. "John, let me tell ya somethin' Ben and Nate and I have never told before. Ya never wanted to talk about the war, either the fightin' or us at home. Ya never knew the

thangs that went on here while ya were gone. Ben
might not even remember. It's time you knew.

When the Yankee solders come through this
county, we got word a little more than an hour 'fore
they got to our place." John jerked his head around and
frowned. "Robert Butler's boy come tearin' down the
road on a horse all lathered up and breathin' hard and
told us they was comin' our way. That boy covered
most all this end of the county before the horse just
plum give out and fell over dead."

****

Martha stood on her front porch watching the
dust hide horse and rider in the road to the east. As
sounds of the hooves faded, she looked to the west
toward faint rattling popping noises. She ran through
the dogtrot to the back of the house and pulled the rope
by the pole, until the dogs howled. As the sounds of the
bell and dogs faded, she stared at the ridge beyond the
barn.

Ben and Nate were working near the house.
They ran to the call of the bell. Martha put her arms
around her sons. "Boys, the Yankees are acomin' and
yer pa and big brother're gone. They're apt to burn the
house and barn, but they'll carry off ever'thang they
can first. It's up to us to save what we can. Go to the
barn and hitch the mules and bring the wagon and be
quick about it."

Nate and Ben started toward the barn. Ben
stopped, looked back, and asked hesitantly, "Ma,
where'll we go? We not gonna try to outrun 'em, are
we?"

"No, we are goin' south to that valley 'cross
Kulumi Ridge, if we can make it. Do ya thank we can?
I've never been, but you boys go there all the time. Can
a wagon make it over the ridge? It's just the three of

us...there's no time to get nobody else. They're movin' this away. Ya better go."

Ben glanced toward the distant sounds and then at his mother, "Ma, it'll be a job and a half, but we can try." The boys fled toward the barn. Martha watched the boys running down the worn dirt path. As she turned to their home, her hands trembled but her face was solemn, and her mouth a tight straight line.

By the time the boys pulled up the wagon close to the back of the dogtrot, Martha had carried out most of the pots and pans, dishes, spoons, knives and forks, and foodstuffs from the kitchen and stacked them near the steps. After they loaded things from the kitchen, they hauled much of the clothing and bedding from the trunks in the bedrooms and piled them in the wagon. They laid John's guns, powder, caps, and shot on the clothing.

As they carried the last load from the trunk, Martha walked past the pictures of John and Jacob. She took them down from the wall and used precious seconds to look at them. *This may be all we have left. I can't leave 'em.* She carried them outside and carefully fitted the glass to the side of the wagon and packed the quilts about them.

Martha went back and looked around her kitchen. The only utensil left was a wooden dough board toward the back of the south table -- its oval shape shaped with axe and adze from the center of a gum log. The middle of the bowl was lighter sapwood and the ends were dark heartwood. She ran her fingers over the edge. It was so smooth and worn that adze cuts by her father could barely be felt. *It's big and I could get by without it, but then... I've used it so long and new dough boards don't make good bread.* She took the dough board.

She and the boys loaded most of the tools from the shed, and drove to the smoke house to load the cured meat. By this time, the wagon was piled high with disorganized heaps. At the barn Martha motioned for Ben to stop.

"The two of ya, run get that old piece of canvas. We can cover our goods with it."

Ben pointed at the animals wandering about the lot, grazing as unconcerned as ever. "Ma, what about the stock? Me and Nate might could drive em, but we'd have to make more 'an one trip. Sheep and cows and hogs'll never go together, and chickens won't go nowhere."

Martha listened to the ever closer rattling and popping.

"Boys, open the gates and run the stock into the woods far as you can. Close the chicken-house door. Knock down that shed where hogs bed down and turn over their trough. Maybe they won't come back. We need our milk cows. I know one is dry, but she'll come in fresh soon. Do ya thank we can make 'em go with us? One of ya has to drive the team."

The two looked toward the ridge and at each other. They turned toward echoes of the now distinct sounds of gunfire. Ben said, "We'll try, Ma. We can get 'em out of the lot. The worst we can do is lose 'em in the woods."

Nate and Ben disappeared into the barn. Ben brought the canvas. Nate came back with his arm under a worn and broken basket. An angry hen sat in it, only because Nate held her by the neck. "Ma, ya said they'd take the stock. This here Dominecker will be the first to go 'cause she's settin'. They can get her easy like. Can we take her?"

"We can't take ever'thang in the county... weell, bring her on, if she'll ride with us. Get that young mule if he'll folla the wagon. Put sacks with some of our thangs 'cross his back, if he will let ya. That will take some of the load out of this wagon."

They set out toward Kulumi Ridge. Ben drove the loaded wagon, the mule following behind with sacks across his back. Trailing the mule were two reluctant milk cows herded along by Nate and Martha swinging four-foot long sticks. The two dogs needed no invitation for the trip. Bess was training her half-grown pup, Bear. When the cows bolted into the woods, the dogs seemed overjoyed to bring them back.

The procession passed through the barn lot, across the pasture and through thin woodland to the foot of the ridge. Martha called to Ben, "I don't see a trail. Are ya'all sure ya know how to get there? I know ya come over here at times, but we got to find a way for a wagon."

"Yes, ma'am," Ben said. "Ya might should drive the wagon while we find it." Ben and Nate pulled saplings and bushes apart to show a nearly hidden path. Martha drove the team through the opening. The dogs encouraged the cows. Ben broke a limb from a tree and brushed away tracks. When the tree branches were allowed to close, there was little evidence of their passage.

Martha climbed down from the wagon. "Nate, you drive now. It's a steep pull with a loaded wagon and yer the lightest. Ben may have to lead the team, and me and the dogs can drive the cows."

Partway up the slope in a level clearing where the trail turned east, they stopped to rest the mules. Gunfire seemed closer now, and rumbles echoed across the ridge. They saw flashes of light in the west. Fearing the sounds might be cannon fire, they set off again. On the steeper slopes, Martha and Ben pushed against the back of the wagon as the mules struggled to pull their burden toward the top. They took off some of the heavier tools and hid them in the brush. The sky grew dark and the wind came in great gusts. It whipped the trees back and forth and tore off leaves and small limbs

to batter the little group. A sudden smell of dust and
then a sense of coolness surrounded them. The cause of
the flashes and rolling sounds became clear: a
thunderstorm was coming. They heard the nearing
sounds and watched the line of heavy rain move up the
slope toward them.

By the time they reached the top of the ridge, the
sky was filled with swirling black clouds, and heavy
driving rain reached them. Now wet pine needles and
new leaves flew through the air and stuck to the people
and mules alike. They stopped at the crest to stare at
the storm swirling about. Angry clouds hid the sun and
what little light remained was fading. On the slope
behind them, a tree fell with a crack and crash. The trail
ahead was a tunnel disappearing under wind-lashed
trees of the dark valley. As the wail of the wind
increased, thunder followed lightning closer and closer.
Ben climbed in the wagon to hold the brake. The boys
cringed at he lightning flashes. The mules jerked
forward and looked about wildly.

Martha smiled at them. "Don't worry. It's
downhill all the way now. God has sent us a
thunderstorm. He will slow them Yankees down for us
to get where it's safe. Ben, you drive and let Nate work
the brake. We best go 'for it gets good dark." The mules
balked, but responded to the familiar voice from the
bench.

The two boys slowly braked the wagon down
the twisting trail into the darkness of the valley. Gusts
of wind whipped limbs that beat against them as they
inched down little more than a deer path. With the
worst of the lightning flashes, Martha ran forward to
lead the frightened mules. The wagon pushed over
small saplings and bushes. Twice, Nate held the brake
and the reins while Martha chocked the wheels and
calmed the mules to give Ben time to chop trees too big
for the wagon to push over. The trail led deeper in the

valley and darkness swallowed them. At times, they welcomed the flash of lightning to show the way for an instant. Martha reminded the boys that lower in the valley the wind was less.

Once they reached the bottom of the slope to almost level ground, the trail turned east and led to a flat area surrounding a spring. Heavy undergrowth kept them from getting close to the water. Ben eased the wagon along and stopped in a partly open area, away from large trees, which might blow over. He stood in the wagon and looked around in the brightness of a lightning flash, "Where's the cows, Ma?"

"When I had to lead the team for a spell 'round that big bend in the trail halfway down, they lit out for the woods and not even the dogs could get 'em back."

As soon as Ben and Nate took the harness off the mules, they fled in terror for whatever security lay in deeper woods. The boys chocked the wheels, tightened the canvas over the wagon and raked a shallow trench to turn the water. Two dogs, a setting hen, and three people on soggy quilts bedded down in near total darkness under the packed wagon. Lightning flashes fleetingly lit the world about them with intense white light, making every tree, rock, and bush appear unreal. After the brightness, thunder crashed. In the brief instant of dazzling light, they saw men, animals, even monsters in the wind whipped trees, or in the deeper shade of black that followed the flash, they thought they remembered seeing them.

Early in the night, they could not sleep. They listened to the anger of the storm, the falling rain, and call of frogs for more rain. Martha kept reminding Nate and Ben that all this was sent to hide their tracks. She talked with them about school and church., work in the fields, crops, work in the shop or anything she thought might distract them from their black and sometimes bright dream world. She kept her quilt pulled up so her shudders did not show in the brilliant light. She spoke slowly and firmly so that her voice did not quaver. Several times, Nate interrupted to ask if the Yankees would follow them. Each time Martha said, "The road goes east and west, but we're to the south. They is no call for them to come our way. And our tracks is hid by the rain."

Martha woke in the early light when fog covered the valley like a cloud. Wisps of mist drifted up from the spring and faded as they reached the treetops. The storm was gone and the wind was still. The air smelled cool and clean. Every leaf of every tree was wet, glistening and slowly dropping its burden of water. The determined hen rearranged herself on her nest and glared at Martha with an unblinking eye, daring anyone to bother her again. In a tree near the wagon, the first mockingbird began her song – strong and insistent. Martha smiled at the sound as she gently shook her sons. "Wake up and hear that happy bird. If she sings like that, this has to be a good place and a fine day,"

Nate asked about the Yankees again and received the same reassurance. Nate said, "I think that we've had about enough rain to hide most of the farm, so I know our tracks are hid."

As they crawled out from under the wagon, Martha said, "Just as soon as ya make yer trip to the woods, come back and wash yer hands and find us a toothbrush tree and cut some limbs. Our good brushes are across the ridge. I'm hard put to tell which has the worst breath -- us or the dogs."

By the time the boys came back, they heard a cow bawling in pain. Nate and the dogs found and herded her to the clearing. Ben milked the unhappy cow, and she joined the dry one browsing in the woods. Warm milk and leftover bread served as breakfast. Nate offered a small piece of bread to the setting hen. She pecked his fingers, but accepted the crumbs he dropped. She left her nest once for a trip to the spring. She walked stiff legged, clucking all the way. The hen fluffed up her feathers, spread her wings and ran at the smaller dog that dared come close as she dipped her beak in the water.

In the night, the noise of battle and storm had faded and sounds of the land returned. After a morning of sunshine, the trail dried enough to travel, so in the early afternoon, Martha sent Ben to spy on the farm from the crest of the ridge. After being gone for an hour, he came running down the trail. "Ma -- Ma, the house is still there! I clumb a tree so I could see good. They's smoke to the east all along the road toward the church. Our house and barn is standin', but curious lookin' folks is ever'where. They're walking 'round big as ya please, like they owned the place. I never seen any before, but they must be Yankees."

Martha nodded. "The storm hit just as they got there. They used our place to get in out of the rain."

"What're we gonna do?" Nate asked. "Are we gonna live here while Yankees stay in our house? I wanta go home."

Martha put her arms around her sons, though Ben tried to pull away.

"If I could, I'd run the Yankees off. The important thang is that we're safe. We got food to last quite a spell. We'll just stay here 'till they leave and hope they don't burn the place. Now while the sun is up, get some wood and about dark, when they can't see our smoke, I'll cook us a hot meal and ever'body will feel better. Tomorrow, when it dries up some, we'll start cleanin' up this place."

Through the day, they unloaded the wagon, hung clothing out to dry, and cleaned tools. Some items they left in the wagon and some they hung on tree limbs. She couldn't cook biscuits, but Martha did make cornbread in the iron skillet to go with the fried ham and stewed peaches for dessert. They spent one more night under the wagon. The night was dry and fair and the moon was clear but new -- its light faint. Toward midnight, Nate shook his mother's shoulder." Ma, I hear a-a-ghost over by the spring. What'll we do? Listen, there it is again, and it's moved! It's one of the Indian spirits that lives here. I know it is! Jacob and his friends told me about 'em."

Martha put her arm about Nate. "Ya know there's no such thang." Then she heard the quivering, mourning, whistling sound. "Why, Nate that's just a little ol' owl. We hear 'em around the house some. This is just a scary place -- that's all. Ever'thang is fine. Just sleep here by me. Do you want to move over here, Ben? You awake?"

"I'm -- ah -- I'm fine here. Ma."

She didn't tell the boys that her mother called that bird the death owl. At daylight when the riotous singing of birds began, Martha woke to find Nate sleeping peacefully beside her. His big brother was on the other side of the wagon between two dogs. The morning meal was cold leftovers and milk. On the second day in the valley, they took the broad axe, small axe, and saw and set to work clearing the flat land about the spring. Ben harnessed the team and pulled the trees and brush into the woods. Over the next few days they worked in the daylight hours and sat down to their one hot meal after dark. As they cleared the land about the spring, they found a large flat rock projecting horizontally from the base of the ridge. A deep hollow under this rock made a shallow cave. As he cleared the floor of their valley house, Nate found arrowheads and pieces of pottery. When Ben cleared the brush blocking the light, they saw faded figures painted on the rock walls. Ben and Nate cut saplings for a frame for the sides of the rock and covered it with pine limbs to make a dry shelter. This was not like home, but with a fire to cheer them at night, they managed.

Each day Ben went to the top of the ridge to survey the house and watch for the Yankees. Each day he slowly walked down the trail and dejectedly said, "They're still there." Some days he said that they had found another hog or chicken or sheep and were cooking back of the house.

The three cleared a large area on the north side of the spring and a small one on the south. The open area now measured nearly fifty feet wide. Nate cleaned out the spring and pulled the brush and weeds from the shallow edges so that water moccasins had no place to hide. The brothers stacked rocks around the western side to turn surface water. The spring was then surrounded by open land but for one tree.

The water bubbled up and the spring cleared itself and mirrored blues and greens like glass. Water spiders and black watermelon-seed shaped bugs swimming in circles disturbed the surface of a spring larger than their own.

The beech in the center of the clearing was too large to fell. They stood on the rug of bright green moss at its base and cut lower limbs and brush to show hundreds of initials and symbols carved in the bark of the trunk. Nate pointed, "See Ma, there's mine and here's Ben's."

They admired their work and Ben said, "If we're gonna have to live here, leastwise it looks purty good."

"Now, boys, those Yankees aren't gonna stay forever. They got homes, too."

On the morning of the sixth day, Ben came running back from the trail to the top. He breathing so hard he could hardly speak, "Ma, they're gone and the house is still there. I can't see nothin' goin' on; can we go home?"

Martha put her arms around her sons. "I don't trust them Yankees. We wait one more day. If nobody is there tomorrow, we go back."

On the next morning, from the top of the ridge the three looked at their house and barn for a long time. Martha could not see well through the branches, but the boys climbed a tree and carefully watched the whole farm. They came down and Ben reported. "Ma, the house and barn is there. We couldn't see no soldiers anywhere."

"Now we have to go check and see have they really gone."

Ben finished dusting himself from the climb, stood unusually straight and said. "Ma, I am the oldest. I'm a full thirteen year old. Lemme go look and see is there anybody there and ya'all watch."

Martha smiled. "Go ahead and check, but you be careful now. Go real slow and look ever'where for them folks. Nate, go back and get yer Pa's shotgun, and thangs. I'll watch Ben. It's mighty long. Do ya think ya can carry it? Leave ever'thang else at the spring."

After several minutes, Nate returned with the gun, the powder horn, a sack of shot, and box of caps. They moved down the slope to a small clearing. From the ridge, Nate and Martha watched Ben as he left the barn. He checked around the springhouse then threw rocks at the privy and waited. The door didn't open. He turned and waved to them as he made his way along the path. He was nearly to the shop when he came to the big mulberry tree. A man stepped from behind the trunk of the tree. He wore no hat and had long yellow hair.

"Look out Ben!" Martha shouted, but he didn't hear.

Both man and boy were startled, but the man had a gun and Ben didn't. The man hit Ben in the head with the stock of the rifle. The boy fell into the weeds and didn't move.

On the ridge above, Martha saw everything. She screamed and began to run. At a bend in the trail, a tree limb struck her in the face and she stopped, rubbed her stinging face, and stared across the fields in horror at the still form on the ground. *I don't know if that man was a soldier. His shirt didn't look like it. But there may be more of 'em -- may be deserters -- that's worse.* She looked up the slope at Nate. He suddenly looked so much smaller and helpless. He was crying softly. *We've not heard from John and Jacob in months. The three of us may be the only ones left. It could be just me and Nate.* She ran back and put her arms around Nate and they both cried. "I won't leave ya Nate. We'll go together."

They held each other and watched the house. After a time, they saw a horse and rider leave from the front of the house and move rapidly down the road to the east.

"Nate, I barely caught sight of him, but that must have been the evil man leavin'. We have to go to Ben, but first, we have to load yer Pa's gun. Ya brought ever'thang didn't ya?"

Nate nodded and picked up the gun. "Now hold it far me, Nate." He held the shotgun up with the barrel at his cheek. Martha took the cap off the horn and poured powder to fill it. She poured a load down each barrel. She poured a small amount of powder in the cap and added it to each side. With the ramrod she packed wadding in each barrel.

"Now hand me the shot, Nate." She took the sack and opened it. "Why there's almost nothin' here. I know that Jacob took some when he went to Mobile, but he left more than this."

"Ma, Ben shot some turkeys in the garden last winter -- so we just about don't have any shot."

"So we can make a noise with this here gun and that's all?"

"Ma, shot is just heavy is all. On the way down the ridge I picked up some little rocks that are might near as round and heavy as shot." He offered her a handful of black rocks. She stared at them in his hand.

"I've never heard of anybody shootin' rocks in a gun." She looked at Nate's hand and then toward the mulberry tree where Ben lay. "I reckon those little rocks are all we got. We'll put a little more than a capful in each side and try it. I've already put in a little extra powder -- like the spoon for the pot when ya make coffee."

She measured the rocks and poured them in each side, then stuffed in the wadding and rammed it in place. She put the strap of the horn over her shoulder, carried the caps and shot bag in one hand and the gun in the other. They ran down the ridge, across the pasture, to the back of the house. Martha struggled with the long gun and called to Nate to slow down and to look behind every tree.

They found Ben lying on his back in a patch of morning sunshine at the foot of the mulberry tree. Blood oozed from the side of his head and ran down a weed to the ground. A circle of ants gathered around the small pool. Ben was breathing slowly, but wouldn't answer his mother's pleading voice as she kneeled beside his head. And he didn't respond to the whine and nudge of the dogs.

"Nate, we gotta get him out of this hot sun. Help me move him. We need to look in the house before we take him there." They dragged him a few feet into the shade. Martha started toward the house. "Nate, see if ya can get the dogs to stay with Ben. They won't go in the house with us anyway."

"What about the gun?"

Martha glanced at the gun she had leaned against the tree. "Thank ya Nate. I most likely would have remembered when I got to the house." She picked up the gun, put on two caps, and eased the hammers down. She moved toward the house carrying the shotgun carefully with both hands.

As she stepped over the shattered iron bell and the fallen martin houses near the back steps, Martha stared at the gun and cocked both hammers, cringing at the sound. She hesitated, looked at an empty window, and then slipped quietly down the dogtrot toward the open door of the small bedroom. The room was empty.

Martha tilted her head to listen. There were faint sounds. *What is that and were is it comin' from?* She wrinkled her nose. *Is it just nasty clothes or...or.* She tiptoed the few steps to the larger bedroom. She took a large step. The gun was so long that Martha could barely hold the barrel up, but with shaking hands she pushed it against the door. As the it creaked open, she looked over the gun and saw the mattress torn and half pulled off the bed, the lard-oil lamp and shelf-clock smashed in the center of the room, but no one was there.

Martha heard scraping sounds and a scream from the kitchen. She ran the few steps to the half open doorway. The man with the long yellow hair she saw by the mulberry tree was in the room and he wore one of Jacob's shirts. The man had an arm around Nate's neck and was dragging him across the floor. With the other hand, he reached for a large knife stuck in the surface of the table. Nate's face was dusky-red, his mouth open and he made strangling sounds as he tried to cry out. Now, Martha screamed. The man threw Nate in the corner and came toward her, waving the knife. The man was big, but to Martha he looked twelve feet tall. His eyes were puffy and bloodshot. He shouted, "I got one, now I'll get the rest of you rebs!" and angry snarling words she didn't understand. She knew his meaning. He rushed toward the door.

Martha was standing in the dogtrot, the gun in her right hand hidden by the doorframe. The soldier was nearly at the door with the knife raised. She took a step sideways, lifted the heavy gun until it was level and pointed directly at him. The barrel quit shaking for an instant and she pulled both triggers -- hard.

The blast knocked her flat on her back in the middle of the dogtrot -- the gun on top of her. From the kitchen she heard a heavy thud. *Lord, let it be that Yankee.* She pushed the gun aside, struggled up and into the room. She stopped, took a deep breath then stepped over the man, lying in a pool of blood that crept along the cracks between the boards. Nate was crying hoarsely, but he was more scared than hurt. She cradled him in her arms and stroked his hair. They heard sounds in the dogtrot and Bess bounded into the room. She came into the house for the first time when she heard Nate cry out.

When she had recovered enough to talk, Martha said, "Now Nate, it's just the two of us. Ya have to help me." As they left the room she held her hand over his eyes to keep him from looking at the body on the floor. They saw no other soldiers about the house, so they went back to Ben by the mulberry tree. Using broken poles from the martin tower and discarded clothing the soldiers left lying about the yard, they made a stretcher. They managed to load Ben, but he was too heavy to carry between them, so the two pulled one end and allowed the other to drag. They moved him across the yard, sometimes imches at the time, up the steps, and into the shelter of the dogtrot. Martha and Nate straightened up wet with sweat, breathing hard and leaned against the wall. Ben moaned and feebly moved his arms and legs, but did not appear to hear them.

"Nate, go fetch my mama. Stay away from the roads in case they's more Yankees. Take Bess with ya, if ya want to. Can ya go? Are ya afraid?"

"No, ma'am. I'll go." Nate left running. After a few steps, he stopped and turned.

"What if they burned the place and she's not there? What must I do?"

Martha was startled at the thought. Worry lines formed as she pinched her eyebrows and considered. *Mamas are always there. But what if she's not?*

"Nate, I don't rightly know where we'd get anybody close by and on short notice. Far as we know, they burned lots of houses. But her place is off the main road and hid in the trees some. Maybe they didn't see it. If you can't find her, just come on back. We'll make out some sort of way. And if ya see any little rocks like up on the ridge, bring 'em. I hope not, but we might need the gun agin." Nate nodded and ran toward the west, through the fields parallel to the road.

Martha picked up the gun in the dogtrot and placed it on the pegs in the bedroom, then hung the powder horn and left the caps and the empty shot sack on a small shelf. These were then the only items in their proper place in the house. She looked though the doorway into the kitchen with revulsion. The soldier lay on the floor, eyes staring at the ceiling. His mouth hung open, and wounds covered the center of his chest. The knife lay by his right hand. Small rocks shot from the muzzleloader at close range had worked. Martha stepped into the kitchen, glanced at the overturned jug on the table and covered the man with a torn sheet. She reached down, but couldn't force herself to touch him with her hand. She used her foot to move aside the man's left leg, closed the door, and sat in the dogtrot at the side of her unconscious son.

She made several quick trips to the front porch to see the empty road to the west. Each time, she returned to Ben and held his hand, muttering to herself that Nate must have been gone half the day already. She was relieved to hear faint conversation along the road to the west. Leaving Ben for a moment, Martha ran to the porch and down into the yard. Nate and his grandmother were moving rapidly down the center of the main road, and Nate was telling her of the days across the ridge and Ben's injury and the rock-shot Yankee in the kitchen. They took the main road because Mamroy Cobb said that no Yankee would run her off *her* road. She carried a basket of quickly packed items. She looked like an older, wiser version of Martha. She carried a few more wrinkles, a lot more gray hair, and a wealth of experience.

Mamroy greeted and hugged her daughter. On the way to the house, they briefly discussed the horrors of the Yankee raid. The Yankees rushed by her house and never saw it, but she knew of the loss of others. Martha asked about Charlotte Emerline. Mamroy said, "Oh, she's fine. She's home with yer Uncle Rufus and Aunt Mary. I'm right sorry their house burned, but they sure have been a comfort to me since yer pa died last year."

At the far end of the dogtrot, Mamroy stooped to examine Ben's wound. She ran her fingers over the tensely swollen area on his head. Thick soggy clots of blood covered the wound, not still bleeding, but not yet dry. She stood and watched the feeble motions of his stupor. The wrinkles gathered about her eyes and forehead and her mouth was a tight line." I agree with ya Martha. We need to move him." She glanced at the ruined bedroom and opened the door to the kitchen. She gasped and stepped back into the dogtrot and shook her head. "Martha, I expected a mess, but nothin' like this -- one of yer boys lyin' in the dogtrot with a broke head, and a dead Yankee in a sight of blood in the kitchen."

"Ma, the three of us can get Ben in bed?"

"I saw them mattresses. I wouldn't put a dog on 'em. They're apt to be full of lice and maybe fleas. I'd throw away the straw and bile the ticks if ya use 'em again. We can clean out a bedroom and put him on a pallet on the floor when ya get yer wagon back. I brought a light half-quilt and some rags we can use fa right now."

They began cleaning Ben's wound with fresh spring water, carefully wiping away clots. The scalp was severely swollen about the open area, but the active bleeding had stopped.

As they finished, Mamroy looked up and said, "Nate, why don't ya go 'cross and get the wagon and ever'thang for ya Ma. Can ya handle it? Ya'll have to drive and brake by yaself. Don't let the mules run away comin' down, now."

Nate was pale and his lip quivered, but he said, "Oh, yes, ma'am, I...uh...I can do that."

"Mama, he's a good boy and big for his age, but he's just nine year old. It took the three of us to get into the valley. He can't do it by hisself. It might take two trips. I'll go with him, if you stay by Ben's side ever' minute."

Mamroy breathed a sigh of relief when she saw the wagon pull up at the barn. When Martha and Nate arrived in the yard, she stood near the back steps and looked over them toward the barn lot. "Mama, we lost the cows this side of Kulumi. Maybe they'll come home by milkin' time. We stopped at the barn, because of that Dominecker hen. We had hard a time roundin' up the mules, but that mama chicken had hatched off them eggs and we had to chase biddies all 'round that spring. We stopped to let her off at the barn. That hen and her biddies may be all the chickens we got left."

They unloaded the wagon and left most in heaps behind the house. Meat was returned to the smokehouse and tools to the shed. With some of the supplies from the wagon, they cleaned the bedroom, moved Ben to a pallet and compressed his wound with poultices. After they cared for Ben, Martha and her mother stood in the bedroom and looked at each other. Each woman opened her mouth to say something, but stopped with nothing more than a drawn out, "uuh." Finally Martha said," Much as it pains me to say it, we got to get rid of that Yankee. I hate to think of what might happen if more soldiers was to come." The women opened the kitchen door and took several deep breaths before going in. The sheet over the man's face and chest was now soaked with blood and spotted with flies. The three managed to drag the soldier out of the kitchen, to the end of the dogtrot and down the steps. Nate pulled on one of the soldier's booted feet and tried not to look back at his face or the wound in his chest.

"Nate, take a rope and tie his feet and take one of the mules and pull him down a ways from the house. I'll show ya where."

Mamroy sat at Ben's side and laid compresses to his wound and poured liquids down his throat when he could swallow. They carried in the possessions that traveled across Kulumi. Martha scoured the house until it was clean, then sat at Ben's other side. Nothing more could be done for Ben but worry and pray.

****

At this point in Martha's story, John slapped the table, making the candles shake and almost fall over.

"Why didn't ya tell me about all this before? Ya *lied* to me!"

"No, we never! Ya didn't want to talk about the war."

He glared at Ben, who seemed puzzled and said, " I don't remember nothin', Pa."

He glanced at Nate. "That is just the way it happened, Pa. Ya always asked what happened to that low place just below the apple trees back of the house. It's level now because a dead Yankee's buried there with his knife and his hat. Took me the rest of the day and into the night to get him under."

Martha said, "John, he wasn't but nine and had to bury a dead man. I did help him some. We kept a little poke of hard money that man left on the table in the eatin' room. I figgered he owed us that for tearin' up the house. It was prob'bly stole anyway. We kept puttin' poultices on the hurt place on Ben's head. He moaned and groaned and waved his arms about for three days while we sat with him. Then he sort of come to hisself, a little at a time. It was a month before he was able to do any work.

He's still got a sunk-in place in his head, but his hair hides it. You know he's different from when you left. Now you know why. He still has pains in his head at times. He speaks up when maybe he shouldn't. He don't remember lots of thangs from before that day. He asks lots of questions and sometimes he has trouble understandin' what people tell him. After that lick on his head, he lost the year in school and then dropped out. He's still our Ben. We need to be patient with him. John, we didn't see war like you soldiers did, and we didn't lose an arm, but I reckon we did see war. Ben like to have died because of it."

John dropped his head and stared at he table.

After several minutes she began to speak again, "We didn't know if we would ever see ya agin. We hadn't heard anything in quite a spell. Ya come back months after the war was over, more dead than alive. I

still don't know how ya walked that far, sick as ya was.
Ya was out of yer head for days and couldn't eat
nothin' but a little bread soaked in pot liquor. Ya didn't
need more troubles to add to what ya had. When ya got
better, me and Nate thought ya still didn't need more
worries.

I had to talk with somebody. I did talk with the
preacher and we prayed over it. That soldier was
liquored-up and mean. He hurt our babies and would
have hurt me, but he was a man. To this day, it scares
me if somebody comes at me right fast through the
kitchen door. I still see his face. I'm sorry I killed
him...but I reckon I'd do it again. I think that God has
forgive me for it. I s'pose I did tell a story about that
stain on the kitchen floor as ya go out into the dogtrot.
It really didn't come from a spilled pot of peas.

John, ya keep sayin' them Yankees whupped us
in the war. I know they did, but I reckon if we stay
bitter and sorry for ourselves all the time, then they're
still whuppin' us. You lost a hand. We lost what they
tore up and carried off, Ben won't never be the same,
but we're lucky all of us lived through it. The war
happened. It's over ... if we'll let it be."

John said nothing. The others fell silent and, as
John did, watched the changing shapes on the kitchen
wall. The wind moaned around the house and the
flames sputtered. Each one from their own vantage
saw different pictures in the shadows. Martha looked
at Nate. She knew they both wished that father and
husband could understand the ordeals of the family,
and know that he was not the only one who had
suffered loss. Nate and Martha both stole quick glances
at John. Martha yearned to hear just a word that they
had been given a great task and handled it well. Ben
appeared to have understood most of the answers to
his questions about the war and life after the war. He
had no memory of the events his mother related,

though he heard himself move within the story. Each event was a wonder to his ears, and now he appeared amazed and bewildered.

After several minutes, John cleared his throat and mumbled, "We better get some sleep. We gonna work can till can't agin tomorrow."

Chapter Four -- Dolly

After breakfast the next morning as Martha was clearing the dishes, John leaned over the table and pointed his stump toward Nate, "How's yer arm? That rag looks a mite wet. If you're up to it, I got a job for you and Jacob."

"I'm fine. I can do a day's work in the field."

"Don't want ya to work the fields. We lost a mule. We need two more, but don't hardly have money fa one. We just about have to have another mule to run this here farm." He looked at Jacob. "I want ya to go to Saturday trade day just this side of New Canaan and see can ya trade far a mule. Load up the wagon wheels we made last winter, and two sacks of seed corn. And ever'body pray that we don't have to replant. I'll give ya what hard money I can spare, which is not much, and sometin' I got out of the bottom of our old trunk early this mornin'." He pushed his chair back, walked to the bedroom, and came back and laid on the table a long bundle wrapped in cloth. It clattered and the covering fell away.

"Wipe it off and use it to trade."

"Pa, ya spent a right smart for that banjo. Ever'body always said it was 'the best they ever seen -- walnut and all carved up like it is."

"It's put up for good reason. I don't need it. No call for a one-armed banjo player. We need a mule."

"Ya could teach one of us to play."

"If I can't play, I can't teach. This ain't no time for such foolishness, nohow. Jacob, I'll give ya a gun to trade if ya have to have somethin' else. I'd hate to part with it."

Martha said, "Surely ya're not talkin' about that little gun ya set such a store by?"

"Where did ya get that little gun from? Ben said. Why are ya so partial to it?"

John jerked around to glare at Ben. "I just got it! That's all ya need to know." He turned back to Martha and Jacob. "I'm talkin about my pa's old flintlock that hangs on the wall in our room. It's not been shot in years, and I'd like to have it for a keepsake, but trade it if ya have to. Put yer goods in the wagon and cover it with that old scrap of a tent so them skinflints can't see what ya got and take out one thang at a time to trade."

Jacob sniffed, turned the corners of his mouth down and sat a little straighter in his chair. "I reckon I know how to trade, Pa."

"Nate, yer the one who lost the mule. You go with him."

"I couldn't help it. I never saw that dog 'till he jumped on me!"

"Don't make no difference. When ya work a mule, yer responsible for him, just like the captain is responsible for ever' man in his company. Ya need ta learn about tradin' anyways. Another day of rest before ya go to the fields couldn't hurt none neither. And sump'in' else, Jacob. Stop by McGregor's store and buy some thangs for your Ma. It's close to where ya'll be. She'll show ya what she needs."

"Now, John, we can get by with what we have. You need shoes worse than Bertha Mae and me need dresses."

"We don't have the dollar and a half fa shoes. I'll patch these a while. Dresses the two of ya have on are so thin ya could poke a broom straw clean though 'em.

They're might near indecent! Ya taken up all Bertha
Mae's clothes after John B. was born. She'll be -- uh --
uh -- needin' a little bigger size right soon. Both of you
women will have dresses."

Martha brought two small pieces of fabric from
the bedroom. "Get me five yards of a cotton print
material, somethin' like each one of these scraps. And I
need thread for the dresses -- she'll know how much --
and bakin' sodey and matches."

"Ma, I don't know nothin' about thangs like
that!"

"Jacob, It's time you did. Ya won't have no
trouble. Give Mary Rose the scraps. Then, just speak up
and talk. She'll know what I like."

John pinted a finger, "And tell that ol' tight
fisted Robert that ya want the cash price. If he puts it
on the books, it'll cost three times as much."

Jacob and Ben went to the barn, hitched the team
and loaded the wagon.

By the light of the kitchen window, Martha
cleaned Nate's arm and the wound on his face and
dressed the arm with fresh rags. "Nate, I don't care
what ya say, that arm can't feel very good. They's some
fever in it and it's drainin' a right smart. I'm uneasy
about ya agoin'. Yer face is red streak-ed. I would feel
better about it if Ben went and you stayed in today.

"Ma, I'll be fine, and like Pa said, I was workin'
the mule when she got hurt. I need to make up for that,
if I can."

Ben stopped the wagon at the front of the house
and stepped down. Nate pulled himself up to the
bench seat with his left hand. Martha watched his face
and saw the clenched teeth.

Jacob drove the wagon west with Nate sitting
beside him, cradling his right arm with his left.

Ben moved the ladder to the front of the house.
He climbed to the top, crawled on the roof, and began

tearing off rotten shingles. More were damaged than expected and the work went slowly. Even early in the year, heat on the roof was fierce. Ben came down once to get water and returned to find his father on the roof drenched in sweat trying to nail shingles with a left hand and a nub. Ben climbed to the top of the ladder and pled with his father to no avail. Eventually, Martha was able to convince John to come down for the noon meal. Both breathed a sigh of relief when he struggled back down the ladder and stood facing them.

"Well, somebody had to put them shingles back. If it rains tonight, it'll flood our bed."

"Pa, I just went to get water."

After the midday meal and usual rest, Ben and John began the work again, this time with Ben on the roof and John carrying shingles in his left arm and his nub on the ladder as he took jerking steps to the top.

* * *

Bertha Mae put John B. in Nate's bed for a nap, well away from the noise of roofing, and she and Martha began cleaning the kitchen. Several times Martha noticed Bertha Mae grabbing at her abdomen.

"Ya don't need to be doin' so much stoopin' over. Do the standin' up work."

"I been layin' off to ask ya about somethin'. I been havin' some pains ever now and agin." Martha put down the pan and turned around. Bertha Mae looked worried.

"Ya not havin' no show are ya?"

"No. Just a few pains ever' few days. Didn't have it like this before. I know ya lost two babies. Was …was it like that with you?"

"Bertha Mae, toward the last I had pains like labor most ever' day, and then I commenced to show. The baby come early -- real early. Rachel Watson -- she's dead now -- she come to help. She was granniewoman for most of the babies about Ebenezer Springs. The little girl was perfect, and the purtiest thing I ever saw, but mighty little. Rachel done ever'thang a body could do, but the baby was just too little to live long. She lasted three days."

"Didn't ya send for the doctor?"

"Doc Davis hadn't come to us then and doctors at New Canaan don't come way out here. About a year or so later, another girl come early, and little bitty. They're buried toward church under that dogwood tree with the fence about it. John wouldn't have me say it, but he cried worse the second time than the first. He tried to hide it from me, but I saw. He wanted a little girl real bad. He said that we wouldn't have more babies, that he didn't want me to go through heartbreak again."

Bertha Mae eased herself down in a chair to listen. "Martha, if I lost a baby, I don't hardly think I could go through it again."

"I felt that way at first, but ya can't say which way ya'll turn till you come to the fork in the road. Doc Davis was here by then and I talked to him. He said that my womb just wouldn't hold the baby long enough for it to get big enough to live. He told me that the only way I might could carry a baby full time is to take to my bed the last month or two."

"I couldn't do that!"

"I said that too, but I did. When we found out that a baby was comin', John was happy as I ever saw him, but at the same time he was scared for me. Toward the end of my time, John and Jacob waited on me hand and foot ... far weeks."

"What could Jacob do?"

"Yer husband was just seven, but he worked, if it wasn't nothin' but lookin' after Ben. When Nate come, he was littler than the other boys, but he was a red head -- hollerin' and strong. Bertha Mae, I try to love 'em all the same, but yer husband was the first, and for that reason was special. Ben was special because he was the last one I thought I would ever have. And he's special because of what the Yankees did to him. But Nate ... Nate was the baby I thought I'd never see. I loved those girls the few days we had 'em. I guess that love was bottled up in me after they was gone. I try not to, but Nate gets a measure of the love I would have give those two under the tree. I think ya feel special about a baby that comes after ya've had a hard time.

If the pains ease up when yer off ya feet, it's not apt to be nothin' but the womb growin', but why don't ya go lie down till they pass. I'll finish this." Bertha Mae lay on Ben's bed. Martha hummed as she finished washing the dishes. She had not spoken to anyone in years of those trying times. Just telling the story lifted a load from her shoulders and made the love she felt for her family even greater.

*   *   *

Well before dark Ben finished the entire roof over his parents' room and a portion of the front porch. As he was taking down the ladder and tools, his father walked farther in the yard to inspect the repairs. John lifted his hat toward the west and shaded his eyes. "That don't look too bad—not bad, atall. Does make that other part look worser though."

Ben left to put up the tools, and Martha and John settled into straight chairs on the porch. There was nothing to hear but the buzzing of insects and the clucking of hens to their biddies as they scratched and pecked their way toward the chicken house. They sat looking toward the west, without speaking. Treetops glowed, but shadows under the oaks grew longer and deeper. John said, "It's late. Time we sat at the supper

table. They oughta be here." He stood and walked the
length of the porch several times. He looked up at the
shed roof then ran his hand along the ten-inch logs of
the cabin wall, squared with broadaxe and adze.
Martha sat in her chair and watched him pace.

"I remember notchin' and settin' every log and
chinkin' the cracks." He stopped as he came to the end
of the porch, rested his hand on the wall and mumbled.
"I know ever' rock in that chimney."

Ben came around the corner of the porch." I put
up the tools, Pa."

John nodded, stepped down from the porch, and
crossed the yard. Bertha Mae looked up when he
passed, but John didn't speak. She had chopped the
few blades of grass and weeds in the packed smooth
dirt under the ring of oaks and was sweeping with a
brush broom. John B. now had the heavy hoe and was
chopping into the trash his mother was sweeping. He
shouted, "Get away!" or "Bad -- bad!" with every
swing.

Martha and Ben quietly followed John to the
road. Martha stopped to speak to her grandson, "You
helpin' your mama chop weeds?"

"Uh huh and uh -- uh -- where Gran'pa goin'?"
He dropped the hoe and ran.

John stopped at the road. Crepe myrtle trees
lined the side toward the house. No longer bushes,
clusters of twisted slick trunks were twenty feet tall
with thick fan shaped tops. John grabbed the largest
one, leaned forward and looked to the west.

Bertha Mae dropped her broom and captured
John B. as he reached the road. Martha and Ben trailed
a few steps behind. They squinted and looked toward
the setting sun. A flock of blackbirds fluttered across
the road. A striped lizard with blue tail scurried away,
leaving a crooked line and tiny dots in the dust.

Nothing else moved. Birds were quiet. Even leaves hung still in the evening heat.

John shook his head and said, "They's all sort of folks about. I hope them boys didn't have trouble with soldiers or maybe get into some sort of foolishness."

"John, they're level-headed boys. They're not in any foolishness. If they don't show up soon, ya may have to go after 'em."

John shielded his eyes against the brightness. In the distance there was nothing but the glare of gold and red setting sun. Streams of clouds were yellow in the far west and violet-purple toward the east. The fiery ball was sinking beyond an empty road. The rest of the sky slowly lost the light.

John B. tried to pull away from his mother." Is my Pa gonna come down that road?"

"Yes. John B. Why don't ya go chop some more weeds? They'll be along d'rectly."

A speck of darkness appeared in the center of the blazing light. Gradually the dark spot became larger, the wavy lines at the edges cleared, and larger moving forms could be seen. Ben said, "Ma, I thank it's them."

Martha sighed.

John squinted against the sunset. "Ben, yer eyes are better'n mine. Is they a mule tied in back?"

"Pa, somethin's behind that wagon."

"Leastwise they didn't take a whole day for nothin'."

"Hope they done good, Pa."

"They better have. If we can ever get ahead a little, we'll get us another one. But for now we got to have at least the three." As the wagon came closer, those at the cabin heard the crunch of the wheels and the plodding of the hooves and faint snatches of words. The road curved and the animal following the wagon moved into full view.

John leaned over, held his hat up to shield his eyes and squinted for a better look. He slapped the hat against his leg and shouted, "That ain't no mule! Them boys bought a horse! They took ever'thang we got and bought a pleasure horse -- a playtoy!"

The wagon moved slower and slower until it was directly in front of the house. "Whoa there, mule," Jacob said in a low voice. He handed the reins to Nate and slowly stepped down to face his father.

Before either man could speak, Martha said, "We are right glad yer back safe."

John B. broke away from his mother and ran. "Pa-Pa! Ya did come back!"
Jacob nodded toward his mother and picked up his son.

"Were you helpin' mama chop weeds?"

"Uh huh. I chopped lots of weeds an'-an' two woofs.

"You did? *Two* woofs? I don't see 'em."

"Uh...uh...they was just little bitty ones."

"That's good, now hush up a while and let me talk to gran'pa." He moved directly in front of his father. "Now, Pa, let me explain. We got a horse -- a work horse." He pointed with his left hand, "This here is Dolly." The twitch of his cheek pulled at his lower lid at rapid intervals.

John's face was in the full glaring light. He crumpled his hat in his hand. "I reckon ya thought I wouldn't notice – I still got both eyes. We need a mule to plow the fields, not some ... some fancy ridin' horse."

"We couldn't get no mule. They was some there, but they wanted big money far 'em. We didn't have near enough to trade. You know stock has been short short since them army mules scattered the glands all over."

"The what?"

"The glands. Some call it the snot. Lots had to shoot their mules." Folks had to kill so many, stock is short since the war.

Nate pointed, "Look at her neck and skin. Nothin' wrong with 'er."

Jacob said, "We did bring the old gun back. Couldn't hardly trade it. Nobody has money to have it changed over to caps. And she's not a ridin' horse." John sniffed and frowned at the small horse. "Course, you could ride her if you was a mind to. We ride the mules now and agin, and she rides a heap better'n a mule."

"I knew it -- ya'all did buy a ridin' horse."

"Now hold on a minute. See how thick her legs is, and look at the muscles on them quarters. She's out of one of them big workhorses like they use up east. Her pa was just a regular horse. Look at them two mules pullin' this wagon. Sam's a little small and Dollie's ever bit as tall as he is, but not quite tall as Buster. Probably thicker than aire one of them two."

John's expression grew increasingly clouded. "Size has nothin' to do with plowin'. If she's from up east, you mean you bought us a Yankee horse?"

"She's not a Yankee horse." He shifted John B. to the other arm." We traded her off Willey Pepper." John looked puzzled.

Nate said, "You know him, Paul Pepper's boy -- the one everbody always called Sneezie. He is a year older than Jacob. He told us how his Pa and his brothers were killed in the war. Nobody left but him, his ma, a sister and her man. And he's one legged."

Jacob said, "The Peppers worked some darkies before the fightin', but most of 'em run off. He borrowed money ever' year since the war. All he could do is pay the interest in the fall when the crops come in and owed more ever' year. He just couldn't keep up that big farm by hisself and lost it to the bank. Carpetbaggers run that bank, and all they're lookin' at is money. They took his farm, but let him keep his stock and a wagon. Carpetbagger bought the farm off the bank, or really stol' it. The bank is like we are -- land pore. They've took over farms all over the county. This here carpetbagger was the only one with money. He was waitin' for the bank to take the farm so he could get it."

John held up his hand, "What's all that got to do with this here horse?"

Nate said, "The carpetbagger, he bought one mule off Wiley, and Wiley sold one to another fella. He had this little horse left. She's all we could get. We was lucky to get anythang in these times. I think Jacob done a good job dickerin' with Willey. She will plow. Me and Jacob tried her to the side of the road where folks was atradin'. She'll pull a plow as good or better'n a mule."

"Ya couldn't work her with a mule."

Jacob said, "We tried 'er with Sam. The two of 'em did work. Ya can team her with a mule...that is if the mule's not too ornery."

"We'd be the laffin' stock of the county if we was to go to church with a mule and a horse."

"Me and Nate figgered that ya could team the mules if ya wanted a matched pair. Mostly we needed a plow horse and she will plow good as a mule, and we can ride her better'n a mule. We could ... uh ...let her visit at the Cooper's and get another horse or a mule, if ya was a mind to."

"She prob'ly made eyes at Nate. He always was soft hearted for stock. Them mules'll never put up with no white horse."

"Pa, she's not really white...she's sorta gray. Not near dark as Maude was, but she's not white...like a sheep. Willey said throw a little dirt on her for a day or so till the mules get used to her."

"He was just tryin' to sell somethin'."

"Now, Pa, Willey has always been fair with us. We could try to get him to take her back if ya want. Don't know how we'd work it out. He's already sold the wagon wheels. We know where he's at. He's gonna work a spell fa Uncle Ambrose."

In a moment of silence, Ben hesitantly said, "I thank she's a right nice lookin' horse."

John glared at Ben, said nothing, turned to look at the little gray horse standing silent and still, but for her switching tail, and then at Nate on the bench and Jacob by the wagon.

"No, a trade is a trade. We are bound by our word. We'll keep 'er, but you two will have to stand good far 'er."

Bertha Mae took the few steps to Jacob, hugged him, said something that others could not hear and, after a struggle, pulled John B. away. She and Martha, relieved at the outcome, left for the kitchen to let the men finish the discussion.

John motioned to Nate. "Go on and put the stock up. We can see what that fancy horse will do next week."

Ben climbed up to the bench. Nate twitched the reins and the team of mules pulling the wagon with the new horse tied in back slowly moved on. As the wagon rolled away, John called after Nate, "And be sure ya put that fancy horse in a stall by herself. She wouldn't want to bed down with a common mule."

John turned to Jacob, "Who bought the Pepper place?"

"Pa, some carpetbagger with a pocketful of money -- not just a Yankee, but some'n' worse -- some kind of fureiner -- just could understand him. He made some kinda funny sounds toward his wife like it meant somethin'. Had his mouth all puckered up like he was suckin' a green persimmon. Sounded like some woman sweet-talkin' a baby. Wiley couldn't call his name just right, but said it was somethin' like Possum-Foot."

"Possum-foot? Possum-foot? What's his Christian name -- his callin' name?"

"Pierre."

"Pee-Air! Pee-Air Possum-Foot? What kind of a fool name is that for a full growed man?"

"Pa, I guess it sounds fine whur he come from."

"Weell, he's not whur he come from. He's in America, and he needs him an American name like the rest of us got. Pee-Air -- why the very i-dee --you couldn't even call his name 'round women folks!"

"It must not mean nothin' bad in his country. We heard his wife call him that sev'al times. He saw your banjo we traded to Wiley and, right off, bought it off him."

"You mean some *fureiner* has my banjo and we got a *Yankee* horse. Thangs are bad all over. Did ya get them goods for yer Ma?"

"Yessir, it's all in the wagon. Nate'll bring 'em or I'll go get 'em. And here's what I had left over." He poured a few coins into John's open palm.

"That's *all* I got back from the two dollars I give ya?"

"Pa, the cloth was 90 cent, the five spools of thread was 25 cent; and the three pounds of sodey was 25 cent and three boxes of matches was 10 cent. That come to a dollar and fifty cent and Robert knocked off 15 cent for cash. I spent a dollar and thirty-five cent. That's sixty five cent change."

"Why did ya get enough matches for half the county?"

"Pa, they was one for five and three for ten cent. We'll use 'em sooner or later."

John looked at the coins in his hand. "Weell, I reckon that was the best ya could do with them tight folks."

As Jacob and his father moved toward the house, Jacob told of other experiences of the day. "Pa, Yankees and all kind of peculiar folks is still ever'where. Luther White was at trade day -- ya know he's pore as Job since the war. He had an old uniform on and two darkie militia come up and seen them Confederate buttons and commenced to holler at him. He flat cut a dido, but it didn't do no good. They held a gun on him and cut the buttons off, and stomped 'em in the dirt."

John mumbled under his breath and said, "They shouldn't oughta do that. It's enough that the country is tore up an folks is losin' their homes. They's a few hot heads left. That sort of a thang could make for a killin'." They sat in chairs on the front porch to wait for supper.

"Pa, do ya reckon we ever gonna get shed of them Yankees?"

"Jacob, Yankee land has got snow four foot deep in winter and big ol' cities fulla trashy folks. When them folks come South and see our weather and the green fields in the spring and ihe peace and quiet of the land, lots don't want to go back. Some Yankees are like a bad case of piles, they come down, but don't go back up." John did not laugh enough to be evident under his beard, but then he rarely did. Jacob gave a half-hearted snicker. They sat in silence until Bertha Mae called them in to eat.

Nate and Ben arrived from the barn carrying the supplies. John B. was being encouraged by his mother and was half through his meal when the others sat down. The adults said little as they ate. John B. stopped eating and chattered away about the snake in the garden, the rabbit the dogs caught, the big catfight and other earth-shaking events on a farm, which fascinate little boys. His smile widened as the adults showed interest in his stories. After the table was cleared and the dishes washed, Jacob and his family left for bed. Martha would not allow Nate to leave the kitchen before she changed the dressing on his arm.

Before Nate lay down, he went to the window and looked out at the yard. A bat flitted across the open sky, an owl called, and far away a dog barked. In the background, the songs of frogs and crickets went on unchanged. Sounds of the night were as they should be – as they always were. He stared into the deep shadows of the yard. Nothing moved; still he was not reassured. He lay on the bed and tried to find a comfortable spot where the straw didn't poke through the ticking. Ben's breathing from across the room was regular and slow. Nate listened again to the voices of the night, but still heard nothing strange.

In the darkness of his room, his right arm throbbed. It had not seemed so bad through the day. He made a fist and bent his wrist to reassure himself that the hand still worked. The fingers moved, but with sharper pain under the dressing. He straightened his fingers and ran them over the mattress. With the hurting arm it was hard to tell, but his sense of touch seemed … near normal. Still, he wondered if the bite of a Devil Dog would ever heal and what the wound could do to his arm or to him. Was that bite different somehow? He sat up several times and looked at the window.

There was a sound that was not part of the song of the night and Nate left his bed and moved to the window, half expecting a dark shape to appear. *Is something out there listening, waiting, and coming for me? Did it scratch on the wall?* He stood several minutes, listening, straining to see into the yard. Nothing moved. Whatever made the noise, there was nothing to see. He lay down again and listened for more than an hour, before exhaustion finally brought sleep.

Chapter Five – Church

On Sunday morning, John milked while Nate and Ben fed the stock. After breakfast, the family made ready for church. Martha laid out a calico dress and dark hat and sat combing her hair in front of a small hand mirror propped in the bedroom window. Jacob and Ben began a major task -- shaving. Since the task was usually a two-handed job, John found it easier to let his beard grow until it was too ragged to be seen at church and Martha chided him into a trim with scissors. Jacob and Ben shaved when they had to, usually once a week. Nate's beard was more promise than reality.

The shavers headed for the good light of the wash-shed. Each took a shaving mug filled with warm water, a basin of water, washrag, towel and straight razor. The men shared a mirror.

They put their things on the washstand. Ben sat on a stump and waited. Jacob picked up a razor that looked like a slim six-inch pocketknife with sides of wood held at each end with pins. He pushed a curl of metal at one end and the blade popped out from the sidepieces. The blade was concave ground, thinner toward the edge.

He began to whet the blade on a smooth black stone on a shelf near the mirror. He moved over to the strop hanging from a peg, and Ben took over the stone. After several strokes, Jacob satisfied himself with the edge by carefully feeling for burs with a finger and cutting a few hairs on his arm. When his razor had been properly honed and stropped, Jacob laid it down on the shelf below the mirror.

His shaving mug was the size of a coffee mug, pinched in the middle, with a spout on the bottom and decorated with a single rose on top and a cluster below. The loop handle was broken. Ben's was plain. The pinched band in the middle divided the mug into two compartments. A shallow bowl-shaped shelf with drain holes at the top held a cake of soap. Most farmers could afford a five-cent bar of face soap that filled the mug more than once. The half circle lip below the waist and looked like the pouring end of a coalscuttle or a cream pitcher. Jacob dipped the brush through this opening into the warm water, swirled it over the cake of soap, and whirled the glob of lather onto the whisker area of the face.

Jacob opened the razor again and began the delicate part of the procedure -- the dangerous part. He moved the sides of his razor three-fourths of the way around and held them out of the way between his index and middle fingers. He held the small curved piece of metal against the middle and ring fingers on the palm side for stability. He directed the metal base of the blade with thumb and index finger. The idea was to hold the area to be shaved flat and taut with the left hand; then draw the razor across the skin with just the right amount of angle and pressure to cut the whiskers at, but not below, the skin level. Jacob changed the angle and method of holding the razor according to the area of the face. He held the skin tight by making all sorts of grimaces, poking his tongue under his lips or pulling his cheek to make odd faces at himself in the mirror. His arms jutted out at strange angles as he held the razor with one hand and pulled his skin with the other. Ben watched and waited his turn at the mirror.

When he was almost through, Jacob looked down to clean the lather off the blade, and saw a flicker of motion in the yard nearby and heard a familiar giggle. Bertha Mae had warned John B. to be very quiet when his father was shaving. She explained that sudden noise or motion might make him jerk the blade against his neck. But the sight of his father with elbows sticking out making a ridiculous face covered with lather was too much to ignore. His mother snatched him up to take him to their room. Jacob smiled to the mirror as he finished shaving and washed the soap from his face.

Ben moved in front of the shelf and mirror. His movements were awkward and he nicked himself on the lip.

Jacob said, "I've told ya and told ya, push ya lip with ya tongue or pull the skin tight some kinda way. Keep on and folks'll think ya broke up a catfight. Just think -- folks in town shave like this ever' day -- waste of daylight hours if ya ask me."

*   *   *

In the house, Martha touched her husband's beard, "John, one of the boys would loan ya some soap and a brush and help ya. I know they's a razor put up somewhere. I haven't seen the face of the man I married in five years."

"The whole company agreed not to shave till we run them Yankees out. They're still here."

Martha sighed. This was the usual answer to a common request. And she knew that it wasn't the whole reason for the beard. "John, ya kept more'n your part of the bargain. Ya can't be blamed for somethin' impossible. Not many of the men in your company are still alive. After five years, some have shaved. I know Matthew and Rufus have." Martha couldn't see the expression behind the beard, but his eyes mirrored the glint of steel in her son's razor.

"We might could trim it some." She held out the scissors. "I'll cut just a little to shape it." Martha knew the beard was a shield to hide behind. She longed for him to drop the barrier, especially with his family.

With one exception, all of the family members passed through the dogtrot, across the front porch and into the yard. Nate stopped the large wagon near the front door. Straight chairs faced backwards behind the fixed bench. Nate climbed down, placed a milking stool by the wagon, and helped his mother up to the bench. Jacob helped his wife and child to the chairs in the back. Ben and John sat by Martha on the bench.

Martha looked down as she settled into the seat, "I sure do wish ya'd come with us, Nate. We'd wait on ya to get ready, if ya would."

"No ma'am, if the rule's not changed, I'll not go. Pa said that we had to go to school and church till we were fifteen. After that, it was our choosin'. I'm gonna go to school, 'cept plantin' time like now and pickin' time and maybe if a Devil Dog bites me, but not to church. Sundee is supposed to be a day of rest. I reckon I need my rest more'n I need to get yelled at."

Nate looked down at the dust in the road. His mother said, "The preacher don't yell ever' Sundee. But then, sometimes people might need to get yelled at."

"Nate, ya might could recollect, I didn't hold to much church goin' before the war," John said. "I got converted early in the fightin' and I been with it ever' since. The church has holp me a right smart, and hasn't hurt one little bit. I did give up a lot for the church -- dancin', and hard drinkin', and cussin', and fightin' with ever'body -- 'cept Yankees. I don't rightly think the Lord would ask me to give up sonethin' like that."

Martha jerked her head around. "John McGinnis, you never did dance!"

"Like I said, I give up dancin'. Ya *can* give up somethin' before ya commence!" Martha peered at John face. He was staring at the mules. The beard hid his mouth and she couldn't see his eyes.

Ben leaned over to look at his father. "And cussin', Pa?"

"Weell now... tryin' to get a mule's attention don't count. It's a heap sight better to say a word or two to a stubborn mule than it is to hit him in the head with a stick of wood. If'n he don't gee-haw just right ya gotta make him listen some kinda way."

Nate still stared at the road at his feet. "I've told ya before. I don't do no sinnin' big enough for me to be hollered at. I did say a bad word, but it was only 'cause that bite hurt so bad. I'll try to remember what ya told me, Ma. I'll hitch the mules to the wagon ever' Sundee, but that's far as I'll go toward church....'less the rules are changed." He lifted his head.

John stared straight ahead. He picked up the reins and gave a little rolling twitch, so the mules could feel them on their back. "Come up, mules, 'fore I have to say hard words on Sundee." The wagon moved away with the wheels grinding, harness slapping, and wagon body creaking as it swayed. Nate watched it slowly disappear around the first bend in the road. Martha looked back just before the house moved out of her sight.

John was solemn and silent as he drove the team. The mules knew the way. There was little for him to do but stare at the road between the flopping ears. One mule was much larger than the other. The team was mismatched, but both were mules. As always, the family watched the sights along the public way. The three-mile drive along the rutted dirt road took them past cabins, some of logs and others weathered boards. Several house sites were abandoned with nothing left but tumbled down chimneys and stone pillars slowly sinking in a sea of weeds and vines. They drove past one larger farm. Fallen bricks lay between four chimneys outlining a large house. Blackened remains of columns overlooked a cracked and broken brick porch.

Four small houses and ruins of others lay to the south. Fields had been recently plowed to the edge of the ruins.

As if he had never seen it before, Ben asked, "Now, who did ya say had this place, and why was them little houses out back?"

Martha patiently explained. "This here was the Gaylord Hampton place. Ya remember, they owned the gin and warehouse where we take our cotton in New Canaan. The little houses are where the colored lived before the war. Mr. Hampton, he was a rich man. The Unions come in and hauled off two thousand bales of his cotton and took his gin. Both his sons was killed in the war. Mrs. Hampton took to her bed when her second boy got shot. She died out a month later. Mr. Ham lost ever'thang. This farm, too. Now most of his darkies live out west of New Canaan. Four colored families come back and sharecrop where they was born. They say in a few years they might could buy the land. Mr. Ham, he lives in a little house he was able to keep in New Canaan -- nobody with him but one of the house Nigras. They say he don't go nowhere and is bad after liquor."

They fell silent as they passed the remains of the plantation. The blackened chimneys stood like tombstones from a lost civilization. Virginia creepers climbed the columns, tangled with vines of poison ivy. The poison ivy was becoming dominant.

As they passed the farm, Jacob said, "Them families have plowed as much land as when all the colored was here. I don't know how they'll pick the cotton and pull the corn, 'less they got a passel o' kids."

John grunted and never turned his head. "East field's laid out wrong. Rows are too wide and the wrong direction. It's already washin' away. Corn is way yonder too thick."

Ben twisted around on the bench to look at remains of homes. "Why, Pa? Why did Yankees burn folk's houses? That didn't have nothin' to do with the war? They was just farmers."

"Ben, Satan and his kin burns ever'thang. Ya'd have to ask the devil hisself why. Them folks that come through the South aburnin' ever'thang come straight from hell."

Their drive brought them to the Ebenezer Springs Methodist Church. A large spring near the church spilled across the road and washed the wagon wheels and mules hooves as they crossed the shallow ford. It seemed fitting to have a church near living water. Water in a well was still; a stream might be polluted, but water that bubbled cold and pure from deep within the earth was seen as a gift from God.

With little encouragement, the mules turned from the road into the chert and clay parking area. Jacob climbed over the side of the wagon and tied the mules to a post near the trees. He helped his mother down from the wagon. Bertha Mae handed John B. down to Jacob, and Martha held the wiggling child while Jacob held his wife's hand as she climbed down.

A few wagons were already on the lot, and others arrived at a steady pace. The passengers nodded and spoke to the McGinnis family as they passed. An oxen drawn wagon passed by slowly and ponderously. John touched his hat and spoke when their wagon was even with his. "Mornin' to the Kellys. 'Spect the millin' business is right slow this time of year." Robert Kelly nodded and drove to a hitching area farther down the line. John stepped down and walked over to the next wagon, pulled by two black horses. "Mornin' Charlotte Emerline -- Mamroy. Mornin', Uncle Ambrose. Hear yer takin' on the Pepper boy for a spell. Mighty nice of ya to help him after he lost his farm."

Ambrose had white hair and beard separated by a crowd of wrinkles. His wife sat on the bench with her husband, holding one-year-old John. She was thin with dark blond hair. Her face was pretty but anxious, her mouth a tight straight line as she looked from the baby in her lap to those behind her. Mamroy sat in a straight chair in back with three-year-old Lavania Violet in her lap and her arm around five-year-old Dove in the chair beside her.

Ambrose nodded, tilted his head back so that he could see under the heavy lids, and said, "He'll pull his own weight or lose the job like he did the farm."

The families moved slowly toward the church. All of these people were well known to the McGinnis family. Some were tradesmen, a few were sharecroppers, but most were farmers who owned their land. Martha answered greetings and spoke with the wives as they walked.

John searched faces in the crowd. "Somebody must be right sick. I don't see Doc Davis."

Most of the visiting took place after church, but some news just couldn't wait. A few of the men had been to town and heard the latest news. Others had read newspapers. All had some personal disaster or victory to share. John greeted Robert McGregor, the merchant, and Dave Campbell, the blacksmith.

As they stood talking, Campbell said, "Heard you had some trouble with that big 'ol red dog." John stopped and told of Nate's account of the Devil Dog attack and the loss of the mule and then the boys' experiences at the trade-day. He listened to stories of crops and life on the land -- some good and some bad. Soon wives were urging their husbands away from the heat and smell of the lot and toward the church as the bell reminded them of the true purpose of their trip. They walked a little faster to the sound.

The church building had straight lines of rough sawn whitewashed clapboard. At the front was a small bell tower with a needle pointing upward barely qualifying as a steeple. Little groups moved up the two steps to the sheltered landing and went in the chapel. Inside, a central aisle separated rows of upright pews without cushions. If sleep happened, it was not from comfort. As they passed the doorway, Bertha Mae stopped John B. with a hand on his shoulder, "Now you know this is God's house and we're here to worship. We must be quiet."

"I 'member—I 'member! If I want somethin', I whisper." He pulled away and ran down the aisle. Jacob caught him and brought him back.

As soon as families were settled, the entire congregation began to sing, with the pastor as director. In an aisle seat, midway back, Ann Cooper sang off-key in a shrill piercing voice. Some of the base singers always sat nearby to try to overcome the sound, sometimes without success.

The preacher was a pleasant, slightly built, clean-shaven man with auburn hair-- a few years younger than John. His only outstanding physical attribute was his eyes. His piercing blue eyes seemed to look within a person's very soul as he spoke. His education was above that of his members, but he never talked down to them. The pastor had served the community for the past two years. They shared Brother Mac, as they called him, with another small church in the north end of the county. He had been their pastor for a short while in 1861 and had left for military service. After the customary two songs, Pastor McDonald began the service. On this Sunday, his face would have been right for a funeral.

"Folks, we measure time from the birth of Jesus Christ. We also measure time from the birth of our nation in 1861 and its death five years ago. Those four years changed Southern states forever. Most of us here today have lived three lives: one of peace and prosperity before the war, one of death and destruction in the war, and one of turmoil and struggle after the shooting stopped. For some in their third life, the image of a time before the war is dim. The conflict is really not over. We pray that we will live to see a better day when strife and hatred fades and abundance returns. We should never forget what happened in the spring of 1865, the death and suffering in those prior four years, and those who never lived to see a new beginning. I have asked the headmaster of our school to say a few words." Brother Mac then sat on the first row.

Edward Allen was a hollow cheeked man of forty-six years who rarely smiled. His most obvious physical attribute was a round scar with ragged edges on his right forehead: the remains of a gunshot wound early in the war. The doctors found no exit wound. Some thought that the projectile had gone through the bone, the brain, the bone in back, and come to rest in fragments under the scalp. Others thought that the musket ball had struck the thick bone of the forehead at an angle, and fragments traveled the surface of the skull without penetrating. Either way, he had a spot on his forehead and lumps under his scalp that had been with him since the swelling had gone down, and would stay forever as marks of the past.

The headmaster's students respected him and feared him. The standard joke among the boys was that you could always tell how mad 'fesssor Allen was by how red his scar was. He was as strict a disciplinarian in school as he had been in the army. Like the pastor and the doctor, he was more educated than most. He was well read, well spoken, and transmitted his knowledge to others.

The headmaster stood and walked to the front of the church. His mouth was a tight straight line as he

mounted the platform and put down a single sheet of
paper. He turned, gripped the lectern until his knuckles
were white, and never glanced at what he had written.
He looked at no one; his eyes fixed on something
beyond the church. The scar on his forehead was ashen.
Words seemed to flow from his soul:

Our land was bathed and blessed in golden sun by day
Cooled at night by ribbons of light in soft moonlight's way.
Both house and barn filled to the brim under God's golden
sun.
Evil to the north, hearts filled with lust –
In their might placed trust –
They question our right to live in the light of the sun.

The evil of the north spread fire through this sunlit land.
Both dwelling and barn were lost to the chastening hand.
They took as they pleased of the land – both goods and lives
From a people who would be free –
Who yearned and burned to be free.
We once had a nation, but it no longer survives.

Fire and death destroyed this land of sun-filled days.
Bare chairs, empty sleeves, sad hearts mark our ways.
The evil of the north are proud of the death of a land.
They magnify deeds –
They justify deeds.
They gloat as they take what is left with a bloody hand.

The proud magnifiers of the northland do not see.
They bear a secret burden and are not free.
The brother whose crime was a wish to live free, they slay.
To hurt gives pleasure –
They increase the measure.
They do not see the mark of Cain, and on them it will stay.

Pained spirits cry to us from beyond their rightful rest.

Their rueful cry is to rebuild the fair land they blest.
Else lives were wasted in the battles they fought for me.
Those who are alive –
Are obliged to strive.
We strive to build with God alone.
None but the dead are free.

Major Edward Allen, CSA released the lectern, stepped down, and sat in a pew without another word. The church was silent but for scattered sobs from women who had lost husbands, fathers and sons. Several men looked to the floor.

Pastor McDonald's sermon was filled with passages about the antichrist, the tribulation and the battle of Armageddon. Except for the occasional gasp or amen, there was rapt attention and silence in the pews. Members had endured desperate days, but they were hearing of events worse than they had seen or could imagine. The implication was that these happenings could begin any time, even during tomorrow's washday.

In the midst of the sermon, John B. spoke out loud enough to draw the attention of those nearby. Bertha Mae blushed, and after trying to quiet him, she pulled her whining child by the hand toward the back door. Martha turned to see her standing on the steps, shaking a finger in John B.'s face. The two returned to the back row, John B. pouting and red-faced.

Brother Mac read from Revelation 19

> *And I saw heaven opened, and*
> *behold a white horse; and he that*
> *sat upon him was called Faithful and*
> *True, and in righteousness he doth*
> *judge and make war....*
>
> *And the armies which were in*
> *heaven followed him upon white horses,*

clothed in fine linen, white and clean.

John leaned over to Martha and whispered, "He sure is abearin' down on them two words. Did *you* tell him to preach on white horses?"

"Hush, John. God is s'posed to tell him what to preach. Maybe He thought you needed it."

When Brother Mac had finished recounting the binding of Satan, the millennial kingdom, last judgment, and new heaven and earth, the noon hour was long past. Brother Mac ignored the old man on the second row who checked his pocket watch several times, then tapped it on the next pew and held it to his ear. But when Uncle Doc Deerman on the third row began to shout, "Glory to The Lord, praise God" and such, the preacher brought the service to a close.

They sang a single verse of the closing hymn and had a final prayer. In cold weather they might have dawdled around in the church. Today, members rapidly filed out of the building. The serious visiting began in the wagon lot. Unwritten rules said that the sermon must be discussed first, then urgent neighborhood gossip, and last of all, national news.

John walked over to the the headmaster." Major Allen, that was mighty fine talk about the war and all. Seemed like ya said an awful lot with just a few words, rhymin' it like that. Sorry Nate didn't get to hear it."

"Tell him that I'll let him read *Ode to The Confederacy* anytime."

Discussion on the sermon ended quickly, and news of the Ebenezer Springs community, the state, and nation began. Several men and women clustered around the school headmaster, Edward Allen, as he explained passage of the Fifteenth Amendment and its implications. Rufus Cooper said, " I can't see that it makes a hill o' beans to us. Since the war, all that's been done. Might make some of them Yankees change their tune some. Four more states are back in the union. Our problem is that lots of white folks still can't vote. Congress has got two colored now and more acomin'."

Eunice and George Roberts, neighbors to the west of the McGinnis farm, stopped to talk. George opened his mouth to speak, but his wife began before he could say a word.

"I just *know* that Sherman is the Antichrist. Don't you think so John? George does."

"If he is, seems yer out of luck. That'd mean that the Rapture has come and you missed it."

"Why John McGinnis, aren't ya even interested in Armageddon and the millennium and all that? Don't ya think it could come soon?"

"It don't make me no never mind."

"Why?"

" I ain't gonna get no vote on it anyhow. God runs thangs. He don't ask me or you when to do what. I reckon He'll do it when he sees fit to. I 'spec it'll be the right time when He decides to do somethin'."

Eunice didn't pursue the conversation. John's blunt somber ways were well known.

Finally, Rufus Cooper got John's attention. "Don't reckon ya heard. A mule run away with Jeff Baker and he fell and broke his arm. Doc set it, but he's gonna be out of the fields quite a spell. They said he was really behind on his plowin'. Doesn't even have his garden all in."

"He's always behind. Serves him right. He drags around 'till summer is half over 'fore he plants. Prob'ly ate his seed last winter."

" I just thought I'd tell ya-- livin' so close and all. He's just a ways east of us."

Ann Cooper was wringing her hands and twisting her handkerchief during the required part of the discussion, waiting for the opportunity to draw the McGinnis family aside. The Coopers lived on land east of the McGinnis farm. Ann was a thin sharp-nosed woman with watery blue eyes and a small-pursed mouth. Her everyday speech was almost as piercing as her singing. She did not consider herself a gossip, because gossiping was sinful. She just made it her business to know everything about everybody. Occasionally, Ann would share that knowledge. Today she could hardly wait to tell her news. Great things had been expected of the boy who had warned of the Yankee raid.

"Martha and John, have ya heard? The Butler's oldest left home and is actin' on the stage in St. Louis!" She moved her head from side to side. "Who woulda' thought it? A whistlin' rooster in that family! Next thang ya know he'll be takin' up with a grass wida."

John nodded. "Do tell! That's a shame, Ann. I don't wonder at somethin' like that happenin' – that's a big town in a border state and fulla all kinda folks. If he don't want to farm, maybe in time he'll come to hisself and take up a more respectable trade."

Social time drew to a close, and families started drifting away from the church. Stomachs audibly complained and small children began running and fighting. One fell and began to cry. Wives tried to guide their husbands toward the wagons. Uncle Doc's shouting faded in the distance. Everybody agreed that his mules must be deaf.

The McGinnis family climbed into the wagon and headed home. John B. was allowed to ride in Martha's lap so he could see his grandfather handle the reins and watch the plodding of the mules. They walked only as fast as reins and words forced them to. Their heads bobbed hypnotically as if nothing else existed beyond the road at their feet.

John B. looked up at his grandmother. "Gra'pa say 'come up' and make 'em go?"

"Yes, John B." The child watched his granfather control the big animals with words and straps of leather. He was quieter than in church. John B. did not see the ruins along the road. He saw bright images that fascinate little boys.

"Gra'ma, look -- dog!"

"No, John B. That's a deer. It's got spots on it, so ya know it's just a baby. See its mama back there?" The boy continued to look in wonder at the world around him.

"See, John B., there's a little rabbit to the side of the road. " Farther ahead of the rabbit, there was movement from the dead limb of a sweetgum tree. Broad white wings with rounded black tips appeared against the sky. The red tailed hawk turned and swooped down. Inherited memory of moving shadows against the sky caused the rabbit to run. The hawk moved his wing almost imperceptibly to change his flight and snatched up the rabbit as it fled. The small rabbit's shriek was not loud. With the helpless prey in his talons, the hawk flapped its wings, climbed into the sun and screamed as if to show his might. The event was a thing of power, grace, and beauty, but at the same time was gruesome and repulsive.

Martha tried to hold her hand over John B.'s eyes to shield him from the sight. He was determined to see. "What's that bird gonna do with that rabbit, Gra'ma?"

"Uh -- he's – uh -- givin' him a ride."

"Huh, his last ride! " John said. "Why don'cha tell the boy the truth. He's gotta know about life sooner or later. They's always somethin' out there that's bigger, and stronger and meaner, and is tryin' to eat ya, whether yer man or beast."

Martha glared at her husband, settled John B. in her lap, and said,

"That bird is takin' that rabbit home to feed babies that're hungry.

"Birds eat little rabbits?"

"Yes, and mice and squirrels, and maybe even chickens. We eat cows and pigs and sheep. But sometimes we eat rabbits and squirrels, too."

"Oh… Who eats birds?"

"We eat chickens. A chicken is a bird. We might eat bob-whites or ducks."

"Who eats that bird?" John B. pointed to the sky where he saw the hawk.

"I don't know who would eat that hawk -- a bigger bird of some kind -- maybe an eagle." Questions and answers flowed until John pulled the reins and turned the wagon into the half circle drive in front of the house.

Nate was sitting in a chair on the porch, reading. The dogs were curled up at his feet and a large yellow cat sat at the far end of the porch, alternately watching the dogs and checking the location of the nearest tree. Nate moved his right arm deliberately, but flinched as he stepped off the porch.

Martha said, "Nate, ever'body was askin' about ya."

"Hope ya told 'em I was fine." He avoided asking about church or events after the service, as if his family had been for a ride for pleasure.

Jacob helped his wife down and then lifted John B. down from his grandmother's lap. The boy ran to Nate, "Unc' Nate, Unc' Nate, we saw a big -- big bird get a rabbit and -- and he flew away like this." He made flapping motions with his arms. He looked to see the effect of his story on his uncle and then just beyond Nate, he saw a hen and biddies scratching and pecking in the dirt. He left running, trying to swoop down on a baby chicken.

Later, as they finished the Sunday dinner, John said, "I reckon we can work the fields a day for ol' Jeff Baker. Jacob, you and Ben load the plows, harnesses and the garden tools into the wagon in the mornin'. Lord knows know how far behind he is, so we best take scooters, shovels, sweeps, wings and middle busters -- so we'll have whatever point we need."

Ben said, "Thought ya said as lazy as he was, he deserved it?"

"True. He's got a sorry streak -- started in the war -- but his wife and chillun will go hungry without no fault of their own. We can spare a day. I 'spec they'd help us if the shoe was on the other foot."

Nate said, "I can do a day's work. Ya want me to go, too?"

"No, if yer able tomorrow, take that fancy new horse and see how she plows, so we'll know how bad we was skint."

No work was allowed on Sunday except feeding the stock, harnessing the team and milking the cow. The rest of the afternoon was leisure time, and the day passed peacefully.

On Monday morning, John, Ben, and Jacob left with the wagon, two mules, and the equipment. Rufus Cooper smiled when he saw John drive up.

Martha was left with Nate in the kitchen while Bertha Mae took John B. back to their room to clean the food from his face and hands and to dress him for his day in the yard. He talked of getting a baby chicken as he left the kitchen. His mother was telling him to leave them alone. Martha dressed Nate's wounded arm.

"I don't think ya ought to be workin' in the hot sun, till that thang heals."

Nate shrugged, "Don't hurt that much, Ma. I know Pa said we're caught up, but they's still a sight o' work to be done."

As Nate left the kitchen, Bertha Mae called to Martha to ask her to listen for John B. while she went to the branch to wash. Martha looked down the dogtrot and saw him playing in the yard. As she finished the dishes, John B. screamed from outside. Martha reached the back steps to find him shrieking and running toward the house.

She picked him up and tried to calm him enough to discover the disaster. There was no obvious major injury. He reduced the cries to jerking sobs, and Martha managed to understand, "Big chicken bite me!" He showed her an index finger with a red scraped spot on each side. There was not enough blood for a full drop. Martha couldn't hide her laughter.

She washed the finger, kissed it, and dried his tears." Now, John B., were you tryin' to get that mama chicken's babies?"

He stuck out his lower lip. "Don' know."

"Didn't your mama tell you to leave them biddies alone?"

"Don' 'member," and the lip stuck out further.

"Go back in the yard and play, but remember that little animals and even little people that look weak an helpless may have a mama or somebody else lookin' out far 'em. And try not to overwork the angel that looks out for you" By this time Bertha Mae arrived short of breath after running from the branch. She left her washing for the afternoon and spent the rest of the morning near the yard trying to keep John B. out of trouble. At midday, they ate and John B. took a nap while his mother finished her washing

Martha was alone in the kitchen when Nate came in. Nate stared out of the window of the kitchen while his mother put his dinner on the table. Suddenly a violent shudder began in his shoulders and passed over his body.

Martha put the plate down and studied him closely. "Nate, that hot sun is too much far ya. There's not a dry thread on that shirt. Ya look plumb white-eyed. Why not quit for the day? Ya've worked way past noontime. Yer Pa won't mind."

"I'm fine. A rabbit run over my grave just now, that's all. I'm doin' alright, Ma." He held up his left hand as if to stop her from coming near. "We need to get the plowin' done. Dolly is doin' real good. I finished up a right smart of it already. If I put my mind to it, I think I can get through with that bottom to the east 'fore dark."

He looked away from his mother toward the window, hesitated, and dropped his voice almost to a whisper. "I did see that Devil Dog again. At the end of the row by the woods he was just sittin' there in the shadows lookin' at me with his mouth open and his tongue hangin' out...like he was laughin'. I picked up a big rock, but he was gone time I got to the woods. I'm gonna carry a stick with me. I'll be fine."

Nate ate quickly and got up from the table and stopped at the door to look back.

"I'd be better satisfied if ya didn't go back in the heat of the day. I just don't feel right about it." Nate smiled at her, waved, and slammed the kitchen door behind him. Martha stepped out in the dogtrot to watch his winding path toward the east. He moved with long loose strides, but he carried his bandaged arm at his belt. She shielded her eyes from the sun and watched him until he was hidden by bushes at the edge of a field. *I reckon John is right; he is big enough to be treated like a man.* She finished cleaning the kitchen and went to her bedroom to work.

Martha looked up from her sewing when she heard slow hesitant footsteps at the end of the dogtrot. She glanced through the window at the height of the sun. *It can't be Nate. It's the middle of the afternoon and plenty of daylight left.* The stumbling steps came closer. She gasped as Nate swayed in the doorway, feeling along the wall with his left hand.

She ran to him, supported him, and led him toward his bed. She felt his forehead. "Why yer aburnin' up!" Nate fell into the bed as she pulled off his sweat-soaked clothes. She fetched a pan of cool water from the kitchen, dipped a cloth in it and bathed his face, arms and chest. He was able to take no more than sips of water. Martha changed the dressing. Pus was to be expected, but now there was swelling along his entire arm and raised red streaks above the elbow, almost to the armpit. She said nothing to Nate about what she saw, or what she feared.

Nate's words were rambling and disjointed. "Ma, I heard a rooster crow 'bout midnight last night. And today...today I heard an owl call in midday...more than once...in the woods by the east field. You know what that means. Those are signs."

"Nate, even if them critters're callin' for somebody to die, it don't mean it'll be you. Everythang is going to be fine, Nate. Yer Pa will get home before long and we'll send for Doc Davis. Bertha Mae can't go in her shape. Just be quiet and still as you can for a bit."

The bedroom door swung open very slowly and John B. peeped around the corner. "Unc' Nate sick?" Martha led him out and handed him over to his mother. Bertha Mae kept John B. in their room. There was no one else to help, so Martha did what she could. She sat and watched Nate and bathed his face and arms with cool water. When Nate was quiet, she ran to the front porch for a few seconds. She twisted the damp rag until her knuckles were white and listened for sounds from the east. *Lord, let 'em come back so we can get some help. I never saw anythang this bad. He's so sick and I don't know what to do.*

A buggy passed once, but it was not Doc Davis or anyone she knew. The others did not arrive until hours later. She ran to meet the wagon as it turned down the little road toward the barn.

"Oh John, that place on Nate's arm is festered terrible and his whole arm is swole and has red streaks runnin' up it. He's burnin' up with fever and is most out of his head. Ya reckon we could send for Doc?"

"Martha, we got no i-dee where Doc Davis is at. It'd be pure-dee luck if we was to find him this late in the day. When he's got a case and dark comes, he stays the night where he is at. We can't wander the county in the dark. We got a little moon, but the sky is so cloudy it's gonna be a dark night."

Ben and Jacob left to put up the wagon and mules as John walked toward the house. Martha tugged at his shirtsleeve and opened her mouth to speak. John pulled away and continued to walk. "I don't see how we can do nothin' till mornin'."

Chapter Six – Journey into Darkness

After putting up the stock, Jacob and Ben came to the kitchen. They both offered to go somewhere for help, even at night. Martha sat at the table across from John and gripped his wrist, "John, he'll be sicker by mornin'. He's got worse since he come in from the field. I'll do what I can, but Lord knows I need help. If we can't get Doc, could we send for my mama? She'll know what to do and we know where she's at?"

John snorted, "Yer mama, why she couldn't treat head lice!"

"That's not so, John. She cured the two older boys when they were so sick last summer."

"Ever'body knows blackberry wine is good for scours."

"She knew to put that white chalky clay and the charcoal in it, too. And when Ben got the itch so bad, she used lard and sulfur and cured it. She's just 'bout good as a doctor."

"Maybe so, but he smelled so bad, he had to sleep at the barn. Anyhow, yer ma can't come that far afoot and ya'll not get our mules to make no nighttime trip."

"Wiley claimed Dolly could be led of a night," Jacob said. "I could walk ahead with a lighter knot aburnin' and Ben could lead the horse. We could take the narrow wagon that we used to haul logs when we cleared land. You know we've floored it to haul mess from the stalls to the fields. She could pull that little wagon by herself. Let us try, Pa. We *gotta* do somethin'."

"John, our youngest is bad sick. Surely w're not gonna just look the other way till daylight."

John looked at the anxious eyes surrounding him. He had no choice. "Jacob, 1 reckon ya'all can try, but Lord help ya if yer grandma finds out she got hauled in a manure wagon."

Ben left to hitch the horse to the wagon Before clouds covered the waning moon, Jacob went to the pile of stumps behind the house. The tangled mound came from virgin longleaf pine, cut years ago to clear land for planting. Each Spring a few more were pulled up and hauled to the house. The sapwood had long since rotted away, leaving the heart saturated with rosin. Jacob always liked the smell on a summer day when the wood was split, and the sticky sap oozed and filled the air with its scent.

Each winter, John and his sons split the stumps into sticks of kindling. A few finger-sized pieces of lighter could start a fire in minutes -- from just a spark. They had to take care, though -- if the sticks were too large a chimney fire could set the roof ablaze.
No one knew how long heartwood could last in the fields. Each year they became a little smaller, but it happened very slowly.

Jacob swung an axe and broke off several long roots. Some had knots larger than a man's fist. He wedged the first of the lighter knots into a U-shaped iron clamp shaped like a wooden clothespin.

When Ben brought the wagon, Jacob loaded the lighter sticks and two buckets of water in the back. He draped an old quilt across the bench. Jacob was quiet and somber as he moved deliberately in the fading light. He stopped and struck a match and shielded it from the breeze and set fire to a splinter on the side of the first lighter. The flame slowly wrapped the stick and swayed over the end.

From the porch, John and Martha watched the eerie procession. Jacob walked ahead with a flaming pine knot in the iron clamp, held at arm's length above his head and a little to the side. He had wrapped his arm and shoulder with wet rags to protect them from dripping rosin that fell flaming to the ground—marking a line of fire dots that slowly winked out. Behind came Ben, his face shining with sweat, scuffling his feet through dying flames, leading a confused Dolly pulling the narrow wagon. She balked and hesitated at times, but with a few soft words and a gentle tug on the reins she went onward. Jacob heard Ben tell Dolly why they were going. Maybe she did understand.

Almost as soon as they left, clouds covered the moon, leaving a gentle glow from the overshadowed body looking down on darkness of the earth. As far as Jacob could tell, the torch he carried was the only light in the entire world. It flowed along the road asif it were a wave of water, pushing a yellow circle into a lake of blackness. The yellow-white light fluttered brightness and shadow on the trees, bushes, and ruts along the narrow road. Stumps, fallen trees, boulders, heaps of dirt at the side of the road appeared strange and unreal in the changing light. Leaves and branches near the road shone brightly, but between them were shadows of nothingness. As they passed, darkness closed about them, their tiny light swallowed by the night.

The ghostly caravan was watched from trees by pairs of eyes reflected in the torchlight. They shone like coals of fire at the bottom of a well. As the wagon creaked along, there was a rustle of leaves and a blink of the eyes and whatever it was gone. Farther along the road, a large set of eyes appeared deep in the bushes near the ground. The coals of fire did not blink. Jacob thought he heard a low growl, and he ran at the eyes swinging the flaming torch. "Get from here, Devil Dog! Nate ain't here!" With a rustle of leaves, the eyes were gone.

They crept forward with agonizing slowness. Jacob wanted to go faster, but his circle of light was small. He cautioned Ben several times not to follow at his heels.

As they passed houses near the road, dogs barked warnings to the families inside. A man would appear in a doorway, most times holding a long barreled gun, silhouetted by candlelight in the room behind.

Each time Jacob called out, "It's just us, Jacob and Ben McGinnis. We got bad sickness at our house and we're goin' to Uncle Ambrose's place to get our grandma. Ya ain't seen Doc Davis, have ya?"

"I got no i-dee whur the Doc is at. Ya'all need help?"

"Nosir, I reckon we'll make it"

And so it went, down the narrow dirt road agonizing foot at the time. Until Jacob spoke, those in the cabins might have thought them spirits of the night.

They were glad to hear the barking at their destination. Several dogs stood guard over two houses, sawmill, and blacksmith shop. A faint light showed through a window of the larger house. Jacob did not have to announce their arrival. The door swung open and against the candleligh a man appeared in the doorway holding a shotgun. The backlight showed him to be tall and stooped with long hair and beard. Even in shadows, the form was familiar. The man spoke to the dogs and reduced their clamor to an occasional bark.

With relief, Jacob called out, "Uncle Ambrose, it's Ben and Jacob! Nate has had a bad backset after that dog bite and is terrible sick. We come to see if Grandma might could come help us."

"Sorry to hear it." He lowered the gun. "Come on in."

"Thankya, but if Grandma can come, we best be goin'. It's a slow trip on a black night. "

Grandma Cobb appeared behind Ambrose in the dim light.

"Course I'll go; let me get my shawl an some thangs. It's a mite airish tonight. Surely yer ma has what we need to treat him. I'll just borrey some clothes from Martha, if I stay long."

She spoke matter-of-factly, but moved rapidly to gather her things into a small bundle and walk to the wagon. Mamroy Cobb had no husband after the war, and like so many recent widows had come to live with her youngest daughter's family. Many homes held several generations in the days after the war, but this was a stranger association than most. Grandma Cobb was younger than her son-in-law. Her daughter, Charlotte Emereline, needed her help. In 1864, Charlotte was thirteen when she married a man seventy-six years old. At nineteen, she had three children and a house to manage.

Uncle Ambrose held the torch while Jacob helped his grandmother to mount and get settled on the seat. At night, clumps of manure were hidden in the corners of the wagon. Jacob hoped that her sense of smell was not what it was the day she caught him and Ben smoking rabbit tobacco behind the springhouse.

Jacob took the torch and raised it again – this time with his left hand. Ben led Dolly and turned the wagon in the circular drive. Grandma Cobb waved to Ambrose and Charlotte.

She looked at the procession ahead and called to Ben, "Is that a horse pullin' this here wagon -- a white horse?"

Ben stood to one side and looked over his shoulder, "Yes ma'am, Jacob and Nate traded far 'er at trade day. She's not really white; she's...well she's sorta gray. We lost Maude. She got a broke leg when the dog bit Nate. Dolly's might near good as a mule, though. She might be better, tonight. Our mules wouldn't make this trip." Ben talked on of the little horse and her virtues while Grandma Cobb gripped the bench with white knuckles.

"Ben, who's drivin' this wagon?"

"Reins are tied right loose there at the front. I'm just leadin' 'er. Ya can hold 'em if ya're a mind to"

The two men and a small gray horse pulling the wagon, with a grandmother who sat straight -- her back not touching the bench-- retraced their steps and were stared at by the same eyes of the night, barked at by the same dogs and watched by the same men standing in a doorway, gun in hand.

*   *   *

There was no sleep at the McGinnis house. Nate shouted a few words now and again, as he thrashed about. Most of the time he babbled randomly.

Martha put her hand on his forehead and jerked it off. She looked across the bed. "John, his skin's so hot it might near burns my hand. It's dry, and I just wet it. Soak some more rags, he's knocked this one in the floor." Martha sat at his bedside bathing his hot skin with water, but at close intervals made trips to the porch to check for a light in the road, a glimmer of hope in the dark. She began a half hour after Jacob and Ben left.

John put his hand on her shoulder as she stood in the doorway staring into the night. "Now, Martha, they're good boys, and if anybody can get through, they can. They'll be here when they get here and not before. It's a fer piece to Ambrose's place. Takes time to make that trip on a night like this." Bertha Mae came again and offered to help, and again was sent back to be with her child.

At last, they saw a glow on distant treetops. Then it reflected on lower branches along the gentle curve in the road. The dancing lights invaded the shadows as they rounded the bend, and Martha and John heard the creak of the wagon and grinding of the wheels. Their own dogs barked as the ghostly figures appeared, but stopped when they rushed up and found friends.

Grandma Cobb greeted Martha and John briefly as she climbed down from the wagon. "Martha, I s'pose he's in the boys' room. One of ya come, and hold a light far me."

John held the candle while the two women removed the bandage and looked at the arm. Martha said, "I put all the sugar we had on it … but that wasn't much." She watched her mother's face.

Grandma Cobb straightened up and said with firmness, "Martha, I'll be fair with ya. It's worser'n the boys would have me to believe. I'd hate to see it in the light of day. See them swoll red streaks up his arm? It ain't just festered. He's got blood poisonin'. I've never seen nothin' bad as this either. Even if we could get Doc, he couldn't cut it off and get ahead of them streaks. We got to do somethin' or he's gone. Get me a vessel or a basket of some sort, and as soon as the boys get back from the barn, send one of 'em out back of the house to hold a light far me."

"I still got one arm, I'll hold the light.." As Mamroy and John left, Martha sat by Nate's bedside bathing his skin with water.

John held the flaming lighter knot as the two walked to the small cluster of peach trees. Grandma Cob worked quickly with both hands and picked a huge basket of leaves.

Returning to the kitchen, she called her daughter from her grandson's bedside. "Now, Martha, fetch me some cornmeal, a right good size frying pan and stir up that fire in the cook stove. I hope ya got plenty of meal. We're gonna need lots." Mamroy set the pan on top of the stove. She made a mush of cornmeal and water. She rolled peach leaves between her palms and dropped them in. She added two pinches of salt and stirred the mix as it cooked.

Ben came from the barn. Jacob went by way of his room, and brought Bertha Mae. All three offered to help. Grandma Cobb said, "Thank ya, but this is a job for one. Yer ma is all the help I need right now. One of ya could bring in some more stove wood and then start a fire under the pot in the yard. Bertha Mae, I don't think this is catchin', but ya best stay out of it, just to be on the safe side. Wouldn't want to mark yer baby."

John sat in his chair at the end of the table and watched as the women worked by the light of the two candles on the small table.

Grandma took the pan off the fire, when she knew it to be done. "Now, Martha, gimme a big rag...white one if you've got it." She looked up to see both grandsons still standing at the doorway. "If ya still want to do somethin', one of ya hold one of them candles over here so I can see to pour."

Ben held the light and Grandma poured the steaming mix into the rag. She tied the corners to make a flattened bag and the two women carried the frying pan and mix into Nate's room while Ben held the candle.

"We got to test this to be sure it's not too hot. We don't want to burn him, too. Martha, wouldn't hurt none to show the boys how to do this." She looked around and saw both boys in the shadows and John in the doorway. "I can stand it on my elbow. I reckon it'll do for his arm."

She placed the dripping peach-leaf poultice over the open wound and the swollen part of the arm. Even in his stupor, Nate let out a long sigh as the heat soaked in.

"Now be alookin' fa more rags. And boys, ya best tend that fire under the wash pot. Most likely we'll have to use the rags over and over and we'll clean 'em and boil 'em between usin's. Don't worry about puttin' festered rags in the pot. Ya can scour it out later."

While the first poultice cooled, the two women made sage tea. "Martha, try to get a little of this down him. At this hour, it's all we've got. At first light, I'll fix a better tea."

And so it went. The women applied poultices of the hot mix to the arm through the night. Ben and Jacob boiled used rags in the wash pot.

As streaks of color appeared in the east, Martha said, "Mama, he's still burnin' up. Just feel his head."

"Martha, ever'thang is worse at night; let's try to hold on till daylight."

When she could see to walk, Grandma went to the nearest willow tree and cut long strips of bark. She brought them back to the house and brewed tea.
"Now, Martha, this is bitter, but I'll try to get some of it down him. Maybe it'll work." She propped Nate up in the bed and offered the steaming willow bark tea, sip at the time. He coughed and sputtered, but drank most of the brew. The swelling of the arm looked a little better, but his fever still raged.

After Grandma managed to get the second cup of tea down Nate, she stood at the doorway to the kitchen where Martha was putting breakfast on the table. "Martha, his fever is broke. Ya'all could change his wet bedclothes. If ya don't care, I'll lie down a spell, but call me if he worsens." She stumbled a little as she crossed the dogtrot to the big bedroom.

By mid afternoon the swelling was down in Nate's arm and the pus turned to thin yellow liquid, spilling onto the bed. His fever was almost gone, and he began to complain, "What time is it? I'm all crossed up. The sun's up...not even showin' in that window. I need to eat an be in the field." Grandma heard voices from the boys' room, looked in, and sent Ben to gather sassafras roots for a tea. They poured teas and soups down Nate while he demanded solid food, a healthy sign that put a smile on Martha's face, even as she ignored his words.

On the following day shortly after daylight, the dogs began barking. John stepped out on the front porch and saw a man walking from a wagon in the road. The man touched his hat. "Mornin', I'm George Allen from over toward the Georgia line and I got bad trouble. I'm on my way to town with a loaded wagon and the ring has broke off my singletree on one side." John called Jacob and the three of them took the singletree off and then to the shop, where they attached a temporary ring to see him to town and back home.

As they reattached the repaired part, John said, "it's a little shorter now, but I thank it'll see ya home. Mr. Allen, ya ought to get a new singletree. If one end rots, the other's not far behind." Jacob left for the house as Mr. Allen shook John's hand.

"I'm much obliged to ya. How much do I owe ya?"

"Just a kind word and a helpin' hand if the shoe's on the other foot, when we're over yer way."

"I thank ya. I best be leavin'." He stepped up to the wagon bench. John started toward the house when Mr. Allen said, "I reckon ya'all heard about that Devil Dog." John stopped in mid-stride and turned halfway around.

"They found him dead in the woods beyond David Harris's place, close to me. They was ascared to lay hands on him, so they covered him with a wagon load of rocks real quick and put a wood cross on the top of the pile. David said it'd keep him from acomin' back... if he really was a Devil Dog. Other folks think he was just a mad dog that was uncommonly big. Had bullet holes in him, but they was healed. The madness is what killed him." Mr. Allen smiled as he gave a twitch to the reins, "So we don't have nothin' to worry about, now that he's gone."

John stared at the wagon until it disappeared around the bend in the road. He walked back to the house and told Martha of the repairs and the death of the big red dog. He said, "Prob'ly died from bein' shot so much."

On the next day, Nate was eating solid food again and walking a few steps. The swelling and redness were even less and the drainage was decreasing, but he continued to complain of pain in the wound and of shooting pains in his whole arm. Even the cool wind blowing through the doorway or window caused sudden pain. And yet he wanted the cool air because he felt as if he couldn't draw a good breath. When the sun was bright in his room, he complained of headache. Grandma Cobb reassured him that the poultice had drawn out the poisons. She said that the festered place looked so much better that it should feel normal soon. Nate was not convinced. He still had a fear of what might yet come of his wounds. He knew that he had heard powerful signs. He worried about who the owl called for and who the rooster crowed for. He knew those things happened days ago, but when the room was quiet in the day and in the blackness' of night, he thought he heard them again. *What was that big red dog -- really? Was he just a big mean dog? Was he a mad dog or could he be somethin' else... somethin' more evil? Why do I keep hearin' them call?*

Toward noon of the third day, Grandma announced to Martha, "Nate is so much better and his arm is beginnin' to mend. Them deep holes are beginnin' to fill with proud flesh. I think I need to go back to Ambrose and Charlotte's place where I have my own room."

Martha agreed and assured her that she could handle Nate's recovery alone. As they left, Grandma Cobb sat on the bench by Jacob and Ben. "Why aren't we usin' that skinny little wagon, like the other night?"

Jacob grinned at Ben. "Oh Grandma, this bigger wagon is so much smoother. We just couldn't handle it in the dark the other night."

On the far side of the bench, Ben said, "Smells better too." But Grandma didn't hear him.

Throughout the week the two older boys did their usual jobs on the farm, but John did not leave the house except to milk and feed the stock. He checked on Nate frequently, but said little. Nate passed his days sitting at his desk, reading for a while, then lying on his bed covering his eyes with his arm and moaning about his restrictions. He sat at the table with the family for meals. His complaint of burning pain in his arm had been slighted, and he could not describe his fear, so he said nothing.

Chapter Seven – Nate's Demon

They finished breakfast on Saturday morning and Martha began clearing the table. John said, "Nate's about well, so me and Jacob and Ben are fixin' to go over to the Roberts'." Martha set the plate down.

"Remember early this spring when ever'body burned the woods? The Roberts let their yard get knee-deep in weeds. Some hot ashes set it afire and it burned slap up to the house, and it caught up and they got burned out. At church last week they said that the logs was ready and most of 'em notched. If the weather holds, we'll raise the house, today. Might even get the roof started. I've talked to Nate and he don't mind us agoin'."

John and the two older boys loaded the tools and left in the wagon, leaving Nate, Martha, Bertha Mae, and John B. About mid morning, Martha opened the door to check on Nate.

He yelled at her. "Close that door right quick! That breeze pains my arm somethin' terrible. And see can ya put somethin' over that winda. Light just kills my eyes."

"I will, Nate, but ya don't have to talk so sharp to yer Ma. That's not like you atall-- to be so ill-talkin'."

Martha went back to the kitchen. About an hour later, she stopped her work to listen to strange noises coming from somewhere in the house. She stepped across the dogtrot to the big bedroom and listened at Nate's door. Now, there was no doubt. Heavy footsteps paced from one side of the room to the other -- slow and few at first, then constant.

As she stood bewildered by the sounds, Nate shouted. "Get out of here—both of ya! I told ya I can't stand the light and all that wind." John B. screamed. The child wondered about the noise and had opened the door from the dogtrot to Nate's room. Martha ran in, snatched John B. up and closed both doors. Bertha Mae dropped her brush-broom and rushed in from the yard.

"What's wrong with my baby?"

"Bertha Mae, he's not hurt, just scared. Take him in yer room for a spell. I don't know what's come over Nate. He hollered out real loud at John B. Commonly he wouldn't hurt nothin'. He can't even kill a chicken. I'll stay and watch."

Bertha Mae comforted the child, and took him to the safety of their room. Martha sat in the large bedroom, to stay near Nate's door. She heard his bed shift and scrape along the floor. Then total silence. She had no idea what caused Nate's strange behavior, but she was uneasy and worried. She looked about her bedroom, feeling guilty about just sitting and and doing nothing. She could not go outside and finish the sweeping or wash because she had to stay where she could watch over Nate. The house was clean, there was food for noontime, and supper was too far away to think about.

To occupy her mind and take it off the noises in the next room, Martha shifted her chair to the corner of the room by an old humpback trunk. She moved a stained and scarred stick, that John had refused to part with after the war, and opened the lid. From the tray at the top, she set aside a tattered stained letter - hardly legible, picked up a cloth bundle and opened it for the first time since the trip over the ridge during the war. In the white cloth were two packets, carefully tied with a red ribbon. The first was a group of notes from John during the war. Martha put them with the ragged

letter. She untied the smaller packet and opened the
first letter. Martha read each word aloud to herself --
slowly. Some words came haltingly and sounded
strange.

> *May 2,1846*
> *Mr. McGinnis,*
> *My Friend*
>
> *I thought not to write you again, yet since you seem to
> insist. I answer this your fourth appeal, only to say: I
> think it silly to write letters, only to be exchanged.*
>
> > *Martha Ann Cobb*

The next one began:
> *"Dear Miss Martha Ann Cobb:"*

Martha smiled as she read the words. Later
salutations from John, when he was courting in earnest,
always began: *"Dear Miss Martha"* and ended as did all
the rest with, *"Your friend, John McGinnis."* This one
was dated August 11,1846, and began:

> *Dear Miss Martha Ann Cobb:*
> *I feel that it is my duty to inform you that I
> am always ready to sympathize with you
> while sick or in distress. You can't imagine
> what a heartfelt sympathy I had for you
> Sunday while there and after I came home. I
> did feel better when Dr. Wheeler returned
> from your home and informed me that you
> only had chills and fever and not that awful
> typhoid. I have had more tender thoughts
> toward you for the last few days than ever
> before and now I must say that it is my wish
> of every hour that you will soon recover from
> your illness and enjoy the great blessing of
> health again.*
> *Your true friend.*

Martha was intent on the letters; as if somewhere in the depths of the words were the answers she sought. *How kind and tender John was. He is now, but hides it -- as if kindness might be thought of as weakness.*

Many were from John when he was young, enthusiastic, read more, had a hand to hold the pen, and before he spent years at hard work and years in the war. He had written letters because her father would permit visits only on some Sundays. He had wooed in person when he could and by letter when he could not. And he had wooed with all the zeal and ardor of youth. The ink on John's letters had turned brown on yellowed paper. Some lines were heavy and some were thin as the ink ran out in the hand-dipped pen. Capital letters had great decorative swirls.

The return letters from her were short and sometimes curt and they made her smile and almost laugh. But the last one dated nearly a year after the first was different. They were all yellow, but this one was worn at the edges and the folds separated.

Home, Monday afternoon
Sept. 7, 1846
Mr. John McGinnis

My Dearest Love:
You will allow me the privilege to express on these pages my sentiments for you, as I cannot feel satisfied until I tell you the whole truth.
Since last night I have not regretted "my promise" in the least. If you knew how much better I feel since I have fully decided to become your wife, you too would be glad, for I am happier than I have been for a time. Were it not for the love that I had for you, I could not leave Papa, Mama, and the children. I think that I have the power to be something in your life.

*With God's help I will add all to your
happiness that is in my power. It is only in
making others happy that I am made happy.
Caring for you as I do, I would be happier
with you, although it may be selfish in me to
think of my own happiness. I believe that I am
doing what God wants me to do. I believe you
to be the very best man on earth, and I have
no fear because perfect love casts out all fear.
Life would be nothing to me without you. I
did not know that I loved you so until last
night. I have ever longed for a kind-hearted
husband when I became married. It has
always been my disposition from childhood to
be easier ruled by kindness than any other
way, and even today I long to be where
everyone will be gentle and kind to each other.
I hope that I may ever prove worthy of your
love and kindness and I hope to never
disappoint or deceive you in the very least
thing.*

*You know that I have the utmost confidence
in you and have never doubted your sincerity.
If you have confidence in me, I feel that we
will be happy together. If I had known that I
would feel as I do, I would have made my
decision long ago, but I was afraid and I did
not know that I loved you so until last night. I
felt that if I said no, it would be no forever. I
realized that life would be nothing to me
without you.*

*Now, Love, as to when we shall get married,
as for myself there are reasons, which cause
me to say that I had rather wait another year.
However when I promised my love, I promised
to live for your happiness and not others.*

Tears welled up as Martha let the pages slip into her lap and thought of the days of youth and strength, filled with hope and dreams. She had felt all the emotions in these letters, but she could never have written these words by herself. Mary Scott, the pastor's wife, had sat by her side, helping and directing her while she wrote every line. Years later, John admitted that the pastor helped him write his letters. They laughed when they discovered that each had used the same deception.

She looked up at the pictures of John and of Jacob in uniform. They looked sullen, as if the weight of the world rested on their shoulders. A scrap of paper tucked into the frame at the bottom of John's picture had several lines of writing, fading into nothingness. It didn't matter. John had read them aloud so many times that she knew the words. At the bottom of the paper, the letters E. A. were almost hidden by the frame. The ink on the paper in Martha's hand was dim, but the image in her mind was crystal clear of the young man who knocked at her door so many years ago. The hair was different, but the smile, the youthful enthusiasm and the shyness that he overcame by persistence were the same, but not the same John in the picture or John now, with his face hidden by a beard. In the image from years ago she saw the face of Nate – different, yet the same.

She was startled back to the present by a thud from the next room. The pacing began again -- faster and louder. Martha stared at the door to Nate's room. She didn't know what to do.

When noontime came, there were no sounding steps. Martha knocked hesitantly on the door. "Nate, it's time to eat a little somethin'. Ya about ready?" She listened at the crack around the door, but heard nothing but heavy breathing. She knocked a little louder. "Ya want to come to the table? I could bring a plate, if ya don't want to come out. It is right airish in the dogtrot."

"No, I don't want a thing."

"Ya got to eat to get well."

"Nothin'." Nate's voice was deep and harsh. The bed scraped and shifted.

"At least try some pot liquor off the greens or peas or just water to keep ya from dryin' up? I'll bring some. Just try it."

"I said I didn't want nothin'."

Martha went to the kitchen and poured off pot liquor from the peas. She broke off a small piece of cornbread, in case she could entice him to eat and returned to the bedroom.

"I'm openin' the door now, Nate. I'll close it soon's I can, so the air don't hit yer arm." Over the years Martha had made many trips through this doorway when her sons were small or when they were sick. But this time, there was strangeness in a room, which made her uneasy. A grumbling groan came from shadows in the corner. She had placed a portion of the only material she could find over the window -- a piece of faded red cotton from the remains of an old dress. As her eyes accommodated to the dim light, she saw Nate standing by the wall away from the window, taking gasping breaths and grimacing in a way she had never seen. His face was a curious color, and he moved toward her with heavy deliberate steps, throwing his arms upward as he breathed.

Within her reach, he turned and began to circle the room. He started talking -- his words rambling, the muscles of his cheek and neck tight, his breaths jerking and labored.

He stopped for an instant and looked toward her, but moved his head slightly from side to side. "How can there be two of you?" He turned and began walking. "That Devil Dog was here again -- lookin' in the winda. Dolly come by once. Tell Pa to put her up. I need a quilt. I'm freezin' to death. And get them dogs outa here when ya go. I keep hearin' that Devil Dog howl and call to me from the woods by the ridge, and that hoot owl was just outside my winda, and it's full daylight!"

Nate stopped near the cloth-draped window; in the mottled red light; his features were harsh and brutish. His eyes darted from side to side, as if he looked for a dreaded pursuer. He jerked his head back and forth as he spoke. His shoulders were stiff and his chest barely moved as he breathed. He raised his arms and strained to take deeper breaths.

Martha was frightened by what she saw and heard. Nate's behavior was beyond her understanding, but she tried to reason with him. "Nate, ya didn't hear that dog. He's dead now and under a pile of rocks. A man told Pa right recent. And I didn't hear any owl." She offered him the only comfort she could, holding out the cup. "Nate, just try some of this pot liquor -- with a little cornbread. It's fresh cooked this mornin'. Ya need to eat somethin' to get yer strength up."

Nate stepped back, but Martha came closer. He moved his hand slowly in a jerking motion, took the cup, and stared at it as if it were some strange object. He suddenly threw the liquid into his mouth as though one part of his being forced another to act. The instant he swallowed, he began choking, strangling and throwing his arms about. The cup shattered on the floor. Nate's face was red and contorted as he staggered and almost fell. Martha reached out to catch him, but he twisted away, took a few steps and fell on the bed. Martha followed him across the room. His eyes were frantic, without reason, as a desperate animal pinned by his enemy. As the violent choking slowed, he was quieter and more lucid. He tried to speak, but Martha understood nothing because of his hoarseness and gasping struggles to breathe.

He rested for a moment, then caught his breath and in a rasping voice said, "I told ya, I don't want nothin'. I don't even want to look at water. It makes me gag, and then I can't breathe. I told ya to get them dogs outa here!" He swung his arm in the direction of the phantoms in the shadow and would have struck his mother had she been closer.

Martha cried as she left Nate's room. She knocked on Bertha Mae's door. "I don't know what's got into Nate. He's not at hisself atall. The way he's actin', he could hurt somebody and not know it. Help me and we'll push the dresser agin' Nate's door to hem him up."

The two frightened women left John B. asleep and went back to the large bedroom. As they strained to push the heavy dresser across the room, they looked through the crack in the doorway. Nate continued to plod back and forth with heavy steps. As each foot struck the floor, rumbling animal-like noises came from deep within his throat. At intervals he stopped, threw up his arms, and opened wide his eyes and mouth as if frightened. He made gasping sounds as he tried to breathe, bands of muscles tightened in his neck, contorting his face and a rigor passed over his entire body. He seemed to exert every muscle in his body trying to breathe. The event was sudden and startling, as if an unseen tormentor in the shadows had thrown a bucket of cold water in his face.

At odd intervals he sat for a minute or two. Even then, his arms and feet constantly moved. As if startled, he jumped up, and the walking began again with more spasms of throwing his arms about, gasping and stiffening his whole body.

Martha and her daughter-in-law stood with their hands on the edge of the dresser as if they could hold back disaster. They watched in fascination and dread.

"What's got into Nate? I never saw nobody act like that."

"Bertha Mae, I don't know for certain what it is, but it's bad. I'm afraid of what it might be. He really don't know what he's doin'. He could hurt somebody while he's outa his head, and not know it. We got the door to our room blocked off. Now we best do somethin' about his door to the dogtrot." The women piled the largest logs they could drag against the door and drove wooden wedges at the edge, then propped a metal bar from the shop against the door. Their work caused no change on the constant steps inside the room.

"Bertha Mae, we've fixed those doors as good as we can. I hope he don't take a notion to come out the winda. I don't think he's apt to. The sun is right in front of his winda. He says light hurts his eyes. The way he's actin' I don't know what all he's gonna do next. But ya can't stay cooped up in that room all day. When he wakes up, take John B. out in the yard for a spell. I'll set in our room and watch. I'll leave the door to the dogtrot open. I don't know what to look for, but if somethin' happens, I'll call out. John and the boys will be back soon ... I hope."

The women spent the early part of the afternoon listening to the maddening sound of heavy footsteps. Bertha Mae and Martha waited in fear and wonder. They didn't know why he paced and why he made the strange sounds. They didn't know who this being was that had been a gentle boy the day before. When the steps stopped and the house was silent, they held their breath and listened in dread of what might come to pass. Neither woman could work. Martha could do nothing but wait at the door and listen for Nate's next move. When he woke from his nap, Bertha Mae would not let John B. get more than a few feet from her in the yard. John B. was oblivious to it all, playing with sticks and rocks and dogs and ducks.

By late afternoon, Nate was circling the room faster, knocking chairs over, jerking the bed around, and shoving a trunk across the floor. At times the women heard violent gasps and grunts that carried well into the yard. Nate pushed against the door to the dogtrot but could not budge the logs. Martha heard him go to the window. He screamed, "Get away dog!" Slow steps came closer to the door where his mother stood, then stopped and the door banged against the dresser. Martha gasped and jumped back.

The grunts grew louder. The dresser moved with a screech and the door opened an inch. Martha ran through from her bedroom, down the dogtrot and called frantically, "Bertha Mae, looks like he's tryin' to break out. Keep a good-sized lighter knot close by! I couldn't use it, but you might have to if he was to get out and come at John B."

Martha went back to the blocked door. The noises became more violent. Bertha Mae followed Martha and helped her push against the barrier. They couldn't hold it back and stepped back to watch in horror. Nate grunted with each push on the door, forcing the dresser farther aside. Bertha Mae stood at an angle to the dresser and watched Nate through the widening crack in the doorway.

"Martha, shouldn't we all run for it? He's might near ready to break out."

"No, Bertha Mae, go back in the yard, and stay. Listen sharp and keep that stick close by. He might could get out if he can push that that door a little bit more. Take John B. and head for the woods if I call out."

During a lull in screeches from the floor and grunts from the room, they heard a blessed sound from the public road: the crunch of wheels and the sound of hooves and harness. Martha fled to the porch and saw familiar mules and wagon in the distance.

She waved frantically as she ran to meet the wagon turning down the lane toward the barn. "John, stop right here and come in the house. Nate's not at hisself atall. He's wild and crazy and is gone to tearin' up his room. He hollered at little John B. and near scared him to death. He's gonna tear thangs up and hurt hisself and anybody else close by. I just don't know what's come over him."

The three men sat as if paralyzed by the news. John said, "Why, he was fine when we left this mornin'."

She was almost shouting, "John, you're not hearin' me! He's not now! He's crazy as a road lizard. We got him pinned up in his room, but ya best come right quick 'fore he breaks out!" As the men recovered from the news, they jumped down from the wagon; Jacob looked at his mother and opened his mouth. Martha said, "They're both fine. They're out back." Jacob tied the team as the others ran to the house.

They crossed the porch in two steps and rushed down the dogtrot. Bertha Mae stood pale and frightened in the open door of the large bedroom. She was pulling John B.'s arm. He had escaped from his mother and was trying to see into the room of strange sounds. Nate had pushed the door partly open, but still not wide enough to get out. Through the opening over the dresser, they saw a boy with contorted savage features and darting eyes. He was raging and pushing against the door with strength no man should have. He pushed in a strange way, using both his legs and his arms. His back appeared to be almost rigid. Saliva ran down his chin and froth circled his mouth.

Jacob ran down the dogtrot and they gathered around the door and watched the terrifying behavior for several minutes in disbelief. Nate gave a louder grunt and push. The door opened more as the dresser screeched and then hung on a ridge on the uneven floor. John stared at the widening opening and rested his hand on the barricade as it trembled and tilted with each push of the door. His mouth moved, but no words came out.

As he stared at Nate, he said, "Somethin' has got to be done...and right soon." John waved his arm toward his sons, "Jacob, send Bertha Mae and the boy to their room, and tell her to put somethin' agin' the door. Ben, get all the ropes ya can find and that old harness at the barn. We can cut that, and use it. It'll hold -- I thank. Martha, go with Bertha Mae."

"No, John, that's my son. I gave him life. He's not gonna hurt me."

"I ain't got time to fuss about it. At least stand back. He's 'bout to break out. Jacob get that ol' raggedy quilt. We'll throw that over him when he comes out and get his arms and legs tied any way we can. The way he's amovin' thangs about we're apt to have our hands full and right quick. We'll hold the door till ya get back."

John and Martha leaned against the dresser. It still hung on the floor, but leaned toward them as the door banged against it. Jacob and Ben came back with the ropes and quilt – both breathing hard. John motioned for Ben to drop the ropes beside the door. John shouted over the scraping and grunting, "Ben, take the quilt, throw it when he comes out; and Jacob, be ready with me!"

John and Martha moved away from the dresser. Nate growled and snarled and in a burst of unnatural strength forced the door against the dresser and with a great scraping sound it jumped over the ridge in the floor. He charged through the door, flailing his arms, eyes dazed and empty.

Ben held the quilt at the ready, but with his mouth open, transfixed, and paralyzed by this apparition. That was his brother charging through the doorway, or at least he had been in the early morning.

Jacob shouted at his dazed brother, "Throw it, Ben! For God's sake throw it, or it's too late and he's loose on the world!"

Ben choked back a cry and threw the old quilt over this strange creature. Instantly, John and Jacob jumped to strike the quilt draped struggling shape and knock him to the floor. John's prophecy proved correct. They had more than their hands full. John shouted, "Martha, long's yer here, tie them ankles together."

The sound of Nate's knee connecting with Jacob's chest was followed by a loud "oof". As soon as he could get his breath, Jacob shouted, "Come on, Ma! It's all we can do to hold him down!"

Over the sounds of scuffling about and animal like groans, John yelled, " If we let up even a little, he starts kickin' us. Tie them ankles. Then we'll work on the arms."

Martha had seen what Nate could do. She threw a rope around one ankle, pulled it to the other. Her hands trembled, but she tied it as tight and fast as fumbling fingers allowed. Eventually they secured the flailing arms with ropes and leather straps.

"Pa, he's tore the quilt with his teeth and I'm scared he's atryin' to bite me."

"Just keep away from his head. We'll tie some lines to his legs and arms so's we can handle him." While Jacob and Ben held the struggling boy under the quilt, John and Martha tied ropes from his legs to the foot of the bed and ones from the arms around a trunk for more stability. After he was bound and a little quieter, mother, father and two brothers threw aside the remains of the quilt and tried to catch their breath, as they stood watching the writhing boy on the floor. Their clothes were pulled at odd angles, torn and dirty, and they were drenched in sweat. Nate kept his trousers, but most of his shirt was torn away and part of the bandage lost. His skin was dry. His face was contorted, and wide-open eyes still showed no reason. Saliva drooled down his cheek. At times he cleared his mouth by spitting explosively. Leather and rope lines held his arms and legs, but he still had the strength to jerk the furniture about.

Jacob looked at his father as he wiped the sweat from his face. " Now what are we gonna do?"

Martha said, "Surely ya won't leave him on that hard floor. Not our own boy."

"I don't rightly think he'll hold there anyways. Let me and the boys get into the little room and move the foot of the bed toward the door. We might could drag him in there and pull him onto his bed."

They placed Nate's bed in the center of the room. They couldn't compete with Nate's strength when they first loosened the ropes to move him. John said, "It'll be like pullin a log, only this log fights back." They tied a rope to his chest and another to his legs, then pulled on the upper rope as the leg rope was slowly released from the bed in the big bedroom. In one of Nate's more quiet periods, they slid him into the room and lifted him to his bed, secured all four limbs to the sideboards and footboard. They passed ropes over his chest and legs and under the bed. Martha loosened the ropes on his arms and legs to apply rags to pad the restraints, especially around the healing wound.

"Now, what, John?"

John did not look up. He stared at this creature, which had been his son and spoke softly. "We got no i-dee what we're up against. No poultice is gonna work on whatever he's got. This time yer Ma can't help. Doc

Davis was at the raisin'. He told us he was goin' to the Camps' house. Ben, go fetch him. We need him real bad -- and today -- not next week. He may not can help us, but we need to know. Ya can even ride that new horse."

Daylight was beginning to fade when the buggy pulled by a large black horse arrived at the cabin. Doctor Samuel Davis was two years older than John. No one remembered what color his hair had been. It was white since the war. His eyebrows and mustache were white. He had deep crow's feet on each side of his eyes and heavy lines on his forehead, not from years in the fields, but from memories of a mountain of arms and legs and thousands of deaths from dysentery and starvation. His gray eyes mirrored care and concern and at the same time, great lingering sadness. In the buggy with Doc Davis was Brother McDonald. Ben had seen him along the road and told him of his quest. He came to be with the family -- as he would have had there been a death. While Doc and others sat in the straight chairs on the porch, John stood in the yard and quickly told the story of the bite of the Devil Dog, the first treatment, the festered wound and swollen streaked arm, its early healing, and the day's happenings. Several times as he talked. Brother Mac and Doc glanced behind them toward sounds of rumbling groans and creaks of the bed.

Doc Davis nodded, "John, I don't think I could have done much better by him. I might have used a flax seed meal poultice while the arm was so festered and then charpie and myrrh when the bite got better, but sounds like what you did worked real good -- maybe better than my treatment. S'pose we look at him."

John, Martha, the doctor, and the preacher crowded into the small room. Ben looked in through the doorway. Bertha Mae and Jacob restrained John B. out on the porch. Nate continued to have episodes of sudden gasping and grimacing. He strained against the ropes and tried to push his arms upward against his bonds as he struggled to breathe. The violent times were followed by periods of subdued groans and pitiful whines. In these relative quiet intervals he appeared to understand some requests, and even said a garbled word or two. Then the violence returned. Doc Davis watched a long while as Nate labored against his bonds. He listened to the sounds from deep within Nate's throat, and looked into his eyes for any sign of comprehension. He watched Nate's deep gasping breaths.

"Martha, let's try some cool water on him." Martha returned from the kitchen and gave a cup to the doctor.

"Now watch close, Doc. He's liable to bite ya." John lifted and steadied Nate's head and shoulders. Doc Davis stood to one side and gently poured the water through twisted lips. This caused instant violent spasms of his neck and throat, coughing, and gagging. Nate spit some of the water across the room, but most splattered on the bed or ran down his neck.

"I've seen enough, John. Let's go back to the porch." Martha sat in the center in the one rocker with Doc Davis and Brother Mac in straight chairs on either side. Ben and Jacob stood to the side leaning against the posts. Bertha Mae sat on the edge of the porch and tried to keep John B. occupied. John stood in the yard facing them.

Before the doctor had a chance to speak, Martha asked, "Doc, has that evil Devil Dog turned our boy into ... into some kind of beast? I never heard of a livin' bein' actin' like that. Preacher, would prayer change him back? I know he's not been to church in a while, but we have."

Doc Davis took a deep breath and began, "Martha, I don't think there's much doubt that he's got mad dog sickness. It's called hydrophobia or rabies. It's caused by the bite of a mad dog. This plague was brought to our country about a hundred years ago and has spread everywhere. 'Possums get it, 'coons get it, cows get it, and people can get it." Doc Davis leaned toward Martha and put his hand over hers as she gripped the arm of the chair. He said gently, but firmly, "Nate has the symptoms."

"Well, what can we do?"

He glanced up at John then back at Martha. He squinted, opened his mouth once, but said nothing as if words wouldn't come. He shifted his chair so he could look straight into her eyes. "There's nothin' that can be done, Martha. He is dryin' up because he can't take water. We could get a little liquid in him by giving him a beef tea enema. You can just picture what kind of struggle that would be. He can't breathe because of the tight muscles about his chest. Morphia might loosen him up some, but I'm afraid it would stop his breathin'. There's not much we can do to help. You could move his arms out some. Maybe slide a board under the mattress and tie his arms out a little. That lets his chest move to breathe better. But you have to understand -- the sickness is fatal, it will take him no matter what we do. There is nothing anybody can do...not even a big hospital... if he could make it that far."

Martha began to cry, softly at first, then with great sobs. Ben and Jacob moved beside their mother's chair, their faces hidden in the shadows of the porch. Jacob held his mother's hand.

John wiped at his eyes and turned toward the purple mountains in the distance. After several minutes, he faced the porch and said, "If they's no hope atall, how long will he last?"

"John, I know you want the truth -- bitter as it is. I'd give a time if I could. It's hard to say...he's young and strong." He glanced at Martha, who was hanging on his every word. "Could be a day or so, maybe five days...might be seven...but I don't think more. And it will be a hard week. Hard on him and harder on you. He is no good to himself or anyone else. He doesn't know he's in the world. He's a danger to those around him. He's worse than a wild animal. A demon rages within him -- not of the underworld, but of sickness. It might as well have been caused by Satan himself, for all we can do."

Doctor Davis stared into the gathering dusk, "It's times like this that I doubt my calling. I call the case and make the diagnosis, but there is so little I can do to treat the disease. If he were a dog or cow, we would put him out of his misery."

"But not a person! Not our boy!"

"Martha, we're kinder to animals than people. As a doctor, I couldn't do anything like that, but it has been done. Just like Nate did to that mule on the ridge."

Martha gasped and twisted the handkerchief in her hand. She shivered, as if a winter wind wrapped about her. When she caught her breath, she turned to the other side, "Preacher, what do you thank?"

Brother Mac shook his head slowly. "I know about mad dog disease, and that may well be what he has -- but that big red dog acted different and looked different than most mad dogs. I saw him once. I could believe that he was straight from the pit. I've never seen a dog that red and his eyes looked like evil itself. And while we were in the room, Nate was cryin' part of the time, but there weren't any tears. I hate to say it, but Satan and his kin don't shed tears. Whatever demon is in him, that's not Nate. He's gone. Whatever that is in the bedroom, it's no good to itself or anyone else. If you turned it loose, it would hurt a lot of folks."

The group turned silent again, each with their own thoughts and anguish. Finally John said, "Doc , we thank ya for comin'. It's late. We won't keep ya no more. Ya know I can't pay cash. I'll have to work it out or trade it out."

"John, there's nothing I can do. You don't owe me a thing. Just give me a kind word sometime or maybe a mess of greens."

"Doc, we appreciate it a right smart, you comin' on such short notice."

As Doctor Davis stood and pushed his chair back, Martha said, "Why did this happen so quick? We thought his arm was healin' up. I've heard of folks getting' bit an' not comin' down with madness for weeks even months."

"Sometimes it does come on fast. Most likely the rabies came from that little hurt on the face that healed over and you forgot. That's the worst place to get a bite."

She nodded slowly. She seemed to have difficulty in forming words, and spoke in a jerking voice. "Let me ask ya one more thang before ya go, Doc. Is they anythang that we coulda done to keep this from happenin'? After he got bit -- I mean."

"Martha, I don't think so. You hear some speak of usin' Hubert's keys. They talk about 'em a lot in the old country. Some have thought they did work if they were used right quick after the bite and called it a miracle if the patient lived. But there's nothin' special about those crosses. You might as well use hot tire metal. And if you had used a hot iron on that wound, whether it it's a cross or metal from John's shop, his face would have been badly scared and the arm ruined. Martha, what's done is done and can't be changed. Don't look for a wonder in our world. We don't see miracles like in Bible times. Don't look back."

As John stepped up on the edge of the porch, the preacher looked up. "Nate is really gone and you're left with a demon. What are you going to do?"

"I truly don't know. I'm thinkin' on it. Somethin' like this, I need to get my mind fixed on it before we do anythang. Whatever we do will have to be tomorrow. We can't take it another day. We'd get all wore down, and then he might get away from us. No tellin' what he would do. Bertha Mae and John B. can't stay hid out."

"What time, John?"

"Soon's the dew is good dried up." John looked at the thin streaks of clouds in the west. "Should be a clear day."

"John, tomorrow is Sunday, but I will be here. I may be a little late for church, but they can start without me. If you don't mind, I'd like to go back one more time before I go."

The group walked down the dogtrot and crowded into the small bedroom. Martha took down the cloth from the single window. Light from the setting sun streamed through the small window, giving radiance to the bed and the bound figure in the center of the room. The brightness made shadows of the corners seem darker. Bathed in the light of sundown, the shape on the bed glowed as though it floated in a sea of darkness. The smooth face of youth was tight and twisted. Redness of evening light marked twisted features and deepened lines and wrinkles he should not have had. Nate could have been a being from another world for how strange and different he looked. As he writhed, fragments of straw fell and clustered about the bed. His kicking feet and digging fingers were slowly destroying the mattress. The falling straw added to the musty smell of the room.

Brother Mac stood at the head of the bed, held his Bible in his left hand and began to pray. "Our Father in heaven: our son, our brother and our friend is gone. And in his stead we have been left a being we do not know and do not understand. We ask that you have pity on the anguish of this family and restore the boy we once knew." Brother Mac very carefully reached over the headboard and placed his right hand on Nate's forehead. "I bid you -- come out of this man you unclean spirit! In the name of Jesus Christ!"

Nate's arms and legs relaxed, features softened, and grimaces faded and he looked like the boy he was, but only for an instant. And then, the grunts and groans and struggling started again. The preacher looked up at the family, "Now, John, Martha, this doesn't mean that God didn't hear our prayer or has no power. It means that it's not his will to change what is. Like Doc said, 'What's done is done. We have asked, and he has said 'No.' Even the disciples couldn't cast out some demons. At least we asked."

The buggy pulled away from the house carrying Brother Mac and Doc Davis, leaving the family sitting on the porch in the gathering darkness. The red and yellow glow of the setting sun lit the western sky and reflected on the grim group. John stared into the fading light for several minutes and then without turning his head said in a low voice," Ben, put a pallet down in our room and get some rest. I got a job for ya, at first light. Jacob, ya best get some sleep, too. We all got a big job in the mornin'...a big job...a bad job"

Martha pulled at his sleeve, "What bad job? We have to help Nate! What're you gonna do?"

John stood and walked away, "We gotta do what needs to be done. I don't know what all, just now. We can't make it through another day like this. We havta do sometin'... and it has to be tomorrow. I'm thinkin' on it. I don't want to talk about it ... can't talk about it. Don't worry me!"

Chapter Eight – Shadows

There was a door to which I found no key:
There was a veil past which I could not see:
                                        Edward FitzGerald

When darkness fell, the others left for bed -- for what sleep could be had with the gasps and creaks and scrapes of the shaking bed echoing through the house. John stayed as far from the struggling prisoner as he could, alone on the porch, sitting in the rocker pushed back against the wall with his feet propped on his grandson's stool. He had slept in worse places in the war, but he was younger then. Early in the night, he prayed for direction, for wisdom to know what to do, and strength to do what needed to be done. He asked for guidance in a tragedy that seemed to have no answer and no end, one like no other. The crescent moon offered faint light. He stared into shadows under trees at the far end of the yard, Answers were not given. Sleep did not come.

Toward the black predawn when crickets tire and are silent and the wind is still, he watched fog roll across the yard like a ghostly wave in the moonlight. The light of the moon was the same, but creeping brightness within the layer reflected against the leaves of the oaks. It glowed and moved like a living thing, flooding the yard, but for the trees. It circled the porch and poured over the boards like a hungry sea, swirling about John's chair and stool as if he rested on a consuming cloud filled with energy and brightness like no other. John stared at the rising waves where the floor had been. *I never seen nothin' like that, not even comin' off the ridge. It's brighter than the moon.* The fog wrapped his feet. Clamminess crept up his legs, then his whole body, and he shivered.

Where the yard had been, great billows swirled to puffs of white. In the distance, smaller tufts of vapor began to whirl into dim shapes. John raised his head and sat up, waved his hand to brush the fog from his face, straining to see. *What could that be? Ain't nothin' man nor beast looks like that.* The whirling masses grew larger and moved from darkness beyond the trees. A wind, which ruffled nothing else, swirled and formed them into shapes with features and they became men waving muskets as they ran. John gave a choked cry as he saw the skirmish line coming. *Lord, just let me get in the house and away from all this.* His legs were like logs and he watched helplessly as a line of men poured from the northeast to meet another from the southwest. Sudden puffs came from the mouths of twelve-pound Napoleons.

Bands of muscles in John's neck tightened. He strained to turn his head, as if against a force he could not see, and watched angry men and motion on all sides. He heard shouts and shots and cries of pain. Men screamed, fell and were swallowed by the unrelenting glowing sea. As they dropped from sight, for an instant he caught sight of faces of men he had known, men in his company, kinsmen, men long since dead. Bullets sang by his head and struck the logs. Chips flew and stung his cheek. Mounted men swept across the scene, shouting and swinging sabers, gleaming in the light from below. One rider, screaming his hatred, came directly at him.

John tried to flee, but his legs would not move. He tried to call, but no sound came. A horseman shouted as wheeled to the left, swung his saber and struck the post with a great clang of metal and shattering of wood. A great chip twisted, turned, and fell in the bright layer at the horse's feet. John knew the place. The battle of Bentonville swirled about and he was a part of it again, with fear, anguish, and death all around.

Just when he thought he could bear no more, a cold wind blew from the north, ruffling his shirt, fanning his beard and chilling his face, though the leaves on the trees hung still. Old wounds ached as though they were new. Men and guns and sound of battle melted into drifting vapors slowly settling, and the fog became peaceful, smooth and quiet. John sighed and leaned back in his chair. *Whatever it was is gone, but was it real? How could it be?*

Then from the glowing layer of white, four whirling columns arose in the darkness to the north. They made no sound as they slowly swirled and swayed ever closer over the blanket of light. John could not move his head; he could not shut his eyes. He watched the columns as if under a spell. *If I'm not dead now, I will be if they come back.* As the four came nearer, shapes became clearer. John saw men walking out of darkness, wading the strange fog, struggling, as if something unseen in the layer held their legs. One shadow moved behind the others. The three in front came nearer still, and he saw the faces of Matthew Owen, Isaac Bell, and Billy Deerman as they plodded through cloud-like vapors. A fourth man stepped from behind the others into the light. He had no right hand. John saw the face. He saw himself as the fourth man. *Lord God, I can't stand to go through all that agin!*

****

Matthew was a year younger than John and taller, with unruly light brown hair and beard. He had the arms and shoulders of an ambidextrous blacksmith. In happier days he was known for the twinkle in his eye, sly smile, and quick wit. Billy was younger, blond, and slight of build. Everyone in the regiment had beards, but Billy's was thin, pale and hardly evident. He was a reader of books, writer of words, and dreamer of dreams. In lulls in the fighting, he wrote of horrors in war, goodness of men, memories of home and dreams of peace. The three were related, though distantly.

Toward the end of the second day, they came upon Isaac Bell, trying to get to the *Two Creeks* community west of Atlanta. The four struck out together -- walking through North Carolina, South Carolina, Georgia and then thirty miles into Alabama. They traveled roads with fellow soldiers, all trying to get home. At times they passed wandering cast out civilians, some moving south, others north. Creaking wagons held women, children, and men too old for war, who lived in hope that a house still stood and a father, son, or husband yet lived to come home. Some traveled roads for most of the war as strangers in their own land. Their eyes were hollow and they barely spoke as the men passed. Flickering hope and dreams of home moved them all.

The traffic began to thin after the first few days. One morning, a rutted path led them to the charred remains of a bridge over a river without shoals for wading. They moved upstream to a swaying Yankee pontoon bridge that appeared usable. The group watched for several minutes and saw no movement on the far shore and began to cross. They were almost in the center, when three Yankee cavalry rode down the far bank and onto the bridge. For the men walking south, the war was over. Two carried sticks to steady themselves over rough ground or to kill snakes. John held a white cloth on his staff and Billy held another. The riders looked toward the walkers, slowed then stopped; one turned in the saddle to speak to the others, and they came closer.

The four walkers moved to the edges of the rocking bridge, leaving the center clear for the horses. John and Billy walked in front and raised the flags. The groups met in midstream. The two troopers in front cantered their horses a few steps, shaking and rolling the floating bridge unsteadying the men on foot. They suddenly drew sabers and held them to the side toward the water. John and Billy had the choice of being cut in two or going into the river. Matthew and Isaac saw the blades ahead and ducked in time. The troopers laughed and never looked back.

John and Billy flailed at the pontoons as they fell. Before Matthew and Isaac could pull them out they were soaked with cold April water. John's haversack with the gun hung on a pontoon, but his second one and both of Billy's were soaked. When they reached the far shore, John and Matthew spread Billy's papers in the sun. They dried wrinkled and empty. The river kept the words. John left one haversack and his soggy Testament by the road. After a few steps down the road, he stopped, leaned on his stick, and shivered in the wind as he looked back to watch fluttering pages. They walked a little slower, so Billy could keep up. He sometimes used both hands on his stick.

After about an hour, John stopped. "Ya'all, wait, look yonder at the sky. It was dusty-red to the southeast, now it's turnin' dark. Curious. After that cold bath, it's seems awful warm. And listen to the birds."

They looked around. Billy said, "I don't hear any."

"That's just it. Not a leaf stirrin'. And the wind was up a while ago. Not a sound anywhere. The air feels...heavy. I'm right uneasy about what's comin'. Let's stay in the open and walk yonder toward that rise south of the road."

As they took faster steps in a new direction, the sky grew even darker and the wind began to blow. Silent birds streaked overhead toward sanctuary. The wind strengthened until it shrieked, whirled leaves and dust and broke limbs with the crack of a rifle shot. They heard the wall of rain coming before they saw it rushing like a skirmish line. The four took cover on the ground next to the bank, holding to saplings, roots of a fallen tree, and to each other, trying to cover themselves with the tent side as they listened to the roaring wind and falling trees toward the east. Small linbs fell all around them. They almost lost the canvas and were drenched. The storm and rain passed over and left as quickly as it had come, leaving silence but for dripping leaves. They could walk no farther that day and slept on damp blankets.

From a hundred damp camps and a thousand nights on the ground, Billy had a chronic cough. After the two soakings he began to cough so violently that he brought up streaks of blood. As the dew fell in the night, sweat dripped from his forehead, soaked his shirt, and he shook with chills. John gave him his blanket and slept under the tent side.

At daybreak, while the others loaded up for the trip, Billy still lay on the ground, picking at his blanket. He mumbled, "So far from home, so far to go...and yet...and yet so near...home."

Between spells of coughing, his cheeks had a healthy glow, but below the sunburned cheeks his neck was sallow. The violent spells left him weak, ashen, and gasping for breath. Ribs showed through his shirt as he labored to breath.

With help, he stood and took several short, stiff steps, but then his knees weakened and John caught him. "Ya'all, he must have lung fever. He can't walk; he just can breathe. We'll carry him. We got no choice." They made a stretcher of saplings, strips of the tent, vines, and cord. Billy protested but was too weak to resist. They loaded him with his blanket over the stretcher, his 'sac under his head, and his stick by his side, and set out toward home with Matthew in back, John and Isaac in front. They changed ends each time they rested. With only one hand, John always carried from the right.

Carrying the stretcher reduced their travel to less than a fourth of the planned eighteen to twenty miles a day. Billy tried walking each day. He did not improve. They traveled in Sherman's fifty-mile swath of destruction. Many homes they passed were nothing but crumbling chimneys and jumbled rocks where pillars and frame once stood. They asked for help when they found a standing house, but families along the way had little food to share.

After the third day of carrying Billy, the four stopped for the night at a spring behind a jumble of blackened logs, once a home. They cooked the last of the cornmeal mush. Matthew gigged two bullfrogs to add to the pot to make a frog leg stew. Billy ate little.

Early the next morning, John, Isaac, and Matthew brought over the stretcher to load for the day's trip. Billy pushed himself up with one hand and motioned with the other. "Don't bother with that thing. Ya'all listen and let me tell you somethin'." He rested between short phrases, but he had less coughing and seemed to breathe easier in this new day.

"I have thought on our fix in the night...while I looked at stars in the heavens...and ones in the water... while I put my words to paper...God gave me a bright full moon... to finish...I've dreamed of words I would write and stories I would tell ...there are so many things I wanted to say...but it's not to be. I didn't go to...but I'm holdin' ya'all back...

John left Isaac holding their end of the stretcher and took a step nearer the spring. "Not much, Billy.

Ya'll be stout enough to walk in a day or so and we'll move faster."

"No, with me along, nobody will make it home...and I know I wouldn't last the trip...Matthew, John.... my new friend, Isaac...you've done as much as a body could do...and more. You are my friends and I love you for what you've done...I thank you... I want the three of you to go on."

John held up his hand, "Billy, hush that foolishness! We're not gonna go off and leave ya. Yer weak as branch water. We'll carry ya. We been doin' it. Thin as you are yer not heavy. We been through the whole war together. We'll take ya home. Let us do it. Ya'd do it for us."

Billy shook his head. "My fever came down in the night...my body is weak ... but my mind is clear...I want you to leave me here ... at this spring...I know I can't make it...I'm weaker by the day, and we're a long way from home." He seemed to grow stronger, his voice clearer, his color better and his breathing slower. His eyes were bright as he looked up at his friends. Isaac started to say something. John turned around and jerked his arm before he could say more than a word.

"Dyin' is somethin' a fella has to do by himself...nobody can do it for you... or go with you. It might be nice to have family and friends around... but I don't have to have a crowd about to come to the end of my days." He turned away coughed violently and began to wheeze and struggle for breath.

"Maybe we could fix somethin' for yer cough," Matthew said. "It was might near dark when we come in last night, but I thank I saw some mullein up by the house. We can't just go off and leave ya."

Isaac looked at him," I didn't see no mullein."

Matthew whispered, "Hush your mouth, Isaac! They coulda been!"

"Oh.... I see."

After his breathing slowed, Billy pointed to the edge of the spring where the water swirled up. "There is living water here...and God is here. I won't be alone. Ya'all do what you think best about tellin' my folks... If you *do* talk to 'em, tell 'em I'm sorry I didn't make it home... that I love 'em and was thinkin' about 'em till the end." His strength faded and he sank down on his blanket. The three watched as his breathing slowed. A thin red stain ran from the corner of his mouth to his chin. Billy stared at the sky beyond and said, "You go ahead and go...Most likely I will be in Canaan before you."

The three saw that his mind was made up, so they moved him where he would be out of the sun and near water. They laid him on his blanket by the spring. They packed brush under his empty haversack for a pillow. John took his knife and awkwardly cut tall weeds next to the water. "When I get rid of all this grass with snake spit on it ya can get to water a little better, and it don't look so scary."

"John, leave the rest. I like to watch the snake doctors light. They are free and can go where they please... If bad times come, they rise up and fly away home." Billy pointed at the flight of a single snake doctor, looked up at John and smiled. "I will do that soon."

Matthew, then Isaac, and John kneeled down, and put an arm around Billy's shoulder, each saying their own last words. They stood and looked down at their friend on the blanket by the spring. Three hardened veterans of four years of slaughter could not keep back tears. All mumbled something about not having a crumb of food to leave.

Billy held a finger to his lips. "Don't worry about that. I couldn't eat anyway. I have my cup. Somebody take my canteen. I don't need it. And please take this letter I finished last night. I've worked on it since we crossed the river. It's the last of my paper and my only chance to send it home."

John reached to take the canteen. The cedar sides, held with bands of iron, were smooth and stained from use. Billy had kept it long after metal ones were common. A word was carved in neat shallow letters on each side. John stared at the thing in his hand, held it against his chest, and slowly ran his fingers over the letters on one side.

"That's where it belongs, John. Take it home. I'll never make it there."

John put the strap over his shoulder. He took the folded letter and stared at the paper against his stained hand. He wrapped it in oilcloth and put it in his haversack. Three dejected men picked up their 'sacks, walked to the top of the little rise above the spring, and turned to look one last time.

Billy mouthed words so softly that none could hear. Isaac said, "What, Billy?"

Billy's mouth moved again and he pointed to the three.

Isaac asked, "What'id he say, John? I can't hear him."

John didn't answer. He stared down at Billy and nodded."God bless you, too, Billy. We'll see ya in the bye and bye."

Billy was smiling and waving. He motioned for them to go on. Suddenly a host of snake doctors appeared. They seemed to come from all directions and fluttered around Billy, their blue bodies and translucent wings shimmering in the morning sun.

John rubbed his eye with the back of his thumb, took a jerking breath and a step down the slope. Matthew grabbed his arm. They turned away, and John was not brave enough to look back again, for fear that he could not leave his fellow soldier, kinsman, and friend.

The men spoke little through the day. In mid afternoon, they stopped to make camp in good light under poplar trees by a small creek. Using hooks and lines they carried through the war, John and Matthew caught fish and roasted them on a stick over the fire. Cool shade and sparkling water brought no cheer. While the men sat silently eating fish in the late afternoon, a snake doctor lit on a weed near John, rested his wings in the last rays of the sun, and suddenly flew away. The men followed his path as the insect faded from sight.

John said softly, "He's flown away home."

They lay down to sleep in the early twilight. Isaac snored while the other two watched the stars in the clear night and listened to night voices along the stream. Matthew said, "John, I been thinkin' on it since we left the spring. I never seen so many snake doctors all in one spot – that big and out this early. Have you? Looked like a flutterby in amongst 'um – maybe two. Never seen 'em mix like that."

"Matthew, we're in curious times. Pe-culiar thangs happen -- thangs I don't understand and might never see agin."

"I reckon so. John... Could we … uh …could we read Billy's letter?"

"He didn't say it was to us. Didn't say who it was to."

"Can we just look and see?"

John stirred the fire, turned his back to the blaze, opened the oilcloth, took out the letter and held it up to the light. He opened one fold to see the first line.

"Matthew, it says here: 'To those in Canaan.' I reckon that's us, or it's where we wanta be." He unfolded the letter and moved closer to the flames. He blamed the flickering light, wrinkled paper, and wandering lines written by moonlight, but he stumbled across words he would puzzle over at noon. He read slowly and deliberately so he could speak with Billy's voice.

To Those in Canaan:

We have seen the red horse and him who rides. We know his name well and have lived in his path these four years. We saw the sun blackened and the moon like blood. We suffered the most evil of all wars. We beheld wounds, cruelty, ruination, and death never before witnessed. Man never had such weapons to hurt his fellow man.

Now we are told that we have lost. We struggled four years for a cause we believed in -- yet cling to. Now we're called to crawl before oppressors and confess what is untrue. Courage, devotion, honor, and perseverance were not enough. A flood of men from strange lands overwhelmed us. We have suffered a deluge of guns, cannon, food, and wagons against starvation and want. Our army fades away. We no longer have a country. Our oppressors are whole. They do as they please with us all. This is what they fought for. I do not know why they battled brothers who wanted freedom.

Now that guns are silent and smoke slowly clears, there are better places to be than bowing to an enemy. I flee the bitterness and look south to Canaan. Homes need those who are left. Our freedom is lost. Our nation is lost. So many friends lie in strange earth far from home. I am troubled by the claim that the flower of the South died in vain.

I say they did not die in vain. We have won! We have proved that men oppressed by brothers can break free and build their own country, even if only for a time. We were a nation for four years. They cannot take that away.

Those who are left must use their strength to heal our land, if the oppressors will allow it. I would have

*been part of that healing, but it is not to be. I endured
his sword and hunger. Now, the shadow of the pale
horse falls on me. I will not see Canaan on this earth,
but my heart is there, as it has ever been. I send but
one pledge: I lay down my arms of my own free will. I
never surrendered. I kept the faith. I kneel to God
alone. I send but one request: remember those who
never return. There will be many. I hold but one
regret: our freedom is not ensured.*

*William Deerman,
Spring 1865*

John carefully folded the letter and put it away.
Matthew turned his head before the tears began. They
lay silent on their blankets as the flames died, sticks
settled, and embers dulled.

Matthew looked back and whispered, "He
didn't say New."

"What?"

"He said Canaan. He didn't say New Canaan.
He don't live in the county like we do; he lives in town.
Did he mean to say he'd be in the town – in *New*
Canaan?"

"Matthew, he meant what he said. Canaan is our
county, but it's also the Promised Land. He *will* be
there before us. We might not be far behind."

Chapter Nine – Agony

John awoke stiff and sore in the coolness of early light. With his neck tight and head still, he blinked and moved his eyes from side to side. Wisps of fog drifted between the trees over bare packed earth. No cannons fired, no soldiers fought, and none lay dying on the ground. In the stillness, John wondered if he could move or speak. He opened his mouth and tried to conquer the lump in his throat. He heard his own voice utter a single word. "Nate."

He sat up with a start, as if a stranger spoke, and something slid to the floor. He did not remember Martha covering him in the night. The sounds from Nate's room began again. The horror of yesterday had not been a dream. And yet, John was strangely at peace. He picked up the quilt and draped it over the chair. As he turned to go into the house, he ran his hand over the post to feel for a wound in the wood.

He walked down the dogtrot and toward the barn. Bear, a great yellow-gray dog with mottled liver spots, left his bed under the house and trotted behind. Sadie did not move from her place, and Nell was on her morning trip around the farm. John stopped at the gate to the lot and put down his bucket. Bear investigated the post with his nose and looked up, as if in question of the man he served. John rested his hand on the post, damp with dew, and stared toward the ridge. Fog hid the foot of the slope. It glowed in the sunlight like the cold fog of moonlight and drifted still and smooth, hovering above the trees. Sam lifted his head from the grass in the lot and stared toward the gate. Without sound, John moved his lips. *I know the thangs I should've done and words I could've said..... No,*

*should've said. I can't change what's been ... I can't change
what is...I know what should be. On the one hand ,.. I could
take him out and... and... On the other hand I could ...* He
reached down and grabbed his stump. *God help me, I
have no other hand ... but can I do it?*

Ben was waiting in the dogtrot when John
finished milking.

"Pa, I've already eat a bite. What do ya want me
to do?"

"Go over to Uncle Ambrose's place and ask to
borry a real light chain thirty four or five foot long or so
and one about eight foot -- it could be lighter. Tell him
we hate to ask, but we're in a bad fix. I know he uses
chains in the loggin' and all, but maybe he can spare
'em a week. Eight days at most. We could even use a
pieced chain. And ask for some links in case I don't
have enough -- four might would do. And mind ya,
stay away from that young wife of hissen. Me and
Jacob will be ready soon's ya get back, so don't drag ya
feet."

"Can I ride the horse?"

"No, you know ya can't carry chains on a horse.
Hitch the little wagon, with Sam ... and that new horse.
And ask if two of them loggers can help us for a spell
this mornin'. They need to be stronger than smart.
We'll be hard put to do this by ourselves."

Ben left for the barn and John sat at end of the
kitchen table with his chair turned so he faced the wall.
Martha placed a plate of biscuits and eggs on the table,
sat in the next chair and stared at her quiet husband.
"John, what are ya gonna do? Surely you'll not treat
our boy like ya did that poor mule? After Doc said
what he did, I worried over it all night."

"What we did for the mule was the kindest
thang we could do. You know that."

The beard hid John's lower face, but a frown
wrinkled and pinched his brow. He turned, stared at

the food on his plate, and pushed it away. "I'm gonna do what I gotta do. I b'leve I been told what and where. If Nate was to get loose, he would hurt you or Bertha Mae or John B. I don't thank I could take that. I got to do what I can for Nate, but it has to be somethin' to keep ya'all safe.

I would give up my other arm and both legs, if I didn't have to do what I have to do this day. I don't want to talk about it. Fact is, I can't hardly thank on it, much less say the words. Nate is gonna get worse. He can't stay. None of us could take it another day. I can't make him well no more than Doc can. But I give ya my word, I will do what I can far him and make it as easy as I can. That's all I'm gonna say."

Martha studied John's face, as he turned away. "I'll have to have faith that you will do what's best. Ya always have. John, I love all those boys. I loved those girls what little time we had 'em, but Nate was always special. He's right good-hearted and the smartest of the bunch. He's always done good in school. Last year, 'fessor Allen talked about him agoin' off for schoolin'. I reckon it's because he's the youngest, and he looks like you. I love him so. I'm hard put to thank about him not bein' with us. We've lost two. We lived through it, but we didn't have thenm for fifteen years."

John left the table, walked to the window, and stared through the wavy pane. After several minutes he said, "Sometimes thangs get out of shape -- like when I look at them dogs through this winda. Bear looks like he goes up and down when he walks yonder. Seems like ever'thang was so clear a way back when. I remember the day Nate was born. Doc handed him to me. I looked at that baby and saw how he would be all grown up. I prayed that he wouldn't have such a hard time comin' up like we did." John sat down by Martha and stared at the window, " I guess God honored that prayer. I didn't know to ask for him to be delivered from somethin' like the Devil Dog." Martha took John's hand and they talked of Nate as a baby, his childhood, and the years as he approached manhood.

* * *

The preacher, Rufus Cooper and Sam Butler arrived almost the same time Ben drove up in the wagon with chains and borrowed loggers. Ben and the two men went in the shed where John was gathering tools.

"Pa, you know John Tom Shepard, and this here is Shadrack. He come to work for Uncle Ambrose durin' the war as a free man. The both of 'em come down from Virginia."

John looked from Shadrack to John Tom with no change in expression. He nodded. "Thank ya for comin'. We need a hand real bad."

John picked up the smaller chain. "Ben, sit on that stump. I need to measure out somethin', and yer might near same size as Nate." He wrapped the chain about shoulders and chest and marked the spots for links with charcoal.

"This'll do. Bad as I hate to say it, we may as well commence. Nobody is gonna do it far us. Now folks, I hope ya eat yer breakfast, 'cause we got us a job. Let's talk a spell 'fore we start. You five fellers and Ben has to hold him, till me and Jacob get the chain 'round him and the links fixed. Then, we got to hook up the long chain to the little chain with a link. Then we move him -- chain and all to the wagon. We're usin' the little wagon so's we can tie his arms and legs a little better. Ya'all understand? Ya ready? We got one chanct. When we turn him aloose from the bed, there ain't no turnin' back. If he gets away, he may end up in the next county doin' death and ruination all the way."

John Tom looked puzzled. "Uh -- uh -- Mr. McGinnis, we'll help you, but what are we chainin' him for? And what are we gonna do with him once he's chained?"

"I s'pose that's a fair question. Ben must not have told ya all of it. Nate is out of his head and right dangerous. Doc Davis says he's got the mad dog sickness. Preacher says it might be even worse. Doc can't do nothin' and Nate won't last the week. He's apt to get loose and do us harm, or hurt the neighbors, or hisself. We're gonna put him the only place he can end his life and not bother nobody. We're goin' over Kulumi. I haven't been in a while, but Jacob knows the way, and Ben might could remember."

The men nodded and offered no suggestions. The somber group walked to the house carrying the chain, the extra links and the tools. John went into the small bedroom with the others trailing behind. Nate's legs were tied to the foot of the bed. His arms were bound to a board passed under the mattress at lower chest level. The ropes were padded with rags. They were thicker around the right arm. With Nate's slightest motion, fragments of straw fell from holes in the mattress ticking and marked a line on the floor. Nate clenched his teeth and muttered. He still breathed with labored gasps, but was not straining at his bonds. His eyes looked to the ceiling and did not move toward the men. Brother Mac, went to the head of the bed and stood ready. Rufus, and Sam followed Ben and Jacob, but stopped just inside the door when they saw the boy tied to the bed. John Tom stood at the doorway. Shadrack stooped to look in. The preacher and the family had seen him day before. The others stood with mouths open, dumbfounded. The room was crowded with silent men trying to hold their breath. Beads of sweat appeared on foreheads in spite of the hour.

"Now ya'all, be right quiet," John said. "And loosen them ropes on his arms and legs. Ben and Brother Mac hold his arms and you hold his legs." He waved his stump at the two inside the door. " John Tom and Shadrack, come on in and slip a hand underneath him and raise him up off'n the bed. We'll put this little chain on 'em right here, while he's quiet. But ya better watch, if he commences to rouse up, he's apt to be a handful."

Four men loosened the bindings on his arms and legs. The ropes fell with a gentle thump. Each gripped an extremity as the other two began to lift his body. Only Nate breathed. John and Jacob stood ready with the chain and links. As his body rose from the bed and its bindings, Nate snarled and sprang to life. He kicked, slung his arms, and threw off men as if they were children. He screamed and was loose in the room. Men cried out, trampled the floor, knocked over chairs, and fell. Rufus turned over the table of books and papers and it fell on Sam.

Above it all John yelled," John Tom and Shadrack, forget raisin' up! Put him down! Don't let him get aloose. If he does, nothin' is safe!"

The two flung themselves on Nate, forcing him back in the bed amid shouts and grunts and a shower of straw and dust. The bed screeched on the floor, popped, and one leg tilted at an angle.

"Now ever'body get an arm and leg agin. This time hold on for dear life. We can't fix 'em in here; just grab what ya can and take him out to the shed."

Nate was quiet and spent as he labored in deep breaths. They carried him through the door, down the dogtrot, across the yard, and held him face down in the shed. Shirts were now stained and everybody but Shadrick gasped for breath. John and Jacob fashioned the chain halter about his shoulders and attached it to the long chain with a link.

Ben was lying at Nate's side covered with the dust from the shop floor. He let go of a shoulder to pull at his father's sleeve. "That chain's gonna hurt him. Ain't there some other way?"

"Ben, he's got madness that Doc can't cure. This is not really Nate. You never saw him act like this. We got to do somethin' to keep him from hurtin' somebody else or hisself. If they was any other way, I'd do it." The men sitting in the dirt, drenched with sweat, holding a wild man, nodded.

"Folks, we got the chain on; let's get him in the wagon."

Nate's back and neck were increasingly stiff, but he had tremendous strength in his arms. They all crowded around, held his arms and legs, lifted and carried him to the log and manure wagon. Jacob, John, and Ben tied his arms and legs to the sides. At the front of the wagon, Sam looked straight ahead and waited for orders. To the left of Sam, Dolly turned to look.

"Jacob, go get yer Ma. I told the women to stay in yer room with John B. till we come far 'em. Bertha Mae don't need to see this atall in her shape -- might mark her baby -- but yer ma's gonna have to say g'by. I'll clean him up a mite 'fore she gets here"

Jacob knocked on the door and called to his mother. She burst through the doorway and fled past him as if he were not there. At the wagon, John caught her and held her back. The men gathered in a silent circle and stared at the boy straining at ropes, gasping, and looking at the sky with eyes that did not blink. Brother Mac stood by the wheel at the back of the wagon near Nate's head and began to read.

"Man that is born of a woman is of
few days, and full of trouble.
He cometh forth like a flower, and
is cut down: he fleeth also as a
shadow and continueth not.

Who can bring a clean thing out

of an unclean? Not one.

If a man die, shall he live again?
All the days of my appointed time
will I wait until my change come.
Thou shall call, and I will answer
thee: thou wilt have a desire to the
work of thine hands.
For now thou numberest my
steps: doest thou not watch over my
sin?
My transgression is sealed up
in a bag and thou sewest up my
iniquity."

Martha struggled in John's arm with tears streaming down her face. "Yer apreachin' his funeral and he's not even dead yet!"

"No, Martha, the shell that looks like Nate is filled with some kind of demon which rages against everything it sees. The boy you knew as Nate *is* dead to us."

"If my boy is gone, where is he? Where did he go? You said we hope for a better life. Why did God take his life?"

"Now Martha, God doesn't -- "

Martha's words poured out. "Ya know he's never been converted. Does that mean he's condemned for eternity? Preacher, we're a family. We live together. We eat together. We work together. We go to church together, and we always thought that we would face judgment together. Was that evil dog straight from Hell? Does Nate act like that because Satan has him now? Are we seein' Satan through his face? Will we see the last day knowin' that Nate is in outer darkness?"

"Martha -- Martha, we can't know all things. This I know; Nate has been out of church a while, but in our sight no better man sits in the pew on Sunday. Who knows what goes on in a man's heart? A man may speak to God in the fields or beyond the ridge. God may answer him. Nate would have come around to the usual way. He may have in his own way. I can't tell you that God takes all those things into account, but I can tell you that He knows these things as surely as I know them. Nate's destiny is the same as ours. It's up to a merciful God."

"I want to hold him one last time if I'm never gonna see him again on this earth."

"Martha, you can't get close to him. He'll spit on ya or bite ya!"

"I'm his Ma. He won't hurt me." She broke loose from John's grasp. Several men reached to grab her, but they were too late. While she held his shoulders, Martha leaned over and placed a mother's final kiss on his cheek.

Whatever being lived in Nate's body became quiet and his shoulders and neck relaxed. He blinked and looked toward his mother. His mouth moved, but there were no words. There seemed to be understanding, but only for an instant. Then he began to strain at his bonds and scream. Martha fled to the house, sobbing.

John did not look back as he pulled himself up in the wagon and sat on the bench. He gave a twitch to the reins and the procession began. John and Jacob rode in the wagon. Ben, two friends from the church, two borrowed loggers, and Brother Mac followed. The three dogs trailed in back and sometimes ran ahead. As the group passed through the barn lot, chickens and ducks scattered. Buster, cows, and sheep stopped eating to stare. Nate's cries were louder each time the wagon jolted over a rut or bump.

The solemn group stopped at the tree line where the pasture ended at the base of the ridge where the woods began. Ben and Jacob found the almost hidden trail and they began the climb to the top. Here, there was no fence. Domestic animals rarely went up the slope and into the valley beyond. They may have feared it with reason. In years gone by, there had been mountain lions, wolves, and bears in the wooded valley. An old Indian told John's father that the ridge, almost a mountain, was Kulumi, which he said meant, *"Where the White Oaks Grow."* And there were many large oaks. The valley beyond was Ochoccola, or *Magic Water."* As they passed, John glanced at the clearing by the road where Nate had led the mule. What had been Maude lay in bright sunlight – shrunken – empty eye sockets - skin stretched tight over bones.

At the top of the ridge, Ben climbed into the wagon and pulled the rope to the lever at the back of the wagon and set the brakes while Jacob drove the team. John stared straight ahead. They creaked down the winding road. Bright sunlight shone through openings in the branches along the trail and in clearings. The trees were so large and the canopy so dense that most of the forest floor had little light until late morning.

At the bottom of the ridge, Ben leaned over the edge of the wagon to see a remembered place. A two-foot wide hole between rocks blew cool air out in summer, and in winter sucked air in. On happier days, Ben and Nate stopped to watch a dry leaf flutter in the gentle stream of air. When he had showed John's father the valley, the old Indian gave the place a name, which nobody could remember, but it meant *Place-Where-the-Mountain-Gets-Its-Breath*. He claimed that at night, earth spirits came through this hole from the heart of the mountain and roamed the valley.

The others did not look down as the wagon passed and turned east toward the clearing around the spring. Since their days in the valley when the Yankees came, Ben and Nate had come into Ochoccola at least twice a year, even though Ben couldn't always remember why they came. The younger boys kept the brush cut in the clearing. They preserved it as a memorial for what it had been.

The area north of the spring was flat and empty but for one tree. Above the open space, the sky had not a wisp of cloud in sight. The water of the spring mirrored the blue of the sky and green of the trees. Around the big beech tree, a new growth of poke sallet filled the clearing like a vast green rug, with broad leaves waving in the wind. There was shade to the west. The clearing looked like a sunlit pasture.

John looked at the sky and said, "Rain in the next three days 'less I miss my guess. Water the stock down a ways and then pull the wagon right next to the tree."

John took the short ladder from the side of the wagon and placed it against the beech tree. The trunk was wavy and smooth, but not glass slick. Toward the base, thick ridges rose from the barrel-like trunk and disappeared in the ground, so that the tree looked like a giant arm with fingers plunged into the earth -- fixed and immovable. Hundreds of letters were carved into the bark; some were by men dead in the war. Ben's, Jacob's and Nate's initials were there. Larger strange carvings were scattered around the trunk. No one knew what these symbols meant or who put them there. Some said they were Indian signs. Others said they were symbols of enchantment. They had been cut before John's father first walked the Ochoccola valley. As the bark grew, the carvings spread and seemed to sink in the heart of the tree. The boys stopped the wagon at the foot of the tree.

John said, "Now wait while I measure the distance to see if what I recollect is true. Hold this on the tree."

He handed the end of an old surveyor's chain to Ben. They stretched out the chain, which was only half of its original length. "I 'spec it's gonna be just right -- 'bout a rod and a half. Can't be too long or too short." He put the surveyer's chain in the wagon and climbed the ladder. "Hand me the end of the heavier chain and a link with a wedge in it, the short sledge and the spikes, one at the time." He struggled several minutes. "After all these years, I never remember that I can't do two-handed jobs. Jacob, get up this ladder and drive them spikes."

Jacob took the hammer and drove spikes in three locations through a link of chain, holding it out of a man's reach while standing at the base. Then at John's direction he connected the loose end around the tree to itself with a link, securing one end of the long chain to the tree. The other end of the chain had been fixed by a link to Nate's chain halter at the shop. The men clustered about the tree, watched and whispered to each other.

"Is that what ya want, Pa?"

"It'll do. Come on down and put the ladder up." John looked around at the solemn group, "Are ya'all ready for this? It may be clost when we turn him aloose."

The men released the bindings on Nate's extremities. Each grabbed whatever he could reach and they eased him off head first from the back of the wagon while he struggled and snarled. When he was clear, John said, "Jacob, pull the wagon clean out of the way. If we don't, he might run into it when we turn him loose." The men then removed the restraints and the rag padding. They were left holding his arms and legs while Nate flipped his body up and down.

"I'd like to set him on his feet. Man oughta go out on his feet, but we can't do that. We'll put him flat.

Ease him down; then I'm agonna count to three. Then ever'body let loose -- and devil take the hindmost."

At three, the men released Nate and fled. He sprang up and raged after the nearest one. The long chain jangled, snapped straight, and jerked him so that he twisted and fell face down. He raised his head and one shoulder, stiffly rolled his body, strained to get up, but could not. He groaned, then collapsed into the leaves and grass, subdued and still.

Brother Mac bowed his head.

"Lord, you have given us this boy, now this man for a very few years, and now you have allowed him to be taken away. We don't understand it, but we thank you for the years we have had. We ask for you to take his soul to yourself and keep him with you. We ask for your hand on the family. They understand it least of all.

> In the sweat of thy face shall
> thou eat bread, till thou return unto
> the ground; for out of it wast thou taken; for
> dust thou art, and unto
> dust shall thou return.
> In Christ's name. Amen"

John moved closer and stared at his son. Nate lay face down, taking gasping breaths. "If ya had ya right mind, I know ya wouldn't hurt a soul. I know ya don't know nothin', but only God knows how much it pains me to do this."

John squatted down. "I want to lay hands on my son one last time." In spite of the urgings of others, he put his hand on one shoulder and his stump on the other. "I know ya can't cry, Nate, but I got tears for the both of us." Nate's strength and rage returned and John would have been injured had not Jacob snatched him up.

John tried to pull away. "My friend an' now my son -- I can't do this agin." Jacob and Brother Mac each took an arm, turned him and led him away.

John, Jacob, and Ben climbed into the wagon. As it moved down the trail the men stared straight ahead at the path, but before they reached the first turn each looked back. John looked more than once. Nate lay crumpled on the ground near the spring. The silent group made the trip up the twisting trail to the top of the ridge and down the north slope past the curve where the mule lay, then by the fields and through the pasture toward the barn.

* * *

Word of the tragedy had spread to many in the church community and a steady stream of wagons came to the McGinnis farm that Sunday morning. Somber men and women stood in small groups waiting and speaking in hushed tones. Several families brought food. Farm wives know that the preparation and offering of food is the same as offering love. The gift was something of themselves, as if food, when cooked, absorbed their love and could be conveyed in a vessel, offered and understood without a word being spoken.

No one could remember a family taking a child from his home to die alone, and yet not one condemned John. Several had seen madness in animals. Uncle Dock had seen it in a man years ago, but he wouldn't speak of it. Women clustered around Martha and Bertha Mae in the back yard. They tried to persuade the two to go in the house and out of the hot sun, but Martha looked toward the ridge and wouldn't budge. Bertha Mae wouldn't leave Martha. John B. played with the older children in the front yard.

Martha watched the procession as it left the cover of trees at the foot of the ridge. She saw Jacob and Ben put the wagon in the shed and turn out the stock.

She watched John's slow and labored steps toward the house.

She met him midway in the path. John stumbled and grabbed a limb of a peach tree to steady himself.

"It's done, Martha."

"Done what? John, what did ya do? Tell me right now? Where is Nate?"

"Come on to the house out of the sun and we'll talk." As John passed, men offered to work the fields in the week to come. John nodded and said, "Thank ya, but we'll manage."

Martha grabbed his arm. "I wanta know now!"

John pulled away. "Have pity. We're about wore out. Let's get out of the sun." John sat next to Martha on the front porch. Bertha Mae sat in a chair nearby and Jacob stood beside her. Ben leaned against a post. Others clustered nearby in the yard, but conversation stopped. John said nothing for several minutes. Then he began, "It's done, Martha -- the hardest job I've ever done."

"What, John, what have ya done with Nate? Ya promised it wouldn't be like the mule."

"Martha, ya know he couldn't stay here. He could get aloose and hurt somebody bad. Ya heard what Doc said. He won't last the week and nothin' can be done. I can't stand to see him go, and I can't let it tear you up by watchin' him go a little at a time. I've done the only thang I knew to do."

John hesitated and stared at the porch floor. He raised his left hand first toward Martha and then moved it to cover his stump. He took a deep breath and said the words rapidly. "He's over in the valley beyond the ridge hooked to a chain, fixed to the tree in the clearin' at the spring,"

Martha grabbed at her throat and gasped.

"Now, Martha, he's got slack in that chain to get water at the spring, if he was a mind to, but not so much reach that he might could fall in and drown. I measured it. The chain keeps him from runnin' into trees and such. Nobody can hear him ahollerin'. Seein' him like that was most more'n we could stand."

"John, how could ya *do* that? Ya took him from his home. He's alone! There's nobody there if he calls out. We've always been there if he called out. I never heard of doin' nobody this away."

"Ya never heard of nobody havin' mad dog sickness, neither." John frowned and stared into the distance for several minutes. He looked into his wife's eyes,

"Such has been done before, Martha...and I've done it. Leavin' Nate at the spring puts me in mind of somethin' that happened a long time ago...somethin' nobody else in the county but one knows. I'll have to tell ya the story from the beginnin'. Then maybe ya can understand why we did what we did."

He told her of Billy at the spring. The memory was as fresh as if it had happened yesterday. After the full account, John stopped to stare in the yard where the strange fog had been. He saw nothing but listening friends standing a little closer, leaning forward, straining to hear every word.

"After that, Martha, I reckon we thought about Billy a right smart -- I know I did -- but we never talked much about him. We had troubles enough tryin' to get home. When I got better, me and Matthew told Uncle Doc -- Billy's brother. The three us went and talked with his folks, so they would know that Billy wasn't never comin' home. I gave 'em his canteen. They'd raised a son for twenty-two year and sent him off to war to get our freedom, and all they got back was a ol' wood canteen with 'Alabama' carved on one side and 'Billy' on the other. His ma and sisters cried and took on some. His pa just sat there and never said nothin', like he'd been hit in the head with a hammer. After a bit, his ma grabbed up that canteen and hugged it like it was a lost child and held it up to 'er cheek. I thought she'd lost her right mind. She gripped it tight, looked at it and said, 'Billy held this in his hands and put it to his lips ever' day. If it's all that comes home, I'll keep it close.' She kissed it and Sarah Ann, that youngest girl, took that canteen and hung it by Billy's picture.

She picked up his plate, knife and fork off the table and put 'em on the shelf. She said, 'The night -- that's the worst time. Toward sundown we always hope and look to the east before we eat." Billy's pa stared at the wall and never moved. They were still sittin' there starin' at that canteen when me and Matthew left.

After we left the Deerman place, we went by the Banner office and told Mr. Wilson that Billy wouldn't be comin' back. Them folks set a great store by Billy and was holdin' a job far him at the paper. I give 'em his letter. Ya might could remember. They put it on the front page. Called it *Billy's Last Letter*. Said it was to us all.

That ol' canteen, one letter and one wore out stick was all that was left of Billy." John stared into the distance and tried to speak several times before words came. "It was all we had 'cept what we remember. I don't know about Matthew, but I can see him yet -- toward the end of the day -- sittin' in front of his tent -- turned to get the last of the light -- readin' a book or writin' letters -- smilin' and wavin' when I walked by. It was bad enough that we had to leave him at the spring, and remember. We didn't tell the family or the folks at the paper the whole of it. We just told 'em that he died of lung fever. I didn't say it, but they sort of thank we saw him go.

Sometimes, when there's no hope of livin' or if folks are dangerous, and if ya can't stay with 'em till the end, 'the only thang ya *can* do is leave 'em. But ya leave 'em with kind words where they can get some comfort in their last days -- in the shade by cool water. Sometimes, all ye can give is kind words and cool water.

Martha, Nate don't know he's in the world. If there's nothin' we can do to cure him and he's a danger to hisself and other folks, this is the best way -- the only way. He won't hurt hisself and he won't hurt nobody else. He won't eat. He most likely won't drink, but if he's a mind to, he could. And like Billy said, he's not really alone."

Martha took John's hand, put her other arm around him, her head on his shoulder and cried. She tried to speak, but words didn't come. Women who listened in silence had wet cheeks. The men's eyes were moist as they turned away.

John looked around at those listening, "I'd be much obliged if ya didn't tell Billy's folks 'bout this. They're grievin' still, and knowin' the whole of it wouldn't help none. They might think hard of us. Like Martha, they'd worry 'bout him bein' alone. Lord knows, leavin' him weighed heavy on the three of us. We done what we thought best -- what he asked us to do."

Brother Mac wiped his eyes and placed a hand on John's shoulder. Friends respectfully backed away while he spoke with the family several minutes and had one last prayer asking for support and understanding.

He raised his head. "John, Martha, Ben and Jacob: You all remember good days -- happy days. They're easy to take, but only the strong can endure something like this. Doc said not more than seven days. Today week you have to go back in that valley. John, you can't go alone. Some of us will go with you. The whole congregation will be here when we get back. I'll have somebody open a grave and we'll go there for the service. I s'pose you want to put him where the babies are? I think it'd be best to do it right away, don't you?"

"I s'pose so... I 'ppreciate ya bein' here. See ya next Sundee right early, maybe a mite earlier than today."

The preacher nodded, walked to his buggy and drove away.

As friends drifted away, John and Martha thanked everybody for coming and for the gifts. The family gathered in the kitchen and picked at plates of food in silence. Most remained uneaten, but like water in the spring, it was there if needed.

Chapter Ten – Far Side of Glory

Is life so dear, and peace so sweet,
As to be purchased at the price of chains and slavery
Forbid it Heaven!

McGowands Brigade resolution

After supper on the day Nate was taken to the spring, Jacob and his family went to their small room. Ben and the dogs crossed the front yard in the gathering dusk while John and Martha sat watching from the front porch. He walked the empty road talking quietly to the heedful dogs. The evening breeze died away and voices of the night had not begun. The air was still and stifling.

On clear spring and summer evenings, farm families sat on the porch, wished for cool breezes and talked as they waited for the heat of the day to fade from the house. The front porch was a seat of conversation, learning, and debate, in many ways as much a school as the one in Ebenezer Springs. Adults talked of days gone by and hopes and dreams of those to come. Children listened to traditions, morals and happenings in the county and nation. Speech patterns went unchanged for generations.

At the end of this day, time moved with crushing slowness and no conversation. To speak of small things was unthinkable and nothing was said of happenings of this day. When dusk hid ruts in the road, Ben came back and sat in the chair by his father. Sadie, Nell, and Bear followed him and arranged themselves according to some hierarchy that only dogs understand. The offended cat at Martha's feet left as a yellow streak. Without speaking, they listened to crickets and frogs almost an hour as full darkness descended. The only movement was that of the dogs when they suddenly left the porch to investigate some real or imagined motion or sound and then returned to the exact spot they left.

Abruptly, Ben spoke and the sound was startling. Even the dogs jumped. "Pa, we gonna go back and check ever' day or in a week?"

"In a week. No call to torment ourselves by watchin' it take place little at the time. Nate wouldn't know we was there. Nothin' we can do there but shed tears."

"Yessir."

Ben was quiet for a time, then looked at his father in the moonlight. "Pa, we lost Nate on account of a bite on his arm. How come ya lost an arm and lived when he didn't? Ya never did tell us about the arm. And after all that, how did ya get home from way off, 'thout no mules or nothin'?"

"I got shot -- then I walked!"

Martha leaned over to glare at John. Even in the dim light, he could feel her gaze. "John, it's been five years. Ya never wanted to talk about the war, so we never asked. Don't ya thank the ones that love ya the most ought to know? We worried about ya ever' day. And when ya did come home, more dead than alive stumblin' down the road in rags, we didn't know who it was till ya was right at the house. Bear tried to eat ya up, but Bess was still alive then, and she knew who it was before we did. She 'bout knocked ya down lickin' and jumpin'. The boys had to take the both of ya to the shed an shave yer head and beard and scrub with lye soap to make ya fittin' to come in the house."

"Ya took ma beard. And I swore to keep it!"

"It was full of graybacks -- and you know it! Jacob might near had to fight with ya to get that old 'sack and canteen away. Bess stayed with ya in the shed 'till we took ya in the house and then she had to come in to see ya ever' day.

"Ben was by the bed when ya was so sick. He loved ya in rags. He asked how ya lost the arm and how ya got home. He never asked about the fightin'. John McGinnis, how *could* ya give him such a short answer?"

John said nothing, but leaned over and looked up at the sky. Martha and Ben followed his gaze. In the faint light he seemed to be counting and measuring stars of the Big Dipper. He finished his survey of the heavens and leaned back in his chair. John cleared his throat, glanced at Ben, looked down and felt of the stump with his left hand and began, this time not so abruptly." Ben, ya remember I was gone four year. Weell, I've seen the elle-funt..."

"A real elle-funt? Where was *that?*"

"Not a real one! Don't be ridic'lous, Ben! Folks say that when they see sights they thought they'd never see -- sights that stay the rest of their lives. I don't call 'em, but pictures of what I saw come back...over and over agin. I know they're not real, but they make me feel like I did when I was there. They might come of a night in a dream. At times they come toward evenin'... when shadows get long. Sometimes they wait in the mornin' fog...when the leaves hang still and wet. That's the worst. The evilest thangs I ever saw dart from fog that circles 'round me. Sometimes they don't come atall, and I thank I'm free. I might go a week or a month or two, and then they're back. If I could work all the hours of the day and night, they might leave me be. When I get quiet and still, they come. I never wanted to talk about the war. If I tried, I don't thank I could've got the words out. War's all about one man tryin' to take another man's life...or part of his life...and the gov'ment says it's right – it's got a reason. It might could be right ...and it may be just...some wars are…we thought ours was…it's not for me to say, but I'll never speak of all that killin'. I will try to tell ya what ya ask.

Ben, toward the end of the war, the 55th was in North Carolina -- it's a long story. In four year of war, we fought across Alabama, Tennessee, Georgia, and South Carolina. In the early spring of '65 we was wore to a nub. The regiment and others was facin' Sherman and all that passel of folks in the Battle of Bentonville in North Carolina. They was ten of them to our one. I reckon Gen'l Johnston did good to hold 'em back, well as he did. We was might near out of ever'thang. A Tennessee regiment come in without a gun among 'em. I reckon ever' man was s'posed to kill a Yankee to get one."

"Why did ya stay if it was so bad, Pa? All that fightin' over slaves."

"Ben, we've already talked on this!" Martha leaned over and looked again. His voice softened. "We wasn't fightin' to keep slaves, 'cause most of us didn't have any. We didn't want them folks from up North runnin' ever'thang and telling us what to do … like they're doin' now. The 55th commenced the war with a thousand men … good men from Canaan County and all around. At the end they wasn't but fifty left that was there at the first. We lost more'n our share 'cause we didn't have skulkers and sneaks. And we lost lots to camp diseases. Nobody from Canaan County left but Matthew, Billy, Jeff, Rufus, and me"

"Wasn't ya an officer, Pa?"

"I was sergeant, but just outside of Atlanta, the captain and lieutenant got killed. The General made me a lieutenant to run what was left of C Company. After the big fight, the Confederate army was northwest of Goldsboro, at Smithfield – places you never heard of -- tryin' to stop Sherman if he tried to join up with Grant. We was hopin' that we could get with Lee and whup one of them Yankee armies. After Bentonville, they pushed us back and took Smithfield and Raleigh. They wasn't no big fights, but the lines moved back'ards and forwards. Folks are just as dead when they get shot in a little fight as they are in a battle with a name. We'd shoot a while and stop. Then, us and the Yankees would just eye one another like two dogs, one strong with a mouth full of big teeth and the other little and all tore up, but not willin' to quit, still hopin' to get his licks in.

One day in early April, we looked up to see Yankee horse soldiers ride through the woods. They got off their horses and come sidlin' up the ridge lookin' down on us. I hollered to the company and we took out after 'em."

****

Amid shouts and shots from the ridge, puffs of dirt spouted in the open field, filling the air with Minié music. The firing stopped and in the lull the Confederates moved to cut off the infiltrators. John was running when a single shot was followed by a loud smacking sound -- the sound of bursting flesh and bone, like a hammer hitting a hog in the head.

John jerked to the right, fell like a wet rag -- face down – and did not move. The men behind screamed, "They got John. They knocked him awindin'." Matthew was at his side in seconds and dragged him behind a stump.

John turned his head and looked up through weeds, "I – I musta fell?"

"John, ya've took a ball through the arm -- right next to the hand -- broke them little bones. Let's tear the rest of this here sleeve and cord it off. It's bleedin' right heavy."

John rolled over, dragging his right hand, and it fell at his side as if it were no longer part of his body. He reached across with his left hand and squeezed his forearm while Matthew tied the tourniquet. He groaned as he propped up on his left elbow and looked at his hand. The bursting wound on the thumb side of his wrist, pointed fingers at an odd angle. He could move the little and ring fingers, but motion came with intense burning that began in the wrist and shot like lightning into two fingers and up the arm. He felt pain in the others, but couldn't move them or feel the rock he could see them resting on. He stared in anguish at the hand drained of color, then lifted his head to direct the rest of the company toward the infiltrators. His voice was almost a whisper and Matthew relayed the words. Men from Company B came and added to the firing. The Yankees left the way they had come.

Smoke drifted over Matthew as he loosened the half-full cartridge box from John's belt. He took the cap box, but left his haversack and canteen. John tried to reach for his Enfield. After he recovered from the pain, for the first time his left hand was dominant. He turned his rifle over. It was bloody, but the ball had only dug a groove in the stock. John fell back on the grass.

Matthew had to lean over to hear the words. "That's a Yankee gun. I've carried it over a year and it's the straightest shootin' rifle I've ever held. I won't never shoot it again. I want ya to have it."

Matthew picked up the gun, gave it to a friend to hold, grabbed John's left upper arm, and pulled him to his feet. "Come on; we got to go. You're too big for me to carry – you'll have to walk. I'm not s'pposed to do this, but ya know I will." He steadied him by holding on to his belt with the right hand and a handful of shirt with his left. John cradled the wounded arm with his left hand. John stared at the pool of blood where he lay. He swayed and knees buckled once, but he stood.

Two of the men from Company B pointed and said, "It's yonder." John leaned against Matthew, and they walked away.

They left the open field for the cover of poplar, dogwood, and bay. They walked by ninebark, sweetshrub, and sassafras bushes covered with the bright leaves of spring and through weeds and grass on a path scuffed by many feet. The way was marked by canteens, cartridge boxes, hats, and spatters of blood scattered among the violets. John weakened as drops fell from his elbow to add to the stains along the path. Whining sounds like bees filled his ears. Needles of light blurred distant objects. The needles converged and burst into terrible brightness. Everything became dim and gray. Consciousness faded for an instant and he moved as if floating in a dream. He dared not close his eyes for fear that he would be swept into a nightmare. He forced them open and looked at the trail as he took each step. He fixed his eyes on anything that would come into focus. The world did not exist beyond his shoe. The two men passed a cluster of bluetts and then one of tiny iris in bloom. John took a short breath."Ever'thang is blue."

"What?"

John took a deeper breath and said, "Even the flowers are all blue."

Matthew grunted to show hearing, but not understanding of the words. The path left the drain and led up a slope. As they climbed, John stumbled and would have fallen, but for the hands holding him. He did little more than lift and shuffle his feet as he was dragged along the trail. Matthew's hat was dark at his forehead and sweat poured down his face. John had no hat. Above his beard, his face was ashen and dry.

From time to time Matthew said, "Hold on, John. It can't be far now," or "We're almost there."

The two miles from the battle line seemed like ten. Through scattered oaks at the crest of the hill they saw a double-pen cabin of rough sawn planks. Like John's home, there was a central dogtrot. From battles of the past, they knew to look for a barn, a house, or a tent. The regimental surgeon and his assistants, carrying instruments and supplies, instantly made any shelter a hospital. The home on the hill *was* the hospital for this battlefield. The David P. Hurt family owned the farm, so the wounded called the building The Hurt House.

Mid-afternoon sun was hidden behind the building, leaving the wounded clustered in the shade of a shed roof. Matthew eased John down at the edge of the porch. He sat leaning against a post to wait his turn. Matthew put both hands on the same post until his breathing slowed.

When the pain of travel lessened and the grimace on John's face began to fade, Matthew put a hand on his shoulder. "Ya know I got to get back to the company, but I'll be back soon as I can. Ya hear me, John? Ya understand? I may have to shoot Sherman hisself, but I'll get back... somehow."

John sat looking down, with elbows on his knees, cradling his wounded wrist with his left hand, taking quick shallow breaths, still afraid to close his eyes, watching drops of blood splattering on the floor. He nodded, but didn't look up.

He waited, surrounded by men and sounds of pain, yet alone. As he steadied the wounded arm, the pain eased enough for him to raise his head. He saw some with trifling hurts he wouldn't have bothered with, but others had twisted ruins of their face, chest injuries or crippling wounds of the extremities. Minié balls had struck most, blowing huge holes, and shattering bones like glass. John stared at his fellow soldiers. *"I've done such to Yankees, and would have this day. Do they hate us that bad? Do I hate them bad enough to give their folks sorrow or take a leg? How could I do that to another man? They are in our land, but -- but they oughta be some other way. I reckon ya just can't reason with Yankees."*

After a time, two men came through the open doorway within the dogtrot and walked the length of the porch. As the steps sounded on loose boards, some men looked up; others lay dejected and still. The steps stopped where John sat. He raised his head to see the faces above the spattered pants. Without speaking, the men helped him to his feet and led him to the north room where the surgeon was working. A man with a wounded leg lay on a stretcher along the far wall. Another, shot in the forearm, sat on the floor and leaned against the wall by the door. The silent men eased John down near the man with an injured arm. Two soldiers with clenched teeth nodded to each other. A few feet from John, the doctor was finishing treatment of a man with a scalp and shoulder wound. The patient was under the window, stretched on a door lying across two barrels, pushed away from the wall just enough to let the surgeon and his helpers stand and work. This operating table was one of three furnishings in the room.

A sudden storm had blown over the battlefield and field hospital. Rain beat on the roof and window, muting moans and screams from the porch and the room across the dogtrot. As clouds covered the sun, light from the window faded. Sounds of The Hurt House died away for an instant and John heard distant shooting above the rumble of thunder.

The door over the barrels was drenched with blood. The floor and wall near the window were spattered. Gray light bordered droplets on the glass panes -- some red and glistening, others dull, almost black -- all in a row. The doctor had blood on his shirt and apron, bare hands and arms below rolled up sleeves. A basin of water sat on a worktable near the suspended door. The water was almost as red as the tub under the table.

When they took the patient away, the surgeon touched his thumbs to his fingers. He washed in the basin and stared as he turned his dripping hands to the light. He said softly, "I'll never be able to wash it all away. "

His assistants were splattered with bright spots over darker stains. A trail of footprints led across the dogtrot and to the porch. Surgical instruments lay scattered on the table beside the pan. The tub under the table overflowed and red crept along the cracks between the boards. The room reeked of sweat and blood, both old and new, and other fluids, some from wounds and some from pain.

Two assistants came from the porch carrying a man on a stretcher. They raised his shirt for the surgeon to see. He seldom looked at patients' faces. He looked at wounds and Zack took their names -- if they could speak. This soldier had a round hole with ragged edges in the upper abdomen. When the patient cried out in pain, fluid drained from the wound. There was blood, but most was cloudy watery fluid with tan and gray flecks and swirling streaks of amber flowing down the abdominal wall and slowly dripping on the floor. The surgeon took a step closer, bent over to look at the wound, touched the tight muscles with one hand, shook his head, and motioned toward the door. The two men carried the stretcher into the dogtrot and beyond.

A third man walked over to the camp supply box, opened it and took out a wicker-covered flask, shook it, then tilted it. He looked up at the surgeon. "Not even any whiskey left."

"Opium pills, sulfate of morphia?"

"All gone. They's a right good sized dose of Dover's powder -- just the one."

"Give it to that poor fella they just took back. Maybe it'll get him through the night. He's bowel-shot and probably liver, too. He may not see sunrise. Then let's get to these others. They keep shooting and they keep coming. Lord, they keep coming. Is there no end to this slaughter?"

Major King was a young doctor from Adams County, north of Canaan, or had been in 1862. Now he looked worn and ageless with a two-day beard and streaks of gray at temples that should have held rumpled brown hair. He dared not lie or even sit or he would sleep as the dead in the fields. He wore brogans to operate because once he stood so long at surgery that boots had to be cut away from swollen feet. There had been an assistant surgeon -- a good man who shared the duties, but was killed in a battle east of Atlanta. A much younger assistant surgeon was assigned to the major, but he had done no surgery since his first tries and was only able to care for those with camp diseases.

The major wore no insignia. In this temporary hospital he was regimental surgeon, monarch, judge, and jury. He had no time to be comforter. He consulted with God alone.

Major King had worked with the same three men for two and a half years. Will and Dan were brothers from Salem County. They were not twins, though some thought they were. Both worked hard and were usually quiet. They had red hair, full beards, and on battle days, flushed faces. They were taller and heavier than the thin major. Zach was shorter than the two, but more muscular. He had thinning brown hair, and tried to stay clean-shaven. When the armies fought, like the major he had several days' growth of beard. He spoke little more than the brothers. As Steward of the drugs and supplies, he wore a sidearm, pushed to the back so he could work at the table. There was little to guard now, but he wore it as a badge and from habit. Others retrieved the wounded, buried the dead, and cared for the sick, but these three helped with the surgery. All were strong. Strength and voluntary deafness were basic qualities for doctor's helpers in a field hospital. They spoke few words, as if each knew the mind of the other.

When Zach came back, the surgeon and three assistants walked over to a man with a hole blown in his knee. He looked to be no more than twenty. He began screaming, "Don't cut it off -- don't cut it off!"

The major leaned over, grabbed hold of his shoulders shook him and said, "Soldier, what's your name?" He hesitated, then looked in the boy's eyes. The wounded man became quiet.

"Tom, sir. Tom Watson, and I'm a farmer. I can't farm without my legs! Please don't cut it off!"

The doctor straightened up shook his head and in a sharp tone said, "Private Watson!"

"Uh -- uh -- yes sir?"

He pointed at the leg crooked over to one side, looked at the boy's twisted face, and in a quiet firm voice said, "Son, there's no choice. If you wanta live, it comes off." Tom began his mournful cry again. Major King turned away and nodded to the men with splattered pants.

Will and Dan moved the stretcher to the operating table and held Tom down while Zach put the tourniquet around his leg. The anguished patient struggled, but could do nothing but raise his head and stare at his leg in panic. As he twisted the knob to tighten the band, Zack looked into the boy's eyes," I wish we had chloroform, but we don't. The major is a good surgeon -- and he's quick." The brothers pushed Tom's head and shoulders down and leaned across his chest, reducing his screeches only a little.

John watched and remembered an earlier day and another battle. He had sat in a different field hospital while Zach treated a saber wound on his hip. He had watched the major at work across the room with Will and Dan. The four were different then. They talked, told stories, laughed, and smiled between patients. As John watched, they all looked worn and old. On this day there were few words and no smiles.

The doctor made one giant circular slash with the amputation knife, severing everything but bone in the lower thigh. John was sitting close enough for blood to splatter at his feet. He tried to turn away, but the knife, blood, and screams held him like a hypnotic trance. The major cut the bone, with a short solid-blade saw. The noise reminded John of sounds at the barn when they butchered hogs. But the hogs didn't scream. He frowned and squinted as he remembered how hard it was to saw bones.

In three minutes, a man's leg was lost. One of the brothers carried the leg beyond the door to the dpgtrot with the shoe and a section of trousers still in place. The boy's cries stopped; he looked pale and senseless. Sounds of the rain on the roof and thunder in the distance returned. The surgeon smoothed the bone, then pulled the arteries and large veins out of the stump with an instrument that looked like a thin crochet hook, took strands of boiled horse hair hanging from the buttons of his shirt, tied the vessels and cut the ends long. The surgeon's assistants wrapped raw cotton on the stump and held it in place with muslin, as Zach loosened the tourniquet. Bloodstains appeared in the center of the dressing and slowly spread. The Major watched until the stain slowed and then motioned to the men.

The brothers carried the man through the door to the dogtrot. John watched every move as they came back and crossed the room to the other man with an injured arm.

Before they could pick him up, there was a clatter of footsteps on the porch and two men rushed in through the doorway with a patient on a stretcher. The man at the foot of the stretcher wore a gray-brown shirt and pants, a misshapen dark hat, and brogans. The front and sides of his shirt were dark and stuck to his chest. His hat was sweat-marked at the forehead. A red wool badge wrapped around his left arm was stenciled in black letters: *Ambulance Corps*. He was splattered with raindrops. The silent man with vacant eyes at the head of the stretcher leaning against the wall near the doorway wore his badge on his hat. The retching screaming patient held a shirt over his abdomen.

The first stretcher-bearer's face was flushed and wet as he stood in the middle of the room. He gasped for breath and had difficulty making himself heard over the noise, "Sorry to bust in, sir, but we thought ya would want to see this fella right quick. It's a shell wound, sir. Several hurt, but he's the worst. His innards is hanging out."

The surgeon motioned, and they placed the man on the table by the window. The assistants held the grabbing arms and jumping legs while the surgeon pulled the shirt away. The stretcher-bearers left. The patient had an oblique wound through the center of the abdominal wall with jutting loops of intestines that formed a globular mass. As the patient cried out and strained, the wet loops farther extruded, twisted, and turned as if they had a life of their own. The surgeon tried to force the loops back. As he threaded one loop in, others escaped and squirted between his fingers.

After the third futile attempt with mounting force and increasing screams, Major King stopped and mumbled, "The hole must be too small." He picked up a curved bistoury and pushed the blunt end beside the intestines into the abdomen. With a few up and down sawing motions he enlarged the opening. More loops came out as the patient screamed louder and retched harder. They were no easier to get back in than when the hole was small.

One brother held the patient's arms and leaned across his chest. The other leaned across his legs. Zach held the intestines to keep more from coming out and watched Major King's face as he took a quick glance at the soldier's face and then stared at the wound.

He muttered, "He won't live long like this. And he's dying in agony." The patient strained and the loops grew larger and darker as they slid from Zack's hands. The wounded soldier still cried out, but now his voice was hoarse and feeble. John tried to shrink from the sight and sounds, but he could not turn away.

"Men, pick him up off the table easy-like and come this way a little. Will, stand that way and hold his feet. Dan, stand at the far end and hold his head and shoulders. Let his body droop so his nates just do touch the floor. Turn him into a U and his muscles will let go."

Between cries and retches, the surgeon knelt and worked the fingers of his left hand between the intestines and the edge of the wound, then slid them into the abdomen. He slipped fingers of his right hand in the other side of the hole, grunted as he lifted the abdominal wall with both hands and shook it. With a little help from Zach, the loops fell back into the abdomen between screams. The surgeon's fingers followed the loops to plug the hole, and then he guided the steward's hand to replace his. He motioned to Will and Dan to lower the patient slightly. He changed to a squatting position, threaded a needle and began to sew.

He glanced at Zach across the wounded abdomen and said, "Don't you dare move, even if I stick you! Hold your fingers just where they are 'till I get to that last stitch."

The screaming and retching faded to occasional groans. When the last stitch was made, Major King nodded to Zach, who drew his fingers out of the hole as the surgeon tied the knot. The repair held and was reinforced by a few more sutures. The silent helpers tied strips of the shirt around the man's body to hold a baked cotton dressing over the wound.

The surgeon stood, moved a foot up and down, stretched one leg, and then the other. He sighed, leaned against the wall. "Take him 'cross the dogtrot. At least now he's got a chance. Get back soon as you can. We've got others to finish before the light fades."

Major King's shoulders drooped lower as he watched the brothers carry the man. "Zach, I still find it hard to believe that one man does that sort of thing to another. They aim for arms or legs, because a wounded soldier is more a burden than a dead one. We wouldn't do that to animals. When I was schooled in Boston, I would have never thought people there could do such to us.

Zack, that soldier they just carried out: I looked in his eyes ... and the boy with the shot leg, too."

"Major, it gives a man courage and confidence if his doctor looks him in the face. There's not a better ... nor a quicker surgeon in this army. As they come in, I talk to 'em when I can because I know what you can do, but them men comin' through the door don't. They're hurt and scared."

The doctor studied his steward's face and shook his head slowly. "It's too much to ask. It's enough to see their wounds – their awful wounds --and hear their screams. Tomorrow ... and tomorrow after that, when I close my eyes, I will see those faces and hear their cries. I cut off arms and legs ... what I have to do if they hope to live. Tragedy needs no face ... no name. It's enough that it comes to our door."

The major groaned as he looked toward the sound of scuffling footsteps on the porch. The same two men of the Ambulance Corps brought in another patient.

The one at the foot of the stretcher was as breathless as before. "Sir. I was wrong, this fella may be worser -- he's more curious anyway. He's fartin' like a mule, but it's acomin' from his chest." The surgeon and Zach looked startled. "Well he is! I don't know how else to say it. He got it when that shell blowed up and got that one with his innards out."

The major motioned toward the table. When the men cane back from the room across the dogtrot, they lifted the man to the door under the window. The stretcher-bearers ran to their mule drawn ambulance. The patient had a small penetrating wound into the chest cavity. A flap of skin covered part of the opening. He was making flatulent sounds when he breathed out, but when he breathed in there was a sucking whistling sound. The wounded man made gulping motions with pursed lips like a fish out of water. His face was blue and his eyes were those of a trapped animal seeing death.

Across the patient, Zach said, "Now, before ya ask, we don't have no lint or collodian."

The Major stared at the blue face for a few seconds. "Get me a piece of ground cloth about as big as two hands. A piece of oilcloth -- from somewhere -- and quick!"

He watched the desperate attempts to breathe and placed his hand over the hole until the oilcloth arrived. The assistants had little to do in holding the patient. He spent his fading energy in trying to breathe. The major placed the oilcloth over the hole in the chest and timed it carefully. When the patient breathed in, the major covered it tightly to prevent air from being sucked in. When he breathed out, the major lifted his hand and allowed the air to be expelled from the chest cavity with whatever sound it chose to make. He encouraged him to blow the air out, or even cough.

When sounds were less with expiration, the major held the oilcloth tightly in the hole and took a quick look at the patient's face. The blue had faded and pink was slowly returning. The corners of the doctor's mouth flickered upward for an instant and his eyes blinked several times. He looked back to the chest.

As the patient gained strength, between breaths, he said, "Them Yankees got us."

Without looking up, the major said, "They've about got us all."

Zach asked, "What are we gonna do now? Ya heard me, didn't ya? No collodian. We can't seal it."

"Just wad up a piece of his shirt about fist sized." He put the cloth against the oilcloth. "Now tear strips of cloth and tie them tight around his chest and bind that pack over the hole. Blood should clot and seal it. When you take him back, make sure that binding doesn't slip. And prop him up real good even if you have to steal a blanket somewhere. And when you're walkin' through the back, call me if there is the slightest noise when he breathes or if he's blue again."

As the brothers carred the man out, he grabbed his steward's arm. "And Zack, not always ... but sometimes it gives the doctor courage to look at a man's face ... and ... and satisfaction, too."

After the brothers returned, the same four amputated the other patient's arm. John watched every move of the men who held and every cut of the surgeon's blade and every motion of the rasping saw. He heard the screams of the boy who wanted to farm, the man who lost an arm, the man with the bowel out, and sounds of agony from the man with the hole in his chest. He saw their tortured faces with eyes that spoke louder than screams. Thoughts and scenes tumbled through John's mind. *It ain't like havin' a broke arm fixed. They're makin' cripples. I can't stand to have an arm cut off like some animal. And even if I could, I couldn't face life without my right hand. I'll die and pass on.*

And then, it was John's turn. The doctor glanced at his arm and never spoke a word. He nodded to the stewards. John didn't ask. He knew the answer. They moved him to the bloodstained table with his canteen scraping across the wood and his haversack hanging off the side. *I can't shoot a gun. I can't hold a plow. I can't work iron, I can't write. I don't want to be helpless, livin' off other folks. But what will Martha do? Her and the boys can't make it by theirselves. I have to go back. What can a cripple do? But then.... if there's life, there's hope...not much, but some. I could do somethin'. I wanta hear voices of my kin. I want to see the sun shine on my own land. I want to live. I havta live. I will live. Lord God above, take me through these next minutes. Help me be a man.*

Major King picked up the twelve-inch long knife with black handle. It looked like a small sword. He moved the blade back and forth through the water in the pan, washed off most of the blood, and held it up to the window. He ran his finger along the edge, frowned at the instrument and handed it to Zack. "That thing wouldn't cut hot butter. Give it a few licks before we start."

Zack leaned over the supply box, picked up the whetstone, rested it on the window ledge and began a slow scraping. Other noises faded and John heard nothing but slow methodical rasp of metal on stone. The pain in his arm grew with each sound of the blade. The grating noise was the same as sharpening knives at hog-killing time in Canaan County. One of the brothers pulled the canteen from under John's hip and leaned it against his belt. The other took off the cord of cloth, tore a piece of one end, rolled it up, and placed it between John's teeth.

"Here, bite on that...when the time comes."

John was distracted only a moment as he opened his mouth. *Quick, what can I let my mind dwell on to take me away from this woe? Mustn't bring Martha and the boys to mind. The sight's too terrible for them.* Zack put the strap around his arm. *There's no time. What can I thank on to take me away from all this?* Three men pushed John down on the table and held his arm in a painful grip. The arm felt as if it would burst as Zach twisted the knob and the tourniquet tightened. John looked up at the stained ceiling with smudges of smoke marks from the fireplace, swirled like fog. *That's it! I can see that cool bubblin' spring, and the mornin' mist over the water that waits by the path toward the barn.* From the corner of his eye, John saw the blade in the major's hand, as if it were a part of his body -- an extension of his being. The new edge gleamed in the light.

John closed his eyes tightly, as when he was a boy and shut out the light to take away demons of night shadows. A startling pain like white-hot iron passed around John's arm. He bit the roll between his teeth and groaned. The cloth tasted of blood and sweat. His arm began to shake and jerk with the grinding push and pull of the saw. Searing agony came in waves to match the sounds. Arms held him like bands of iron. His vision of the spring faded, and he heard his own cry added to others. His world dimmed and vanished.

Release of the tourniquet caused a flood of pain, then a sensation of cool liquid and a burning which forced him back to the world he fled. He heard a voice that seemed to come from far away.

"Sir, that's the last of the carbolic acid. The next ones will just have to stink."

When the intense pain passed, John forced his eyes open enough to see shapeless forms moving about him. Shadows touched his throbbing arm. They touched his back and he had the feeling of floating through air. *I didn't know the end would come like this.*

Chapter Eleven – Beyond the Door

John opened his eyes to a world of blackness with flickering red and yellow lights. The light moved, glowed, and for an instant filled a doorway. A shadow hovered and was gone. Low voices, then groans and a scream told him that all this was a nightmare. And then he moved his arm and knew the pain was real. *Has it been hours or days? I'm alive somewhere... I thank, but the house must be afire. I can't move. It'll be over soon.* He tried to sit up, but pain and weakness forced him back. The light faded and shadows covered him.

He woke in the grayness of an overcast day lying on the floor, his head on his haversack. He began hearing cries and sounds as if they came from a great distance. He blinked and strained to know what surrounded him. He saw long shadows almost in a row. Some shadows moved. John blinked and squinted to see cheesecloth holding bloody cotton at the end of his right arm. The slightest motion of that arm caused pain in fingers he did not have. As sounds grew louder and forms clearer, in this room with one window and one door, he saw wounded soldiers lying like scattered stove wood. By day, the room was beyond a nightmare. There were no beds. Men lay in a row around the room almost touching each other, each with his head to the wall and his feet, or foot, toward the center of the room. Some had beds of loose straw. John and others lay on their blanket. As the wall spaces were filled, two men added wounded to the center, leaving a narrow path to walk. Some on the floor moaned; some still bled; some babbled of home; others had their eyes closed, still in the blackness of night. A boy, no more than sixteen, laughed -- the hysterical laugh of one who knows all is lost. At the far end of the room lay a Yankee. He was no longer an enemy, but a man who lost a leg. John saw men that he knew, but Tom wasn't there. He said he couldn't farm with one leg.

Will and Dan brought another man in on a stretcher and put him down across the room along the wall with the window. The patient next to him raised up and said, "What's he doin' here? Darkies don't belong!" He grabbed the steward's sleeve. "Why ya bringin' colored? He ain't no soldier!"

The man pulled away, said nothing, turned, and walked through the doorway to the dogtrot. The irate soldier shouted after him, "He's got no part in this war."

The old man next to John, propped up on one elbow and raised his other arm.

"He does so, Luke. Colored worked as cooks and nurses and drivers and body servants in the whole war. Some places they're armin' colored. Most likely he's from that Georgia regiment that's got a colored band. That makes him as much a soldier as you. From the looks of that bandage on his leg, I'd say he's here 'cause when he gets shot, he bleeds red, same as you."

The wide-eyed new patient nodded vigorously and said nothing. The complainer muttered and turned his head.

At the same time the new man was brought in, the patient with the abdominal wound from the day before woke from his Dover's Powder and began screaming. Luke raised up again. "That ain't no man. He oughta be home hanging onto his mama's coattail."

The man in the corner answered, "I couldn't see who it was last night. I know that boy. Claims he's fourteen one day and fifteen the next."

The man who lost his arm before John said, "That's Pink Walraven's boy. Sammy's always been a right smart size fa his age, but he can't be no more than twelve."

Over time, the boy's cries -- higher pitched than the rest -- grew weaker and he called, "Mama! Mama! Help me! Please." Droplets of amber soaked his shirt and trickled down his side.

Lying next to John, the defender of the musician with a gunshot injury of his shoulder and a wound of the scalp watched the boy and listened to his cries. After several minutes, he rolled on his side, got to his hands and knees and slowly stood. The years made him stooped, and he swayed and held to the wall until he gained his balance. He grimaced in pain as he moved across the room to the boy under the window. The man had a white beard and hair but for a streak of dark gray – almost black. Dry blood matted his hair on one side. He was a large man with thick features that spoke of age. He grabbed the window frame and stood, looming over the frail boy. John knew him to be a man from Salem County, a sergeant in D Company. No one knew how old he was, but most called him "grandpa." He lived in the same county as Sammy. He leaned against the wall with one hand, eased himself down, sat at the boy's side, took his hand, and tried to calm him. The boy looked up at the old man through eyes fogged with pain and said, "Daddy?"

Sammy asked again. Sergeant Grandpa's beard quivered. He moved his lips, but no words came. He took a deep breath and said, "Sammy, I reckon I can be yer daddy this hour."

"Daddy, it hurts so bad. I can't stand it. I got to have somethin' for the pain."

"Son, listen to me. Yer mama loves ya. Yer daddy loves ya, and God loves ya. Try to breathe slow and easy-like and be quiet as ya can. Don't wake baby sister, now. I promise, soon there will be no more pain."

"No pain?"

"No pain, I promise. Yer daddy wouldn't lie, would he? Now let's pray together."

Sergeant Grandpa leaned over to whisper near the boy's ear so he could hear above the din about them. Those not unconscious or irrational sat up and watched the two. The old man moved his lips near Sammy's ear and the boy's shoulders and neck slowly relaxed. He closed his eyes and mouthed words.

The man in the corner who lost his arm before John said, "I can see their mouth move, but I can't hear words. Yer closer. What are they sayin'?"

"Yer not s'posed to hear," John said. "The old man and the boy hear one another, and God hears 'em both. I can might near hear Him weepin' over it." Soon, the motion of the boy's lips became slower and then stopped. His face went slack, one hand fell to the floor, and there was no more pain.

The men in the room had seen death and caused death. But they saw a soul depart far short of three score and ten. The room became strangely quiet as men forgot their wounds and pain -- watching Sergeant Grandpa holding Sammy's hand. While they looked, storm clouds cleared and light streamed through the window. The old man's hair and beard looked softer and whiter, and the boy's face, framed by light blond hair, was pale, thin, but peaceful -- almost smiling. Every conscious eye in the room was on the old man and the boy. They all saw the death of a young boy. John saw the death of all the hopes of the young nation he served. Sergeant Grandpa folded the boy's hands across his chest, struggled to his feet and moved back to his place. He sat by John and stared through the open window. He didn't bother to wipe the tears streaming into his beard.

John sank down on his blanket and the world around him faded. When he woke, the man and the boy, one too old and one too young for war, were gone. The man in the corner said they had carried the boy beyond the door and Sergeant Grandpa picked up his haversack and blanket and followed. Dan and Will said they saw him headed toward the battlefield, to find Sammy's drum. The wounded Negro man was with him.

John listened to the commotion for the rest of the day. He watched the stewards bring new patients and carry some away. Once, he saw a man carrying a leg down the dogtrot. There was no food. Men were expected to reach their own canteens. One soldier, years short of twenty, cried over and over, "Just a sup of water – please -- just a sup of water!" Bloody cotton covered his arms and eyes. Zach gave him water several times until his cries slowed and then stopped. Will and Dan lifted him up and took him through the door and down the dogtrot.

The room smelled of yesterday's blood and last week's sweat. Overpowering this was the acrid scent of rancid meat. The window and door were open, and flies swarmed to the stench. Some men did not bother to brush them away. Once, Zach promised that they would be taken to a hospital in Charlotte, but it never happened.

Slowly, some of John's strength began to come back. He felt in his haversack to find his clothes, knife, a sliver of soap, his Testament, and the pistol still there. He looked about and found a cartridge box a few inches from his head. A deep gash scarred the AVC of the oval brass plate. *That matches my scar. That's my box! Matthew has been here!* The twenty rounds were gone. Light began to fade, and shadows deepened. There was no candle for the night to come. Sounds around him seemed louder and louder until they were deafening. *If*

I stay, they will haul me out that door and down the dogtrot by daylight. Matthew couldn't stay, and there's no help here. Home is a long ways off. I havta get out, but can I walk? He saw a chest-high stick leaning against the wall within his reach. *That musta belonged to somebody they carried down the dogtrot.*

He threw his blanket and ground cloth over his shoulder and looped the haversack strap over his throbbing right forearm. He grabbed the stick with his left hand and pushed himself up with his back against the wall. He weakened and fell with his elbow on his haversack. Sounds faded, then returned louder than ever. John pulled his feet under his body. He took a deep breath, clenched his teeth, and pushed up again, this time with his forearm on the right and with the stick on the left. No one noticed one more moan and cry. A thousand live coals shot through fingers he did not have, but he stood -- with his shoulder against the wall. He leaned over to try to pick up the box with the slash, but there was no hand and sounds of bees and needles of light burst forth around him.

John straightened up again, clung to the stick and forced his eyes open. When the room stopped spinning, he moved away from the wall, staggered through the door and left the room of screams and death. He could not see clearly as he stumbled down the dogtrot dragging his haversack, but his feet pretended to be at home in Canaan County. After leaving the room with one window he squinted against the light ahead. John lurched against the wall, but could not stop. He knew he would fall if he did. He was startled by a sight from the back porch, faltered, and could go no farther. He swayed, leaned against a post by the steps and stared at a mound of cut-off arms and legs in the brightness of the setting sun with long shadows pointing toward the room with one window and one door. Feet stuck out from the tangle, a few with brogans and others bare. As the glow of sunset touched them, some fingers seemed to move and twist to mirror the scream of their owner. Stains from the base of the pile were dark circles in the dirt; the top layer drained red. The stench was stronger. *I've got to go past that...that testament to war. And somewhere in that pile is.... is part of me.* He looked at the ground and leaning on his stick, dragging his haversack, moved the left foot to the top step, then his right foot to the same step. He took the next step then moved both feet to the ground, staggered, turned his head and walked away.

The storm had passed and it had turned off clear. Beyond the corner of the house he stopped, propped on his stick, took deep breaths of cleaner air, blinked and squinted. Some of his far vision came back. At his left he saw remains of a burned-out barn. Two tents stood about a hundred feet to the right, where a small flag appeared gray or maybe yellow in the fading light. A man walked from one tent to the other, but within the tents there seemed to be little activity. Occasionally, a man left for a visit to a nearby sink. *That's a pesthouse for camp sickness. No better than the place I left.*

Beyond the tents he saw a campfire near a large oak. Men were scattered about – some propped against the tree, most lying down. In the fading light, John couldn't see what their injuries were or even if they had wounds. In the early darkness, fog rose from the rain-soaked ground, creeping and hiding everything before him. As the clamminess reached him and swirled around his legs, he walked to the warmth of the flames in the center of an island surrounded by white. Drifting fog pushed in, only to be burned and tossed upward by the shielding heat.

John threw down his blanket in the last vacant spot around the fire. He spread the corners with his stick." I hope you fellas don't mind. I'd like to join ya. I can't take it in that house no more." They said not a word. John mumbled to himself, "I 'speck they are as wore out as I am."

As he eased himself down with his stick, John thought he heard singing, but he couldn't be sure because of the sounds from the Hurt House. Then the noises of pain faded and he heard a clear tenor voice. He thought it came from the battlefield, but the words seemed to surround and drift from the fog.

"There is a balm in Gilead to make the wounded whole...."

He lay down, rested his stump on the letters of his buckle, closed his eyes and listened.

"There is a balm in Gilead to heal the sin-sick soul. Sometimes I feel discouraged, and think my work's in vain.."

The song faded, the fire warmed him, and John slept a dreamless sleep like those lying in the fields.

When he woke, the fire was out, but he was warm, his pain was less and he felt stronger. He sat up and looked about. Most of the men had gone, but others lay around the heap of ashes as they had the night before. John shook the shoulder of the man next to him to rouse him. The arm was stiff and cold. In the light of day he saw the wounds of the men under the tree. Only John breathed.

He fell back on his blanket and shut his eyes. *It's all about me, no matter where I go. I've walked to another place of death. Could it be? Am -- am I dead, too?* After a time, even through closed lids, he knew that he was looking into a bright light and heard birds singing. He opened his eyes and glanced at the still men and up at blinding patches in the tree branches and the rays through smoke of a dying fire. *I can see the light. I'm under the sun. I'm alive! I don't belong here.*

He pushed himself up, picked up his haversack and blanket, turned his back on the circle of death, and slowly walked back to the house, leaning on his stick. He stopped several times to adjust the dragging blanket and to catch his breath. Each time he looked around, unsure of what to do. There was still moaning and the occasional scream from the The Hurt House. He watched men working behind the house. In the early morning, they had dug a hole big enough for a small horse and were throwing in arms and legs. John stopped at the edge and watched parts of men's lives fall in the pit. When one of the men looked his way, he said, "Folks cuttin' one another, shootin' holes in one another, burnin' homes, and starvin' folks to death. I figger war must be a taste of what Hell is like. Don't see how Hell could be much worse. If them Yankees would have just let us be, a lot of good folks would be alive today … on both sides." The men must have heard, but said nothing, and never stopped.

John stood watching an arm, then a leg fall. *Part of me will never see the light of day agin… What if I saw my own hand? If I did, I might…. Would I know my hand, if I saw it in that hole? Can a man know his own hand if it's not there at the end of his arm, if it lies outside his reach, if he can't thank on it and move a finger, or hold water in his palm and feel wetness?* He stared at the pit, then his left hand as he turned it over. *Yes, I would know your brother, even if he's cold and still …in that grave. But, I don't know what I might do if I saw him. I don't want to look on it.*

He turned from the falling parts. He had no thought but to leave the funeral of limbs. He saw a little spring near the barn and headed toward the water, leaning on his stick. He discovered how difficult it was to travel uneven ground holding one arm up and dragging a blanket. John squatted at the edge of the spring, filled his canteen and drank. Seemed like he hadn't had water in a month. He put his left hand in the water, waved it back and forth, brought it up dripping and stared at it, then at the stained wrappings on his stump. He stood and looked toward the circle of still men under the tree and at the house of pain. Three men with shovels were throwing dirt over the limbs. John didn't know what to do or what path to follow, but he knew he couldn't stay. He placed the strap of his haversack over one shoulder and adjusted the satchel-like part at his waist. He fumbled with his hand and after several tries rolled the blanket and placed it over his shoulder.

John looked one last time at the Hurt House. He raised his left hand. "I'll see ya in the bye and bye." He walked west toward the woods beyond the spring in the direction of sporadic shooting in the distance. He walked with faltering steps -- alone. By the time he reached the shelter of trees, his stride was stronger and his shoulders straighter. John never looked back. He walked toward home.

He entered a land of shadows. Some shadows moved. John stopped and leaned against a tree and watched soldiers drifting into a clearing. With relief, he recognized Confederates, wounded or lost from their unit. With a whispered greeting, he joined the group. Most were from the 55th, but some were separated from other regiments. They walked through an open area where men had fought, past dead horses, swollen with legs held at odd angles. They carefully stepped around shallow graves. Some had wooden crosses with scratched letters saying how many lay below in their final sleep and which side they came from. The only sounds were a few whispers and shuffling feet along the paths and through the grass. There was stillness and an oppressive scent -- of gunpowder, smoke, dead horses and, above it all, a curious frightening odor.

They passed the marks of death and came upon the battle line – now quiet. Yankee pickets never looked toward the Confederates. The federals were dressed in new uniforms. They had good wagons and tents and food cooking. It appeared to the southern boys that they were passing around a bottle and celebrating. The breeze brought smells to remind John that he hadn't eaten in two days. Suddenly, his knees were weak. He stopped and leaned on his stick. The soldier walking beside him reached out and steadied John's shoulders until his feet began to move toward home again.

They walked a hidden drain and entered a clearing beyond the woods. Some turned south with John, toward the 55th standards. Others went north, looking for familiar flags or friendly faces. John found what was left of his company. The men looked up from their meager meal. One said, "The Lord, look yonder, there come some of the boys through Yankee lines and one of 'em is John."

Matthew and the rest of the company ran to meet John, welcomed him and put him to bed, if a blanket on the ground can be considered a bed. Matthew said, "He needs real food -- not this slosh we're eatin'. Somebody in D Company killed a deer this mornin'. Go tell 'em if they don't give us some meat for John we'll tell the rest of the regiment and they'll lose it all."

Over the next few days, John improved rapidly. He looked at his wound for the first time as Matthew cut the ties from the vessels. The surgeon had left short open flaps to cover the ends of the bones of the forearm. The wound had a small amount of pus, little smell and was rapidly closing. But the fingers he knew so well were gone. The hand that pulled the trigger in war, held the hammer in peace, the one he offered in friendship lay in the darkness of a pit. In their place, he was left with pain in fingers he did not have and a life of ineptitude.

From his right sleeve there was no hand, but something like a stick with raw meat on the end. He stared at the wound. "When I wake up ever' day, seems like I have to find out all over again that it's gone. In that house, I prayed to live. I might coulda been wrong. Yankees may as well take my life as my right hand. I'm not fit for nothin'. I'm ruint." He looked in the distance and appeared not to hear the words of his friends.

When John was stronger, less dejected, and was up and about more, he began to ask about the lull in the war. Matthew shook his head and said, "John, we don't know for sure. We heard that Lee surrendered to Grant on the ninth. Then we heard that Johnston surrendered us to Sherman on the eighteenth with terms that would let us hold our heads up when we got home. Today, we heard they turned it down."

"Who turned it down?"

"Them pisspots in Washington -- that's who! They said surrender complete or nothin'. We got to give up and let 'em do whatever they want to with us and our homes."

"What's gonna happen to us? Yankees are thicker'an lice on a hen. We saw 'em when we come through."

"John, some says we'll all get shipped north, when it's all over."

"North! Some place like Johnson's Island? They may as well shoot me now. I'd never make the first winter."

"Some says we get put in a prison camp close by. So them two generals are dickerin' about. Nobody has asked the ones that shot the guns four years. 'Course, I ad-mit our supplies are mighty low. Just sittin' around lookin' at one another is puttin' everybody on edge. Must be a dozen card games goin' on. Some folks got some pop-skull they're passin' around. Some are fightin' amongst theirselves. The regiment is comin' apart with nothin' to do. I'm gonna go over and see if I can find out somethin' from one of them folks that works for the general."

As Matthew left, Billy Deerman limped over from a nearby tent, leaning on a staff, sometimes using both hands, with the right on a little crook near the top and the left below.

"Mornin', Billy. Glad to see ya movin' about better. That hole in yer leg must be about mended. Most of our folks made it through that last little fuss, but I've not seen Rufus and Jeff since I got back."

"Same day you got shot, Rufus took sick, probably the continued fever. A while back, Jeff was cavortin' around with some of those loose women and he's sick too. I reckon he's got the pox. Both have gone Company Q. Yankees probably have 'em now, since we fell back."

"I sure hate that, Billy. I had hoped what's left of the company could make it home. Them two have been with us from the first. Rufus might could get better, but Jeff has fixed hisself real good -- and him with a family and all."

"He talked about takin' his gun and walkin' toward the Yankees."

" If he lives to get back, he may not be worth much. I don't see how he can face his wife with that cloud hanging over him."

Billy and John were still talking when Matthew came back with a grave look. "The word is that we're gonna give up complete in the next day or so." Matthew turned away so his face was hidden. There was a catch in his voice. "After four years, it ends like this. We all gotta throw down our guns, allow we was wromg, go over and sign a oath and get paroled before we can go."

Billy shifted his stick and looked from Matthew to John. "What do you think, John?"

He looked at Billy for a time, as if he had not heard. He glanced at the Confederate camp and then stared at the Yankees in the distance. He frowned, squinted and moved his lips, but there was no sound. When he did speak, his words were soft and deliberate." Why don't the two of ya go over and see can ya beg or borrey all the food the three of us can carry, a little cook vessel and a side of an old tent or some more oilcloths. We need somethin' for a shelter, but somethin' light, and some matches. Be sure to get matches and maybe some light rope and cord. Wouldn't hurt none if we had a extra haversack apiece."

"John, we'd be deserters!"

"We fought four year and watched our friends die to get our freedom. They deserted *us*." As John's anger increased, he dropped his stick and stood straighter. "And now we got to go over to them Yankees that tore up the South and crawl like a beat dog and sign a paper sayin' that we were wrong and then beg for a parole like some criminal? I'm s'posed to kiss the hand that pulled the trigger on the gun that took my hand! Do you think that I'm gonna do that? Not hardly! If the Yankees thank that, then the butter's done slid off their biscuit!"

Matthew said, "If the end is that close, shoudn't we stay till it's settled?"

"No! If the war is over in the next few days, thangs will get clean out of hand right quick. We need to be out of here so we can get a head start before the ruination commences. Some are leavin' ever' day. Ya know thangs won't wait till next Mondee. They gonna sign any day now. We need to done gone by then. If ya'all can get them thangs, I mean to talk to the major. I wouldn't leave without it."

"He'll have you arrested for desertion," Matthew said. "They catch some ever' day."

"We've give 'em four years. I give my right hand. We never had cannon fever. My name's been on the Roll, and yers, too. If there's no hope, I'm agoin' home. But I aim to tell the major before I go. We owe him that much, even if we are givin' up."

Matthew and Billy got a small cook-pot, a worn tent side, some salt pork, a few pones of cornbread, a little meal, a metal box of matches, rope, lanyard cord, and a small axe. When they arrived with the supplies, John was standing in front the major's tent. The officer, sitting on a folding camp chair at a small table, wrote on a piece of paper and handed it to John. He walked around the table, reached out to take John's hand and put his right arm about his shoulder.

John walked back to the other two. "Did ya'all get them thangs?"

"Yes, and we found out that when the generals sign the papers and we sign the parole, it's all over and our army is gone... and our country is gone. They're gonna give us some rations and about a dollar specie and tell us to go home ... best way we can."

"Hallelujah, we can buy us a pair of mules and a wagon when we get there! Folks, when the generals sign them papers, we need to be down the road a piece. Are ya gonna go with me or stay?"

Billy glanced at the tents and then at John," What did the major say?"

"The major said right much. First off, said he was right sorry about how all this come about. The war is might near over and we didn't know it. Lee give up the day before I lost my hand. The word just took a time to get to us. He said that papers about my commission still hadn't come through, even though I been runnin' the company for months. Said he was supposed to be promoted too, but his papers never

come either. Said if he didn't have to stay and speak for
the regiment he'd go with us. He thanked us for our
service till the end. He give me a o-fficial order." He
held out the paper to Matthew and Billy.

April 24, 1865   *1st Lt. John McGinnis*
                                             Cpl. Matthew Owen
                                             Pvt. Billy Deerman
        The above three men are on a mission for this
regiment and may pass picket lines.
        Edward Allen, Major, C.S.A. 55th Alabama Infantry

"This will get us by our lines. Then we're on our
own. And we're not really deserters. We'll be
accounted for at roll call. "Matthew glanced at the
paper and handed it to Billy. He read the words of the
pass and turned it over. On the back was written:

> *Duty has compelled us.*
> *Purpose has sustained us.*
> *Pride has bound us.*
> *Hardship has plagued us.*
> *Victory has shunned us.*
> *If all else be lost, let us hold to honor.*
>   *E.A.*

He studied the words on the back a second time
and handed it to John. He turned away and rubbed at
his eye with his thumb.

"What's our mission?"

"Whatever we want it to be. Mostly we need to
check up on thangs in Canaan County, if we can figger
how to get there. Prob'ly go 'bout the same way we
come. Need to stay away from the towns where
Yankees are. Major helped some. He gimme a little
map."

Matthew looked at the map and nodded, "I've studied on it while we was gettin' these thangs. I'll go, John. I ain't too good at lickin' boots, 'specially Yankees'. I don't think Billy has made up his mind. Is ya leg sound enough to make the trip?"

They looked at Billy staring at the Yankee lines beyond the rows of tattered Confederate tents. After several minutes he said very softly. "Now, we're called on to crawl." He shifted his stick and faced his friends. His knuckles were white and his eyes moist.

"What should we do?" Matthew said. "We oughta be together on this."

Billy turned toward the south horizon. He began again with emotion spilling over at times. "Each man must do what his heart tells him. We could stay and let them deal us what they will. There is no dishonor in that, but there is certainly no honor. My heart says go, and let the Yankees drown in their oaths and papers and rations. I will not sign a paper saying that I gave four years of my life for a cause, which is wrong. I will not sign a lie. My leg hurts, but the pain would be in my heart if I stayed. I think I can keep up."

"Then it's agreed, we'll go! Can we tell some g'bye?"

John leaned on his stick and looked at clusters of men gathered by their tents, waiting for the end. "Most of them folks yonder are fine folks, good friends. One or two of 'em ain't worth ...."

"Ain't worth a fart in a whirlwind," Matthew finished for him.

"True. If they heard we're leavin', they'd strew it ever'where. We best go and say nothin'. If anybody asks, we tell the truth that we are on a secret mission for the major, and got a paper to prove it."

Chapter Twelve – Desperate Journey

> *Once more be hungry and eat;*
> *once more tired and rest;*
> *once more cold and wet*
> *let us sit by the fire*
> *and feel comfort creep over us.*
> *Carlton McCarthy*

John laid out articles on his blanket and packed them in his haversacks. With one hand, he wrapped a Colt Baby Dragoon in an oilcloth along with caps, balls, powder, ramrod, and nipple pick. John glanced up at the other two watching.

"That Yankee didn't need it any more. It's little and light. A new-made left-handed man can hide it and might could use it if he has to. When we head south, we're gonna be in a bad row fa stumps. We can't carry a long gun, but we need some kind of weapon. Wrap them matches in some of this oilcloth like I'm doin' my gun, so we can keep 'em dry."

Matthew nodded and said, "Yer right, John. We'll be on our own. No tellin' what we'll run up on." Matthew tilted his head to read the words on the folded cloth on John's blanket: FOR LIBERTY WE STRIVE.

"John, them are the regimental colors."

"It's not heavy. We followed it four years. Better for us to take the flag than let some Yankee get it. I told the major, if we all get home, he can have it, if he wants it."

Billy nodded his approval. The three loaded their haversacks and placed one strap on each shoulder so that one 'sack hung on the right hip and one on the left. They rolled food and supplies in their blankets and covered them with an oilcloth and tied the ends to make a U-shaped parcel. John fumbled unsuccessfully several minutes and reluctantly let Matthew tie his. They looped the round end over the right shoulder with the blanket roll hanging across their chest and back and the tied end resting on the left hip. They carried a canteen over the right hip. They wore shapeless blue pants, faded tan shirts, and brown-gray shell jackets.

They left in a westerly direction, moving slowly because of illness and injury as well as the burdens they bore. Matthew had just recovered from a bout with the flux. Billy limped and leaned on his stick. John held his stump across his belt and used his stick to try to keep his balance on rough ground. Near the edge of the camp two pickets blocked their path. The nearest one came toward the three. He carried an Enfield in his right hand and had a Remington Army in his belt.

"Lemme walk on ahead," Matthew said. "If he tries to stop us, I'll whup 'em before he can say God with his mouth open."

"No, Matthew, stay back. We'll play by the rules." John leaned his stick against his chest, pulled the pass from his 'sac and handed it to the sentry before he had a chance to speak. The soldier squinted in the morning sun, read the pass, and inspected the three from hats to boots.

"Two war-bags apiece, a blanket and canteen. Maybe somethin' in the blankets. Looks like yer loaded down. Where ya'all agoin'?"

"You know better than that, Abner. Ask the major. We can't say." Abner blinked, said nothing, handed the pass back and waved them on.

They arrived at the rail line as a train was being fired up. They slowed to measure the cars by steps, then walked as fast as Billy's limping would allow down the track about a mile, piled brush on one rail, retraced their steps about five car lengths and hid in the bushes by the track. When the train loomed in the curve to the east John whispered as if those on the train might hear, " Ya'all be ready when the time comes."

The locomotive came toward them at the usual ten to twelve miles an hour, puffing a stream of black smoke and trailing steam. A coal car, a car filled with men and one packed with tools and supplies swayed and rattled by the men huddled in the bushes. The train screeched and moved slower while the cowcatcher pushed the brush aside. All eyes were on the track. Matthew climbed in first, and then pulled the other two into an empty car at the end of the train. They moved away from the side and lay on the floor with their head on their 'sacks.

As the train picked up speed, Matthew looked out at the trees moving against the sky. "It still don't seem right. We're agoin' west but a little to the north."

"The major told me the line turns south after a mile or so, and that's where we wanta go."

The rhythmic click and rumble of the wheels lulled them to sleep.

John woke as Matthew shook him. The car was silent. "How long we been stopped?"

"I don't rightly know, John. I walked toward the engine to see what was goin' on. This is a work crew. Ahead of us, the track is tore up. It's in bad shape. They ain't gonna get it fixed 'fore dark. Might not fix it tomorrow."

"How many soldiers they got?"

"Not a one. That's a colored crew up ahead with a white foreman carryin' a shotgun. He's not army. He's just wearin' work clothes. Some more men come by walkin' down the track goin' south like us, and he didn't say pea turkey to 'em."

"We may as well go, if we can get Billy up. We'll walk the track 'til we come to a town, then take a road."

They walked until nightfall and began again the next day. On the second day, they found a solitary walker going their way. The men stopped in a shade to rest and talk at midday. Isaac Bell was older than John, with a hawk-like nose and small squinting eyes with permanent wrinkles to the sides, even in shadows. He had thrown away his hat and tied a butternut colored cloth band around his forehead and ears to protect them from the sun. It covered most of the streaks of gray in his brown hair. His beard was full like the others, but his voice was high pitched for a man and it was pinched like his eyes. He was a gaunt farmer, stooped from the years behind the plow, recently transferred to the 55th from a disbanded Georgia unit. The other three had only seen him at a distance.

After introductions and a little discussion about early departure, John said, "Well now, sounds like ya got a day's start on us. We tried to ride a ways on the train. The tracks are all tore up, so that's might near a lost cause. We're just gonna have to walk. It's right at five hund'erd mile to Canaan County, as the crow flies -- more the way we have to go on all them dog-legg-ed roads. Accordin' to my way of thankin', at fifteen -- twenty mile a day we can make it in a month if thangs go good -- six weeks if we get slowed up some. That is, we can make it if we can get somethin' to eat along the way. We couldn't carry thirty days rations on our back, even if we coulda got 'em."

Isaac nodded. "That's the way I figger it too. I got to get home to get a crop in or the family wont have nothin' to eat this winter. When the war commenced, I volunteered and jined up with this here army. Now I just sort of ...well...un-jined. The army ought to understand that. The Confederates were trying to un-unite with the Union. Hit's might nigh the same thing. I'll go with ya, and be glad fer the company. I will have to cut north a-ways this side of the Alabama line though." He pointed a finger at John. "Ain't that a cavalry hat?"

"I lost my old hat when I got shot. Matthew give me this. In that last big fight some of them horse soldiers went down right in front of the company -- musta been 'fore you come. We put 'em under and Matthew saved the hats -- boots and britches too. It was either this or one of them stove lid hats that are plain no 'count when the sun is up."

A few minutes into their walk the next day, they heard a commotion ahead. There were desperate shouts, stamping of hooves, cry of mules, and constant barking and snarling. They ran over the rise in the road to see a pack of dogs around a team and wagon. The mules were tied to a tree and a man had fallen at the side. He was striking at the dogs with a small stick, but several had bitten him and were tearing at his clothes. The four ran to the melee. John handed his stick to Matthew and Isaac found his own. Three men began beating the dogs back. More than twenty bird dogs, coon dogs, great deer-hunting hounds and guard dogs circled the group, and several together rushed in to attack the man lying by the road. They were not intimidated by soldiers with sticks.

John snatched his Dragoon from the haversack, steadied his left arm with the right, and fired at the dogs nearest the men. The first shot kicked up dirt beyond the pack. The second shot and third wounded dogs that the men with sticks finished off. The fourth knocked down an enormous red dog. The great creature tumbled, then jumped up with a snarl and fled with the rest of the pack to the shelter of the woods.

The men helped the traveler sit up and used their canteen water to clean his wounds. Billy calmed the mules.

When the man was able catch his breath, he said, "I was right proud to see you folks come up. I think they would've got me. My name's Luther Hill." He reached out a hand.

Matthew grasped his hand and pulled him up. "Where did them dogs come from? I never seen nothin' like that."

"Yankees tore up folks' houses and run 'em off their land. People was gone or dead and the dogs lived. There wasn't nobody to feed 'em so they banded together in packs to wander the countryside. Some follered the Yankees, pickin' up scraps. Don't reckon the Confederates left scraps. Yankees run the dogs off, and now droves of 'em are all over, pullin' down game, stock and even folks.

I been to trade fer some cotton seed and stopped to rest the mules. I reckon ya'all are tryin' to get home. Tell me yer names and we'll go to the house and have a bite of breakfast. That's all the pay I can offer ya for what ya done."

The walkers enjoyed the luxury of riding in a wagon for three miles before arriving at a weathered clapboard house. They washed at the back of the house and entered the kitchen to meet Mrs. Hill. They gathered around a table set with real dishes, knives, forks, and spoons and even coffee cups. As they were adjusting their chairs, Mrs. Hill brought a steaming pot to the table. Matthew said, "Ya'all got coffee -- real coffee? I can't hardly believe it!"

"This here is Confederate coffee. We make ours with real thin slices of parched sweet taters." She filled the cups and set before them platters of hot biscuits, ham, and scrambled eggs. As she sat down she offered them a bowl with a spoon. "Sugar, anyone?"

"Sugar -- real sugar?"

"No, we just call it that. We've not seen coffee or sugar in four years. We used honey 'til it ran out. This here is dried figs all ground up. Tastes right good in tater coffee." As they ate, they forgot that the coffee was not real.

After the platters were emptied, the last stains on the plates were sopped clean, and many cups of Confederate coffee drunk, Luther said, "Me and the wife fed lots of folks fer a spell, but we can't keep on 'cause we just don't have the food this early in the year. Ya'all just ate the last of our ham. Can't kill a hog. We got no salt to cure it. What's in the bowl there is from the smoke-house floor. It's not too white, but tastes salty. Not enough of it to do more'n a side and maybe a shoulder. This spring we've fed all sorts goin' ever which away, even a crazy man carryin' a drum."

John sat straight up in his chair, "A what? When was that? What'd he look like?"

"Oh, I 'spec it was two -- maybe three weeks ago. Said he was, but I knew he wasn't no soldier. He was too old with all that white beard and hair 'cept one dark streak. And that drum? He wouldn't let it out of his sight, and it tore up, too. Hole blowed clean through both sides -- prob'ly a musket ball from the size of it. Tried to ask him about it, but he wouldn't say nar' word. He was right peculiar. We was scared of him, but we fed him anyway."

John stared through the window to the south. In his mind's eye he saw the determined old man trudging southward with a drum strapped to his back. John spoke softly as if to no one in particular, "Be not forgetful to entertain strangers: for some have entertained angels unawares."

"What?"

"Oh, nothin', Mr. Hill, he was a good man -- foot-sore and full of trouble -- but a good man who wouldn't hurt nobody. He was a soldier and one of the best men I know. I don't doubt for a minute that he will make it home with that drum."

The next day they met the Yankees on the bridge and that afternoon were drenched by a storm. Three days later they left Billy at the spring.

The three were glum as they made their way home again. Men streamed south, and attitudes changed. People in the small towns had heard that Johnston surrendered on the 26th, and some wanted to avoid bitter memories of a lost cause. Some had no food to share with the flood of men who passed their door. Others feared bearded scarecrows spawned by war and burned by wind and sun. Canaan seemed an unreachable goal to men on foot with holes in their boots, no food, and ragged clothes. Some of the roads they trod were marred by the relentless traffic of the armies. Their rate of travel was not what they hoped for.

They began to be passed by other southbound travelers -- not walkers, but riders. The first group had a major, a captain and two lieutenants from a Georgia regiment. They rode horses with saddlebags in place and swords at their sides. They threw up a hand as they passed.

The Major nodded to the men. "These are sad days, boys."

After the officers came common soldiers riding mules and workhorses. Most were horse soldiers, artillerymen or drivers of wagons who managed to take an animal at the end. A wagon passed so crowded with men that the mules struggled to pull the load. Some men in the wagons were missing limbs. Some had eyes and faces covered with soiled rags.

Late one day, a rider named Robert, stopped and shared a meager meal with the three. He tied his mule out to graze as the men watched. Just under the jawbone there were swellings on the animal's neck and open sores on its skin.

"What's wrong with yer mule?" Isaac asked. "She looks right porely."

Robert shrugged and frowned. "Don't know. She was the best I could do there at the end. Yankees took ever'thing else. I hope she makes it home. I sure need 'er to work with my mules." The next morning, the mule carrying Robert walked slowly, but still faster than men on foot.

The weeks wore on and late one day as John, Matthew, and Isaac stopped to rest, they saw a long line of people crossing the evening sun. These northbound walkers were in the open, but the three south-walkers were hidden, waiting and watching behind bushes in the shade of a white oak. The column moved along slowly, their shadows flowing up the slope toward the trees.

John and his friends saw men and women, young and old, and several children. Two women had babies strapped to their chest. Mules that had seen better days pulled a battered wagon with wheels askew, laden with bundles, plows, garden tools, tables, and chairs, all secured loosely with ropes. One long bundle wrapped in a quilt lay behind the driver in an empty space. Women trailing behind the wagon wore tattered print dresses and had cloths tied about their heads. Men had patched pants and coarse shirts. Most wore hats in various states of disrepair and carried packs on their backs. Many of the women held bundles in their arms or on their heads. They walked single file and by twos and threes. Two small spotted barking dogs brought up the dusty rear. The tall man in the lead carried a shotgun. Several toward the back of the group were singing:

Way over in Egypt Land, You shall gain the day!

March on and you shall gain the victory!
March on and you shall gain the day!
This is the year of Jubilee, You shall gain the victory!
The Lord has set his people free, You shall gain the day!

John's stick hit the ground with a thump, scattering dry leaves at his feet. Isaac jumped, then said, "John, ya see that gun?"

"I see it. I'm not used to seein' 'em carryin' guns, but times they are achangin'. I got my hand in my war-bag."

The men in the front of the line hesitated when they saw the south-walkers in the shadows. The words of the singers trailed off and stopped. The man carrying the gun took it from his shoulder and held it across his chest with a finger on the trigger. They stopped to speak to each other, pointed toward the three in the shade, looked around to see no other route for the wagon, and resumed their march along the road. The group moved slower and slower until the first man was a few feet away. The marchers stopped and several toward the back dropped their bundles and sought shade. The eyes of those in front were fixed on the south-walkers.

The man in the lead adjusted his grip on the shotgun, looked from one man to the other and then directly at John. "Evenin', white folks. Ya'all musta come from da wah? Ya goin' home?"

"We're tryin'"

"Whure ya goin'?"

"Canaan County, Alabama. Where ya'all goin'?"

"We free now and kin go anywhur we wanta go."

"We heard that. So, where ya goin'?"

"Don't rightly know. Tol' us down in Macon they's givin' forty acres and a mule to colored at da Jubilee up noth. Ya'all know whur that be?"

"Don't know nothin' about that. Times like this, I figger folks ought to stay home where they were raised up. Food is hard to come by on the road."

"Yassah, we done fount that out. Uh – rah – jus' lookin' at ya, don't look like ya'all got nothin' to spare neither?"

The three shook their heads. The tall man with the gun said something to the man beside him and then motioned to those behind. Men and women picked up their burdens and the group began their walk again.

The man with the gun turned to John, "We best be goin'. Sister Jenny's old daddy been right sick two – three days and he done passed -- middle da afte'noon. We got to have a buryin' soon's we find a restin' place."

John nodded. "Hope ya'all make it to wherever ya're goin'. They's water about three mile up ahead, just south of the road. House is tore up, but the well is good."

The man put the shotgun on back his shoulder, "We thank ya. It's dry—dry--dry, way ya'all agoin. Not even a puddle in a wagon rut fa miles."

The men and women of the line were covered with sweat and dust, but they smiled and waved as they passed. The three touched their hats and nodded. The singers began again, livelier than before. In the middle of the column, a man with a deep booming voice sang the first words and others joined in the refrain.

Gonna lay down my sword and shield,
> *down by the riverside,*
> *down by the riverside,*
> *down by the riverside.*
Gonna lay down my sword and shield
> *down by the riverside,*
> *Ain't gonna study war no more.*

Matthew stared at the singers and said, "That's 'bout like I feel, too."

The column stopped and the singing ceased. Several men rushed to adjust the load, which had shifted when the wagon hit a deep rut. The north walkers moved on and the singing resumed.

I'm bound for the promised land.
I'm bound for the promised land.
Oh who will come and go with me?
I'm bound for the promised land.

The ragged column of people and barking dogs disappeared around the bend in the road, the sounds of the singers faded, and the dust slowly settled.

"Least we know where we're goin' an they got no i-dee," John said. "Pore folks. They got 'bout as much chance findin' the end of a rainbow as a Jubilee where they're givin' away land. Truth is they're chasin' somethin' not real." He brought out his pistol, wrapped it in the oilcloth, placed it back in his 'sack, and stared at the bend in the road. "Leastwise, I hope they're not gonna take our farms and give 'em to colored. None of us had slaves."

"Wonder whur them darkies got the wagon and gun and thangs."

"Isaac, they might ask where we got what we got."

"We worked four year fer what little we carryin'. Hit's pitiful enough pay."

Isaac turned to see John's eyes fixed on him. "Oh, I reckon I see what yer athankin'."

John said, "The day's 'bout gone. Why don't we camp here the night. Maybe we can find water tomorrow."

No one offered help in the small community they passed the next morning. In mid-afternoon they walked a desolate road. Years of wagon ruts and heavy rains had cut deep into the clay making high banks lined with trees and brush on each side. They spoke in whispers, in fear of what might what might be unseen above. As they stepped in silence, they heard a voice. "How's the war agoin', boys?"

The three looked for the man who spoke. The voice seemed to come from above. The sun shown around a vague shape in the center of blazing light shining through an opening between the trees. Matthew shielded his eyes. "I can't tell where he is at. Is that a man standin' yonder in the sun?"

John held up his hat to the light and squinted. "Walk up a step or two. Maybe we can see a little better." Low branches blocked some rays and the form became clearer. They could see that the sun shown around the shape of a man holding a long object, which looked to be a rifle.

"Ya'all goin' the wrong way. Ya're not runnin' away are ya?"

Matthew whispered. "If he's one of them folks that catches deserters, and he don't know the war is over, we are in bad trouble. He's above us with a gun."

"Nothin' to do but try the truth." John squinted up at the form in the sun. "Sir, the war's over. We're atryin' to get home."

The shadow in the sun moved the long thing, but did not speak for a full minute. "Over? Surely we didn't lose. Did we sign a peace treaty?"

"No sir, we give up complete. *We* didn't. Them generals did. They never asked us."

The voice from above hesitated again, then said, "Walk on down that road a piece, and ya'll come to a place where ya can come up to where I'm at."

After a whispered discussion, they did as he directed and came to a path sloping upward. They climbed the bank and turned east to meet the shape in the sun. They walked around the last bush and came upon a man with white hair and beard. They now saw how old and stooped he was. He leaned on a hoe.

"I'm Lafayette Higgins. Most folks call me 'Fate'. You boys got names?"

"I'm John McGinnis. This here is Isaac Bell and Matthew Owen."

He studied them several minutes. There were snags and tears in their clothes. Hats drooped like the face under the brim. Shirts had spots from sweat. John still had dark bloodstains across his shirt and britches. "Ya'all look to be in bad shape. Could ya use somethin' to eat?"

"Yes sir. We would be right proud to have anything ya could spare. We'll eat and be on our way."

"Walk that path toward the house and we'll talk about it." He followed the three as they went single file. "I've not been to town in a month or more. I didn't know about the war. It's hard to b'lieve. If our army has give up, what'll happen to us?"

"I reckon them Yankees will do as they please," Matthew said. "That's why we need to get home. Our army is gone. There's nothin' between us and the Yankees. They'll be after our land next."

They walked past a large garden, small fields of corn, and a cutover wheat field. The other land was grown up in weeds, brush, and small trees. Arriving at a cabin almost hidden in a cluster of oak and sweetgum trees, they found yards swept clean and two straight chairs sitting close together on a neat front porch. Others were tilted backwards toward the wall. The house was smaller, but much like John's. They walked around the side of the house to a washstand by the well.

"Wash off in one of them tubs there and come on in the house. I'll tell the wife to fix extra."

"Thank ya kindly," John said. "But there's not enough water in that tub to make us fitten to go in your house. If it's not too much trouble, just hand the food out and we'll eat in the yard. We don't want to be no bother." Fate Higgins said nothing and disappeared down the dogtrot.

Almost an hour later, Mrs. Higgins came from the house with steaming platters in both hands and set them on the wash bench. She wore a brown print dress and an apron. She did not bother to wear a bonnet over her white hair and squinted in the afternoon sun. Her face was faded like her dress, and shadows filled every wrinkle. When introduced, she nodded to the men and said little. Fate brought plates, knives, and forks. The three men sat on overturned buckets and tubs pulled up to the bench. They stared at full platters of cured ham, greens, new potatoes, cornbread and a pitcher of buttermilk.

John slapped Isaac's hand as he reached for the bread before Fate asked the blessing. They bowed their heads and John closed his eyes. With the sounds of plates, the warm smell of foods and words of thanks, he was home. He opened his eyes to see tattered britches and knew that Canaan County was far away. They raised their heads after the few words were said. John glanced sideways, stuck an elbow in Isaac's ribs and whispered, "Isaac! Wait 'til they pass the platters." They tried to eat slowly and with manners, but it was impossible when they saw food on their plate. The Higgins insisted on eating with them and asked about the war and spoke of fears and hopes for the future.

Food worked wonders on the spirits of the tired men.

Matthew asked, "Just you two live here?"

"Our only son, his wife, and their younguns lived here and they was gonna take over the place. War come and he left out fer the army. Didn't hear much fa a spell. Then, they was some fightin' just to the east. Few days later, folks come bringin' him home in a wagon, all shot up. His wife and the two of us done the best we could. He healed up some, then come down with the continued fever. The doc come an give him what quinine he had. About two weeks later he died. His wife stayed a few months, and then left out fer her folks' house. Took the grandchilun with 'er. We've not seen nor heard from 'em since."

He looked away and was silent for several minutes. Fate looked down at the table and used his fork to toy with a scrap of food on his plate. "We don't try to put in a crop no more. We have a garden, grow a little wheat and corn and a hog or two." Fate's face seemed to sag and he looked older. Gray eyes were moist as he stared toward the setting sun.

"The two of us are waitin' our turn to go." He turned back to the three. "We are right proud to have holp ya get to yer folks."

They thanked their hosts and picked up their 'sacs to leave. Fate held up his hand." I've studied ya right close. Ya'all are in no shape to leave right here at dark. Sleep in the barn tonight, and in the mornin' I'll see if I can squeeze a egg or so out of them hens. We'll feed ya breakfast, and then ya can be on yer way."

John and Matthew slept on loose hay and Isaac on the shucks in the corncrib, a luxury to them. Their snoring kept the cows awake.

Fate was good as his word. For breakfast, they ate eggs and a mountain of biscuits and gravy. They filled their canteens, loaded their 'sacs with left-overs, shook hands with the Higgins, and thanked them again and again.

"I'm sorta 'shamed to say this," John said. "But with all sorts passin' through, ya'all don't need to be so trustin'. The three of us wouldn't do nothin', but some that come might when they see two folks up in years by theirself -- ever which side they're from."

Fate smiled for the first time. "Ya don't live long as I have without learnin' to judge folks right quick. Ya might could remember that I didn't stand too clost when we first talked, and I had a hand in my pocket. Only thang our son left me, when he died out, was this, and I carry it ever' where I go." He flinched as he pulled out a Colt pocket revolver. It had a short barrel with no sight to hang in clothing and was even smaller than John's gun.

"I wouldn't have said nar' word to ya if they was more than three in that road. I carry this little gun in case I see some no'ccount folks. I was in a war, too. We had flintlocks back then. Thought I'd never get used to these here guns. I know ya meant well. Thank ya for thinkin' of us. We'll be careful."

John looked at Fate's arm as he talked. When he brought out the little gun, his sleeve fell back showing a scarred withered forearm. "That come from the war?"

"I got shot in the battle of New Or-leans, weeks after the peace treaty was signed – we just didn't know it. I thought I was ruint. I moped about fer a spell, but I been able to make it these years."

"I see. Good thang it's ya left hand. I lost...."

"I'm left handed -- or I was. Had to learn to do everthang with my right, except shoot this little gun. Can't aim with my right eye. I'm slow and it hurts some, but most times I hit my mark."

John nodded and said nothing. He stared at Fate's arm again and then his own. The three said good-by one more time, walked south on the path, down the bank to the road, and moved rapidly west. They did not look back and tempt themselves to stay another day.

Chapter Thirteen -- Friends, Enemies, and Renegades

They moved on, catching fish or bullfrogs when they crossed a stream, poking around empty houses for forgotten dried fruit or beans, and searching forsaken gardens for volunteer garlic, turnip greens, onions, or potatoes. Once they made a stew of a large rattlesnake. They ate lamb's quarter, sassafras buds, poke sallet, wild onions and garlic until they could hardly stand to look at them.

As they picked over a meal of the greens one night, John said, "At least we don't have scorbutus. Maybe General Lee was right. I sure would hate to have that –whatever it is."

"After eatin' this mess, if we coulda got close enough to the Yankees to blow our breath in their face, we might have won the war," Matthew said.

The three men spent most of one day building a raft for a river crossing. Isaac announced that the shore they reached was Georgia. They rested that night and began their daily walk the next morning. Heat was an increasing factor as the days of May slipped by. Canteens were always dry when they found a stream or spring. At the end of some days there was no water to fill them.

They entered a remote area with few occupied houses, though they were now north of Sherman's path. As they walked the old corduroy road, Isaac said, "I see smoke yonder." We ain't eat in a spell. Let's cut to the north and see what's there. I believe I'm hungry enough to beg fer a handout."

Smoke drifted from one chimney of the weathered board dwelling. Recently plowed fields skirted the sides of the house, though weeds in the front yard were waist high, almost hiding a broken plow and a brush broom leaning against the side of the building. Dogs that left the porch to meet them had great chests with skin stretched over jutting ribs. Their bark had a hollow ring.

The men did not go near the house, but stopped on the main road. Isaac cupped his mouth with his hands and called out, "You folks in the house there! War is over. We're from the 55th Alabama, and are atryin' to get home. We sure could use somethin' to eat -- just anythang."

The dogs continued to bark and run forward, snarl, and slink back when John raised his stick. Isaac called out again. This time the door opened wide enough for a gun barrel. A man's voice said, "Git off our land or I'll sic the dogs on ya and give ya a load of shot!"

John said, "Come on, Isaac. I'm not worried about them dogs. Puff of wind would take 'em out. That gun is apt to be loaded."

As they walked away, Matthew turned back to shout, "Thanks far yer hospitality. Ya'all come see us sometime." He mumbled, "Sorry no 'count goober-grabbin' scalawags." He jerked his head around to look at Isaac, "Now I don't mean that about *all* Georgia folks."

Isaac shook his head. "I can't dispute ya about that man. Fella won't give a starvin' man a cold biscuit ain't much."

"He don't have to feed us or even let us come on his land if he don't want to," John said. "I've never had to beg before. Maybe we're doin' it all wrong."

A mile down the road they came to another house. The thin stream of smoke from the chimney marked it as occupied. Fields were grown up in weeds. The yard had been swept and a small garden grew north of the house. A single dog barked as Isaac began to call out the request for food.

Matthew grabbed Isaac's shoulder and stepped ahead. "Lemme try it this time." He didn't need to put his hands to the sides of his mouth. His voice boomed out, "You folks in the house! We're from the 55th Alabama and we're tryin' to get home. We're might near starved to death -- don't believe we could make it 'nother mile without somethin' to eat. Could ya spare anythang?" And then in a quieter tone toward his friends, "Is that pitiful enough? It's not far from true."

As before, nothing happened until the second request. The door opened just a crack. A woman's voice called out, "Get in here, Sergeant!" The door opened wider for the dog to go into the house. Through the opening, the men had a glimpse an older woman with a shotgun standing behind the one at the door. The opening changed to a crack. The young woman answered, "We don't have nothin' to give out to strangers." The door slammed shut. There were no other dwellings in sight. Their hunger had not changed.

John moved closer so that his voice could be heard. "Ma'am, most likely ya've got a man in the war. If he's alivin', he's tryin' to get home. Ya can't do nothin' far him. I sure hope somebody along the way feeds him."

The three turned to leave. The door opened barely an inch. The younger woman said," Wait right there." Several minutes later, the woman reached an arm out the door and shoved a cloth and a pan onto the floor of the dogtrot.

"Leave the pan. " Her voice was halting and husky. "Ya can take the cloth. Some is yesterday's leavin's. That's all we got. Mama's holdin' a gun on ya. Take it and go." Isaac and John walked across the

porch and one step into the dogtrot. They emptied the
pan into their own and picked up the cloth.

As they straightened up with their food and
turned to leave, they saw the woman behind the voice.
She wore a faded yellow print dress with long sleeves
and looked to be in her early twenties. She was pale,
blond, and rail thin. Her face was wet with tears as she
held back a small child trying to look at the men.

The three stopped in the dense shade of a poplar
tree and dropped their 'sacks and blankets. Matthew
said, "Isaac, what'd we get from the pan?"

"They's yesterday's beans and some carrots --
some cooked carrots. Just look at 'em! Hit's been a
coon's age since I seen any. The rag has got a few
biscuits. They're still warm from breakfast, but this
here part of a pone of cornbread is a little dry -- prob'ly
from yesterday."

"I don't care when it was cooked. Heat them
beans and carrots and we'll eat like kings." Matthew
built a small fire and heated the vegetables, beans on
one side of the pot and carrots on the other. They
divided the hot food and the bread and sat around the
fire. As Isaac emptied the last spoon into his cup,
Matthew said, "John, ya give her some pain."

"Pain and hurt was already there. I brought it to
mind." John looked down at his portion of food. "I
mean to say words over this 'fore I eat." They bowed
their heads. There were no sounds but the crackle of
flames and shifting of the sticks in the fire.

"Lord, wherever that woman's man is, we ask
ya to see after him -- and maybe somebody could feed
him like she done us. We don't know his name, but
You do. Thank ya for this food. Amen." They ate, but
not like kings. They were not bound by rules of
etiquette.

One night in June they slept in a barn near a
burned-out house. At first good light Isaac drew their

breakfast from the well. The three men drank their meal of water, picked up their haversacks and began their daily walk, with the sun at their backs. After the coolness of the heavy dew of night, warmth soothed aching muscles. Each time they passed a fork in the road, fewer Confederates walked within their sight, until finally the road was deserted but for the three. They passed abandoned fields and destroyed homes. They saw no game and the streams were empty, as if a curse had been placed on the land.

About an hour into the trek, Isaac said, "I know we're a ways into Georgia. Hard to tell just where we are at. Sherman didn't leave no road signs." They nodded and walked a little slower. They had fallen behind their schedule, but no one spoke of it. The day passed with nothing in their mouths but canteen water. They stopped for the night by a small branch. There were no bullfrogs. Tiny minnows twisted to the light to show a flash of silver. Others along the bottom had a touch of red.

Matthew stared at the fish when he gave up hunting frogs. "The whole school of them minnas wouldn't make a mouthful for a midget. Anyhow, silversides and redhorses might nigh rot from the water to the pan."

The three built a fire from habit and for comfort in the cool evening. They sat and stared at the flames and listened to the crickets. Something moved in the bushes by the branch. In the distance, a Whip-poor-will called. Isaac stood up, shivering. "That's uh...uh lonesome sound." He added to the fire.

"It's a shame they   ain't no Yankees about," Matthew said. "All through the war if we got hungry enough we just drove 'em back a little and took their goods."

Isaac nodded and John said, "With one little bitty gun and a stick, we wouldn't drive nobody back." Their empty stomachs complained, but they slept.

Just after daylight, Matthew woke the others with a whisper. "They's a rabbit yonder. I'm gonna slip around and see can I run him toward ya".

John whispered, "Lemme go. You swing a stick better than me." John crept cat-like on elbows and knees. A breeze rustled leaves to cover what little sound he made. Every few hops, the rabbit stopped, sat on his haunches, wiggled his nose and jerked his head from side to side. His attention was directed to a large moving shape against the sun. John squinted against the brightness. It looked like a dog—a big red dog. John stood when he was beyond the rabbit. The dog ran into the sunrise. The rabbit fled toward the two at the branch, turned and ran along the bank. Matthew threw a walnut sized rock that struck the animal a glancing blow, knocking him into the water. He floated downstream, kicking violently.

Three men plunged into the water with shouts of, "Don't let him get away! Grab 'em! He's a big 'un! If he gets to the bank he's gone for sure!" After much splashing and shouting, Matthew caught the struggling rabbit by his hind legs and swung him so that his head struck a rock at the edge of the branch. Three men stood with water dripping from them, looking at the limp soggy animal. The rabbit trembled when Matthew picked him up. Now the men trembled. Before them, hanging from Matthew's hand, was the first food they had seen in days.

John reached in his haversack. The knife he took from its sheath and gave to Matthew had a six-inch blade with hand-whittled handle. The guard was an iron plate with the end curled toward the hand on the sharp side of the blade and away from the hand on the other. Ambrose said that he was too old to go to war, so he would send a blade from his blacksmith shop in the hand of kin.

Matthew skinned and dressed the rabbit with great ceremony. He threw the guts far into the field to the east. He said, "I don't know 'bout ya'all, but I'm not quite hungry enough for rabbit chitlins... not yet anyways." He cut the rabbit into small portions and put them in a vessel of water. John and Isaac watched every move.

"It's a pity we got no grease and flour. We could cook up some slosh. All we can do is cook it right slow and have us a stew."

They built up the fire and set the pot on stones. The men busied themselves with their morning activities. Each rolled up his blanket and ground cloth and tied the ends to make a loop to fit over a shoulder. Matthew offered to roll John's blanket.

John said, "I thank ya for the offer, but I best be learnin' to do with what I got left. They'll come a day when yer not around." Matthew threw rocks at bushes, trees, and floating leaves and when John wasn't looking tightened his blanket roll.

Isaac sat by the fire and watched the pot as bubbles began. John unwrapped his pistol, turned it over slowly, wiped the surface, and polished a small stain on the brass trigger guard. With a ramrod he found each load in place. He pulled back the hammer of the small gun with his left hand and rotated the cylinder with his right forearm and checked the caps as they passed the opening on the right. One nipple was empty. He carefully placed it under the hammer.

Isaac turned from the pot and watched closely. "Why no cap on that one?"

"I just might drop it or hit the hammer and shoot the gun when I didn't aim to. I lose one shot, but I figger if I need more than four, I'm gone anyway." He practiced with his left hand, pulling the gun from various places and aiming it with a thumb on the hammer. At times, he had dry-fired it on a spent cap to convince himself that he could pull a trigger. The day after they left the Higgins's house he wasted a shot to satisfy himself that he could fire the gun and hit his mark in close quarters. He did not have Fate's choice. He turned his body and head slightly to the left, supported the gun with his stump and aimed with his right eye. His pull was slow and the shot not quite on target, but there was no powder for more practice.

Isaac said, "John, ya check that little ol' toy gun ever' day like yer lookin' for the war to commence agin. Hit ain't big enough to kill a gopher, noway"

John wrapped the Baby Dragoon and put it away in his 'sack. "Yes, I do. A gun that won't fire is worse than no gun atall. It'll get ya killed. If we was to need it, we might need it bad. Course, we need a good hand to hold it."

Whatever they were doing, their gnawing stomachs brought them back at short intervals to watch the bubbling pot and sniff the increasing aroma. Matthew said, "When ya're down wind by the branch, ya can 'bout taste that rabbit. I may drown, my mouth is waterin' so."

John looked up and saw a flicker of movement on the horizon. He stood for a better view. "Folks, we got company: maybe three men leadin' some kinda beast -- looks like a mule. They're movin' right slow, but headed right towards us." The other two stood and looked across the branch. "They're movin' east, not likely our side. I don't see no colors." They forgot the rabbit stew and watched the moving shapes grow larger.

Matthew said, "They're goin' the wrong way. I can't make out no uniform or mark on 'em. Looks like they got on some Yankee and some Southern thangs.

That pore mule is might near broke down. Look at him stagger. Don't look like he will make it long."

Isaac said, "Ya reckon they might could be ours from out west?"

The three were closer now. John spoke in a low voice, "They've spread out like they're lookin' to worry somebody. I don't doubt they've seen our smoke. The one to the left is carryin' a long gun. The man in the middle has a pistol. It's big, but I can't make out what it is. Most likely they's four if not five shots there. That's a little bitty long gun -- might be a Spencer. If it is, he could shoot us twicet apiece and not reload."

"I see 'em," Matthew said. "And the one to the right has a blade...right heavy...looks like one of them short swords. Look at that pitiful mule. They have beat his hin' end 'till it has bled down his side. He just can make it. We best move out of the open. We don't know what we're apt to get into. Let's back up a ways from the bank. They's a big tree down back yonder and cover if we need it."

When John passed his 'sack, he stooped down and reached in for an instant. As they were slowly easing up the bank, the three strangers moved faster than expected and arrived on the opposite side of the branch.

Long Gun raised the rifle and in a rasping voice said, "That's far enough. You three stand right where you are. You over there, I mean for you to stop, too." He pointed the gun at John. He stopped and turned part way around with his right side toward the branch. Long Gun looked at the nub with a red scar hanging from the sleeve and moved the gun toward Matthew. The six stood and stared at each other. The branch ran clear, the minnows played, the pot bubbled, smoke drifted across the branch, and the smells grew.

Pistol dropped the bridle and struck the mule with a heavy stick. The animal flinched, crossed the branch, staggered at the water's edge, then walked stiffly to the top of the rise and stood as if he could go no farther. The three strangers waded the water without a word and stopped on the eastern bank and stared at the three beyond the steaming pot.

Long Gun stood to the left a few feet in front of Matthew. He was the tallest of the three and wore a Yankee Cavalry hat pulled low, shading his face and hiding his eyes. Hair hung down his neck -- straight and crow-black. Stubble on his face said that he had shaved recently. His pants were blue and his shirt came from neither North nor South. As he talked, a scar on his chin pulled down the corner of his right lip, showing yellow teeth. One was tall and pointed.

Pistol stood in front of Isaac. The squat man with flushed bloated features wore a Confederate hat over dirty blond hair and beard. His pants and shirt were blue. John faced Short Sword, in butternut shirt and gray pants -- the thinnest of the three. His beard was rounded and short. Tufts of red hair stuck out from his uncovered head and sheltered his ears. He frowned and squinted in the sun. All had clothing in good repair and looked well fed for the times. Each carried a canteen and a weapon, but nothing else.

Long Gun wrinkled his nose and glanced at the pot. "Pretty good smelling pot you have there. We haven't eaten since noon yesterday."

John said, "We ain't eat in three days -- maybe four." Long Gun kept the Spencer pointed at the three with his finger on the trigger and thumb on the hammer -- first at one man, then the other. Pistol dropped his mule whip and held his hand on the handle of the gun in his belt. Short Sword gripped the hilt of his blade -- his left hand -- squinting until his eyes were slits, all the while leaning forward, stealing up the bank in slow creeping steps, never taking his eyes off John. The branch ran muddy, the minnows fled, and the pot bubbled away.

Long Gun said, "We mean to have that stew. You can watch us eat, if you like."

Matthew clenched his fists. " We ain't gonna stand by and watch ya eat our food and us astarvin'! We worked hard for that rabbit! You're not takin' it! Get your own rabbit!"

"I was hoping you would say that." He smiled a crooked smile. "We can arrange it so you won't have to watch." He swung his rifle directly toward Matthew and pulled the hammer to full cock. The sharp metallic noise was harsh and penetrating in the morning air. The opening of the barrel suddenly looked huge. Three men watched his finger tighten.

In the split second that the cocking sound reached John's ear, he let out a yell -- one he hadn't used since early in the war, when Confederates were charging the Unions and pushing them back. Long Gun swung the rifle from Matthew to John and pulled the trigger. As he yelled, John stooped and reached toward his left boot. He heard the shot and felt the jolt and burning pain in his right shoulder as he brought up the Dragoon with his left hand. He staggered back one step, steadied the barrel with his stump and fired. The bullet struck Long Gun in the neck and he fell, gurgling, strangling, and waving his arms.

John swung the gun toward Pistol. The short man frantically dug at his weapon with both hands. His second shot struck Pistol's chest. John jerked the gun toward Short Sword, but the creeping man had moved farther right, to the shade of a blackgum tree. John saw the blur of the blade and drew back. The swishing-smacking blow and jarring pain in his cheek knocked his head backward. Short Sword stepped closer to get another swing. Blood spurted from John's cheek and flooded one eye. He sank to his knees with his pistol barrel in the dirt. John forced his eyes open and tried to lift the gun. He saw the raised sword falling like an axe and closed his eyes.

John heard a thud and a bursting sound, as if a watermelon had been dropped. He strained to open his left eye and saw Long Gun, Pistol, and Short Sword lying on the bank. Long Gun gurgled and bubbled and writhed about, clawing at the ground. Pistol had a wound in the center of his chest. His hand gripped the gun handle. Still eyes looked to the sky through flowing water. Short Sword had a small bleeding wound on his forehead and his temple was caved in. He and his weapon lay at the water's edge. The branch streamed red.

Matthew and Isaac were at John's side in an instant. They took off John's shirt and jerked cloths from around their neck to put pressure on his wounds. Matthew said," John, it's not too bad. Opened up the top of ya shoulder. Didn't go through it. Just touched the bone. Don't think it's broke. One of them blood veins is agoin' pretty good if I don't keep pressin' on it. Right smart sized gash on ya face. It's bleedin' sorta heavy at the upper end."

John said, "If it don't quit, ya know what ya'll have to do. Ya may as well get ready. Take that blade off'n Short Sword and heat it up. Big as it is, it'll about fit. "

Isaac pulled off fingers locked on the hilt, picked up the weapon and wiped the blade on Short Sword's shirt. He stirred the fire and raked glowing coals over the end. After several minutes of feeding the fire and blowing the flames, Isaac took off his shirt, wet it, and wrapped the hilt. Using both hands with his arms outstretched, he brought the smoking sword with glowing red tip. The bleeding did not stop. John sat up, turned his head to the left, held the pack on the cut on his face, clinched his teeth, and forced his eyes closed.

Matthew jerked the pack away from the shoulder wound and grabbed John's upper arms. He nodded to Isaac and the hot iron made a great frying sound as it touched the raw furrow in John's shoulder. Isaac pushed the blade across the wound from back to front, twisting it side to side as it sizzled and scraped the bone. John groaned through clinched teeth and in spite of his efforts cried out in pain as the blood spattered and smoke curled around his head. His chin fell and his arms went slack. His chest didn't move.

Matthew shook him, "John —John ya hear me?" He raised his head, took rapid shallow breaths, blinked, and closed his eyes again. "John, we done it. Looks like fried white-meat, but it's not bleedin' now." John's hand with the pack had fallen away from his face and blood spurted. Matthew put the cloth back. "I'd hate to do that to your face. It'll make a bad scar."

After his breathing slowed, John opened his eyes and said," Matthew...keep pushin'...it may stop."

While Matthew held pressure, Isaac put the sword back in the fire, went to the mule and pulled the load off his back, slapped him on the hindquarters, and sent him off to graze nearby.

"Lookie here! Lookie here! They's candlesticks and forks and spoons and all kinda thangs. Looks like lots is silver." He emptied more sacks. "Matthew, somethin' else here. They even took some woman's sewin' basket." He held out the box.

Matthew held the pack on John's face with one hand and sorted through the materials with the other. "They is needle and thread here aplenty, John. What do ya thank? It's this or the hot iron."

They helped John to the shade and put his haversack under his head. Matthew wiped his hands on his shirt, sat on a rock at John's right side and threaded cotton thread through a large needle. He hesitated and stared at the wound as Isaac took off the rag and blood flowed.

"Its got to be done, Matthew. Do it!...I'll do the best I can, but Isaac, you best hold my head so I don't jerk about."

Matthew motioned to Isaac, "Keep pushin' on that squirting part so I can see to do the rest." He pushed the needle through and John grimaced. After the third stitch he groaned each time. The looks on Matthew's face were more pained than John's; and sweat poured down his face. He wiped his forehead, leaving a smear of bright red.

"I tell ya, John, I've sewed socks and I've sewed britches, but sewin' meat...weell, it's differ'nt." Isaac took the rag off the end of the cut. The line of stitches reached the spurting part of the wound and as suddenly as it started, the bleeding stopped. They wiped the blood from John's face and chest. Matthew handed the shirt and cloths to Isaac." Why don't ya put these in the branch to soak? I thank I better sit here a spell to...uh...uh...watch John. He's lible to get weak and let a faint."

Isaac took the blood-soaked cloth. "Ya don't look none too peart, yaself."

After several minutes, Matthew said, "Yer color is better. Ya feel stout enough now?" John nodded and his friend pulled him up by his good arm, first to a sitting position then standing. John blinked, swayed, and reached for a stick that wasn't there. Matthew held his arms until he was able to take a few steps toward the branch. Isaac handed him his stick.

Long Gun had stopped gurgling. He lay ashen and still in the midst of claw marks on the bank. Long hair streamed in the water. Minnows picked at the rippling strands. The others had not moved since they fell. The pot was quiet over a dying fire. Smoke lay low on the bank and drifted across the water.

They stared at three dead men on the ground and at each other. Isaac said,
"I don't know about ya'all, but if we face t'other way, b'lieve I could eat some of that rabbit stew."

John squatted at the water's edge, threw water on his beard and squeezed it out. They divided the stew, sat facing east, ate the meat, drank the juice, and cracked the bones for the marrow.

When he spooned the last drop from his cup, John looked at the still men at the branch and then back to his friends. "We have to do somethin' about them three. We don't even know which side they come from. Couldn't tell from what they were wearin', and they never said."

Matthew snorted, "Long Gun sounded like a smart mouth Yankee to me. They was gonna shoot us. They thought we couldn't help ourselves. Them three were prob'ly some of Sherman's bummers. We broke 'em from suckin' eggs. That's *all* we need to do."

"Pistol and Short Sword didn't say more'n a grunt or two," John said. "They could have been Confederates. That sword come from the South."

"You mean runnin' with the enemy?"

"Curious things happen."

"Don't know what else he was, but Pistol was dumb as a froe. Carried a gun big as a cannon, but couldn't get it out of his britches. And Short Sword was redheaded and left-handed. Ya know what they say: man like that is a child of the devil. Even looked like he had horns, the way his hair stuck out. John, leave 'em. They wouldn't have done nothin' fa us."

"No. They're men. I'd like to think that we're better'n them. We'll put 'em under."

"We got no tools."

"True, but where that tree is down, they's a big hole where the roots been pulled up. We'll put them there."

They dragged the three to the hole. Isaac stooped down and tried to pull the gun from Pistol's belt. He loosened the belt and tore a piece of cloth hung in the weapon. He pulled out the heavy pistol. "What kind of a gun is that? They ain't no hammer. And somethin' is on the side. Look at that trigger!"

John took the pistol in his hand and turned it over. "This here is a Confederate gun. I was over at headquarters tent one day last year and one of them generals was showin' one off. That metal arm to the side of the barrel is a ramrod. Most likely he got somethin' hung in it. And he may've hung that double trigger under the guard in his belt. Takes two fingers to shoot it -- one to cock it and one to let the hammer fall. See? They is a hammer. It don't have no ear. I b'lieve he called it ah – Tram – ah -- Tranter, or somethin' like that." He threw it in with Pistol.

Matthew brought the Spencer from the bank where Long Gun fell. The trigger guard-lever was pulled forward to push in the second round. "This is one of them load-on-Sundee-and-shoot-all-week guns. Ya might near havta to be a mechanic to use one. They won't get it with a full load." He levered out the shells and they fell on the men in the pit. He threw in the Spencer and the short sword.

"We can't carry those guns, John, but what about all this from somebody's house? If either side catches us with it, we're in trouble. They'll say we stole it."

"Put that in the hole too."

Isaac and Mathew threw the sacks in the hole. Isaac pointed at their feet.
"John, I'm fer puttin' them thangs in, but what about the brogans? Them folks ain't worth nothin' cept fer what's on their feet. They could come out of them shoes, and never miss 'em."

"They're way yonder too little for Matthew. He couldn't get in one if he got a runnin' start."

"But me and you sure could use 'em. Them three ain't gonna need 'em. Shame to waste 'em. My boots is wore out, and walkin' in 'em has about eat my legs up!"

They picked the two best pairs and left the other beside the downed tree for the next homeward bound soldier. With flat rocks, they raked a sprinkling of dirt over the three and carried stones from the edge of a field and covered the bodies with several layers. Matthew used vines to tie two sticks together and make a cross and he placed it on the west side of the rock pile. They stood and stared at the mound covering three men they did not know.

John said, "I s'pose we outa say somethin'." They took off their hats and stared at the ground in awkward silence.

Matthew took a sideways glance. No one offered to speak. He grinned and looked to the ground. He held a hand to the side of his mouth and shouted, "Ya'all can light the fires now!"

Isaac scowled, "Now, that's not very Christian!"

"Well then, you say somethin'."

"I can't think of nothin' good to say about them no 'count folks and not make myself out a liar. John?" They lowered their heads and were silent again.

John squinted, frowned, moved his lips without sound, then at last said, "Lord have mercy on these three sinners." The others raised their heads just high enough to glance at John. His eyes were closed and his head down. "And have mercy on these three sinners standin' here lookin' down. And forgive us for killin' three men over a mess of rabbit stew. Amen." John raised his head.

Matthew said, "John, they was gonna kill us."

"Book says if a man wants ya coat, let him have ya cloak also."

"The Bible don't ask us to stand and be killed. We have run out of cheeks to turn these last four years."

Isaac said, "We better be goin', if we aim to cover any ground today." He shuffled down the bank and began to load up for the walk.

John looked away from the mound of stones, took a few faltering steps, and sat on the trunk of the uprooted tree. He leaned over with his elbows resting on his thighs and stared at the ground. "I've shot men and seen 'em fall -- but they fell a long ways off. They didn't have a face. This time it was up close. I saw Long-gun's mouth move and I looked in the eyes of the other two. We caused sorrow...somewhere."

"John, snakes don't grieve over their kin."

"True, but folks are different. Just 'cause a man is mean as a snake, don't mean his mama is."

"She probably knows him, what he's up to, and how he'll wind up."

John's voice dropped almost to a whisper, "Without a right hand, a man's soul goes black and bitter. War is over and here we are killin' agin. I wonder if I can be with reg'lar folks any more. I don't thank I'm fittin' to go back... too much hate in me. ...I may belong in that hole, too. They can't be any love left."

Matthew sat on the log and put his arm around John's shoulder, carefully avoiding the wound. "John, ya buried 'em when most would have walked on. And somethin' else, why did ya give that big yell a while ago?"

"He was gonna shoot ya."

"You thought ya was ruint when ya lost the hand. With one hand, ya did what few coulda done with two. The book also says, 'Greater love hath no man than this, that a man lay down his life for his friends.' John, ya never even thought about it. You yelled and took the shot meant for me. That's love. I owe ya my life."

John glanced at Matthew, then stared toward the branch for several minutes. His voice was low, almost a whisper, "And I owe you mine for that rock you flung."

"Isaac throwed the first one that hit him on the forehead. John, we do have love for one another, but we have been away so long and seen so much evil, there is a tenderness and a gentleness that's missin'. When ya're with ya wife and family a while, the true John will come back."

John stood and stared at the pile of rocks and then toward the sun.
"It'll be a late start, but I'd like to fill our canteens and make as many steps toward home as we can 'fore night sets in."

In the heat of early summer, they traveled by moonlight. When the nights were dark they walked in cool mornings and late afternoons. The midday sun drove them to shade. They had eaten little since the stew three days before, and their strength was ebbing. They lost the tent to Billy's stretcher. They shed jackets and extra clothing, when blackberry winter was past. Now, they left the cook pot by the side of the road. Several weeks into their trek, well into June, they stopped midmorning to rest. They sat in the shade of a withered pine, standing alone in a field given up to saw-briers and stunted blackberry bushes. There was no fruit and the ground was as dry as their canteens.

John groaned as he looked down the road ahead to see a column on horseback. He stood and pointed to the line. "Yankees. And band box soldiers ta boot." John reached into his 'sac. He threw the gun and knife into the briars. "I'm removin' temptation and puttin' 'em out of sight. If them folks are like the ones on the bridge or at the branch, I'd be mightily tempted to shoot 'em, and we're bad outgunned."

John dropped his stick. The three men stood without moving. The Yankee column arrived with weapons drawn and walked their horses around the group.

They stopped so that the three had to turn slightly and face the sun. The young lieutenant said, "Are you soldiers and trying to get home?" They nodded, squinted and glared at the riders.

"Is one of you an officer in charge?"

John said, "I'm actin' lieutenant."

"I don't see insignia".

"Toward the end of the war we did well to have shoes, much less decorations to show off. I wouldn't wear none of them chicken guts, even if I had 'em. Yankees shoot the officers first."

"Let me see your papers."

John handed the pass to the sergeant, who passed it to the lieutenant.

"I'm John; this here is Matthew."

The lieutenant glanced at the pass and looked up.

"And that would make the other one Billy?" The men nodded. "This just proves that you aren't deserters. Where are your parole papers?"

"The war ended while we were on the mission. They's no army to go back to."

The sergeant took the pass from the lieutenant, hesitated, and turned it over to look at the back. He raised his head and studied each of the three men. He read the back again, folded it, and returned it. As John wrapped the paper and put it in his haversack, the sergeant watched him closely. John looked up without sign of recognition.

"Everyone has to be paroled. You will have to turn around and go with us to get your papers. You are a pretty sorry bunch. Where do you think you are going?"

"Few miles the other side of the Alabama line."

"And you think you will make it?"

"If they's breath left in me."

The sergeant spoke, "Beg pardon Lieutenant, look at these men. If we make them go fifty miles out of their way to get a piece of paper, they will never make it home. Can't we forget we saw them? The war is over."

"That's not our problem. They are rebels and will take what we give them." He stared at the three in tattered clothes. "They would slow us down if we had to wait on them. Sergeant, I am putting you in charge. Take O'Riley and Schultz and escort them for processing. The rest of us will go ahead and meet you at the dock where we are to be shipped north. If they get away, you will answer for it." The column rode away, leaving three men on horseback looking at three standing.

The sergeant moved his horse a few steps so those on foot did not have to look into the sun. He still stared at John as though hypnotized. John looked at him without blinking. The soldier's eyes never left John's right arm and in a barely audible voice he said, "I once shot a man in the right hand and saw him fall." He reached into his saddlebag. "I have two days rations here. It's yours. I hope you make it home."

Matthew looked at John. He didn't move. Matthew reached to take the food and mumbled his thanks. The sergeant motioned and the three riders began moving away.

John called after them," What battle?"

The sergeant turned in the saddle, "I didn't say. Let's keep it that way." John stared after them.

"If that don't beat all. Thay is some good Yankees," Isaac said. "Sides dead ones -- I mean."

John nodded his head. "And that's one of 'em. We're in a dry desolate land like the children of Israel. Last night I prayed for manna from heaven. Who woulda thought He'd send it by a Yankee."

"Them folks sure did talk funny"

"Isaac, if we'd had mor'n a nod 'n grunt out of you, they might've said *you* talk funny."

Matthew pointed to the briers. "John, get yer gun and knife and let's get out of here before they change their mind and come back."

"I thank I know that sergeant's mind. He's not like the lieutenant with fuzz on his face. He's prob'ly a farmer, too. Most likely he's been in the war from the first and knows that it could have gone the other way after that hot Sundee at First Manassas. It could have been him in our place at the little end of the horn. That day seems so long ago. Leastwise, we can make out another few days."

Chapter Fourteen -- One More River to Cross

"Today I saw the dragon-fly
Come from the wells where he did lie,

An inner impulse rent the veil
Of his old husk; from head to tail
Came out clear plates of sapphire mail.

He dried his wings; like gauze they grew;
Through crofts and pastures wet with dew
A living flash of light he flew."

Alfred Lord Tennyson (The Two Voices)

Two days' rations for one fed three for two days. On the morning of the third day, when there was light to see the way, they began their walk. A veil of mist lay heavy in low areas, hiding the ugliness of the deserted road. Their shoes scuffed trails through heavy dew on grass and weeds. The fog parted and swirled as they passed, then morning heat dried the dew and burned away the fog. Their paths vanished as if no one had ever come this way.

Isaac began to see familiar landmarks and knew he would be home soon. The sights brought rambling words about the home-cooked meal waiting. Isaac's spirits climbed with the sun. He walked several steps ahead of John and Matthew and was ready to begin again almost as soon as they stopped to rest. He had a spring to his step; his eyes were brighter, and he talked more -- all strange behavior for him.

Along the road they saw untouched houses in the distance, but they also passed burned out ruins. John and Matthew glanced at each other for an instant, but said nothing. Isaac did not see, or pretended not to see, the destroyed homes and farms. He talked all the more of his wife and children, of cathead biscuits, ham and eggs, his own well water, and his own bed under his own roof. He shouted and pointed to a white oak with roots wrapped around an immense moss-covered rock on the south side. They left the main road and walked north. Isaac walked through the weeds in the path as if they were not there. "Ya'all, just 'round this bend is my cabin! I can picture it in my head. I can smell smoke from the breakfast fire. Just a few more steps and I'll be home. I can't hardly wait to see it!" He rushed ahead with strength he had not known in weeks and disappeared from view.

For a moment from beyond the bend in the road, they heard no greeting, no shouts of joy, no sound of any kind. Then, they heard a wailing screeching sound -- a strange blend of mourning and rage. Matthew and John didn't run -- couldn't run -- but took steps quick enough to cause their 'sacs and canteens to slap their sides and rounded the curve in the road to see Isaac, head down, stumbling through blackened ashes between two chimneys. The limbs of circling oaks were burned and dead. He stood several minutes in the midst of desolation while John and Matthew watched, not knowing what to do or say.

Isaac's shoulders and hands shook; he clenched his fists and whirled about to walk rapidly to his friends." John, ya'all are close to home. Lemme have ya little gun. I'm goin' back. I'll kill many as I can."

"Isaac, ya can't do that! War's over. Just wait. House and barn are gone, but that don't mean ya folks are. What's that sticking up yonder in the middle of them ashes?"

As John picked his way through the ruins, there was a crunching sound and the breeze covered his shoes with black ash. His nose filled with the stench of burned wood and cloth that hangs like a cloud over tragedy. In the center of desolation, a green stick the thickness of a finger had been driven into the ground. The stick projected into the neck of a small bottle. John lifted it from the stick and read the fluttering label before the wind blew it into the weeds: *Dr. Parks Balsam of Wild Cherry and Tar.* Isaac stood at the edge, watching every move. Streaks of ash and dust coursed down his cheeks into his beard. His eyes were on the bottle in John's hand as he came near.

John held it out. "Isaac, they's a note inside."

"Well break it, and quick!" He grabbed at the bottle.

John pulled it away. "That'll tear the paper. Let Matthew get it out. It'll take two hands."

Matthew slid two thin twigs in the bottle, twisted the paper, and drew it out in a tight roll. As he watched, Isaac pulled and twisted the strap of his haversack, then broke a dead branch from the oak tree. Matthew handed it to a shaking hand. "Careful, don't let the wind take it."

Isaac unrolled the paper held it flat with the stick and stared at the lines. He squinted and turned it to the light. He held out the note. "John, I'm so tore up I can't seem to make this out. See what you can do."

John took the paper and read the lines silently to himself, moving his lips as he read. The letters were drawn with watery ink and the spelling was novel. He looked up, "I see what ya mean. Must have used polkberry ink or some such. He began to read aloud.

Deer husban
We have went to yer Pas house
i got yer mules an wagun an plows an dogs
Me an th clillun are tolable well
Yer wif Sarah

Matthew shouted, "Praise the Lord!"

Isaac threw the stick to the ground, "Well blame it all! Now I got to ast Him to forgive me, 'cause I was fixin' to go to killin' Yankees agin."

John put the note back in the bottle and handed it to Isaac. "How far is it? We'll go with ya."

"It's four mile straight north. No need to go out of yer way. Let's just say g'bye and ya'all be headin' west to yer own place. I thank ya for the company and help. I wouldn't never have made it without ya." He blotted his eyes with his sleeve.

The three spoke a jumble of words about the war, family, friendship and the long walk home. Isaac held out his hand. Matthew took it and pulled him forward, crushing his friend in a great bear hug. John shook his hand and placed an arm without a hand around his shoulder. Isaac sniffed and tried to speak, but words wouldn't come. He wiped at his eyes again, whirled about and walked the almost hidden road between abandoned weed-covered fields. The two watched until he was out of sight. He slowed once, turned to one side, then ducked his head and jerked his shoulders. He raised his hand to wave, but never looked back.

When Isaac disappeared beyond a clump of trees, John said, "First they was four of us, then three and now two."

Matthew nodded and without speaking they walked to the main road, then west toward the setting sun. About four miles later they stopped to rest by a small branch. John stared blankly at the moving water, so Matthew said nothing. After several minutes of silence, he cleared his throat and said, "John, ya wanta stop here fa the night, 'stead of chancin' finding a good place down the road?" John nodded.

Matthew gigged one bullfrog, which they roasted over the fire. The frog was large, but one leg apiece was not very filling. They ate, said nothing, and propped on their haversacks looking toward the fire. After several minutes, Matthew asked, "What're ya studyin' on?"

John stared at the flames as they slowly died away and the coals dulled.

"Matthew, when them generals give up, there wasn't no more hope of winnin'. When there wasn't nothin' there, we left. Nothin' worse than a place where thery's no hope atall. We left to go where they was hope -- to our homes. When he rounded that bend in the road, Isaac saw what he counted on ... what he lived for ... all those miles ... burned to the ground. A man can't say what somethin' like that does to a fella 'less he's been there. Isaac's wife is a right smart woman. She put hope in a bottle, and left it on a stick for him to find. I b'lieve that on the way to his pa's place, he will take out that bottle, look at it and know that house and barn can be rebuilt. What he holds in his hand is what's important. That's his hope. He's luckier than some that have ashes on the ground and don't have a bottle on a stick."

Matthew nodded, said nothing as he poked at the dying fire. After several minutes he added softly, "And we don't know what we got waitin' in Canaan County." John was asleep.

Just after daylight, they drank from the branch, filled their canteens, and began their walk in the cool of the morning, before the June sun became unbearable for exhausted men. The road became wetter, stickier, covered with brush and weeds hiding wheel ruts, and steadily fell away before them until they began hearing sounds of water. The tracks they followed dipped down and disappeared in a ripple-marked sheet of mud. They climbed the dry bank by the side of the road and stared at swirling muddy water where a bridge or ford should have been. The body of a horse floated along the opposite bank. They watched its path as it hung an instant on a sandbar. Water spilled over the body, it tumbled, sank into a deep pool, bobbed up, and sped around the bend and out of sight.

"Matthew, see them marks on the trees and brush? It's come a flood through here right recent—even wose than now. It musta rained a lot upstream in the last few days. That's why nobody's travelin' this road. No sign of a bridge. Clean washed away deadwood we could use for a raft."

"John, this must be one of the Tallapoosas, prob'ly the Little."

"No shoals to wade, too fast to swim, and nothin' for a raft. It'll be days before that flood goes down."

"We could cut some trees."

"*You* know, well as I do, that it takes a heap o' greenwood to float us across. And us with nothin' but that little hand-axe, and little enough cord left." John dropped his haversack, sat on a rock and stared at swirls in brown water. "It's all I can do to carry my 'sack, blanket and canteen. I'm plum' wore out. I don't know if I can manage water movin' that fast. Ya may have to leave me this side of the river."

"Come on, John, it's just one more river to cross. It's not very wide. We crossed the Savannah, the Chattahoochee, and rivers we couldn't put a name to. We can cross this 'un. One *last* river to cross, and then home."

"Billy said 'So near yet so far.' I know what he meant. I feel like I'll never see home agin. I'll take my turn with the axe, but I may not be up to a trip 'cross high water. It'll take a man with two hands to raft that flood."

"I'll do the chopin', John."

"No, I'll do my share. I need to train this left hand for such. I'd just as soon ya go first."

Matthew picked a tree near the water and began. John lay on the grass in the shade. He put his hat over a hollow in a rock and eased his head down. Lulled by the murmur of water and steady chop-chop-chop of Matthew's axe, John closed his eyes and was asleep instantly.

As he walked a muddy road, a storm surrounded him. Dense clouds swirled about and wind-blown rain stung his face and soaked his shirt. Lightning flashed, struck, and ran along the ground in a great ball of fire, blasting and felling trees in its path. He lifted his hand to protect his eyes, but there was no hand. Clouds thinned and he saw formless movement in the tumult about him. His legs were held by hands he could not see. The blackness parted and he saw himself on a road with shadows shaped like bodies on either side. There were many. Some raised a hand to beg for help. A wind blew the darkness away and the road around him was empty and quiet. Far in the distance he saw Martha, Ben, and Nate looking toward him. A dim figure was beyond. *Reckon that's Jacob?* He looked down and struggled to pull his feet from whatever held him. Each time he looked away and then down the road, Martha and the boys were farther away. Martha was wringing her hands, but she did not see him. Her mouth moved, but he heard no voice. He tried to call her name. No sound came from his throat. Desperate to break free, he threw his arms about. He woke to the sound of his shouted words, "I'm comin'!"

As his arms stopped moving and he blinked himself fully awake, he heard the crash of a falling tree. The chopping sound continued at a slow steady pace. John sat up, felt his right sleeve and trousers and found them dry.

John left his blanket and 'sac and stepped carefully through the brush toward the steady sounds on the bank overlooking the mouth of a small branch.

The chopping stopped as John neared. Matthew's face and shirt were wet. He was taking short rapid breaths. John leaned against the tree, and looked toward the river.

"Did ya hear a tree fall?"

"Wish I could, but I got a long way to go. I've not more'n scratched the tree with this little axe."

"I've studied on it some, Matthew, and I'll try the crossin', but I wanta look into somethin' before I take my turn with the axe."

"John, ya just had the mulligrubs. I wouldn't have left ya anyway. I knew ya'd come around."

John nodded and turned away. "I'll be back d'rectly."

He walked a deer trail by the branch. The chopping sounds began again. The path led through dwarf cane and brush to a thick growth of hardwoods. As he entered the heavy shade, a breeze surrounded him with a wave of coolness and wetness of a body of water, but not a dirty river. He rounded a bend in the trail and saw the tree that fell. A brown-coated animal waddled away from a pile of chips and slid effortlessly into the water with hardly a ripple. A great blue heron beat the air with its wings, rose from shallows, circled to gain height, and gave a single cry as it sailed over the trees trailing long legs. John looked around and gasped.

He put his index and little finger in his mouth and split the air with a come-here whistle. The chopping stopped and Matthew appeared at a fast pace, but not running.

"I didn't dream it Matthew. One did fall. There's the tree on the ground. And better'n that, that beaver cut two more that hung a little ways up -- a long time back. He never could use 'em and they're nice and dry."

John and Matthew looked and listened to the faint sounds of water spilling over the dam of tree trunks and branches woven together and packed with mud. The structure held a rounded triangular pond almost two acres, surrounded by hardwoods and stumps. A single tree, too large to fell, stood in the center, dead twisted limbs reflected in water so smooth that image and reality blended. The glasslike water mirrored the trees beyond and the deep blue of the sky.

John pointed at the dam. "Just look at that. It's a wondrous thang that a little animal can build somethin' that 'll hold back a flood."

"True. If we coulda found beavers big enough, we might've held back them Yankees."

"Matthew, the trees are already cut far us, and two are dry."

"Them trees are small. It'll take a heap of 'em to float us. And we don't have much cord left."

"We can tie two poles together over the ends of the logs. We just need four ties. It may hold. We'll tie to ever' log if we've got the cord. Matthew, just thank about it. He cut them trees months ago -- right in our path. Wouldn't ya like to ask 'em if God whispered in his ear a while back?"

They accepted the gift of dry wood and trimmed sections of poplar and gum, hauled them to the riverbank, and fitted them together to make a raft. There was just enough lanyard cord to tie the ends of four poles holding the small logs.

"John, do ya thank...weell I reckon we could try it any time."

John shook his head." Let's test it first."

Their raft was upstream of an outside bend of the river. The river was eating away the far bank and dumping sand and gravel on a bar across the channel inside the bend.

"We got to push into the river as far as we can so that the flood will carry us to that sandbar on the side towards home. If we miss it, we chase after the horse. Lord knows where we'll end up." They used limbs trimmed from the logs as a test. Each time they shoved a stick into the water, it missed the mark and went rushing down the river and disappeared around the bend.

"John, we have to try sonethin' or stay with the beavers. We could cut some long poles. Paddles wouldn't do much, if we had 'em."

"I'm for tryin' it, but I'd as lief wait a spell as to go now. I saw some right fat perch in that beaver pond. Whatever happens, I'd like to go with a full belly."

Several fish took the crickets they offered and ended up on a stick over the fire. They sat on a log by the pond and ate their fill in silence as the fire faded and died. They listened to the muted sounds of water and the buzzing of bees in the sourwoods. A jay overhead was offended by a mockingbird and gave several harsh cries. Across the pond a woodpecker pounded incessantly against a tree and gave his ridiculous call as he flew.

Matthew sighed, leaned against a tree too big for the beaver to fell, and looked upward toward the blooms. "Ya can smell them sourwood blooms clean down here. Prob'ly a bee tree right close. Shame we don't have time to look far it."

"They can have their honey.   I been stung enough for a while."

A sudden whirring surrounded them. Two large snake doctors fluttered, tumbled over each other, hovered, then one landed on a dry weed and the other on John's stick propped on a bush by the pond. They rested, their straight blue bodies with translucent web-like wings outstretched, motionless except for the black heads, which twitched in vigilance toward the water.

As if by prearranged signal, they left as they came in a fluttering darting path and were gone, skimming over the water toward the river in a blur of motion and color.

"Some says them thangs walk about under the water and then sprout wings and fly off. Do ya believe that, John?"

"It's true. When I was just a boy, one summer mornin' I was fishin' and I watched this ugly worm-like thang crawl out of the water onto a weed. He crawled up toward the top and sat there, just a dirty worm with a big ugly head. He didn't move. I thought he was dead. He dried off some in the sun. Then that thang commenced to wiggle about; his back split open and a snake doctor crawled out."

"A snake doctor with wings and ever'thang come out af a worm?"

"Might near had to fold hisself up to get through. Wings popped out and he sat there a long time soakin' up sunshine and lookin' at marvels of a world he'd never seen. All of a sudden, he flew off, just like he'd been doin' it for years. I picked up what he left. Nothin' but a holla shell. He did live in the mud for a time and then left that old body and flew off. I wondered how he knew to come out of the water that day and who called 'em."

"John, reckon how long them thangs live? Do they go back in the water or just live on? I never seen a dead one."

"I thought I did once. One day in late fall, not even a month 'fore Christmas, I saw three of 'em side by side sunnin' themselves on a gate. Didn't hardly have no color to 'em atall. Ya could might near see through that long part. Looked like ghosts. That time of year most other bugs were gone. I thought they were dead and reached out to touch one and see was it real.

They flew. Looked like they flew straight up. Don't know what I saw or what it means."

"John, you remember all them snake doctors when...... "

"I remember. I try not to, but I remember." There was silence again but for the sound of water spilling over the beaver dam and the song of birds overhead. The heron flew over and settled to fish in shallows at the far side of the pond. After several minutes, Matthew stretched and leaned back further. "With a full belly and all this peace an quiet about, seems like there never was a war ...no killin' ... no hate. I could lie here and sleep a month."

"True, but that river's not goin' down no time soon, and the day is wearin' on. Dog Days will be on us, if we don't move on. We may as well try it. Maybe we can make it 'cross Dead Horse Bend. Let's cut those poles, and then we'll go."

Matthew cut a ten-foot hickory sapling. John cut a thinner one seven feet, leaving a strong crooked branch about a foot long at one end. Matthew looked puzzled as he watched. John said, "I can't handle one no bigger with one hand."

"And that hook on the end?"

"Hook is to hold on with." With the axe, John split off a slab of wood from the side of a log and shaped a crude handle on one end.
They took off their shoes, tied them together, and hung them around their necks.

John said, "Hope we don't lose 'em, but I walk barefooted a sight better than I get my breath under water." They pulled the small raft down the soggy slope into the edge of rushing water, leaving half of it on the bank. Water spilled over the end, shook the bindings, rippled and rattled the logs. They held to short limbs on each end to keep it from being sucked away.

Matthew stared at the waters swirling over his feet." River wants our raft."

"Wants us, too."

"We got to get on it and get in that flood and cross to the other side before we get to the bend. John, I want to tell ya in case we don't make it...."

"Don't say it! I know what ya was about to say. We been helped by soldiers, farmers, merchants, even a Yankee and now a beaver. We *will* make it!"

While they held to alders, Matthew squatted in front and John sat on the left at the back. The logs moved up and down as they got settled, and almost sank to the level of muddy water as they slowly edged into the stream. They put their blanket rolls in the middle of the raft with John's stick, placed their poles against a rock in the bank, and with a shout pushed away into the flood. As the raft shot down the river toward the bend, they plunged their poles in muddy water.

From the front, Matthew shouted, "I got bottom!"

John could reach nothing with the shorter pole. He put it down in the raft, held it with his foot, and began to paddle with the slab, pulling with his hand and pushing with the stump. Matthew bent the slender pole and pushed the raft toward the opposite bank. With each shove of the pole they moved across the currents directly toward the sandbar. As he gave a great push, the pole held fast in the mud, pulled Matthew over and his chest fell in the flood. Muddy water covered his head. Before he let go of his pole, the raft jerked about and began a slow spinning. The raft tilted with Matthew's weight and water poured over it, loosening cords and separating logs. They twisted out of control away from the bank.

As the rushing flood rattled the logs, John looked up to see the sky and muddy bank slowly revolve about him. He glanced ahead at water spilling over the sandbar not twenty feet downstream. Just ahead, he saw a rapidly approaching snag hanging from the bank far out over the water. John dropped the paddle and grabbed up his pole with the hook and caught the dead wood as the raft passed underneath. The trunk groaned and broke with a sound of a rifle shot. The pole jerked out of John's hand, but the spinning stopped and the raft swung hard toward the bank, shot along the edge of the current, and grounded on the sandbar, throwing Matthew partly out of the raft. He coughed, took a deep breath, caught the limbs of a willow and pulled the raft up on the edge of the sandbar.

Matthew took John's right arm and pulled him to the landing. As he climbed off, he snatched up his stick. With the release of weight, the raft turned on its side and tumbled away, breaking up in churning water downstream. A jumble of logs clattered against the bank, fell back in rushing water and disappeared around the bend. Their blanket rolls and poles churned with them. John's paddle, and Matthew's hat followed.

They pulled on tree limbs and hauled themselves up from the sandbar. The two stared at the flood from the top of the western bank. "John, that was a near thing. Ya done it again. Man with three hands couldn't do more. That mighta been us headed toward Mobile." John nodded, took a few steps, sat on a log and began to pull on his shoes. Matthew took his from around his neck and poured water out. "Guess I'll go barefooted a spell."

"Matthew, yer warbag looks to be full of water, too."

He tilted it and poured a stream at his feet. He took out the box of matches and opened it. "We didn't have many, but now they're wet. Box didn't hold. Didn't have tallow to seal it."

John opened his haversack. He brought out his gun, knife, the pass, and Billy's letter wrapped in a ground cloth, still dry. With them was Martha's last letter, now months old. Each night he held it, read it, moved his fingers over the words. He had opened it so many nights that the edges were frayed and the paper parted at the folds. Some of the words were dimmed and gone, but it didn't matter. He could recite the lines from memory, but the message wasn't the reason he carried it all these miles. Each night his hand held something Martha had touched. The ragged letter was a reminder of her and home. It was his hope.

His 'sack had nothing else but a worn toothbrush, a small stone, and a piece of metal. "Matthew, I've got flint and iron here, but that's a slow way to go for a fire. Looks like we'll sleep in the grass with chiggers for a spell. Maybe your shoes'll dry by daylight. I'm right glad mine didn't get wet. I've got a cut on my foot and I don't need to get dew-poisonin' to add to our troubles."

John adjusted the strap on his shoulder and moved to the bank to stare into the swirling muddy water. "*That* river don't flow out of the throne of God."

"What?"

"That's an evil river. I'm about wore out, but before we bed down let's get down the road a ways where we don't have to see it or hear it." He took one last look at the water rushing around the bend. "Hate to lose the flag. It was in the blanket. I reckon it wasn't meant to be for us to take it home. Least it's headed south."

They each had a haversack, a canteen and a wet fishing line in a pocket. Straps across their shoulders were padded with strips from castoff jackets. Matthew lost his hat to the river and walked on bare feet with wet shoes around his neck. John's hat was hardly more than a rag from five hundred miles of sun and rain.

As they left the sounds of hungry waters, Matthew said, "Why don't ya cut yaself a new stick, ya've about wore that one to a nub? Axe is at the bottom of the river, but you got a knife."

"When we left him, I took Billy's stick and left mine. If I get back to Canaan County, Billy's stick does, too.

****

John stopped his story and stared at the night sky. "Ben, only God knows why one man lives and another man dies. In that farmhouse I prayed to live, but I 'spect Tom did too. God let me live... and I still don't know why. I thank Him ever' time I see the sun come up, just like He was givin' me life one day at the time. I never felt the call to do nothin' curious after He let me live. I've done the only thang I knew how to do: I took care of my family and farm the best I could and tried to be fair with folks.

I saw men fall in war and others die tryin' to get home. Most were good men ... hard workin' men with families. They didn't deserve to go like they did. I still can't understand why all them men died and we lost. We just wanted to be free. I don't know why the Stewards picked me from all the shot-up soldiers on that front porch of the Hurt House. I don't know why I lived and other folks died. And I don't know why Nate has to go. We have to believe that there is a purpose in all this – and a meaning. We may not understand it, but we have to believe it, or we couldn't live in this world."

Ben mumbled, "Yessir, they is lots of thangs I don't understand." They listened to tree frogs and crickets. After several minutes, Ben asked, "After ya crossed the river, how did ya get home? Ya was still a long way off."

"Ben, I don't rightly know how I made it home. We had creeks to cross and one more river. We walked in the hot sun and sometimes in the rain. At times we were lost because the roads were tore up. The only thang that kept me goin' was thinkin' about my family waitin' and lookin' far me. I could close my eyes and see yer faces. I could see the house and the fresh plowed fields. I could see mountains in the north with the clouds kinda low ... almost touchin' the tops. In my mind, I could look to the south and see the spring and how cool it was, and the barn and Kulumi Ridge with the mist driftin' down from the top, like it does. And I could hear the crickets and frogs and katydids ahollerin' and dogs bayin' at the moon. I tried not to think on yer ma's cookin'.

I knew that I had to get home to live. It was like when I got shot and tried to get to the hospital. I had to look down at the path and think of nothin' but one step at the time. When I got real weak after we crossed Dead Horse Bend, I'd go to countin': one ... two ... three ... four more steps toward home. Not more'n a whisper -- ever' time my stick hit the ground. Sometimes, Matthew would hear and counted with me. As we got closer, I'd raise up and look around ever' bend thinkin' maybe I could see our place and ya'all waitin', like in the dream. But thangs changed since we left. I remember tellin' Isaac that I'd get word to him, but I wouldn't promise to visit. I told him that if I ever got back to Canaan County, I wouldn't never leave again. I don't remember much after we crossed the river in Georgia. I don't even remember gettin' home. I don't remember Matthew's folks bringing the wagon to get him.

I remember a little of the restin' tree, a mile or so this side of the Alabama line. Me and Matthew was aimin' to rest by the spring under that big beech tree where it's so cool. We could see folks already there. I didn't think I could make it another mile. Matthew pointed, and up in a tree by the spring was words. He pulled me closer so I could read 'em. Fresh-cut letters said:

JOHN
ALL WELL
COME HOME
LOVE
MARTHA

And below in smaller letters:
BILLY AND MATT, TOO

Matthew held me back so he could fill the canteens. I remember leavin' while them folks looked at us like we was crazy for not restin'. I don't remember nothin' else."

John had never spoken of this before and could go no further. After a time, he began again -- his voice softer and the words halting.

"Some nights I remember them cuttin' off a leg and an arm on those two fellas while I was waitin' my turn. I hear hollerin', rain on the roof and shootin' in the distance. I close my eyes and see that room and all the folks in it, and the blood. Blood was ever'where. And I remember walkin' the woods with the curious smell. I know now that death has a smell all its own. I remember the long trip home like a dream – a dream that woudn't end. And on bad nights I see Billy wave and smile and hear Sammy call his mama." There was silence, but for the voices of the night. John wiped at his eyes with the back of his thumb.

"What is hope, pa? How can ya put it in a bottle?"

John stammered and searched for answers.

Martha put a hand on John's arm. "Can I tell Ben somethin'?" John nodded.

"Ben, ya wish for somethin' ya want real bad. Ya can't see it out there, but ya thank it'll come. Hope is a feelin' in yer heart. It's always there. It's sometimes covered up by bad times, but it's still there. Ya can't really put hope in a bottle or on a tree. But ya can put a note in the bottle and words on the tree that makes ya remember, and then hope wells up in ya. Nate couldn't go by hisself so we asked Uncle Dock, yer shoutin' uncle. He was a wicked cussin' man before he went to the river meetin' and got santified. He took Nate with him to that tree. Ya was still havin' pains in yer head and couldn't go. They chopped limbs to make a place and stood on the back of the wagon to cut words on that big beech. It was the only thang we could thank of to do. We knew yer pa would come that way. Through the war, I hoped that Jacob and yer pa would come home whole. If not whole, then I hoped they would come home in some shape. And if they didn't come … then I knew I'd see 'em in the next world. Even if ever'thing you see is awful, ya have to have hope to keep goin'. Hope is always there. Mine is low these last two days, but it's still here." She touched her chest.

Martha took John's hand and smiled. "Thank ya for tellin' Ben. It did me and you more good than it did him. Maybe talkin' about it will help ya get over so much of the hurt and hate of war."

After minutes of silence, Ben said, "Ma, if you don't care, I'll still sleep on that pallet in yer room. Our room is a mess. 'Sides, I ain't ready to stay in my regular bed quite yet."

Chapter Fifteen -- Doldrums

On Monday, John milked and came to the kitchen. He sat at the table, picked at his food several minutes, then gave up any pretense of eating and walked down the dogtrot. He stopped at the steps to watch the ridge. Beyond the top, huge birds circled on motionless wings.

Later in the morning, the dogs began barking in a stranger-approaching way. John walked around the house as a buggy turned off the main road. He ordered the dogs away and stood in front of the porch. A well-dressed man stepped down from the buggy and came toward the house. He offered his right hand. John twisted his arm thumb down and accepted with his left. "Mr. McGinnis, my name is James McKay."

"George McKay's boy?"

"Yes sir. I didn't know if you would know me or not."

"I remember ya."

"Mr. McGinnis, you were always a good friend to my pa before he died. I work at the courthouse in New Canaan, and I thought you should know what is about to take place. On the first of the month, your farm and others are to be sold for back taxes at public auction on the courthouse steps. Folks in the tax office say that they notified you and got no hearin'. I've written down where you go and the amount due, in case you didn't get a copy. If you can pay it before the first, everything will be fine."

John took the paper, stared at it, and handed it back. "I am much obliged that ya come out of your way to tell me. Could ya come in and set a spell? I just brought fresh water from the spring."

"No sir, thank you for the offer, but I need to be gettin' back to town. Just remember, the deadline is the first of next month."

John stared after the buggy as it disappeared down the road to the west.

John ate little of the noon meal. He sat at the table and stared at the wall. As Martha scraped John's plate into the pan for the dogs, she asked, "What did the man want?"

"What man?"

"The one that come by in a buggy, a while ago."

"Told me they was gonna sell our farm fa taxes."

"I know ya been savin' to pay em'. How much more do ya need?"

"Eleven dollars."

"They wouldn't take away a farm that feeds a family for eleven dollars -- would they?"

"Don't make no difference if it's eleven or eleven hundred. We're short the full pay. They're sellin' farms all over fa taxes. By the hundreds. Our taxes are three times what they were in '60, and times are worse. Ten years ago they were taxin' slaves. Now they get that money by raisin' our taxes. The fed'ral gov'ment takes our money to pay Yankee soldiers we fought and their families. The state taxes us to pay Confederate widows. We had to pay for the war when we had it. We're still havin' to pay far it – the ones that are livin', that is."

Martha nodded. "I know we're payin' our side and the Yankees', too. But I can't believe they would take a home for that little bit of money."

"Martha, farms are lost for 50¢. You know we didn't have much of a crop in '63 and had a drought the year the war was over. Then in '68 the Union gov'ment passed that tax on cotton. Times have been pore since the war. Nobody has any money, and prices of cotton and corn are low."

"Is they any way we sell somethin' or could one of the boys take a job?"

"In good times, eleven dollars would be a month's wage for a field hand. I could hire out — if somebody wanted a one-armed man -- or one of the boys could, but these aren't good times. Nobody has money to pay field hands. If folks can't farm their land, they sharecrop it. Folks at the courthouse want our farm so they can sell it."

"What are ya gonna do?"

"I'm gonna thank on it, and pray on it. I've studied it some -- about losin' the farm my pa had before me and us bein' on the road with the others. It's most more'n I can stand. I have thought some about sittin' in the road with my gun. At least I would be gone and wouldn't never have to see my family turned out. But that wouldn't do ya'all no good. I've been on the road without food and nowhere to turn for help. I don't want my family to live like that. Folks with money left the South after the war. They're goin' to South America and Mexico to get away from thangs like this. Pore folks are leavin' all over Alabama 'cause they lost their land. Most are goin' west."

Martha washed and dried John's dishes, rested her hands on the table and looked around her kitchen at the pans, stove, dishes and her mother's dough-board. "If we had to, we could, too. You and me, the boys, Bertha Mae, and John B. would still have each other."

"Some will starve on the way. Martha, we built this place and made it what it is. Ya'all and this place is all I could thank on when the shootin' was over. This is home. Jacob and Ben like it. Those two girls won't never leave, and I don't reckon Nate will. We're not supposed to have more than we can stand up to. We loose two babies, our son and now our home." His voice broke and he barely got the words out. "I don't want strangers to have ever'thang we worked far and own the graves of our kin."

Martha sat down beside him." Could we ask some of our friends to help us a little?"

John got up from the table abruptly and walked out of the kitchen, down the dogtrot, and into the yard. He stopped and looked to the south. The circling birds were gone. John looked away and shuddered. In his mind he heard his own words. *A man has to do what a man has to do. Them are buzzards. And buzzards have to do what buzzards do. That's all they're doin'. Buzzards and skippers, they're all part of God's plan.*

Martha walked down the back steps carrying her load of clothes and rags toward the branch." What's the matter, John?"

"Oh nothin', I jus' got somethin' in my eye. Gnats are bad right early this year."

Monday was washday and washdays were always long. This one seemed longer. Tuesday was little better. John and Ben dragged the torn mattress out of the boys' room and pushed it under the house for the dogs to sleep on. They smelled it and fled as if something evil were in it. John pulled the straw mattress into the yard and burned it. Bertha Mae and Martha cut and sewed a new ticking and John cleaned new straw and placed it inside the ticking spread in the center of the bedroom floor. After it was tightly packed, the women sewed up the openings, forced tufting threads through and tied them in place. Martha and Bertha Mae scrubbed the bedroom.

Jacob straightened the two collapsed legs of the bed, drilled them and drove new pegs. He pulled and tied new cords to replace those broken. John put the new mattress on the cord bed and Martha covered it with fresh bedding. They arranged books and papers on the table as they were before Nate's madness.

That night at supper they offered the new mattress to Ben. "If ya don't care, I'll just keep mine. It's already broke in. Them new straw mattresses rattle and stick so bad that ya 'bout can't sleep for a month or so. Leave that fresh one for company to break in."

As John predicted, Wednesday brought rain, not heavy, but enough to discourage field work. The men worked in the shop, next to the wash shed. This sheltered area contained a jumble of tools and materials for working in wood and iron. On the farm something was always broken or worn beyond repair, but nothing was ever thrown away. Even if the part were worn out for its original use, it might be used for something else. The space was cluttered with an assortment of worn or broken metal parts. New tire metal shone in contrast. Toward the east side, stacks of wood slowly dried for the years to come. In the center of the shed a hood sheltered a small forge and anvil. Tools for simple metal work hung on walls and were scattered about the dirt floor. A drawing table and a foot-operated lathe stood near the south wall.

The three men began by shaping seven-inch hubs of dried hickory on the lathe. Jacob drilled the central area to accept the metal cap of the axle and John carefully marked fourteen squares about the edge of the hub. Jacob drilled and cut them with a chisel. He tapered each one slightly toward the inside of the hub. They patiently helped Ben cut two of the mortises.

John said, "Now remember, ya don't cut but twelve for a front wheel." John and Jacob fitted, heated and forced four iron bands over the hub in proper position to bind the hub on either side of the spokes and on the edges. Ben dipped the hub into water to shrink the metal to a snug fit.

While Jacob was finishing the hub, John marked wood for the spokes. Ben roughly sawed them and placed them on the drawing table. Jacob shaped them with a drawing knife. He cut the tenon end with knife and chisel. Ben tried one but could not shape it to fit. John and Jacob then drove the spokes into the mortises of the hub.

"Ya see, Ben, they have to fit real tight or they won't work," John said. "Practice on some of them scraps and maybe ya can do some next time."

John placed the pattern for the felloes of the rim over the oak board and marked it. Ben cut the pieces with a band saw suspended in the center of a wooden rectangle. Jacob shaped the spokes to a dowel-like end and drilled holes to fit in the parts of the rim.

John glanced at the fading light and said," Let's quit for now. Next rainy day, we'll fix the rim on the spokes and put the tire on. Ya know that the both of ya need to know wheelwright work. Pair of good wheels will bring a right smart at trade day...if ya don't get skint."

As they left the shop in the rain, John stopped and turned to look through gray skies toward the ridge and valley beyond. The sky was empty but for streaks of dirty clouds sinking and settling on Kulumi. *Wonder if it's happened yet? Whether it has or hasn't, I hate to think of him in this weather. Least it didn't rain much.*

Skies were clear enough to do the usual jobs on the following day. There were cows to be milked, the stock to be fed, and fields to be plowed. Thursday, Friday, and Saturday crawled as if hours had been added to the day.

Even easygoing Martha had a harsh word. She shouted at Nell as she chased her out of the yard with a broom." John, what has that dog rolled in? She smells like pure dee kearn!"

John defended his dog, "Now, Martha, she thinks she smells good. Don't have a conniption fit!" But Nell had to endure a lye soap bath in the branch.

When the sun was low on Saturday, Ben looked at shadows in the garden and said, "Pa, don't ya think supper's 'bout ready? We're caught up here."

"It's past time it was ready. And if it ain't, I mean to raise a fuss!" The men washed for supper as they did every Saturday of the year. John entered the kitchen with a scowl and sat at the table. Supper was on the table and steaming hot. John knocked his chair over as he got up abruptly.

"I'm not agonna eat a bite of it. I ain't hungry." He stomped across the floor of the kitchen.

Martha was startled." Now, John, don't be so fractious. Sit down and eat." He slammed the door and stalked out into the fading light of sunset. He walked through the early twilight and in the blackness of night, but could not flee the images of his mind.

Chapter Sixteen – Sad Journey

John slept through troubled dreams in the hours past midnight. The day began like any other Sunday. He was up at daylight and at the barn to feed the stock and milk the cow. Ben was waiting to help. They finished the work without speaking, walked the path to the house and ate in silence with the others.

John pushed back from the table and stared at the wall for several minutes." Well, I guess we better get the wagon out and the stock hitched. Folks will be here right soon. We need an iron to pry the chain off the spikes and a wedge and hammer to take a link out" A pained expression came over his face and he added, "And that scrap of a tent fa a cover."

Martha struggled to get the words out," We'll need his... his Sunday clothes. I hope they still fit." She buried her head in her arms on the table and sobbed as the men left. Bertha Mae laid one hand on her shoulder and wiped her eyes with the other.

As Ben and John left for the barn, wagons and buggies began arriving. Men tied teams in the shade of the oaks. Men and women streamed toward the house, some carrying chairs and some carrying food. Children played and fought in the yard. Two ox drawn wagons lumbered up and joined the mix under the trees. The women gathered around Martha and the men wandered toward the barn.

With Ben's help, John was harnessing the mule and horse when two arms encircled him from behind in a viselike grip. John was startled, then said, "Not but one bear hug like that in Canaan County." He turned to face Matthew.

"Ya knew I'd come. I wooda been here last week, but I didn't know a thang about it 'till a peddler come by Friday. John, I'm truly sorry. I'm the only one in the county that knows what yer sufferin'. No man should go through somethin' like this twict in one lifetime. Me and a neighbor put together a coffin – didn't figger you had one. It's rough and not much to look at, but it's all we could do on a day's notice."

"Thank ya for the … uh… coffin. I couldn't bring myself to make one. Thank ya for comin' Matthew. I had to tell Martha of Billy at the spring, and other folks heard it. I reckon half of the county knows about Billy and Nate now. I hope word don't get back to the Deermans. Ya just don't know how much I 'preciate ya bein here. Ya can't really understand somethin' like this if ya don't live through it."

John looked around him at the growing crowd and said, "Let's get agoin'. The sooner we get there, the sooner we get th'ugh."

Jacob sat on the bench of the narrow wagon and drove the horse and mule mismatched team. John sat beside him. Jacob had insisted that he ride to save his strength. He had slept little in the past week. Ben, Brother McDonald, Matthew, a throng of friends and the two loggers who had come again, all clustered behind the wagon. Bear and Nell made the trip with the men. Sadie stayed home with new puppies.

The climb up the trail to the top of Kulumi Ridge seemed longer than a week before. As the wagon passed the clearing where Maude lay, several men looked toward the opening. They shuddered and turned away.

At the top, Jacob stopped for Ben to climb in. The wagon with the three McGinnis men made a slow descent into Ochoccola Valley along the winding path.

It snaked back and forth to make a gradual slope down the ridge. Only the creak of the wagon, crushing grinding of wheels, plodding hooves, and occasional slap of leather harness and clink of the chains marked their passing. Some disasters cannot be prevented. Storms cannot be turned away or rivers held back. Some illness cannot be treated. But each man must have wondered why? *Why is it God's will for this to happen to a young boy and to his family as they struggle to survive?* Only Ben asked the question of his father.

After he asked the second time, without turning his head, John said,".....how unsearchable are His judgments, and His ways past finding out!"

Ben worked the brakes while his brother drove the wagon through turns and narrows. John slumped on the bench, staring straight ahead. He said nothing and appeared to see nothing. They reached the bottom of the valley and Jacob turned Dolly and Sam east toward the spring. Scattered along the trail behind the wagon, men spoke in whispers. The still low sun shone through trees, making long flecks of brightness along the trail and deep shadows to the side. Morning mists floated in low places and lazy fingers reached for the trail. Beams of light through vapor shined like bars of gold, which might be gripped and held against the darkness of trees. Stillness and sunlight on fog made the wood they entered seem a peaceful enchanted place.

They rounded the last bend and came upon the spring with the clearing to the north and one beech tree in the center. The open space was circled by woods in deep shadows. A shaft of light penetrated the canopy of trees to the east and glowed in mists over the spring and clearing. As Jacob pulled the reins, Ben tugged on the lever and braked the wagon to a full stop. John climbed down and walked toward the tree. He moved slowly, hesitantly, with great effort, as in a dream. The men's eyes were fixed on the tree.

Matthew motioned to the others and whispered, "Stay back. It's his son. He may need to grieve by hisself fa a spell."

The men clustered around the wagon and would go no farther. An uncommonly large snake doctor left a weed at the spring's edge and with a gentle whirring fluttered across John's path. He stopped, raised his arm to the sound and the small being turned in flight and came to rest on his scarred stump, holding still web-like wings out from an iridescent blue body. John stood motionless, holding his breath. He looked at the little creature on his arm and the snake doctor twitched its eyes and looked, too…somewhere. It rested a moment, then flew toward the tree and out of sight.

John raised his head, glanced at the tree and spring and said, "Curious…downright pe-culiar. Never seen one light on a man."

He stared at the beech in the clearing. The chain hung motionless from the tree. A circle as far as the spring surrounded the beech where plants and leaves were not. Poke sallet and grass grew lushly about the ring, but not within. There was no body lying on the ground shrouded in mist. He looked from one side of the clearing to the other. Nothing was in the circle but the tree.

The wagon creaked forward a few inches. Jacob and Ben held the team still. The other men followed a few feet behind John, stepping hesitantly, carefully, so as to not snap a twig. John moved into the drifting cloud. Bear, the biggest and meanest dog, went with him. As John came closer, he saw in the mist beyond the tree a vague upright shape, hidden until then. The morning light glowed around the tree and the shadow. The figure was not on the ground but unmoving, upright, leaning against the tree.

Those following took slower shorter steps. John Tom Shepard whispered, "Preacher, could a man die leanin' against a tree, and not fall down? That couldn't happen, could it? What *is* that?" The sun glared around the shadow making it appear spectral. The men pointed and whispered to each other.

Bear did not believe in ghosts. He walked to the tree ahead of John, looked up, and wagged his tail. A hand reached out in a jerking motion from the shadow to pet his head. To their everlasting shame, three men shouted and left the group at a dead run up the trail and over the ridge. One was far ahead of the other two, who stumbled on a log and fell in a yelling pile of thrashing arms and legs.

John stopped and stared. The mists cleared, and he saw his flesh and blood son. Alive! *Nate was alive*! He couldn't be, and yet he *was* alive! John shouted, ran the last few feet and threw his arms around Nate.

"I wondered where ya was, Pa. I had about give up on ya. I heard ya come up. I didn't say anything 'cause I thought you were still mad over all that fuss I made." His words were halting, but clear.

The men clustered about, asking a thousand questions. Nate was thin, but in remarkable condition with no evidence of the madness of the week before.

Brother Mac recovered from his astonishment and began to pray.

"Lord God, we don't understand it, but then miracles are not to be understood. Thank you for the return of this boy to his family."

John kept his arms wrapped around his son and begged his forgiveness as tears streamed down his cheeks. When he finally stood back, sniffing, still holding his son's shoulder, he said, "Let's get ya back home where ya b'long. Nobody's mad! What are we waitin' far?"

"Pa, I'm hooked to that tree. I tried to get loose, but I can't."

Jacob, Ben, and Matthew propped the ladder against the tree, while John continued to ask his son's forgiveness and understanding. Jacob shook badly and could not work for looking at Nate. The twitch of his cheek was so severe that he tried to cover it with his hand. Matthew replaced Jacob on the ladder, beat two spikes down with a hammer, used a bar to pry the chain off and it fell to the ground. Men pushed John aside and crowded about Nate. They took the link off the chain around the tree, but a dozen fumbling hands and a clamor of voices could not get the one off Nate's back.

"Don't make him walk; he's weak as branch water." John said "Just load him into the wagon, chain and all. We'll get it off at the shop where we got better tools and maybe steadier hands."

As the wagon moved away, the men clustered around it and began to shout and rejoice. Voices became louder and happier with each step. If the wagon moved too slow, the men pushed and shouted. The team heard the voices as sounds of encouragement and pulled harder. John had embraced his son, shed tears of joy and begged his understanding, but now he could not sit still. Jacob stopped so his father could climb down. When they reached the top of the ridge, this somber inexpressive man ran beside the wagon, threw up his arm and the sleeve with no hand, and shouted at the top of his lungs, even louder than Uncle Doc. Brother Mac shouted almost as loud as John.

The journey down the north slope of the ridge should have been slow and careful. Braking, not pushing, was needed. Ben and Jacob began that way, but the farther they went, the louder the men shouted, and the more excited and enthusiastic they became. Soon they were running ahead, yelling, and looking back at the slow-moving wagon. Ben left the bench, propped his feet at the back of the wagon, grabbed the brake lever and pulled with both hands to try to keep from running down the team. The men urged the wagon to move faster. The dogs were barking and running in great circles, adding to the melee. More excitement and joyful gratitude filled this group than in any revival in the history of Canaan County. After they made the turn at the clearing halfway down, the speed became unsafe. The team knew it. They were straining to keep out of the way of the wagon. And the more they pulled, the faster the wagon came, sometimes bouncing and jerking the two brothers on the bench, the one at the back and rattling Nate's chain. Jacob struggled with the reins; Ben wrestled with the brake lever. Nate sat by Jacob, the calmest and dryest on the ridge. But a man delivered from death should feel secure.

*   *   *

At the house, women tried to talk to Martha and distract her by speaking of sewing and cooking or happenings in the community. She insisted on moving to the south side of the house to watch the path down the ridge. They brought a chair. She ignored it and stood, staring toward Kulumi. After many minutes of stillness in the distance, she began walking the path toward the barn, slowly and then faster, never taking her eyes off the Ridge.

Ann Cooper called out," Martha, don't ya thank ya better wait at the house? Ya don't need to be out in this hot sun. We'll check on thangs far ya, the very minute they get back. They've not been gone long."

Martha walked as if she did not hear the shrill voice. Her eyes were fixed on the ridge. A few women followed behind Martha. Some took their own advice and stayed in the shade to pet the cats. As she moved into the lot and beyond the barn, Martha began to hear noises from the ridge -- strange noises. She heard distant sounds, but they were sounds of a team and wagon coming off the ridge faster than any should travel. The overhang of the tree branches hid the trail and she could see neither wagon nor men. As the noises moved down the ridge, clouds of birds took flight to mark passage of something down the trail. And their cries added to the clamor.

In the jumble of noises, Martha heard voices. Faint at first, and then stronger. She could understand nothing in the tumult. The sounds grew louder; some sounded like shouts. *But what were the words?* She cupped her ears with her hands and strained to hear. The wind changed, and she clearly understood, "God's perfect circle!" She had no idea what this meant. Oddly, the voices sounded happy, even jubilant. And then in the distance, she heard John's shouted voice, saying something she couldn't understand, and then she could. One single startling word:

"*Alive!*"

Martha lost her bonnet. She ran toward Kulumi as if she were a child again. Sounds were louder now. There were shouts and screams. The team and wagon burst forth from the woods and almost ran Martha down as Ben braked the wagon to a grinding stop. The men milling about the wagon were covered with dust and sweat. A stranger would have thought these staid people deranged. All tried to talk at once. She looked beyond as if they were not there. All she saw was the thin boy on the bench. Beside Jacob sat Nate, very much alive, with chains about his chest and shoulders. The long chain hung from his back to a pile in the back of the wagon.

John was still running around the wagon shouting his happiness and thanks to God. He yelled, "Just see what we brought back!!"

The two dogs chased around in the same circle, barking constantly. The men were smiling, grinning, slapping each other on the back and cheering along with John. Birds don't smile, but they were singing. Ben later claimed that even Dolly was smiling. The other men were shouting and rejoicing, but not like John. He would have done cartwheels if he'd had another hand. Men from the house ran to the celebration. Several volunteers pulled and pushed Martha into the wagon where she threw her arms around her youngest son and covered him with tears of joy. Martha sat on the bench by Nate. Ben released the lever and Jacob drove the wagon the rest of the way home. What began as the saddest journey imaginable ended in the most glorious rejoicing return ever conceived.

Most of the congregation of the little church was gathered at the house and workshop when they arrived. The incredulous news was staggering, and the shouting and rejoicing were contagious. Nate was passed down to the crowd. His foot was not allowed to touch the ground. Men crowded about him and carried him into the shop trailing his chain. Martha was left on the wagon. Everyone's eyes were on Nate as he was eased down by the stump.

Matthew grabbed up the tools and said, "Lemme do it, John. It'll make me feel better about Billy." He put the link on the stump, opened it with a wedge and took it off. The chains fell to the ground and Nate was freed of their bondage.

John jerked off Nate's shirt to examine the skin. There were red stripes, a few shallow ulcers and abrasions, but no major damage. He breathed a great sigh, and looked at the crowd of faces. "Where is John Tom and Shadrack?" The crowd parted to make a path for Shadrack.

"Mista 'Ginnis, yo' son look right nicely now, but back yonder in da valley, I sho' thought he were a haint. Das why I lef' out... sorta sudden like."

John handed him the chains. "Tell ol' Ambrose that these done the best job in the history of the world. We're athankin' him."

As the loggers left, voices from all directions offered food and comforts. Most of the women watched from the back steps or the yard near the house. Men crowded around Nate, his father, and brothers until they thought they would be crushed. As some moved close to touch Nate, John held up his hand and said, "Move back a mite. He can't hardley get a breath." He turned to the boy by the stump.

"Nate, don't ya want to lie down and rest? We got a new bed."

"Pa, I been lyin' down most of a week."

"Somethin' to eat?"

"I could use somethin' to eat."

Martha's voice was uncommonly loud. "Let me through!"

The murmur of voices stopped and men moved aside to let her pass. When the crowd ignored her and carried Nate away to the shop, she had left the wagon for the kitchen. From the food brought by friends she filled a plate with fresh venison, beans, and bread. She smiled as she brought the plate and cup of sweet milk to the son thought to be dead.

Behind Martha through the jostling crowd came Bertha Mae carrying John B., squirming, trying to see, and calling, "Unc' Nate! Wanta see Unc' Nate!" Martha held the plate while John B. sat in Nate's lap

Bertha Mae pulled John B.'s arms from about Nate's neck. "We're all right proud to have ya back. John B.'s cried most of the week. He couldn't understand where ya was. He kept sayin' that ya'd come back."

The two women smiled and watched Nate. The clamor of the crowd subsided and men spoke in hushed tones as they watched a man thought to be dead as he ate every bite, as though he were performing some wondrous feat. Even these country people knew that it is rude to stare, but when a man returns from the dead, there are no rules. As Nate passed the empty plate to his mother, several in the crowd said, "Oh, he's through now."

Nate wiped his mouth with the back of his hand. "Pa, if you don't care, I would like to clean up a mite, since we got company and all."

Spectators were ushered out, and John and his older sons helped Nate wash and dress in clean clothes. Nate's steps were unsteady and he almost fell as he tried to walk from the shed. The crowd swept him off his feet and carried him in a straight-chair to the shade of the front yard. John, Jacob, and Ben tried to keep loving friends from crushing Nate with concern and kindness. A jumble of voices asked about his memory of the trip over the ridge and seven days alone chained to a tree. John and Martha insisted that Nate not answer questions, but go in to rest.

Nate smiled, "I've not seen another human bein' for a week. It's sorta nice to have some about."

Questions about his ordeal persisted, now louder. He began to speak and the crowd was instantly silent and still. For the first time Nate saw the new wood of the coffin shining against the weathered wagon under a tree. He stopped, stared and moved his mouth without sound. He lifted a hand to point for an instant, then turned back to the crowd and began again. The words came slow and strained. "When I was tied on that bed ... then when ya'all took me 'cross the ridge, I could hear some thangs, but not clear. There were spells like somebody threw cold water on me and I had a rigor all over. My muscles all knotted up, and I

was scared 'cause I couldn't get my breath. I hurt
ever'where. I guess that's why I kept throwin' my arms
about. I hope I didn't hurt anybody. I tried to tell ya'all
somethin', but it was like a demon in me that run my
arms and legs and mouth. I was inside, but I couldn't
say it. The harder I tried, the worse my mouth hollered.
The worst was when Ma told me g'bye. I tried my best
to talk right, but I couldn't."

As Martha stood beside Nate, she stifled sobs,
but then wept openly. Ben stood in the midst of the
crowd and smiled. Jacob was beside Bertha Mae and
John B. He held his hand over his left cheek. John
remained toward the back of the crowd. Gnats seemed
to bother him again.

"Ya left me at the spring -- and I don't blame ya -
- I know I was like somethin' wild. Ya'all took me there
to die, and I *thought* I was just before bein' dead. The
next mornin', I was surprised to see the light of day.
When I woke up good, I sort of come to myself a little. I
stood up and tried to run. The chain jerked and I fell on
the ground. I was at myself enough to cry. I looked
toward the spring, and a deer was grazin'. My head
was still crazy, but I thought if that deer can eat grass
and such, why can't I? Right next to me was poke sallet
all wet with dew, so I ate it. That day about dark, I
crawled to the spring and commenced to drink water.
Seemed like I hadn't had a drink in a month. Grass and
poke sallet was all I had to eat for the week. There was
even a clear place where I was lyin' that first night. I
must have eat poke sallet and not remembered it."

"Ya was there a week. What did ya do all that
time?"

"I tried to get loose from the chain, but I couldn't
even find a rock to beat it with. I couldn't go anywhere
'cept in a circle 'round that tree. I crawled about at first,
but I learned to walk by holdin' on to the chain and
playing it out little at the time. It was so quiet ... seven

days without hearin' another person speak. It rained some toward the middle of the week. And the dew was right heavy ever' night, but I dried off soon as the sun come up. As my head got better I talked to myself and I thought on the last few days, where I was, and my home and my family. I read the names and looked at the signs on the tree -- over and over. I know every letter on that tree. I watched catbirds feed their babies in a nest. I watched a big fat 'coon and her little 'uns. I watched the minnas in the spring. Ever'thing drinks at that spring. I talked to the critters that come by. Some come real close like they pitied me 'cause I wasn't free like them. And I talked to God. I figured He lived in that valley just like other places. Maybe He comes to the spring, too...like ever'thing else. At times, it seemed that somethin' or somebody was close by, maybe behind that tree. I never could see anything when I looked around it. I called out, but I never heard words I could understand. I had 'bout eaten all my sallet when ya'all come back. That purty much took care of the week." The last words were raspy and faint.

A few members of the Ebenezer Church were always late. They arrived in the front yard as Nate spoke. Others had come from the graveyard when no one showed up. As each entered the crowd, there were exclamations of astonishment. "Why Nate ain't dead! He's up and about. Looks right peart for a fella tied to a tree all week." Each one wanted to hear the story again, in every detail.

Even Doc Davis came. He was the most incredulous of all to see a man who had survived rabies, untreated and alone. Doc Davis and John discussed the situation. They agreed that Nate would be exhausted by attention and curiosity. John announced to the crowd that Nate had eaten, changed clothes, and spoken to everyone, and now on doctor's orders he was to be put to bed on his new straw mattress. Several men picked up Nate in his chair and carried him to the porch. Martha and Ben and Jacob took him to his own bed. When they returned, there was a constant rumble of voices telling the story over and over and adding to the known events. Now that Nate had gone to bed, several asked, "What was it like when ya fount him, John?"

"If ya'all will back up some so's I can see the light of day, I'll tell ya'."

John began the story of the descent into the valley. After he had related the events and those who had made the trip with him interrupted to add their version, Brother Mac moved into the center of the crowd and offered a prayer of thanksgiving and began to sing. Others joined in.

> *"God moves in a mysterious way*
> *His wonders to perform;*
> *He plants his footsteps in the sea*
> *And rides upon the storm.*
>
> *Ye fearful saints, fresh courage take;*
> *The clouds ye so much dread*
> *Are big with mercy, and shall break*
> *In blessings on your head."*

As the last note echoed in the circle of trees, he began again:

> *"O worship the king, all glorious above...."*

When they came to *"our shield and defender,"* the crowd almost shouted the words. They sang *"Rock of Ages cleft for me, let me hide myself in thee."* Hymns followed hymns, one after the other. The words came alive with new meaning. The main crowd was on the porch and in front of the cabin. But children and more adventuresome adults climbed the oaks. The circle of trees to the north side held a row of singers on the lower limbs. The happy people were in a natural amphitheater, and the sounds swelled and filled the countryside like an angelic chorus. The joyous singing drifted to neighbors over a mile away. In years to come, those not at the gathering told of sounds that seemed to come from the sky itself. And who is to say that an angel of joy or two did not add their voices? Besides, two women kept Ann Cooper busy in the kitchen while the others sang.

Most of those at that gathering had brought food. They spread it upon the back of the wagons and ate between songs. Bear and Nell wandered about the group. Bear offered to sing once and was quickly shushed by John. Several chickens and three ducks wandered about the edge of the group. A group of young boys had discovered a large frog hiding in a cool corner near the house and had chased the girls with it until corrected by parents. They were now clustered about the poor beast, encouraging him to jump. Women brought over plates loaded with food for John and Martha, Bertha May, Jacob, and Ben. Sarah Baker set a plate of fried chicken, beans, bread and a slice of onion in front of John." Martha said that ya've not eat nothin' in might near a week -- eat up. They is more whure this come from."

John checked one more time on Nate, and then he did eat, and had a second helping. Ann Cooper arrived from the kitchen with fried peach pies. After the second pie, John leaned back in the chair and shook his head when offered another.

"No, thankya ma'am. I've eat a gracious plenty. More'uld be a dog's bate."

In the midst of this noisy event a man and his wife stopped their buggy in front of the cabin. Matthew walked over to move a wagon so that the strangers and buggies and asked, "Has there been a death in the family?"

Matthew smiled. "No, there was a death here last week. Today, there is a life in the family."

As the strangers drove around the tangle of wagons, the man glanced back at the crowd and said to his wife, "I don't understand these Alabama people."

Family members took turns checking on Nate, as they would an infant. He was sleeping like a baby. Bertha Mae let John B. look when he promised that he wouldn't say a word. The clamor outside and loose straw in the new mattress seemed to bother Nate not at all. After many hymns, prayers, hallelujahs, shouts and "Praise Gods," the pastor announced that the family needed rest. Everyone came by and said a few words of happiness and joy and offered help. One man insisted on doing the night milking for John.

He reluctantly agreed. "Now if ya milk her wrong, she'll kick like a mule."

The crowd eventually drifted away, leaving a mountain of food in the kitchen. John B. slept in his mother's arms. From the porch the others watched the yellow and gold and red of the sunset as if it were the first they had ever seen.

When John was about to get into bed, he said, "I tell ya, Martha, I'm plumb wore out. I don't know what it is. I ain't hit a lick at a snake all day. I must be agettin old."

Chapter Seventeen -- Fresh Regard

After breakfast on Monday, Martha took dirty clothes to a large pool in the branch beyond the spring. As she began wetting the clothes, she was surprised to see Nate trailing behind.

"Pa won't let me work in the field. I got to do sonethin'. Can't I help?"

"Ya need to stay home and eat and rest...but this is in the shade. Wet all them shirts and britches, soap 'em up, and spread 'em on that big flat rock. Let me show ya how to use the battlin' stick."

She picked up the three-inch wide wooden paddle. This short handled tool was slick and bleached from years of use. "Now look close, if ya hit too easy it won't get clean, if ya hit too hard it tears up the cloth." Nate finished the battling and began to rinse.

"Ya're not washin' out that lye soap. That shirt will eat ya alive, first time ya sweat." Martha rinsed them all again and piled them in a basket. Nate brought them to the yard where his mother hung good clothes on a line and rags on a bush.

No one ever visited on washday. Tuesday the parade began. Wagons and buggies arrived at intervals throughout the day. Some of the people had been at the farm on the previous Sunday. Others were Baptists, Presbyterians or non-churchgoers who had heard the startling news and wanted to see for themselves. Most were country people in their Sunday clothes. A few came from New Canaan and some from across the county. Most brought some small gift as an excuse for the visit -- usually food. The guests talked with Martha, but they really wanted to see Nate, watch him blush, and hear him say a word. The most persistent were husbands and wives bringing a daughter, or even daughters, of Nate's age or younger. The girls said hardly a word as they sat on the front porch with their parents, Nate and Martha. Their faces flushed as they looked at boards on the floor while adults talked. Nate tried to be busy so he would not have to be involved in these visits, but Martha usually managed to find him since he was restricted to the house area.

After several visits Martha asked Nate what he thought of the girls. Nate said, "Well, I tell ya, Ma, they look pretty good when they're all shined up in their Sunday clothes, but that last one sure can be a mean 'ol thing in school."

On Thursday, a couple arrived with their daughter. They had made an earlier attempt to visit, but Nate had managed to hide. When they left, Nate volunteered an opinion. "Ma, I don't wonder they made two trips. That girl is ugly as homemade sin."

"Now, Nate, he's just tryin' to look after his daughter. Young men are right scarce in the South. My own sister at thirteen married your Uncle Ambrose when he was seventy-six 'cause there wasn't much choice in the war."

On Friday a widower arrived with his daughter. Three times he made it clear that this daughter was his only child, and he had a large farm. When they left, as usual, Martha asked Nate, "Well, what do you thank?"

"Ma, I've seen his farm. It's not near big enough to get rid of that girl. She's so ugly, she'd snag lightnin'."

Martha put a hand to her mouth to try to hide her laughter and said, "Ya're as picky as yer pa."

On Saturday Nate announced that he would be glad to see Monday come so he could go back to work.

Chapter Eighteen -- Ingratitude

"I fled Him, down the nights and down the days;
I fled Him down the arches of the years;
I fled Him down the labyrinthine ways
Of my own mind; and in the midst of tears."
                                        Francis Thompson

Sunday morning brought the usual care of the stock and milking. John had dismissed the substitute milker at midweek, after he was kicked twice and production went down. Ben and Jacob labored through their weekly shave and all began to dress for church. All but Nate. Martha reminded him that they would be ready to leave soon.

Nate said, "I'll bring the wagon around and ya'all can go like usual."

"Ya mean after last week ya won't go and thank God for yer life and all? We better tell Pa about this."

Nate flushed, as redheads do, and looked through the window toward an oak, and said in a halting voice, "I -- I don't have to go to church for that. We can tell Pa, but 'less he has changed the rules, ya'all can go without me."

John sadly admitted that he would not change rules he had made, but he too could not understand Nate's ingratitude. The wagon pulled away with Jacob, Bertha Mae, John B., Ben, Martha, and John. Buster and Sam pulled the wagon. They left early, expecting more conversation about events of the past week.

As the wagon rattled down the road with wheels grinding, Martha looked back at Nate on the porch. When he disappeared from sight, she turned her head and dabbed at her eyes with a handkerchief. When the family arrived in the church wagon lot, they were surrounded by well-wishers. They were astonished at Nate's absence.

Brother Mac greeted the family as they entered the church and looked behind them. "I don't see Nate? Surely he's comin'."

"No, preacher, he's not. I'll not force him to come. Said he could thank God at home. Said he didn't see nare soul for a week, then saw every'body he ever heard of last Sundee. Said he was about wore out with folks. I reckon he's still thinkin' on what happened to him."

Service began with two hymns. Announcements were followed by prayer, with no mention of Nate and his experience.

*   *   *

Wiley Pepper arrived late in the churchyard. As he walked from the wagon lot toward the little church, he saw a familiar gray form. He could not help delaying a little longer to walk over to the far end of the hitching post. "Dolly, old girl. What are you doin' here?" Dolly looked at him, but wouldn't say.

*   *   *

Inside the church Brother Mac began to read:

"While the word was in the king's mouth, there fell a voice from heaven, saying, O king Nebuchadnezzar, to thee it is spoken; The kingdom is departed from thee.

And they shall drive thee from men, and thy dwelling shall be with the beasts of the field: they shall make thee to eat grass as oxen, and seven times shall pass over thee, until thou know that the most High ruleth in the kingdom of men,and giveth it to whomsoever he will.

The same hour was the thing fulfilled upon Nebuchadnezzar: and he was driven from men and did eat grass as oxen, and his body was wet with the dew of heaven, till his hairs were grown like eagles feathers, and his nails like eagles claws.

At the end of the days, I Nebuchadnezzar lifted up mine eyes unto heaven, and mine understanding returned unto me, and I blessed the most High, and I praised and honored him that liveth forever, whose dominion is an everlasting dominion and his kingdom is from generation to generation.

"Now folks, I never knew that poke sallet grew in Bible lands, but it must have. Ol' Nebuchadnezzar went mad and ate grass like an ox and was healed. At times, God does use means to accomplish his purpose. Miracles don't come like they did in Bible days with a flash of lightning and a clap of thunder. Curin' with herbs like poke sallet is just as much a miracle as if God had sent one of his angels down in a flash of light. And what better place for a miracle to happen than on a tree? Who directed John to that clearin' at that spring and why was the place so clear and free of brush and covered with poke sallet? And how do we know that God didn't send down an angel to oversee the whole thing?"

Wiley Pepper tiptoed into the back of the church on the right side. The church was packed; even the front row was filled. Some had to go back to their wagon and bring straight chairs and put them in the aisle. Others were very late and stood behind the pews at the back of the church. Wiley looked down the section to the left and finally saw John and Martha, but no Nate. He moved over to the right corner where he could lean against the wall and hear the sermon.

Brother Mac began to read again, but as he did, something caught his eye in the dark far corner to his right. There were no windows toward the back of the church. A latecomer might arrive and slip into the shadowy corner and stand unseen by those in the pews, especially if he looked toward the floor.

Red hair is almost impossible to hide. The preacher saw Nate. Now he looked at him and spoke every word directly to him. Sooner or later Nate would have to look up, especially if he were stared at long enough.

"And now, behold, I loose thee, this day from the chains which were upon thine hand. If it seem good unto thee to come with me to Babylon, come; and I will look well unto thee: but if it seem ill unto thee to come with me into Babylon, forbear: behold all the land is before thee: whither it seemeth good and convenient for thee to go, thither go.

Nate, who do you think loosed your chains and set you free?

God setteth the solitary in families: he bringeth out those which are bound with chains: but the rebellious dwell in a dry land.

Nate, you have been freed from your chains. You're free to go and to do what you will. It is your choice. God gives us the choice like your Pa gave you a choice about comin' to church, but we answer for our choices one day. Nate, do you remember when Elijah was lookin' for God after he defeated the prophets of Baal? Do you remember how he ran?

And, behold the Lord passed by, and a great and strong
wind rent the mountains, and brake in pieces the rocks
before the Lord; but the Lord was not in the wind; and
after the wind an earthquake:
And after the earthquake a fire; but the Lord was not in
the fire;
and after the fire a still small voice.

Nate, folks don't see God, but he's there. He may come in a still small voice, or he may come in an earthquake, or a presence you can't see. He comes in a way that you can understand, if you will. He comes when you'll take heed. He may fix it so you can't run away and have a long time to think about nothin' but Him. Now God may pass by and not be seen. Some folks wouldn't know the spirit of God if it jumped up and bit 'em on the arm.

Nate, any man with a Mac in his family name has a lit-tle stubborn streak. I did. Your Pa did. It took killin's in a war to get his attention. Nate, who do you think put you in chains? Your Pa did the work, but who arranged it? Who bound you, so you could be set free and know who delivered you? If that big ol' red dog with eyes like fire had come up to you and licked your hand, you would have patted his head and paid no more mind to him than you did Bear when he came up to you at the spring.

What we thought was Devil Dog was really The Hound of Heaven. It looked like that hound was after you...and he was. He was sent. He got your attention. He put you at the spring. What looked like a curse was a blessing.

He that is our God is the God of salvation; and unto
God the Lord belong the issues from death.

Nate, you were put in chains so that you could be set free and know who runs this world and...."

Brother Mac stopped in mid-sentence to run down the aisle and meet Nate, taking halting steps with head down. The two men embraced vigorously. Both shed tears. All of the women cried and some men did. Most of the men began to shout, "Glory hallelujah, Praise God" and the like, clapped, threw their hands above their head, and stamped their feet. Uncle Dock was loudest of all. Even that was not enough to express the intense emotion of the moment. Several Rebel yells were thrown in.

Two men from the eastern end of the county were driving their wagon past the church. They later claimed that the building was actually shaking. They stopped the wagon, thinking that some great disaster had taken place, ran up the steps into the back of that little church to behold a wild melee of shouting rejoicing people, two men standing in the aisle, others slapping them on the back, and women sobbing, They saw all this and still didn't know what was going on. They left before they were caught up in a celebration they did not understand.

When the tumult settled somewhat, Brother Mac led Nate to the front of the church. Baptisms were never scheduled. In this church, they were carried out when the person was converted. Brother Mac asked the usual questions about accepting Christ's works. He stopped several times and asked the people not to cheer when Nate answered. He picked up the dented pewter pitcher from the table by the pulpit. Yankees took the silver one, but this one, filled with spring water, stood always ready. He said the words of baptism and poured the water over Nate's head, drenching the left side of his head and body. The preacher held up his left hand and church members managed to restrain themselves to stifled shouts.

Brother Mac backed up a step and looked intently at the boy.

"Nate, the whole right side is dry. Long as it took you to come down this aisle, I mean to make certain of this baptism." He shifted hands and poured the rest of the pitcher on the right side. "I want you to *know* that the Holy Spirit has been poured out on you this day. You are drenched with it." There could be no restraint. The shouting, yells, and stamping began again. When the group finally filed out of the little church, many on this warm spring day looked as damp as Nate.

The McGinnis family took their places in the wagon for the ride home. Nate rode Dolly alongside. Martha could not keep her eyes away from her youngest son and shed a few more tears. Most of the members of the congregation hinted at another Sunday visit, until they were officially invited. Several wagons joined the McGinnis family to make a caravan down the narrow dirt road. The happy group parked under the trees and along the road on both sides. Other families stopped to pick up supplies from home and arrived a little later. Food was laid out and shared from the backs of wagons. Like the previous Sunday, singing began again.

As friends were clustered around the McGinnis family, two men parked a buggy and made their way through the crowd. The taller man, in his mid twenties, had the tanned face and loose loping walk of a farmer. This was Wiley Pepper. The other was a smaller man with a soft round hat-like thing with no brim, pushed to one side of his head. He was not Negroid, but his hair was black and the skin of his clean-shaven face was darker than those watching him. The man was dressed far better than those in the crowd. He was squinting in the afternoon sun and grinning. He carried something wrapped in a cloth, holding it crossways with both hands.

John said to Ben, "Who is that feller with Wiley agrinnin' like a jackass eatin' briers over a rail fence?"

"Pa, I don't know that fella from Adam's house cat."

Martha leaned over and whispered, "Now, John, be nice. He's a stranger."

The two walked to the family and stopped directly in front of John. The murmur of the crowd ceased. Everyone stared at the strange man and Wiley.

"Mr. McGinnis, this here is Mr. Pierre uh ... Possum-foot. He wants to meet ya and tell ya somethin'."

"How -- are -- you, Mr. MaGinies?" John did not change his stern countenance.

"About like common, Mr. Possum-foot."

The stranger took a step, held his bundle with his right hand and raised his left a few inches, as if he would offer it in friendship. John made no move, so Pierre dropped his hand.

"Mr. McGinnis, he wants to give ya somethin'."

Pierre took the cloth away from the object and thrust it toward John. "I want you have theese!"

The stranger held John's old banjo, freshly polished and strung. He pushed it forward in the position it would have been held, when John had two hands to play.

Ben looked first at Mr. Possum-foot and then at his father. John's expression did not change and he made no motion to accept the gift. Ben took the banjo, held it in place and gently pushed it against his father.

"I can't hardly take no hand-out. Not from a ...a carpetbagger."

"Oh, Mr. McGinnis, it wouldn't be a hand-out. This here man was a farmer where he come from, but he don't know nothin' about the kind of farmin' we do 'round here. He's got that big farm of ours, but he don't know the first thing about farmin' corn or cotton or even beans and 'taters for that matter. Several have told him that yer 'bout the best farmer in the county. He wants ya to learn him how to farm our way, so's he can do it on our -- that is -- his farm. He needs to watch ya most of the summer. He's got folks workin' far him, but he don't know what to tell 'em to do."

"Weeell, if he's a farmer, what did he grow where he come from?"

"Lemons, olives, and currants – whatever they are."

"Well now, I do declare! If that's all he growed, his chillun must have been pore as Job's turkey. I just don't know about this." He looked down for the first time, raised the arm without a hand to support it, and allowed his fingers to glide along the polished surface of the old banjo. From the memory of years gone by, his hand took the neck and pressed the strings. Ben watched his father's face and drew his fingers across the other end of the strings, making a nameless tune. The sound penetrated the silence about the four men.

"And that's not all, Mr. McGinnis, he's willin' to pay ya ten dollars ta boot." John's mouth opened. Then Wiley added, "In add-vance."

Ben caught the banjo. John's body went slack. One knee buckled and he swayed backwards. His lips moved, but he said nothing, Parents hushed children. In the stillness, a drake cried his harsh rasping, trailing sounds, "*Wuaaack-waack- waack- wack-wack.*" No one looked.

Pierre raised his left hand again and extended it toward John. "Agreed?" All eyes were upon the two men.

John was motionless, pale, and speechless. He raised his hand a few inches, stopped, then grasped his stump. His face was covered, but his beard quivered.

He glanced at his family standing nearby and then to the house behind him and the fields on either side. He stared without expression, not at Pierre, but over his shoulder and beyond the oaks at mountains to the north. In his mind he saw painful glimpses of the Hurt House with the blood and pain. Images filled his mind of the long walk home, Billy at the spring, Isaac in the ashes, and Nate at the spring. Gentle visions followed of wheat, cotton, and cornfields full and mature in the bright sun. John saw his family around the table with heads bowed. Images of what had been were crushed and crowded by what might be: a vision of his family on the empty dusty road leading away from home. He remembered hope in a letter, hope in a bottle, and he saw again hope on a tree. He saw something he hadn't seen in a long time. He saw hope within and hope within his reach.

John looked back at the stranger and said, "Weell, Pee-air, I'll tell ya -- I recken we could. Agreed!"

He dropped the stump and took Pierre's hand. The stranger pumped it vigorously and grinned even more. The crowd clapped and cheered.

When the clamor subsided, John said, "Now if yer gonna learn farmin', we start right after sunup. If ya don't get here till midday, ya won't learn but half what ya need. And somethin' else -- if ya don't get some kind o' hat with a brim, ya won't be able to open yer eyes wide enough to learn nothin'."

"I weal be here early weth a hat."

"Wouldn't hurt a thang if ya brought the ten dollars, too."

Pee-Air Possum-Foot shook hands one more time, grinned one once more, and said, "Yesss." The two turned to walk to the buggy.

"Ben, come help me put up the banjo."

"I'll put it up far ya, Pa."

"No, it'll take the two of us! Do what I tell ya. Come on!" The two went into the house.

The murmur of the conversations in the crowd returned. They spoke of yet another miracle. Three quarters of an hour later, friends and family looked up to see two figures coming from the house, one was obviously Ben. The other man wore no hat. His trimmed gray hair, slicked down with water, contrasted with the pale strip of forehead below his hairline -- the part that a farmer covers with a hat. The face about the nose and eyes was springtime-tan. Below the nose the cheeks were a sickly pallor. At least some parts were pale and white. Others were scraped and cut and there were scattered patches of dried blood. This man was as unfamiliar as the one who left in the buggy. He was grinning -- not like Pee-Air -- but he was grinning. Martha almost fainted.

With Ben's help, John had submitted to a haircut and shave. Ben grinned too, not because John promised to teach him to play the banjo, but as he told his mother, because there was happiness in his family once more. Jacob was as amazed as everyone else, but not at his father. His twitch could not happen with a smile.

Large hands gripped John's shoulders. Matthew leaned over near his ear and whispered above the murmur of the crowd, "I tol' ya so, John." He turned to his old friend with a puzzled look. "The real John has come home."

The strangers from last Sunday came again and couldn't get their buggy past the crowd. As Matthew moved a wagon for him, the man asked,

"The crowd is larger than last Sunday and quieter. There *must* be a death in the family."

"No. There's a renewed life and renewed hope."

The stranger told his wife as they drove away, "We're going back north. I have no idea what these people are talking about."

Afterwards

The shooting had stopped, but the war was not over. Generations would pass before differences would be settled. Scars would remain always, but on that day, on that farm, for the people of Ebenezar Springs, Canaan County, in their third life, healing had begun. It began because a carpetbagger named Pee-Air reached out his hand to a struggling man. A one-armed farmer was delivered from an even slower death than a boy bitten by a rabid dog. The first life would never return to the people under the trees, but on this Sunday they saw hope for a miracle of recovery from the ashes of defeat just as they had seen the miracle of life returned to the boy and hope returned to the man.

The crowd gradually drifted away, reluctant to leave, as if they feared that on Monday they would wake and find that it had all been a dream. Never had there been such a day or such a week. The story of Nate and the Devil Dog was told and retold, and over the generations was almost lost. Controversy raged over interpretations of the events. Robert McGregor thought the little valley with the mist draped spring and sky-blue water was enchanted. He remembered stories about magic springs in the old country. The strange symbols on the tree proved it -- or so he said.

Ann Cooper said, "He never had madness atall; he was just aputtin' on."

There *is* hysterical or false rabies. But Doc Davis said, "The Devil Dog and others sure had rabies. Besides, how would a farm boy know what symptoms to have, even if he were the world's best actor? Maybe uncommon things *do* happen like in Bible days."

Brother Mac never questioned a miracle in the bite of the Hound of Heaven and the return from madness and freedom from chains. Others said that it just happened that Nate was put where he could get to the herb that cured. The preacher answered, "Is it any less of a miracle that God directed him to be put where poke sallet grows? God uses means in his miracles sometimes, means that we least expect. Remember that Nate was tied to a tree. The greatest miracle of all occurred on a tree, a long time ago."

The matter was never settled, and much of the story was lost, but a tradition was left for generations to come. In the spring when the sky is blue, fields are green and leaves burst forth in the rush of spring, but doldrums of winter persist, someone goes down where poke sallet grows and gathers a basket of the bright green leaves.

Now everyone knows that poke sallet cannot be eaten raw. How did Nate survive it? Some said that the poison in the poke sallet drove the madness away. Some said the plant was different in that valley. Everyone agreed that you had to be mad to eat it raw. The herb must be cleaned and cooked and the liquid poured off – maybe twice to be sure --and then the greens are eaten by all.

As Grandma Cobb said, "It strengthens the body, purifies the blood and for sure cures madness." Every spring, the people of Ebenezar Springs in Canaan County ate poke sallet -- except Nate. He said that he had eaten a lifetime supply.

Author's Request

And so -- if madness strikes, whether it be madness that comes from the bite of a dog or madness of disease or age, if I am of no use to myself or anyone else, or have become a danger to others -- do not put me in an institution where strange people poke tubes in all my natural orifices and make unnatural holes for stranger yet tubes. I may breathe and my heart beat, but that's not life!

Be kind. Leave me at the spring. But try to do it in summer, or better still in spring when the sky is clear and blue, fields are green, leaves burst forth on trees, birds sing, and the air is filled with hope. I really hate cold weather. And try to put me down where poke sallet grows. There might be something to the story about that herb. It worked on one McGinnis. It might work on another.

Glossary of Nineteenth Century Speech, Southern Words, Idioms and Expressions

Typical -ing words which lose the –g
bleedin'   nothin'
beginnin'   dyin'
dyin'   somethin'

"a" added on words of ongoing activity
aburnin'   atryin'
agoin'   amovin'
astandin'   atearin'

Typical words which lose the first letter or syllable
'bout---------about
'fore----------before
'splain--------explain

Southern Words

acrost------------across
afar--------------on fire
aim to (go to)--intend to
airish------------cool
apt---------------likely
backset(or setback)—
   relapse
bottom-----------low land
   frequently along a
   stream
branch-----------stream
   too small to have a
   name
Bu-ro------------Bureau
clost--------------close
commenced-----begin
Domineker-------
   Dominique chicken
d'rectly---------not now,
   but shortly
ever------------every

fer---------------far,
   sometimes means for
festered---------pus filled
fix----------------situation
flutterby------- now
   called butterfly
   In old English the
   insect was called
   flutterbee or flutterby
grass widow----
   divorced woman
fixin'to-------about to
   or prepairing to
fount---------found
flux------------to make
   liquid (diarrhea)
Free'man----Freedmen's
growed-------grown
graybacks----lice
heap sight----a lot

holler----------hollow
(valley)
holp-----------past tense
of help -- holp and
holpen in the time of
Chaucer
hissen----------his
i-dee-----------idea
pronounced I-dee
kearn----------carrion –
pronounced kee--arn
leaders--------tendons
lighter---------heart pine
filled with resin
lief--------------willingly
or gladly. Dates
back to Anglo-Saxon
leof (beloved)
pronounced leave.
nar'-------------(nary)
not one
mite-------------a bit
muiligrubs-----dejected,
dispirited
Nigra-----------Negro
passel------------large
number
peart----------lively,
probably
pronunciation of
pert

piece------------distance
plum------completely
(also slap or clean)
proud flesh –
granulation issue
purdy-----------pretty
rurn (ruint)----ruin
(ruined)
recken-----------reckon
shed-------------rid
skippers--------maggots
snake doctor --type of
dragonfly which
frequents streams
and ponds
spell-------------while
stob-------------stake
swole------------swollen
sut---------------soot
toothbrush tree—
blackgum tree
towhead--------very
blond -- like flax
usually in young
children
yer---------------you

Southern Expressions and Idioms

at first light------------------------daylight enough to see

aputtin' on -- or let on like------pretending

battle clothes-----------------------to strike the clothes
   with a batler stick or battling stick--a three inch
   wide wooden paddle with a short handle. See *As
   You Like It*, Act 2, Scene 4, Line 48)

can 'till can't----------------------from when you can see
   until you can't (daylight 'till dark)

conniption fit--hysterical exhibition over circumstances

corded off--------------------------to apply a tourniquet

didn't go to------------------------didn't mean to

dog's bate--------------------------bate means a sufficiency.
   A dog's bate means gorged to excess

flat cut a dido----------------------In this context flat means
   absolute, cut means to perform or execute, dido is
   showy foolish or mischievous behavior

gee and haw-----------------------right and left, said
   forcefully to a mule

heap sight--------------------------a lot

hard put----------------------------it would be difficult

if he was a mind to--------------if he wanted to

if I put my mind to it------------if I make a determined
   effort

I ain't hit a lick at a snake-------I have done no form of
   work

it's comin' up a cloud-----------a rain cloud is coming

layin' off to-------------------------meaning to, putting off

paid him no mind---------------paid no attention to him

might near--------------------------almost

no call to---------------------------no reason to

no'count----------------------------no account. of no value

not worth a fart in a whirlwind-------
                              the ultimate uselessness

pea turkey--------------------------nothing

poke sallet--------------------------young leaves of the poke
   plant

pretty quick------------------------almost immediately
puts me in mind of----------------reminds me of
rabbit run over my grave--------explanation for a
    sudden generalized tremor
right smart----------------------------a lot
root hog or die----------------------make your own way or
    starve
so ugly she'd snag lightnin'-----the ultimate ugly
sets a great store by---------------thinks very highly of
that away------------------------------in that fashion or in that
    direction
they is (they's)---------------------there is
till good light is gone-------------twilight, too dark to
    work
toothbrush tree---------------------blackgum
ugly as home made sin-----------second most ugly state
uneasy about-------------------------worried about
used to could----------------------something could be
    done in the past, but not now
whistlin' rooster-------------------*A whistling rooster and
a crowing hen, both will come to no good end.*
white eyed----------------------------appearance after
    working to exhaustion
would go to ---------------------------would begin to

Blended words

gonna----------going to   t'other---------the other
mor'an--------more than   they's-----------there is
soon's----------soon as   wooda----------would
have

Lost Central Sylable or letter

b'leve-----------believe   th'ugh -----through
ever'where----everywhere   s'pposed—supposed
gov'ment------government

Historical Notes
Chapter One
Butternut dye is made from copperous (ferrous sulfate) and walnut hulls.

Matthew 5:30

Chapter Two
Side- meat is country bacon. It was sliced with a knife and was quite thick.

Froe or frow is an ancient cleavage tool used to split wood. Earlier than 1600 it was called a frower.

Chapter Three
Ulrich B. Phillips, *Life and Labor in the Old South*. The census of 1860 reported 46,274 households owing twenty or more slaves. Three times as many held five to nineteen slaves. Five times as many owned or hired one to four slaves. This leaves nearly six of the eight million whites out of proprietary touch with the four million slaves.

James Ronald Kennedy and Walter Donald Kennedy, *The South Was Right*, The *Desire*, the first American slave ship, was built in 1637 and sailed from Salem, Massachusetts. The slave trade, based on rum. slaves and molasses, continued legally or illegally two hundred years. Most of the cargos went to the Caribbean or South America. Slave trade to the South primarily occurred before 1800. Virginia was the first state to outlaw the slave trade October 8, 1778. In 1865 few slaves could remember Africa.

Deo Vindice -- God will vindicate or defend. On the Great Seal of the Confederacy. Later used on memorials or markers.

Chapter Four
George Lewis, DVM, "Preparation For Disaster," *Conference on Civil War Medicine*, 1998. Fredrick, Md. Glanders is an incurable usually fatal disease of horses and mules. It involves the nose, lungs, or lymphatics. Swellings of the neck are common. More chronic

involvement of skin is called farcy. After the war many infected army animals were sold and spread the disease throughout the country. Glanders was not eliminated in this country until 1932.

Chapter Five

Ebenezer Hearn founded Methodism in Alabama. Many churches were named for him.

Ambrose McGinnis was born in 1788 on the David Fite farm on the east fork of the Catawba River in Lincoln County, North Carolina. Ambrose was my great-grandfather. He died in 1874 two months before the birth of his fifth child in his second family. My grandfather was two when Ambrose died.

Charlotte Emerline Cobb married Ambrose in1864. I have spelled her name as it was pronounced and written. When her husband died, she waited the usual two-year mourning period and remarried. I have spelled her mother's name as my father remembered it and wrote it. Courthouse records say it was Memory.

The Fifteenth Amendment states "suffrage shall not be denied because of race, color, or prior servitude." Georgia, Mississippi, Texas, and Virginia were readmitted when they ratified it in 1869.

Chapter Seven

The letters in this chapter were written by Bertha Mae Swann and Luther Lafayette Owen, my grandparents.

John Brooks Wheeler, *Memoirs Of a Small Town Surgeon.*, 1935. There was no knowledge of the relationship of bacteria to infection and no concept of sterile technique in 1870. Charpie is loose linen threads. Myrrh, as used at that time, was one part of tincture of myrrh to five or ten parts of water. Myrrh was said to be astringent and stimulating.

Chapter IX of Dr. Wheeler's book is entitled *A Case of Hydrophobia.* He had the rare opportunity to observe a patient from admission until his death. The author was a "house pup" (house pupil, or what we would call an intern or resident) at Massachusetts General Hospital in 1878.

Alabama Rabies Control and Bite Management Manual, Alabama Department of Public Health, Montgomery, 1997. In medieval Europe, rabies was a terrible threat. People who were bitten often turned to St. Hubert, the patron saint of rabies victims. If they could not visit the shrine at Liege, they used the keys or crosses of St. Hubert. Usually they were heated red hot and applied to the animal bite. Sometimes keys were carried as amulets or placed on the walls of houses. This belief existed was common until late nineteenth century

Chapter Eight

Pus was not known to be related to infection, but was thought to be desirable for healing. It was sometimes called laudable pus.

Lung fever is pneumonia. Galloping consumption is a strong possibility in Billy.

William Deerman was brother to Sara Ann Deerman, my great grandmother, and was left at a spring by two family members on the way home from the war.

Revelation 6

The usual interpretation of the four horses of the apocalypse:

White Horse-----------Conquest, victory
Red Horse-------------War
Black Horse-----------Famine, calamity
Pale (Ashen) Horse—Death

Chapter Nine

J. T. Shepard and a free black did come from Virginia during the big War and worked for Ambrose.

Job 14:1-4, 14 – 17

I *saw The Place-Where-the-Mountain-Gets-Its-Breath.*in St Clair County about 1940..

A surveyor's chain is sixty-six feet or four rods. Rod intervals of 16 1/2 feet are marked.

Genesis 3:19

Chapter Ten
Skulkers or sneaks. When the battle raged, those cowardly soldiers hid in a ditch or behind a wall and could not be found until the battle cleared. They claimed that they got separated from the others in the noise and confusion.

The Union Minié, or conoidial ball, from the Springfield or Enfield was .58 caliber.

Ether was used as an anesthetic in the war, but chloroform was preferred because it was not explosive.

Dover's powder was named for T. Dover (1660-1742) English physician. 1 part opium, 1 part ipecac, and 8 parts lactose. Still listed as an analgesic, sedative, and diaphoretic

H. H. Cunningham, *Doctors In Gray*, Louisiana State University Press, Batton Rouge, 1958. Oiled silk was unavailable in the South. Boiling horsehair made it pliable and accidentally sterile.

The hook used to pull out vessels is a tenaculum.

The preferred dressing of linen lint was in short supply. Confederates used oven-baked cotton. Baking also sterilized the dressing.

A bistoury is a knife with a long cutting edge of uniform width, either straight or curved with sharp or blunt tip.

With a penetrating wound of the chest, as the ribs are moved upward and outward to expand the chest cavity to breathe , air is sucked through the hole and collapses the lung on the injured side. When the ribs move down, the air is then expressed through the hole. In addition, when the air rushes into the chest cavity, the mediastinum is shifted over to partially collapse the normal side.

In 1865, the usual treatment of a sucking wound of the chest was a plug of lint sealed with collodian.

Stewart Brooks, *Civil War Medicine*. Charles C. Thomas, Springfield, Illinois, 1966. When available, potassium permanganate, sodium hypochloright, bromide, iodine, carbolic acid or alcohol were used as deodorants, not realizing that they were antiseptics.

Chapter Eleven

Alabama militia was called Alabama Volunteer Corps. They wore oval brass buckles and had a smaller similar plate on the cartridge box.

Johnson's Island was a small bit of land in Lake Erie three miles off shore near Sandusky, Ohio. A prison facility imprisoned as many as three thousand Confederate soldiers that the Federal Government refused to exchange toward the end. Many southern soldiers did not survive the 20 below zero winters.

The great pox is syphilis.

Company Q means disabled due to illness, probably in the hospital.

Lincoln was assassinated April 14, 1865.

General Johnston surrendered to General Sherman April 26 near Durham Station N C.

When soldiers demonstrated bravery or accomplished some extraordinary deed they were listed on an Honor Roll. Lists might be read to an assembled military unit or published in a nearby paper. Commissions were given to some men.

Chapter Twelve

A Colt Baby Dragoon was a .31 caliber muzzle-loaded five shot percussion revolver. Two thousand were made in 1847.

Chapter Thirteen

H.H. Cunnningham. *Doctors In Gray*, In the spring of 1863, General Lee ordered that a detail from each regiment gather these antiscorbutics each day to try to prevent scurvy: wild onions, garlic, lamb's quarter, and poke sallet.

Carlton McCarthy. *Detailed Minutiae of Soldier Life in The Army of Northern Virginia*, University of Nebraska Press, Lincoln and London, 1993. When supplies were low, bacon was fried to produce a pan of grease. Flour and water were mixed and poured into the boiling grease to produce slosh or coosh (cush). If available, pieces of meat, cornbread or biscuit were added to the stew. Slapjack might be produced by mixing less water and grease to make a batter to be cooked as a pancake.

A Spencer carbine was a lever-action repeating rifle holding seven rounds of .52-caliber ammunition in a tube in the stock.

Chapter Sixteen

Romans 11:51

Verses from songs in this chapter were taken from my great grandfather's songbook published in 1842.

Chapter Seventeen

To battle means to beat wet clothes with a paddle as they are turned and twisted. Many years later a mechanical contrivance called a washing machine would be invented to swing paddles automatically and strike the clothes with the proper force. See *As You Like It*, Act 2, Scene 4, Line 48.

Rags were hung on bushes to save line space. A farm wife, when asked if she had been busy, might answer, "They's a rag on ever' bush!"

Chapter Eighteen

Daniel 4:4-31

Jeremiah 40:4

Psalms 68:6

Psalms 68: 20

I Kings 19:11-12

References

Ahladas, John, Curator, The Museum of The Confederacy, Richmond, Virginia. Personal communication.

Bartlett, John G., *The Civil War In North Carolina*, The University Of North Carolina Press, Chapel Hill, 1963.

Blethen, H, T., and Wood, Jr, Curtis W., *Ulster and North America*, University of Alabama Press, Tuscaloosa, 1997.

Brooks, Stewart, *Civil War Medicine*, Charles C. Thomas, Springfield, Illinois, 1966.

Chambers, William Pitt, *Blood & Sacrifice*, Blue Acorn Press, Huntington, W. Virginia, 1994.

Crow, Mattie Lou Teague, Editor, *The Diary of a Confederate Soldier, John Washington Inzer,* The Strode Publishers, Inc., Huntsville, Al., 1977.

Cunningham, H.H., *Doctors in Gray*, Louisiana State University Press, Baton Rouge and London, 1960.

Denny, Robert E., *Civil War Medicine*, Sterling Publishing Co. Inc., New York, 1995.

Eaton, Clement. *The Waning Of The Old South Civilization 1860's - 1880's*, University of Georgia Press, Athens, Georgia, 1968.

Fisher, Miles Mark, *Negro Slave Songs*, Russel and Russel, New York, 1953.

Johnson, James Weldon, Johnson, J. Rosamond, and Brown, Laurence, *The Book of American Negro Spirituals*, The Viking Press, New York, 1923.

Kennedy, James Ronald and Kennedy, Walter Donald, *The South Was Right*, Pelican Publishing Company, Inc., Gretna, Louisiana, 1994

Lacey, Mark , Methodist minister. Personal communication

Lerer, Seth, Professor Stanford University *The history of the English Language* audiotapes

McCarthy, Carlton, *Detailed Minutiae of Soldier Life,* University of Nebraska Press, Lincoln and London, 1993 (reprint of 1882 edition)

McCutchen, *The Writer's Guide To Everyday Life In The 1800's,* Writers Digest Books, Cincinnati, Ohio, 1993.

Merck Veterinary Manual, Third Edition, Merck and Co. Inc. Rahway, N.J., 1967.

Millor, Rex, *The Forgotten Regiment,* Patrex Press, 125 Brierhill, Williamsville, North Carolina, 1984.

Montgomery, Michael: *How Scotch-Irish Is Your English?,* The Journal of East Tennessee History, vol 67, Knoxville, 1995.

Morgan, John, *The Log House in East Tennessee,* University of Tennessee Press, Knoxville, 1990.

Owen, L. L. and Swann, Bertha Mae, Letters (In the author's possession)

Phillips, Ulrich B. *Life And Labor In The Old South,* Little Brown and Company, Boston, 1929.

Randall, J.G., *The Civil War And Reconstruction,* Boston, D. C. Heath and Company, 1937.

Watson, William, *Life in The confederate Army,* Louisiana state University Press, Baton Rouge and London, 1995.

Wheeler, John Brooks, *Memoirs Of A Small Town Surgeon,* Fredrick A. Stokes Company, New York, 1935.

Work, John W., *American Negro Songs And Spirituals,* Bonanza Books, New York, 1940.

Wiley, Bell Irvin, *The Life of Johnny Reb,* Louisiana State University Press, Baton Rouge and London, 1943 (1993 printing).

Sacred Songs for Family and Social worship, American Tract Society, 150 Nassau Street New York, 1842

Wigginton, Eliot, *Foxfire 2,* Anchor Press/Doubleday, New York, 1973.Watson, William, *Life in The Confederate Army,* Louisiana State University Press, Baton Rouge Louisiana, 1995, (originally published 1887).

Owsley, Frank L., *Plain Folk,* Louisiana State University Press, Baton Rouge, 1949.

Noyes, Alfred, *The Highwayman.*

McPherson, James M., *For Cause & Comrades,* Oxford University Press, New York and Oxford, 1997.

About The Cover

The cover illustration was taken from the cover of the *Alabama Rabies Control and Bite Management Manual*, published by the Alabama Department of Public Health. The original came from a rabies vaccine brochure published 65 or 70 years ago.